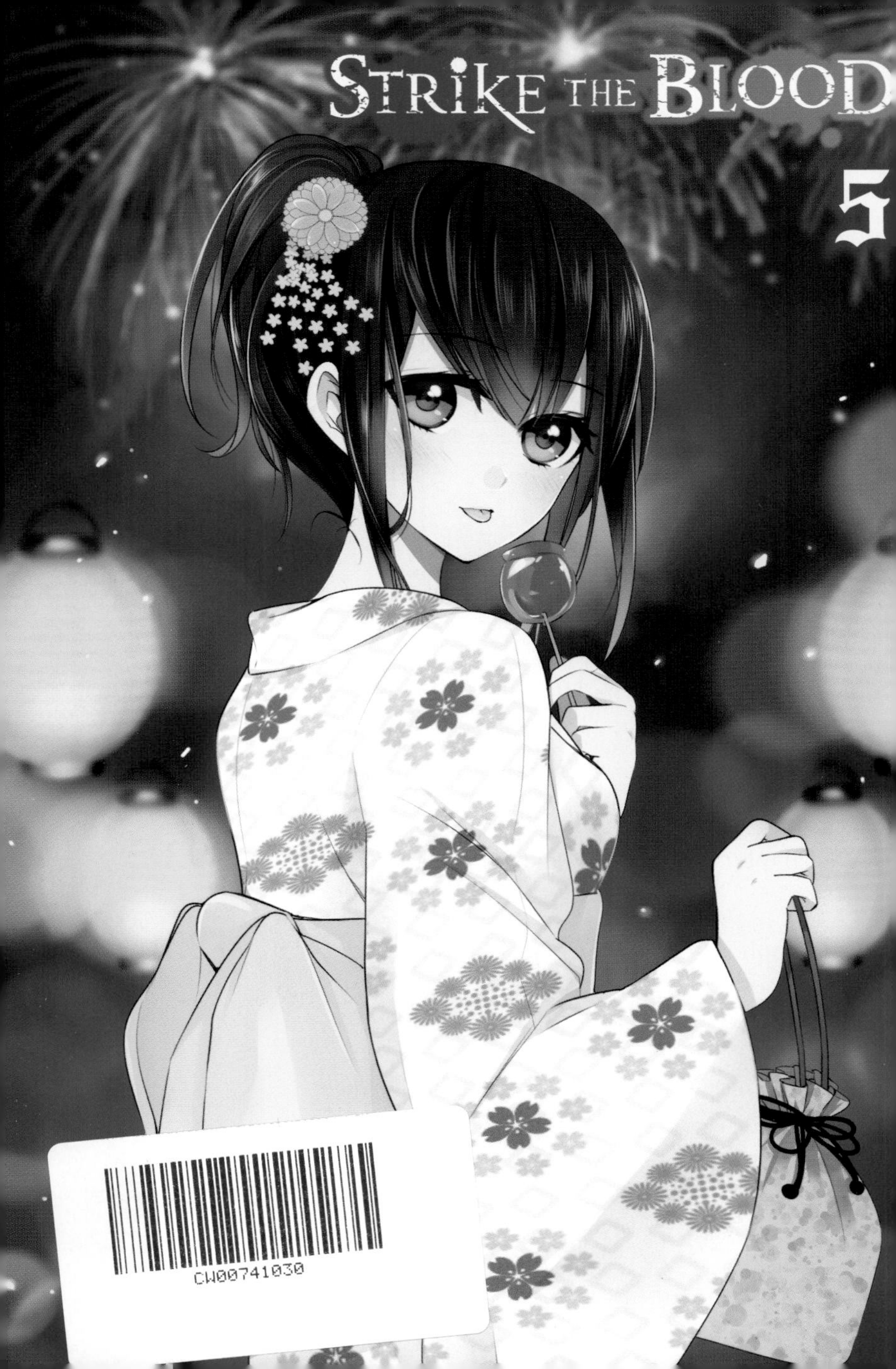
STRIKE THE BLOOD
5
CW00741030

5

STRIKE THE BLOOD

The Fourth Primogenitor is immortal and indestructible. Rejecting his vampiric brethren, he does not desire domination, but only the service of the twelve Beast Vassals that are disaster incarnate, the sipping of blood, carnage, and destruction. The vampire is said to be ruthless and heartless, completely beyond the doctrines of the world, a monster who has laid waste to innumerable cities in the past.

CONTENTS

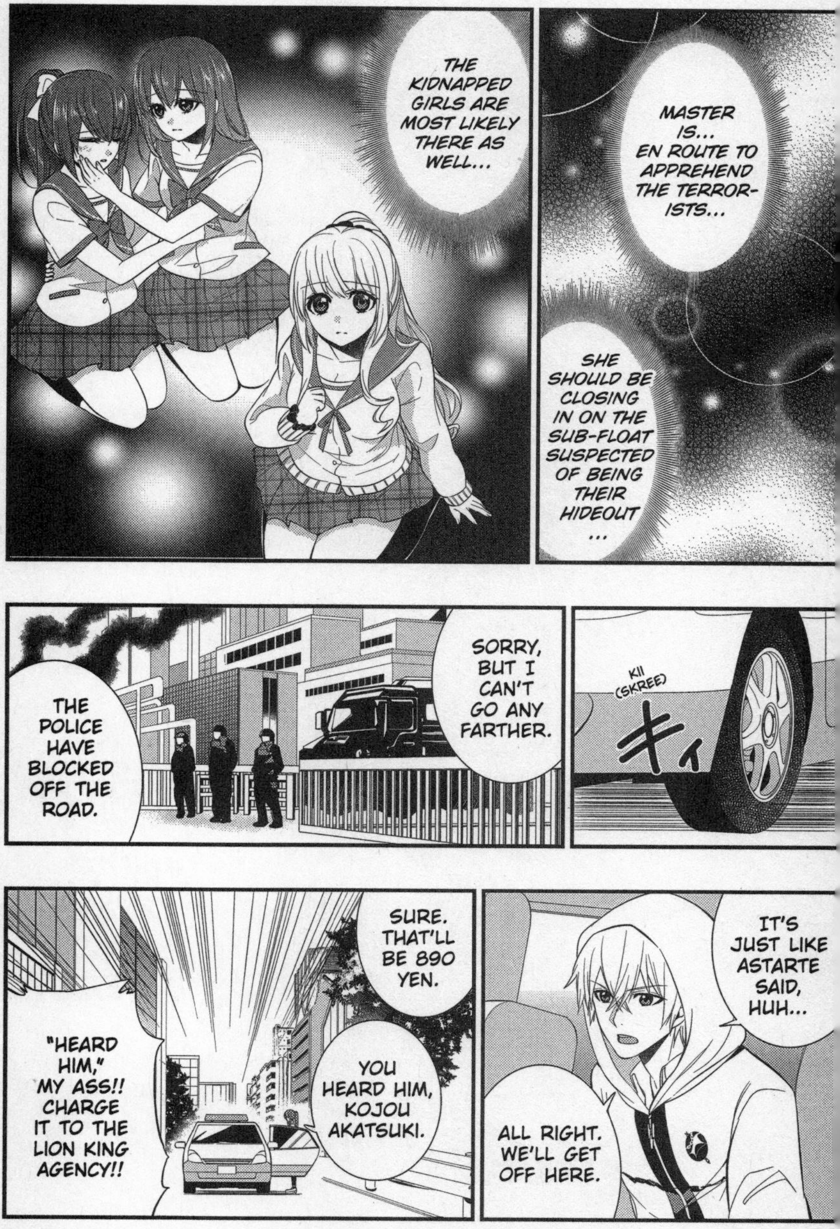

MASTER IS... EN ROUTE TO APPREHEND THE TERRORISTS...
SHE SHOULD BE CLOSING IN ON THE SUB-FLOAT SUSPECTED OF BEING THEIR HIDEOUT...
THE KIDNAPPED GIRLS ARE MOST LIKELY THERE AS WELL...
KII (SKREE)
SORRY, BUT I CAN'T GO ANY FARTHER.
THE POLICE HAVE BLOCKED OFF THE ROAD.
IT'S JUST LIKE ASTARTE SAID, HUH...
ALL RIGHT. WE'LL GET OFF HERE.
SURE. THAT'LL BE 890 YEN.
YOU HEARD HIM, KOJOU AKATSUKI.
"HEARD HIM," MY ASS!! CHARGE IT TO THE LION KING AGENCY!!

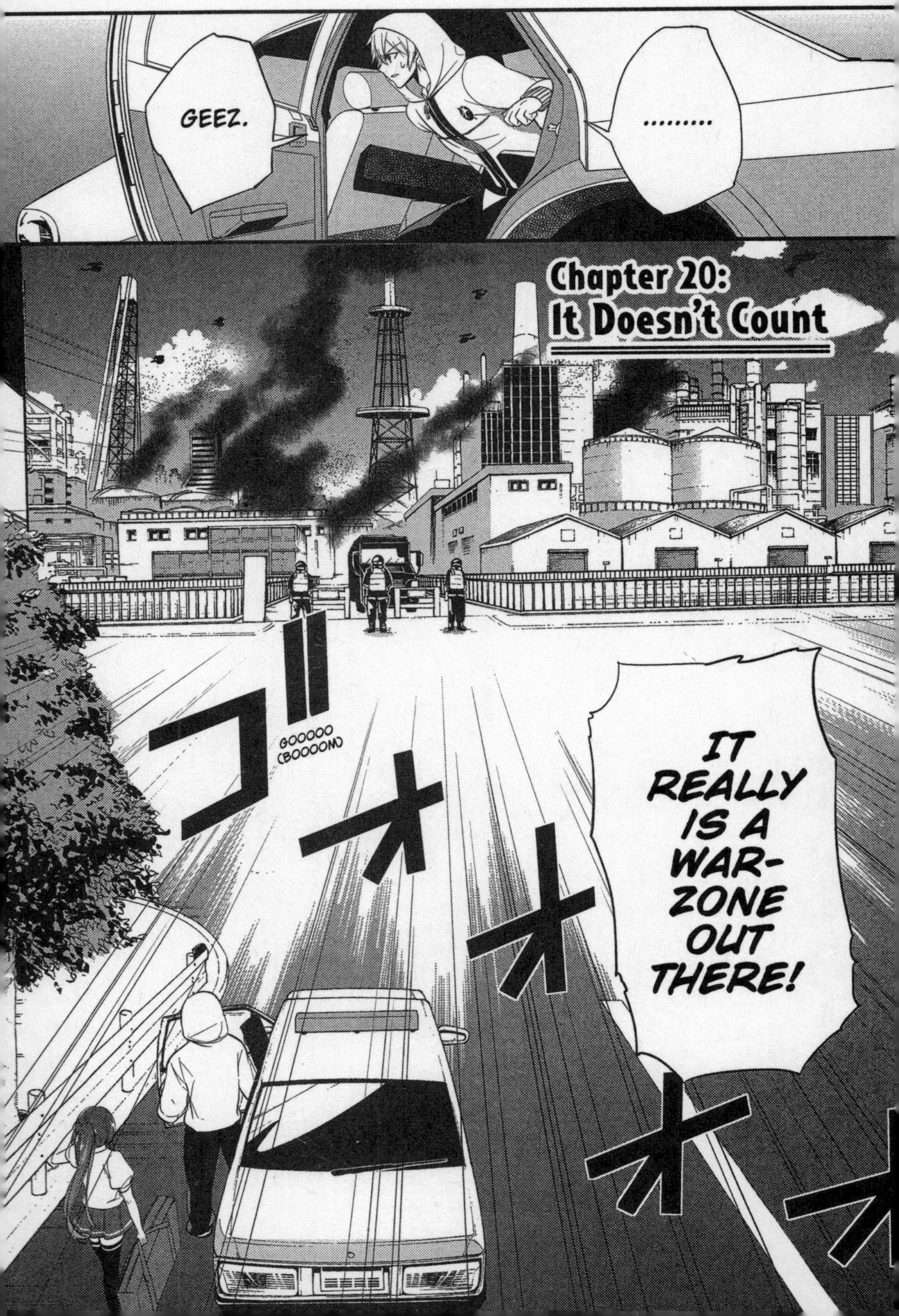
....
GEEZ.
Chapter 20: It Doesn't Count
IT REALLY IS A WAR-ZONE OUT THERE!
GOOOOO (BOOOOM)

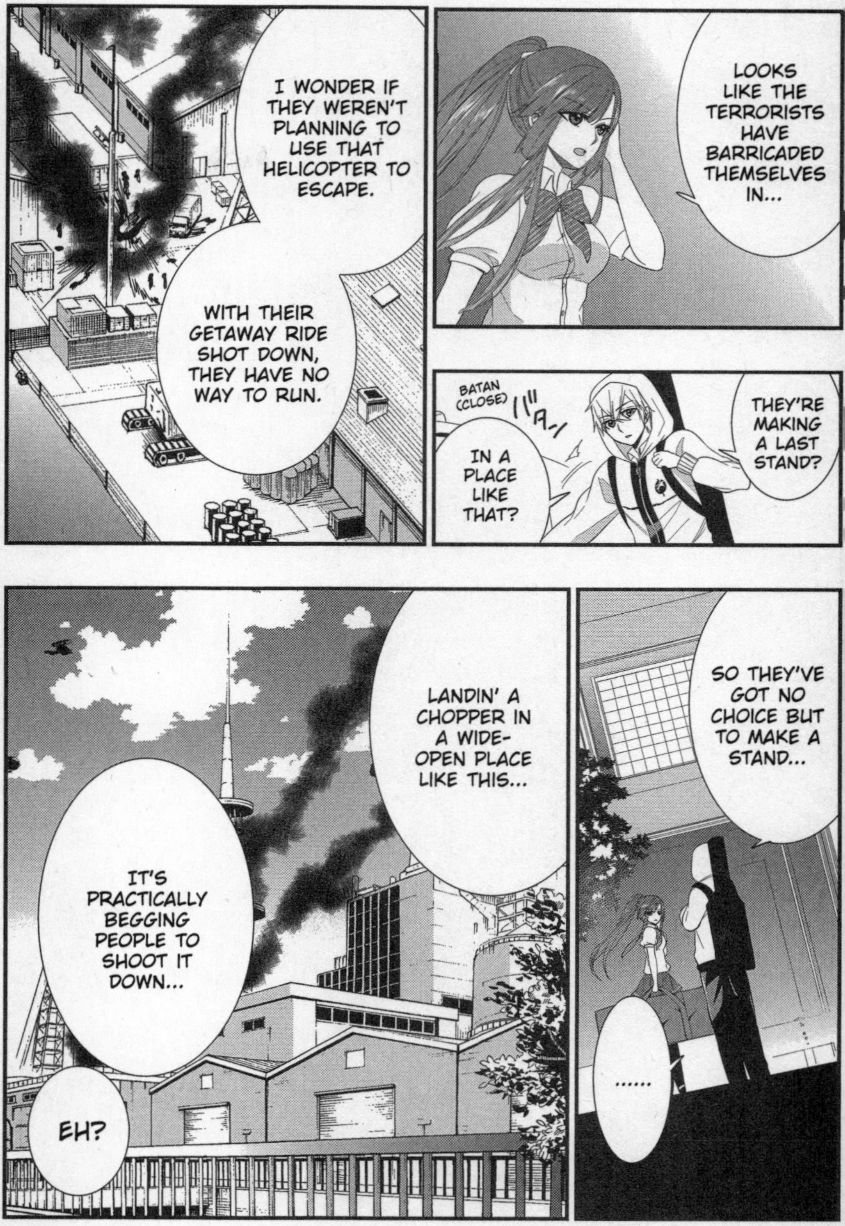
LOOKS LIKE THE TERRORISTS HAVE BARRICADED THEMSELVES IN...
THEY'RE MAKING A LAST STAND?
BATAN (CLOSE)
IN A PLACE LIKE THAT?
I WONDER IF THEY WEREN'T PLANNING TO USE THAT HELICOPTER TO ESCAPE.
WITH THEIR GETAWAY RIDE SHOT DOWN, THEY HAVE NO WAY TO RUN.
SO THEY'VE GOT NO CHOICE BUT TO MAKE A STAND...
......
LANDIN' A CHOPPER IN A WIDE-OPEN PLACE LIKE THIS...
IT'S PRACTICALLY BEGGING PEOPLE TO SHOOT IT DOWN...
EH?

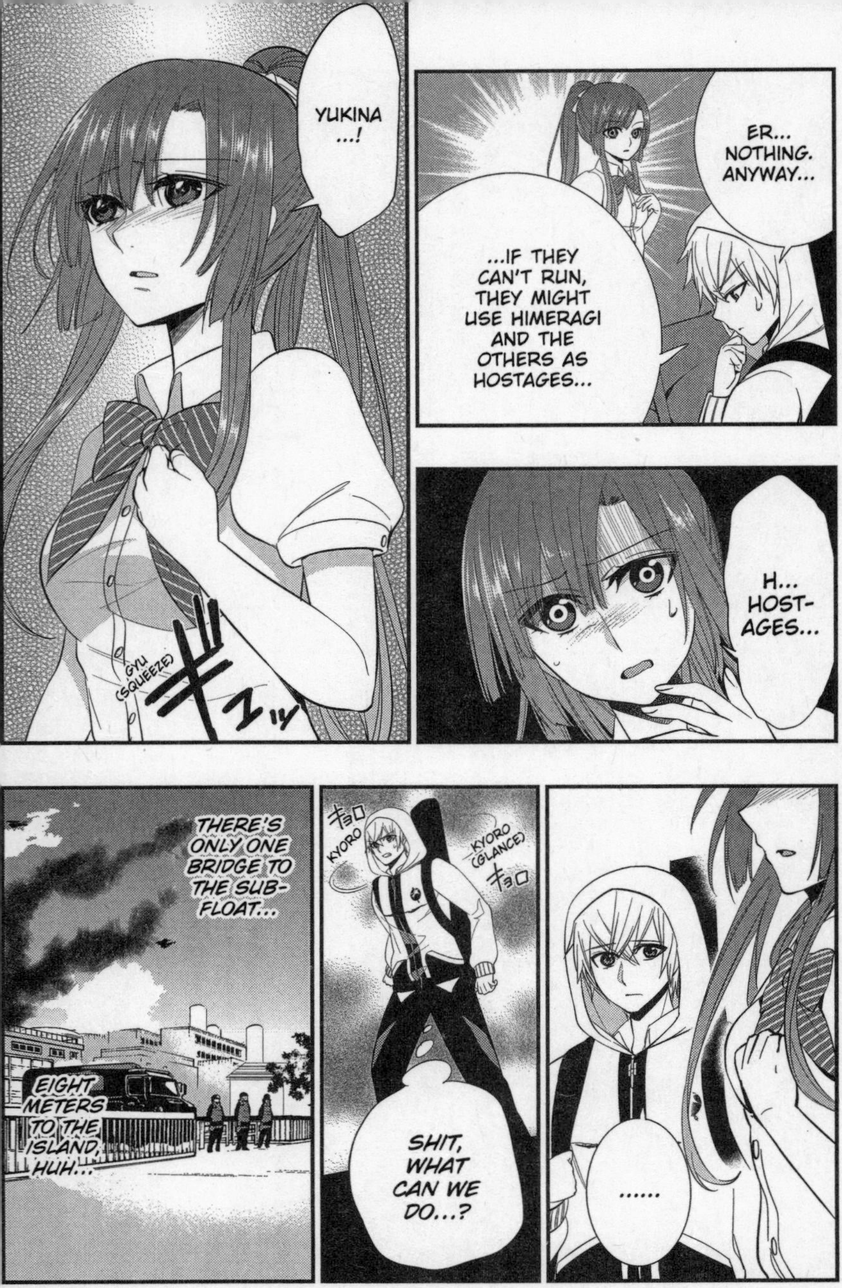
ER... NOTHING. ANYWAY...
...IF THEY CAN'T RUN, THEY MIGHT USE HIMERAGI AND THE OTHERS AS HOSTAGES...
H... HOSTAGES...
YUKINA ...!
GYU (SQUEEZE)
......
KYORO (GLANCE)
キョロ
KYORO
キョロ
SHIT, WHAT CAN WE DO...?
THERE'S ONLY ONE BRIDGE TO THE SUB-FLOAT...
EIGHT METERS TO THE ISLAND, HUH...

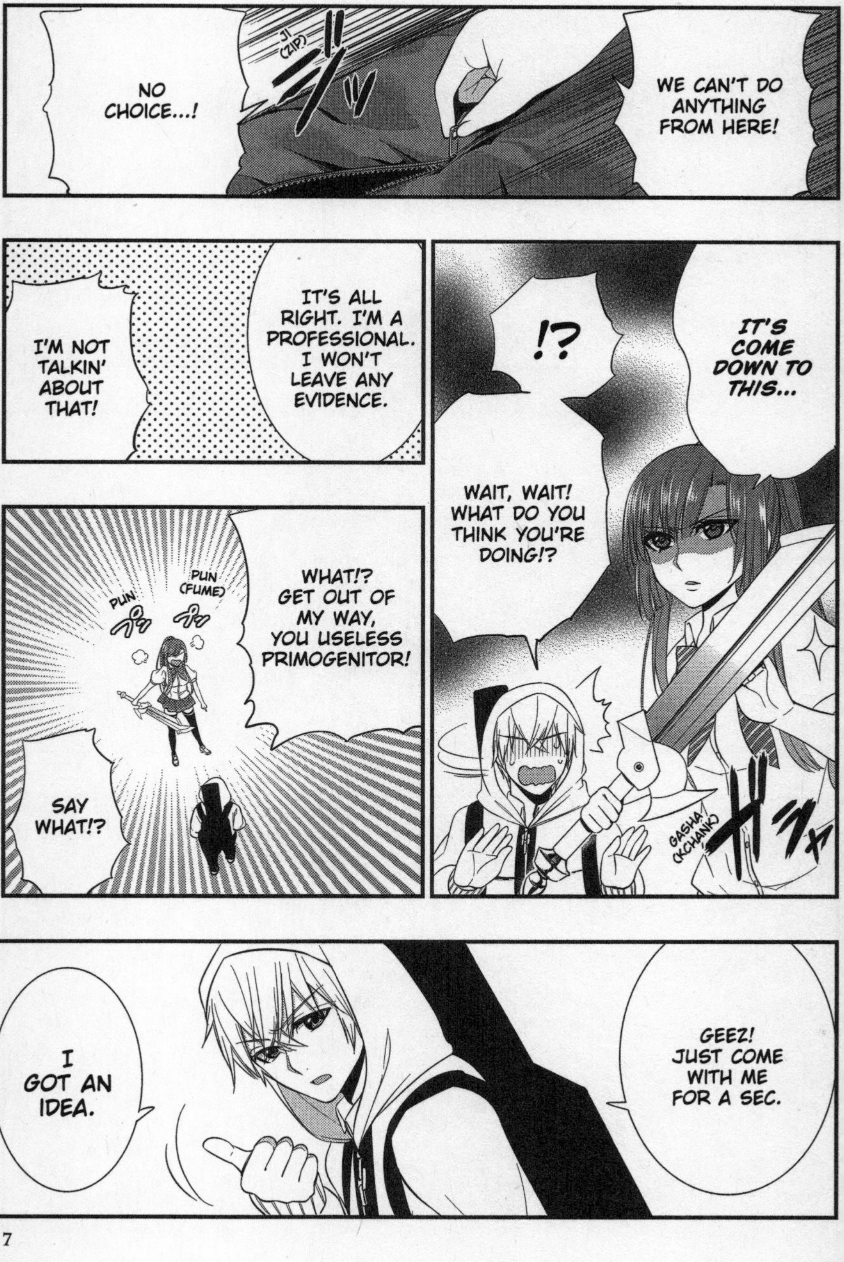
WE CAN'T DO ANYTHING FROM HERE!
JI (ZIP)
NO CHOICE...!
IT'S COME DOWN TO THIS...
!?
WAIT, WAIT! WHAT DO YOU THINK YOU'RE DOING!?
GASHA (KCHANK)
IT'S ALL RIGHT. I'M A PROFESSIONAL. I WON'T LEAVE ANY EVIDENCE.
I'M NOT TALKIN' ABOUT THAT!
WHAT!? GET OUT OF MY WAY, YOU USELESS PRIMOGENITOR!
PUN (FUME)
PUN
SAY WHAT!?
GEEZ! JUST COME WITH ME FOR A SEC.
I GOT AN IDEA.

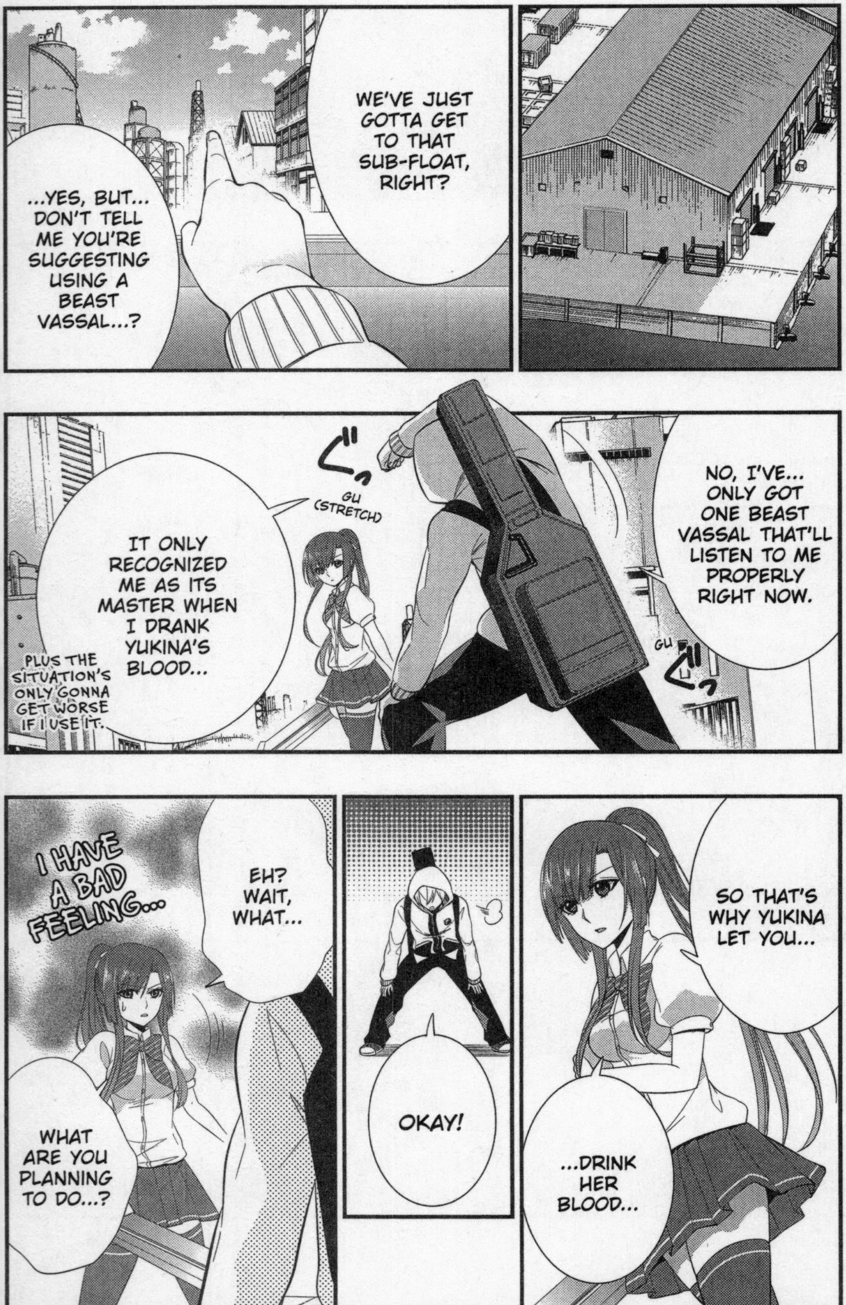
WE'VE JUST GOTTA GET TO THAT SUB-FLOAT, RIGHT?
...YES, BUT... DON'T TELL ME YOU'RE SUGGESTING USING A BEAST VASSAL...?
NO, I'VE... ONLY GOT ONE BEAST VASSAL THAT'LL LISTEN TO ME PROPERLY RIGHT NOW.
GU
GU (STRETCH)
IT ONLY RECOGNIZED ME AS ITS MASTER WHEN I DRANK YUKINA'S BLOOD...
PLUS THE SITUATION'S ONLY GONNA GET WORSE IF I USE IT.
SO THAT'S WHY YUKINA LET YOU...
...DRINK HER BLOOD...
OKAY!
EH? WAIT, WHAT...
I HAVE A BAD FEELING...
WHAT ARE YOU PLANNING TO DO...?

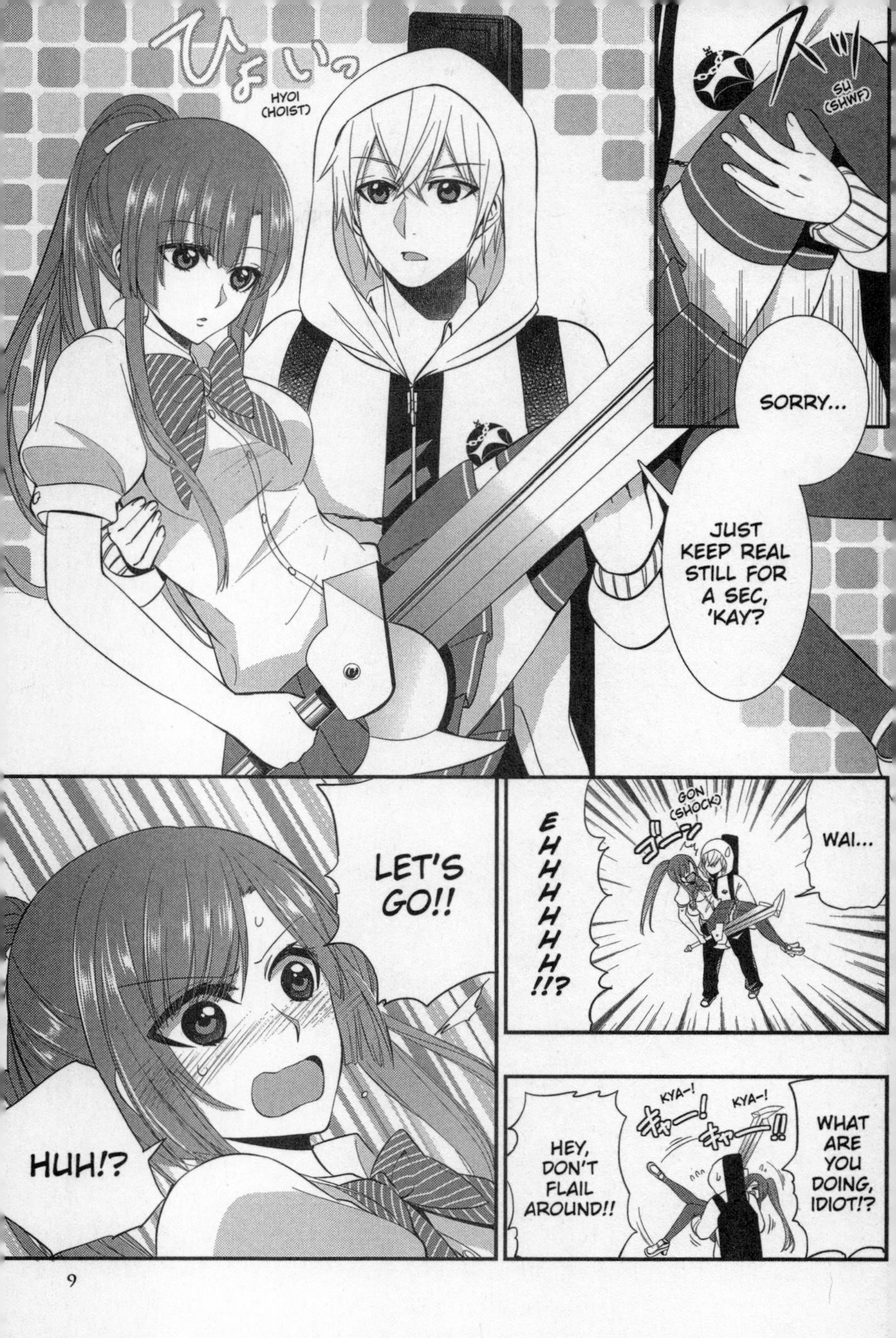
SU (SHWF)
SORRY...
JUST KEEP REAL STILL FOR A SEC, 'KAY?
HYOI (HOIST)
WAI...
GON (SHOCK)
EHHHHHHH!!?
WHAT ARE YOU DOING, IDIOT!?
KYA-! KYA-!
HEY, DON'T FLAIL AROUND!!
LET'S GO!!
HUH!?

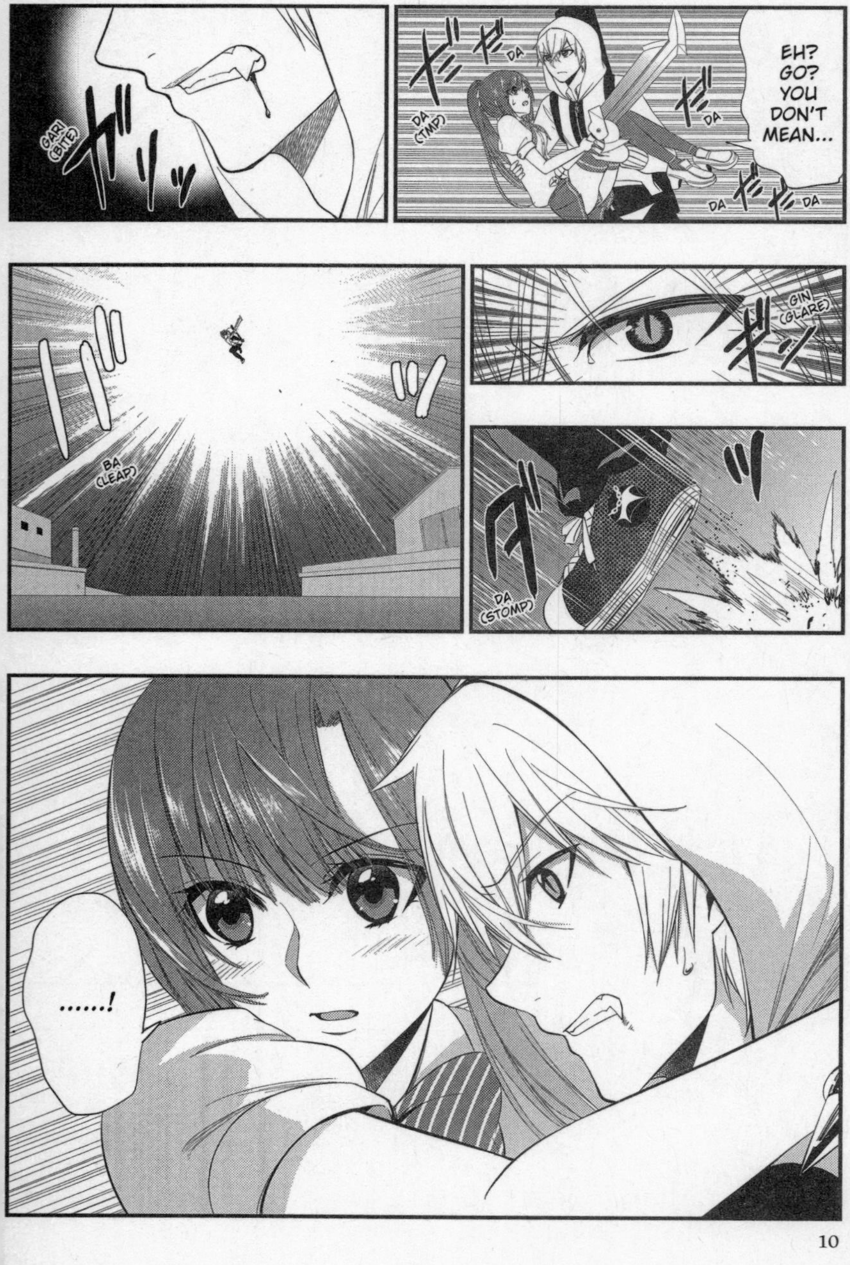
EH? GO? YOU DON'T MEAN...
DA
DA (TMP)
DA
DA
DA
GARI (BITE)
GIN (GLARE)
DA (STOMP)
BA (LEAP)
......!

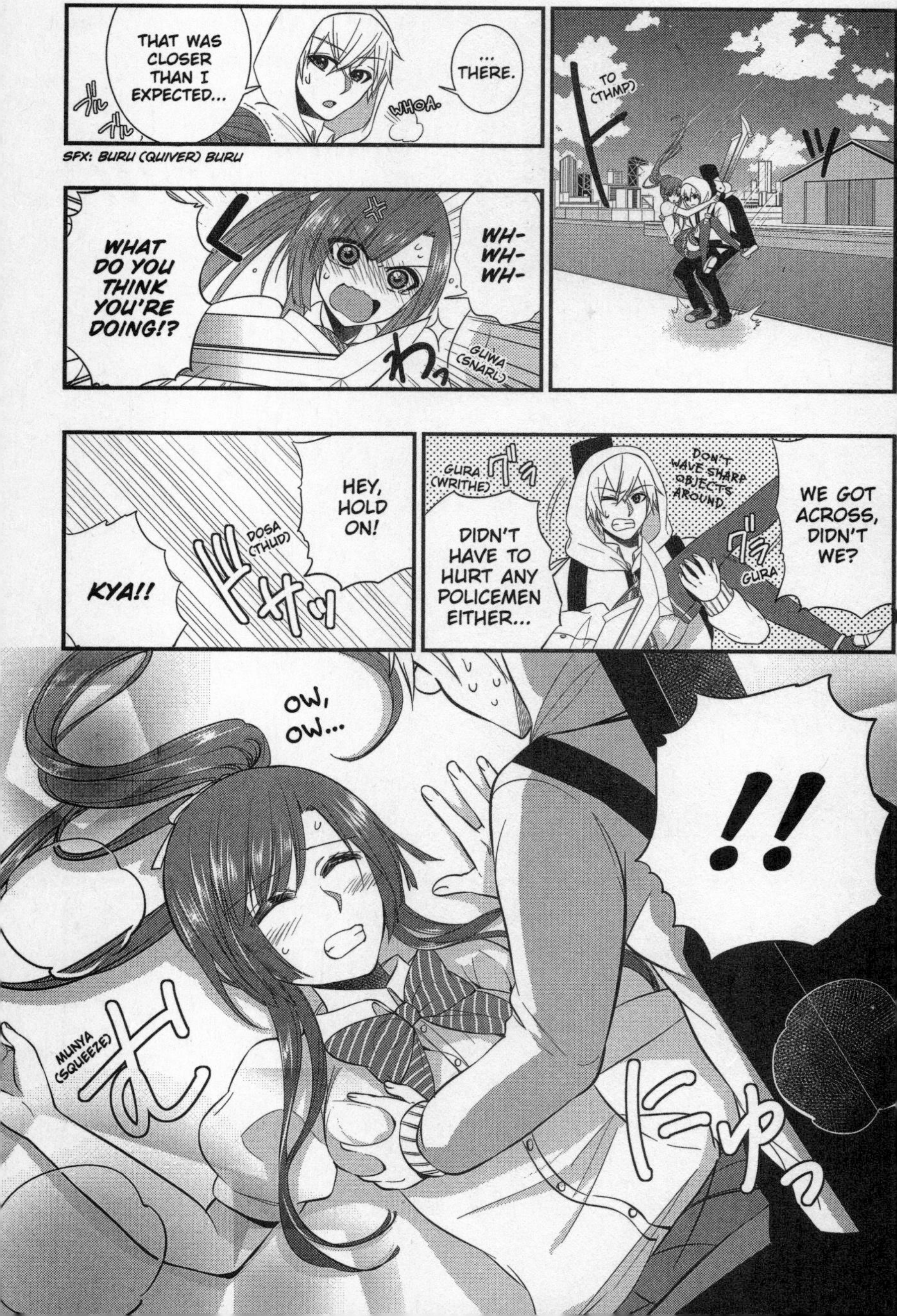
TO (THMP)
... THERE.
WHOA.
THAT WAS CLOSER THAN I EXPECTED...
SFX: BURU (QUIVER) BURU
WH-WH-WH-
GUWA (SNARL)
WHAT DO YOU THINK YOU'RE DOING!?
WE GOT ACROSS, DIDN'T WE?
GURA
DON'T WAVE SHARP OBJECTS AROUND
GURA (WRITHE)
DIDN'T HAVE TO HURT ANY POLICEMEN EITHER...
HEY, HOLD ON!
DOSA (THUD)
KYA!!
!!
OW, OW...
MUNYA (SQUEEZE)

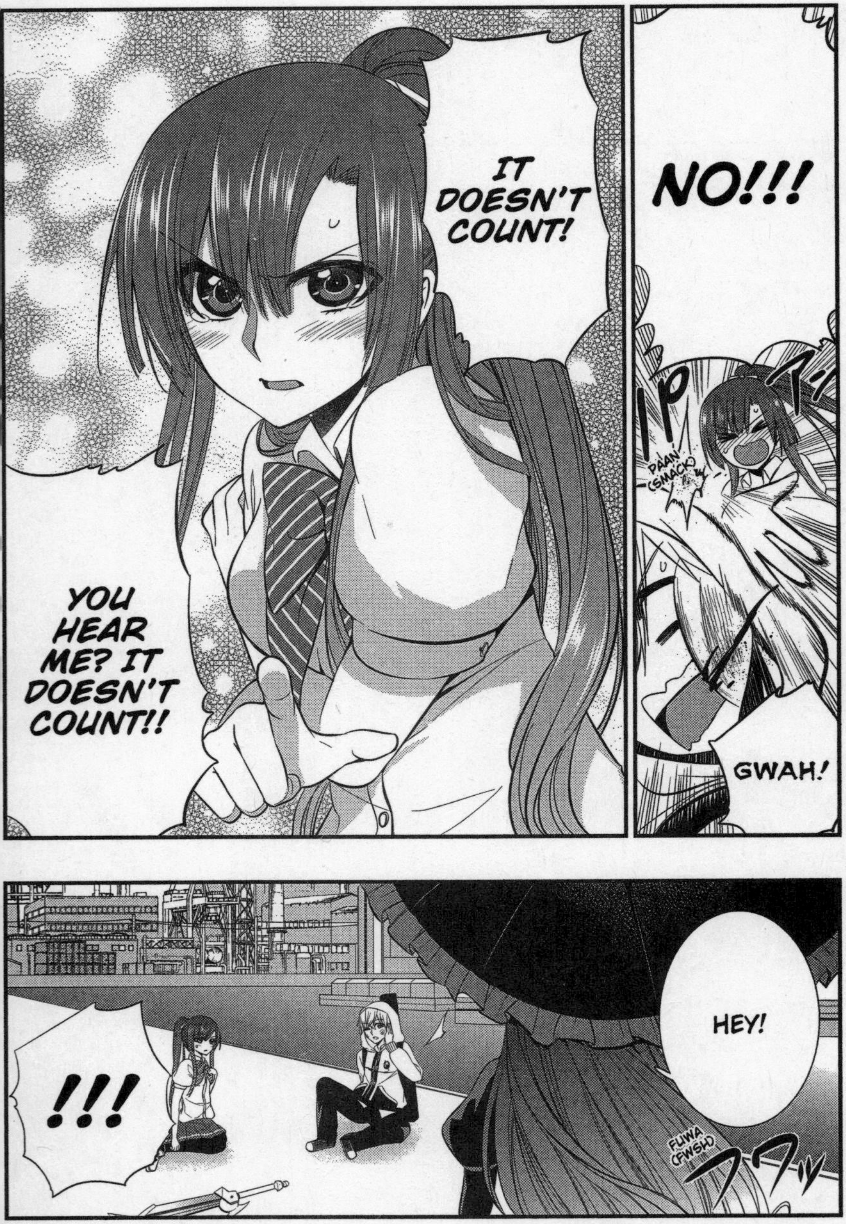
NO!!!
PAAN (SMACK)
GWAH!
IT DOESN'T COUNT!
YOU HEAR ME? IT DOESN'T COUNT!!
HEY!
FUWA (FWSH)
フワッ
!!!

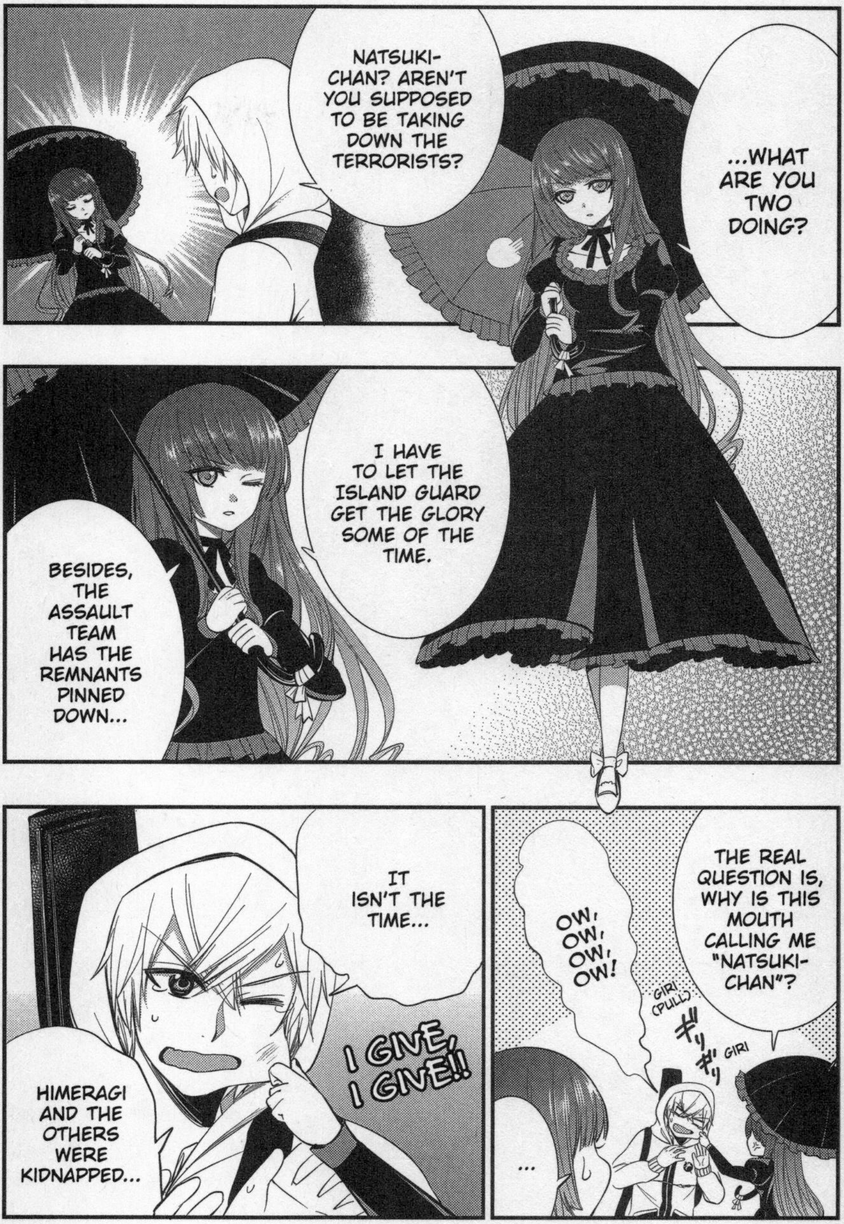
...WHAT ARE YOU TWO DOING?
NATSUKI-CHAN? AREN'T YOU SUPPOSED TO BE TAKING DOWN THE TERRORISTS?
I HAVE TO LET THE ISLAND GUARD GET THE GLORY SOME OF THE TIME.
BESIDES, THE ASSAULT TEAM HAS THE REMNANTS PINNED DOWN...
THE REAL QUESTION IS, WHY IS THIS MOUTH CALLING ME "NATSUKI-CHAN"?
OW, OW, OW, OW!
GIRI (PULL)
GIRI
...
IT ISN'T THE TIME...
I GIVE, I GIVE!!
HIMERAGI AND THE OTHERS WERE KIDNAPPED...

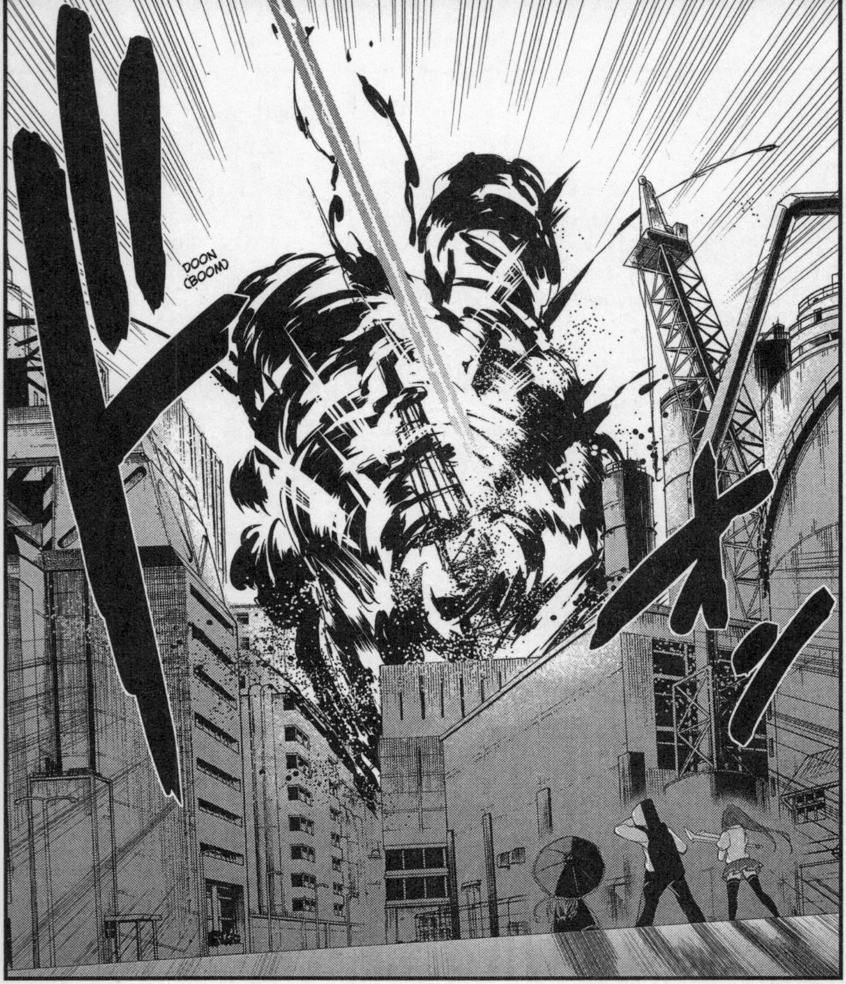
DOON (BOOM)

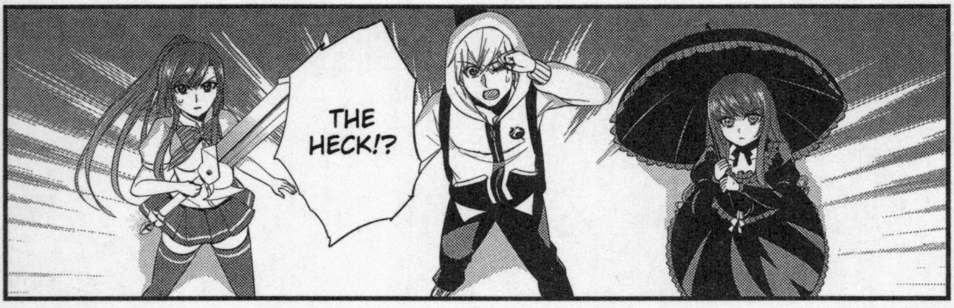
THE HECK!?

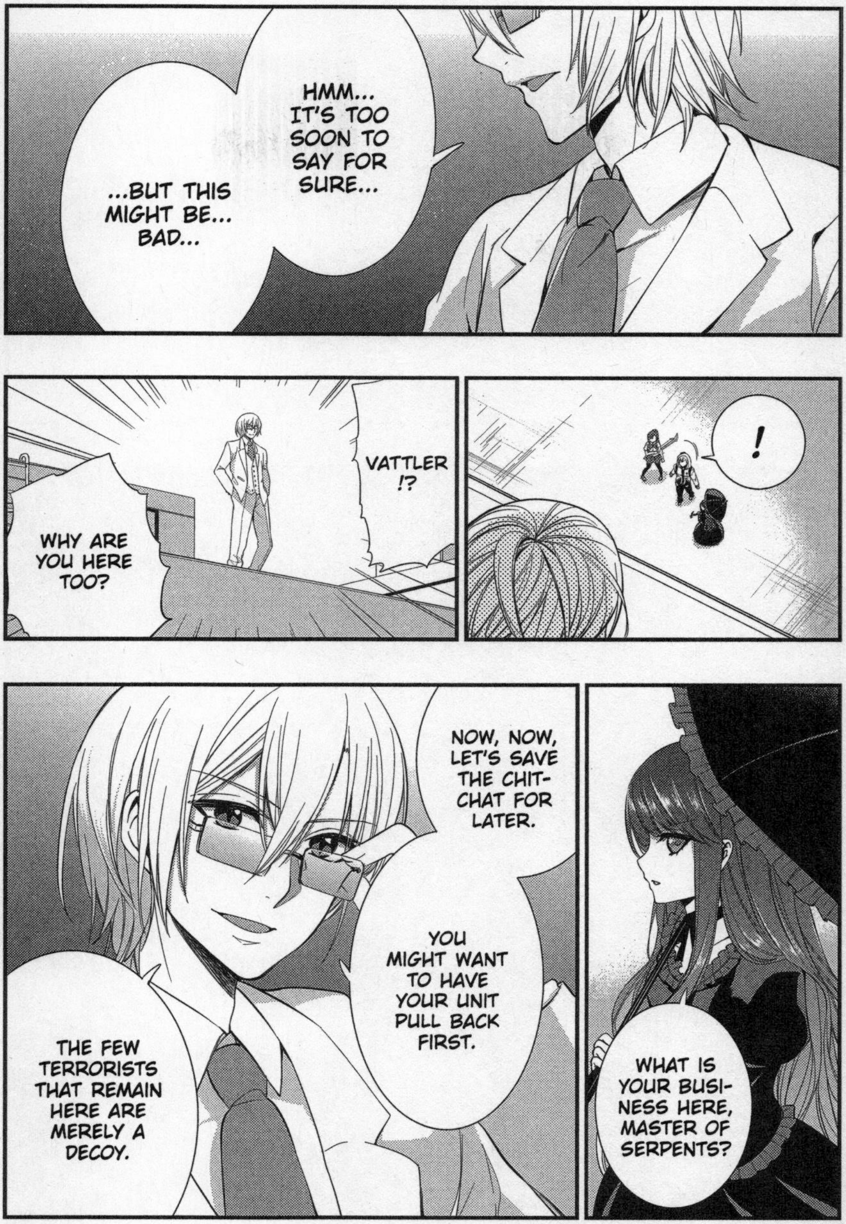
HMM... IT'S TOO SOON TO SAY FOR SURE...
...BUT THIS MIGHT BE... BAD...
!
VATTLER !?
WHY ARE YOU HERE TOO?
WHAT IS YOUR BUSINESS HERE, MASTER OF SERPENTS?
NOW, NOW, LET'S SAVE THE CHIT-CHAT FOR LATER.
YOU MIGHT WANT TO HAVE YOUR UNIT PULL BACK FIRST.
THE FEW TERRORISTS THAT REMAIN HERE ARE MERELY A DECOY.

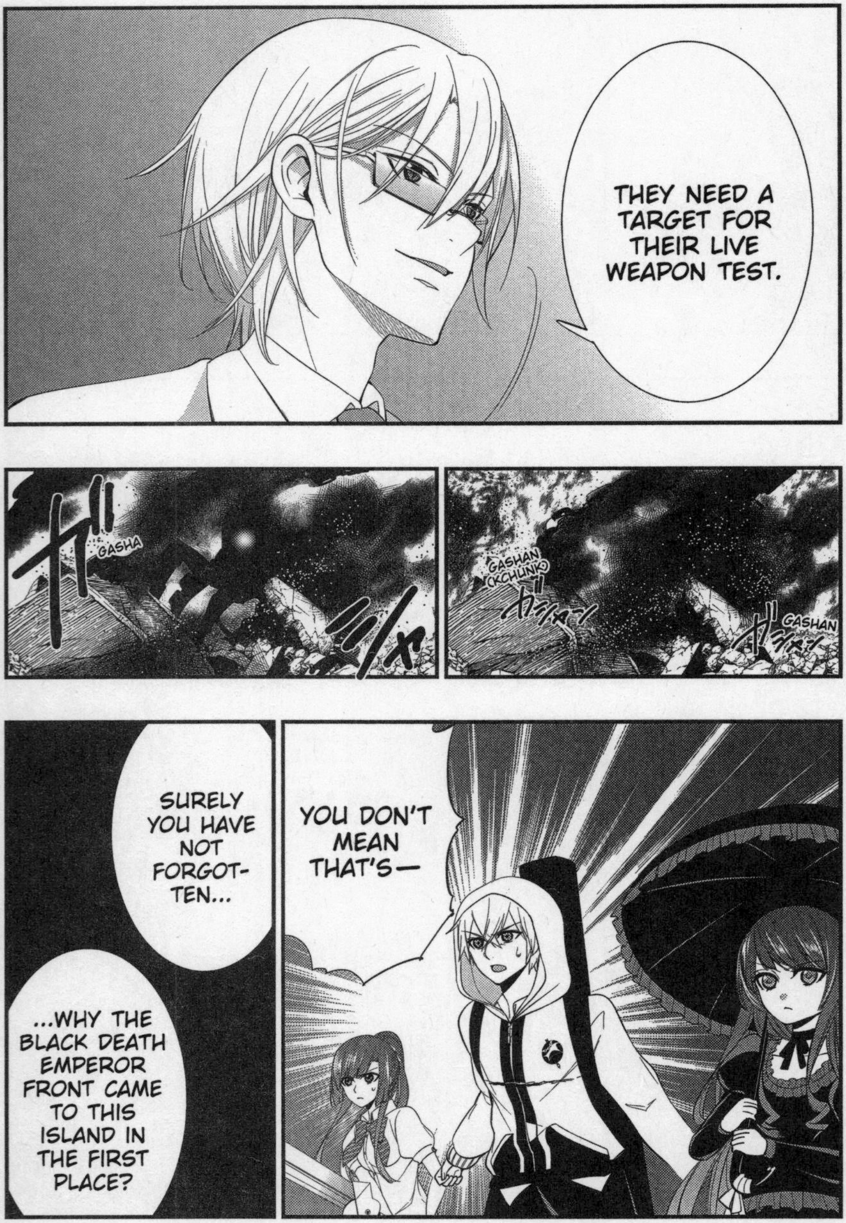
THEY NEED A TARGET FOR THEIR LIVE WEAPON TEST.
GASHAN (KCHUNK)
GASHAN
GASHA
YOU DON'T MEAN THAT'S—
SURELY YOU HAVE NOT FORGOT-TEN...
...WHY THE BLACK DEATH EMPEROR FRONT CAME TO THIS ISLAND IN THE FIRST PLACE?

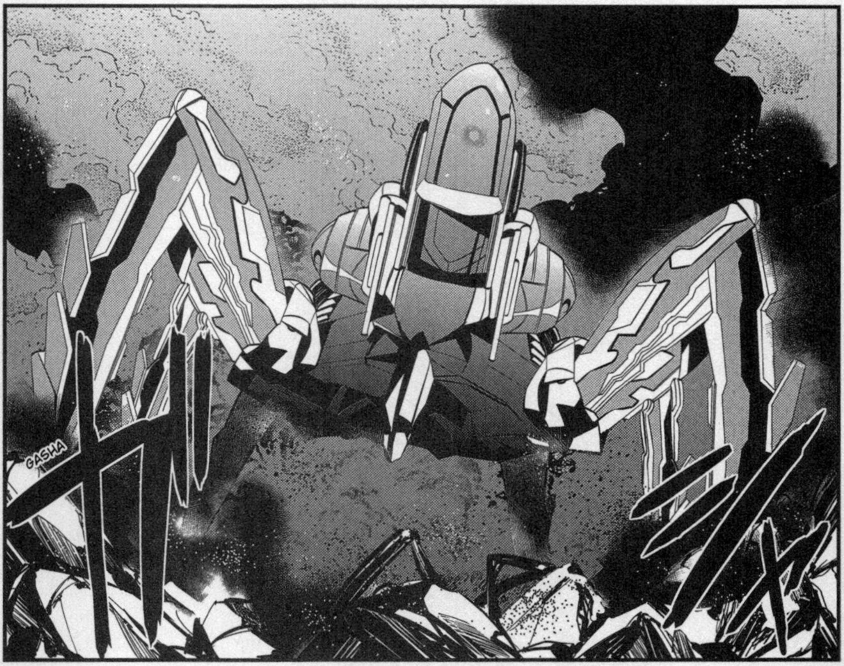
GASHA

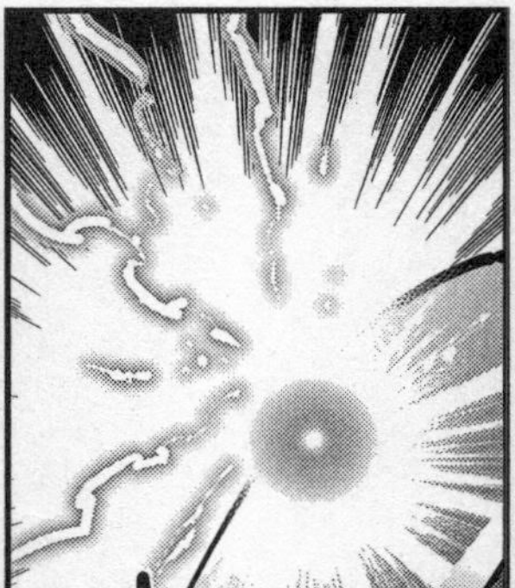
GYUIII
(VWEEN)

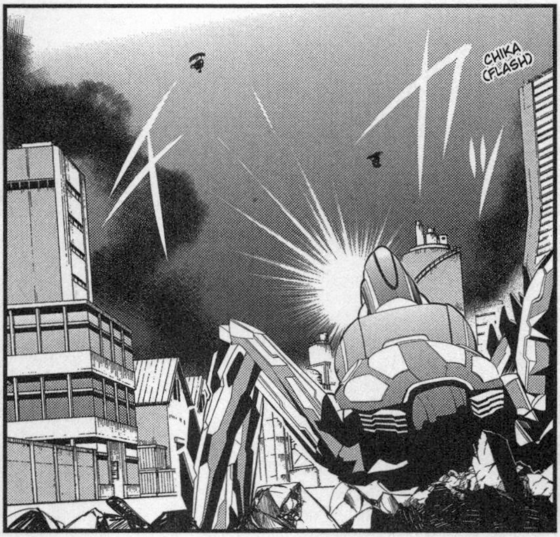
CHIKA
(FLASH)

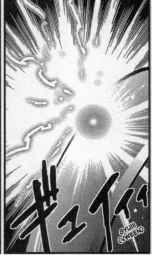

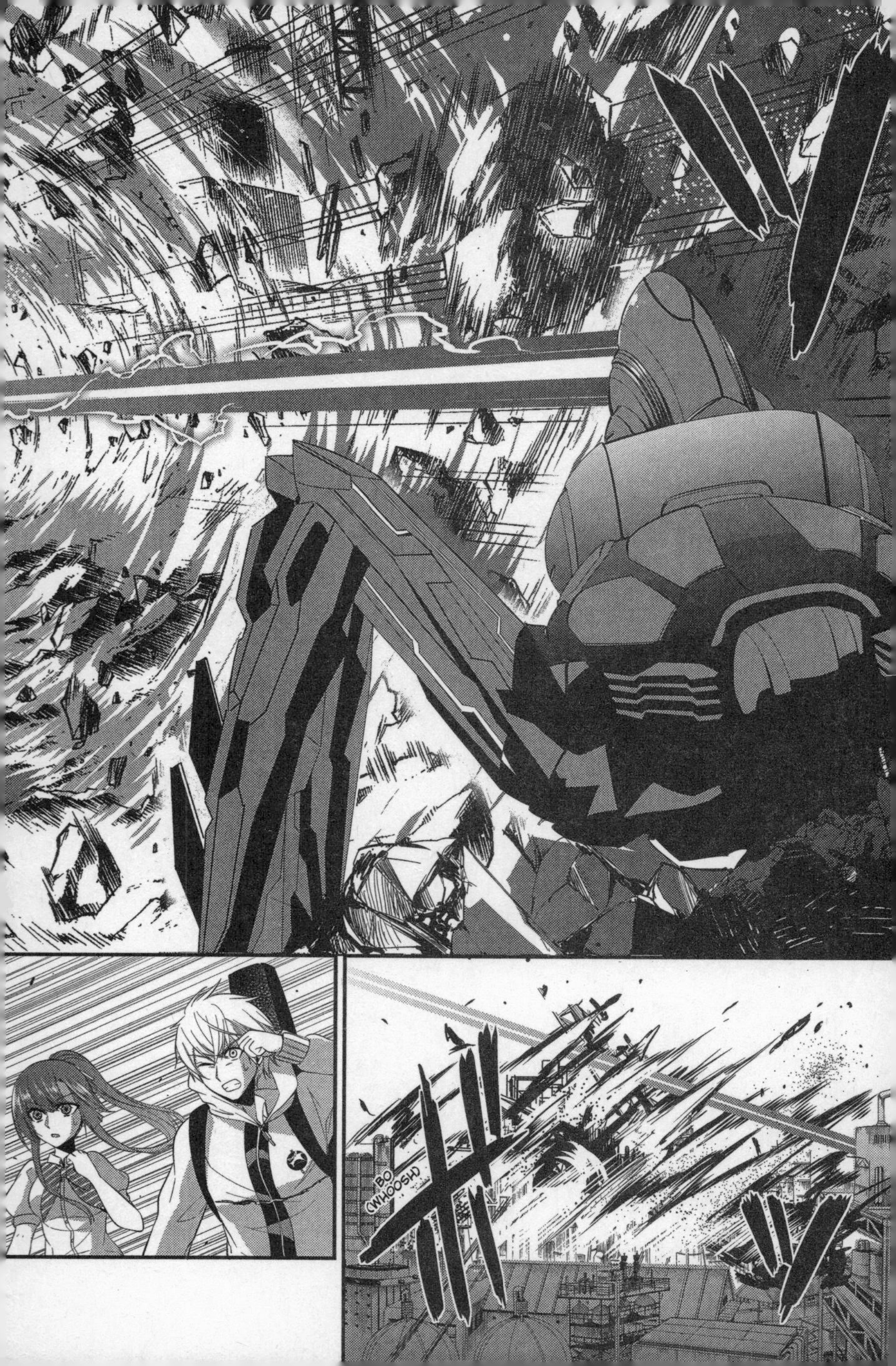
BO
(WHOOSH)

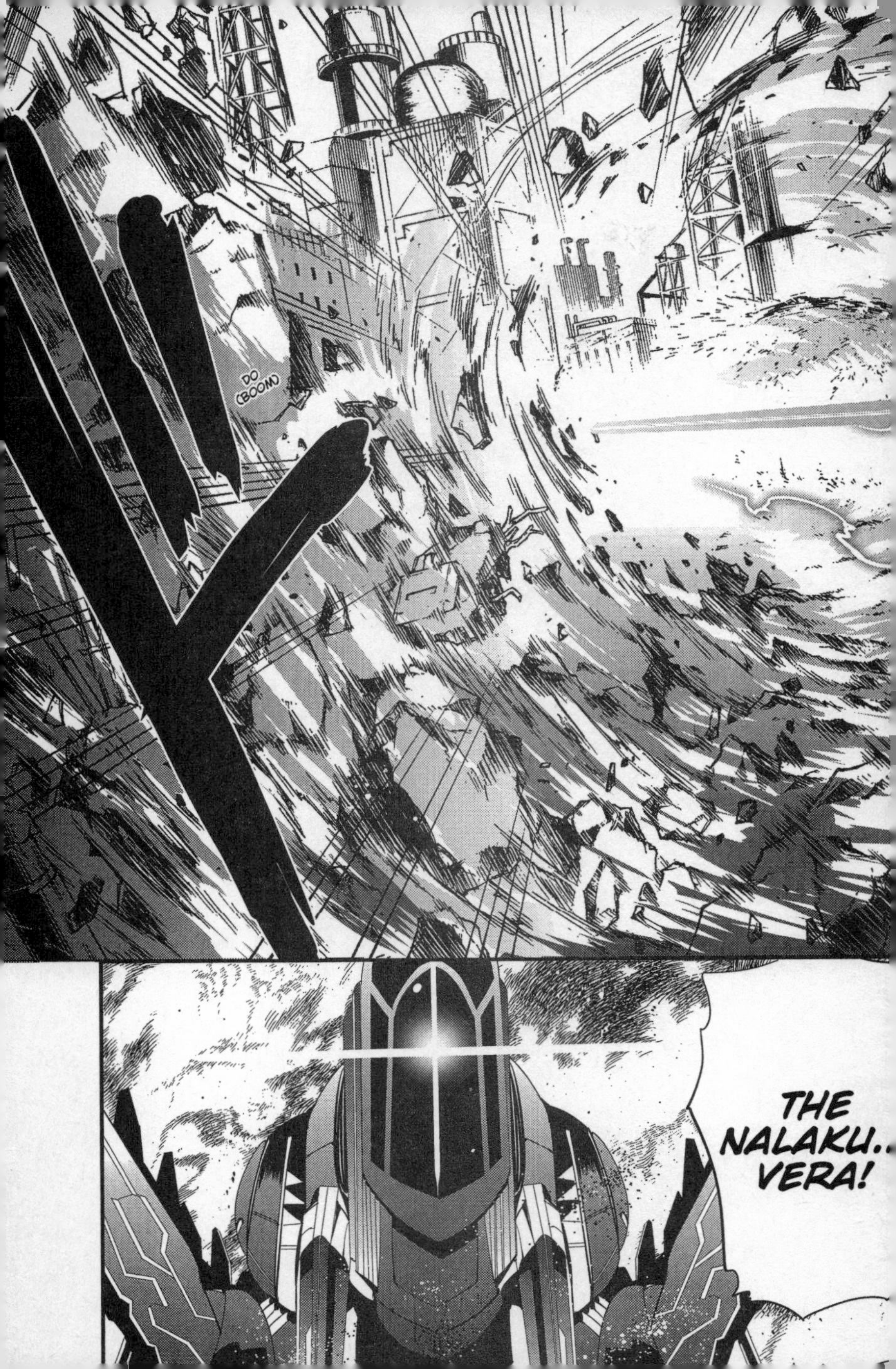
DO
(BOOM)
THE NALAKU... VERA!

STRIKE THE BLOOD

DEFINITION

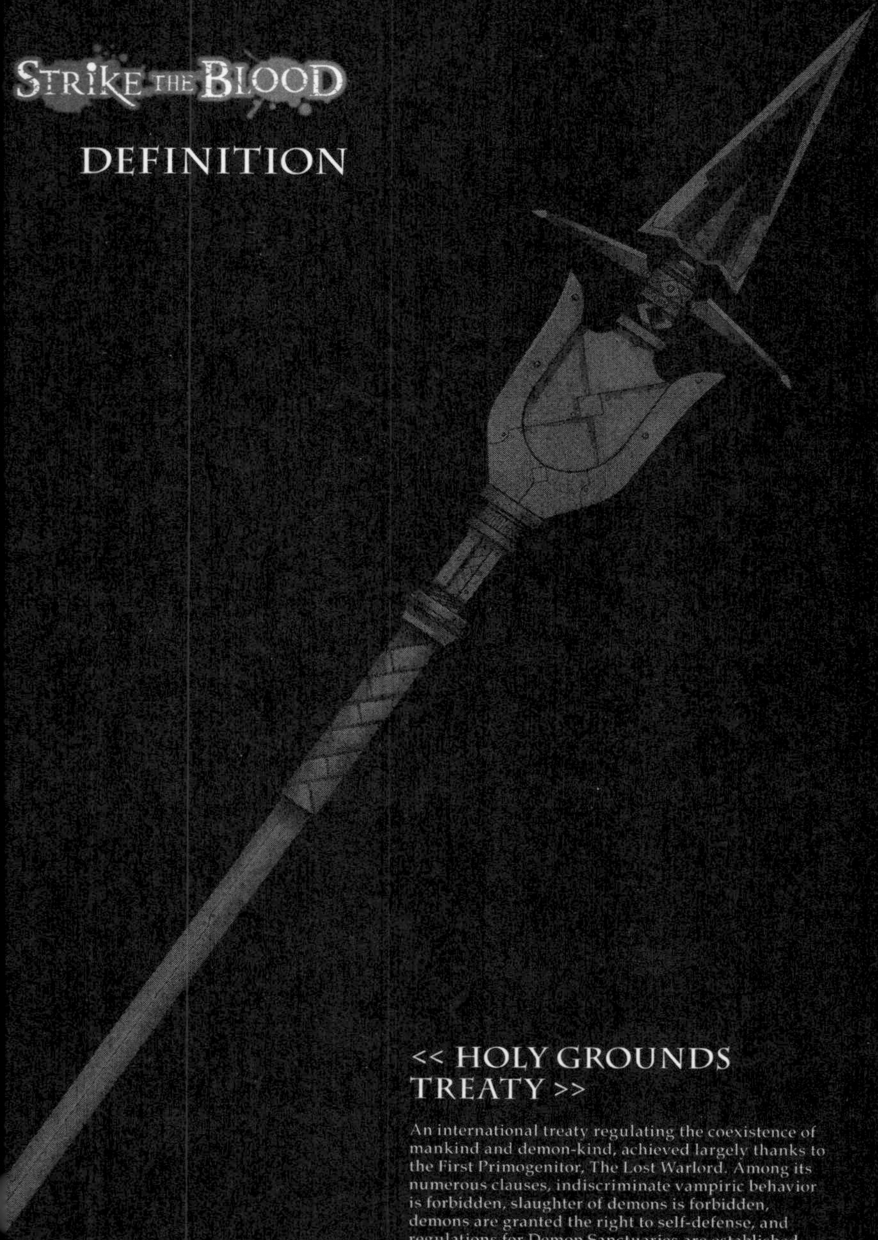

<< HOLY GROUNDS TREATY >>

An international treaty regulating the coexistence of mankind and demon-kind, achieved largely thanks to the First Primogenitor, The Lost Warlord. Among its numerous clauses, indiscriminate vampiric behavior is forbidden, slaughter of demons is forbidden, demons are granted the right to self-defense, and regulations for Demon Sanctuaries are established.

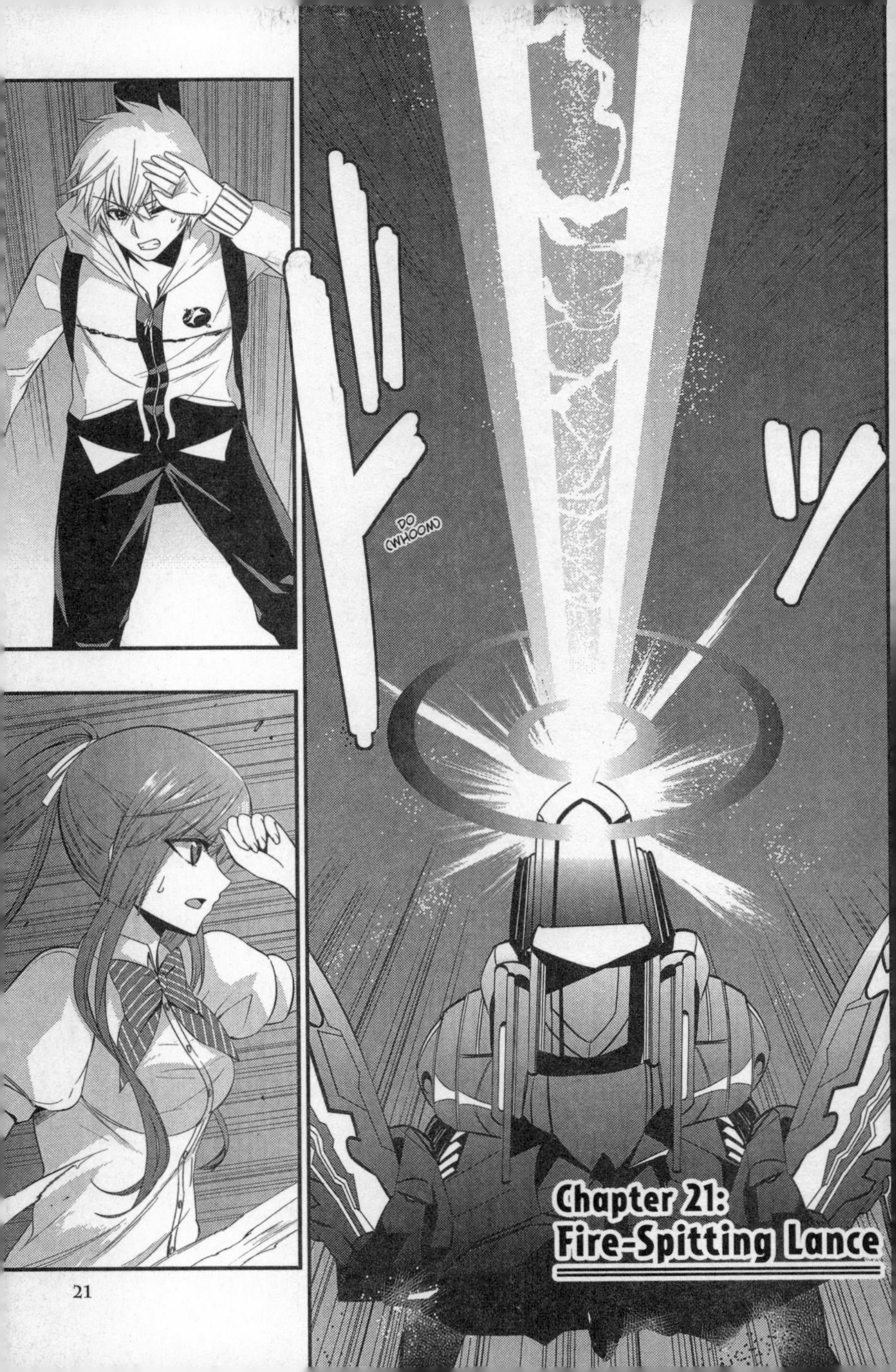
DO (WHOOM)
Chapter 21:
Fire-Spitting Lance

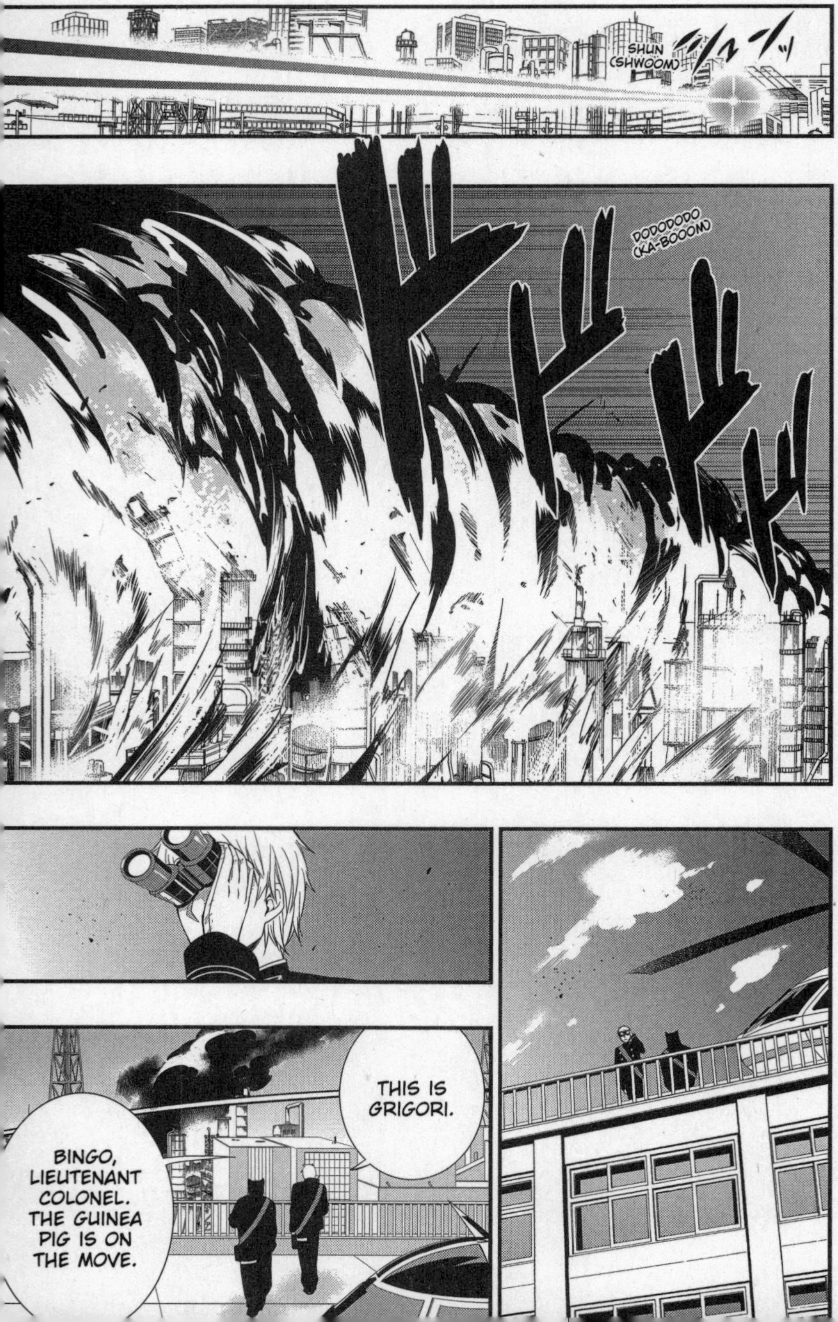
SHUN (SHWOOM)
DODODODO (KA-BOOOM)
THIS IS GRIGORI.
BINGO, LIEUTENANT COLONEL. THE GUINEA PIG IS ON THE MOVE.

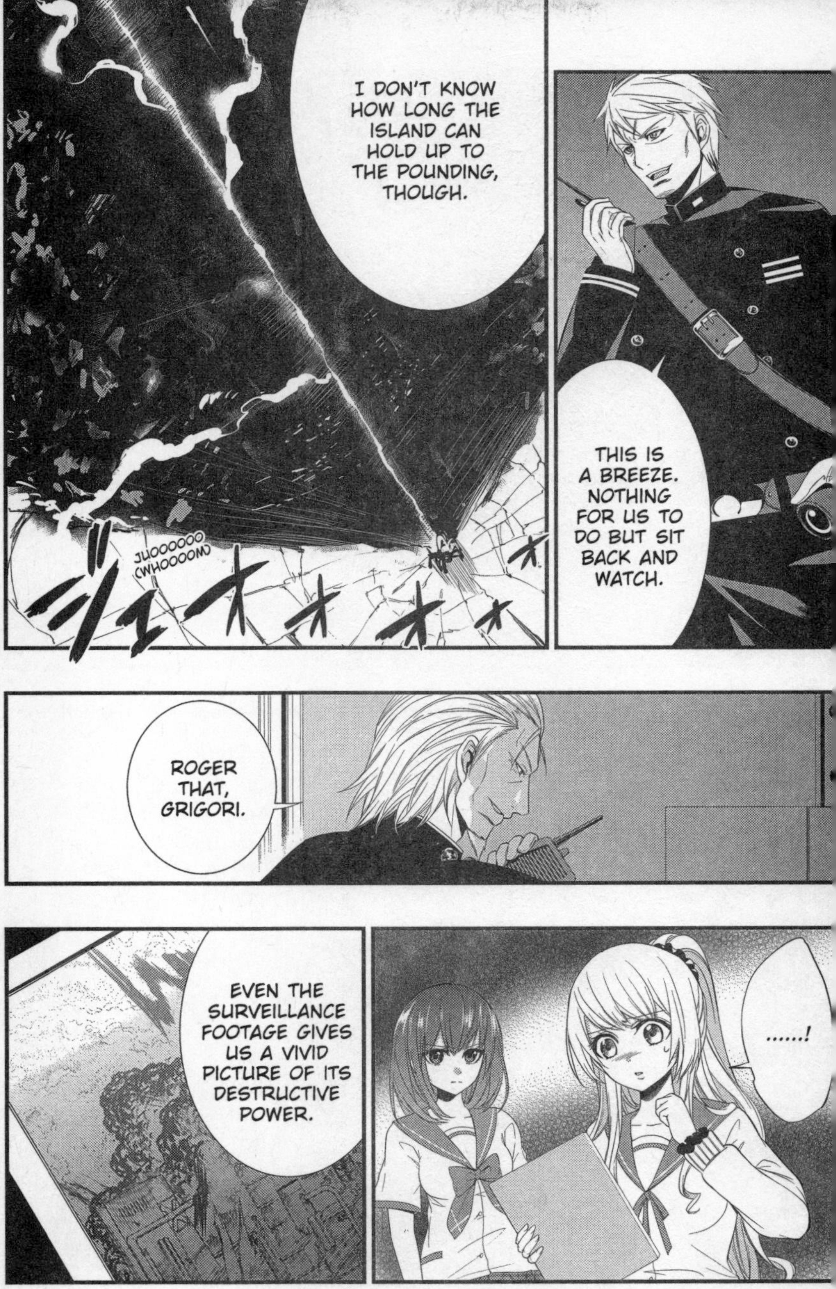
THIS IS A BREEZE. NOTHING FOR US TO DO BUT SIT BACK AND WATCH.
I DON'T KNOW HOW LONG THE ISLAND CAN HOLD UP TO THE POUNDING, THOUGH.
JUOOOOOO (WHOOOOM)
ROGER THAT, GRIGORI.
......!
EVEN THE SURVEILLANCE FOOTAGE GIVES US A VIVID PICTURE OF ITS DESTRUCTIVE POWER.

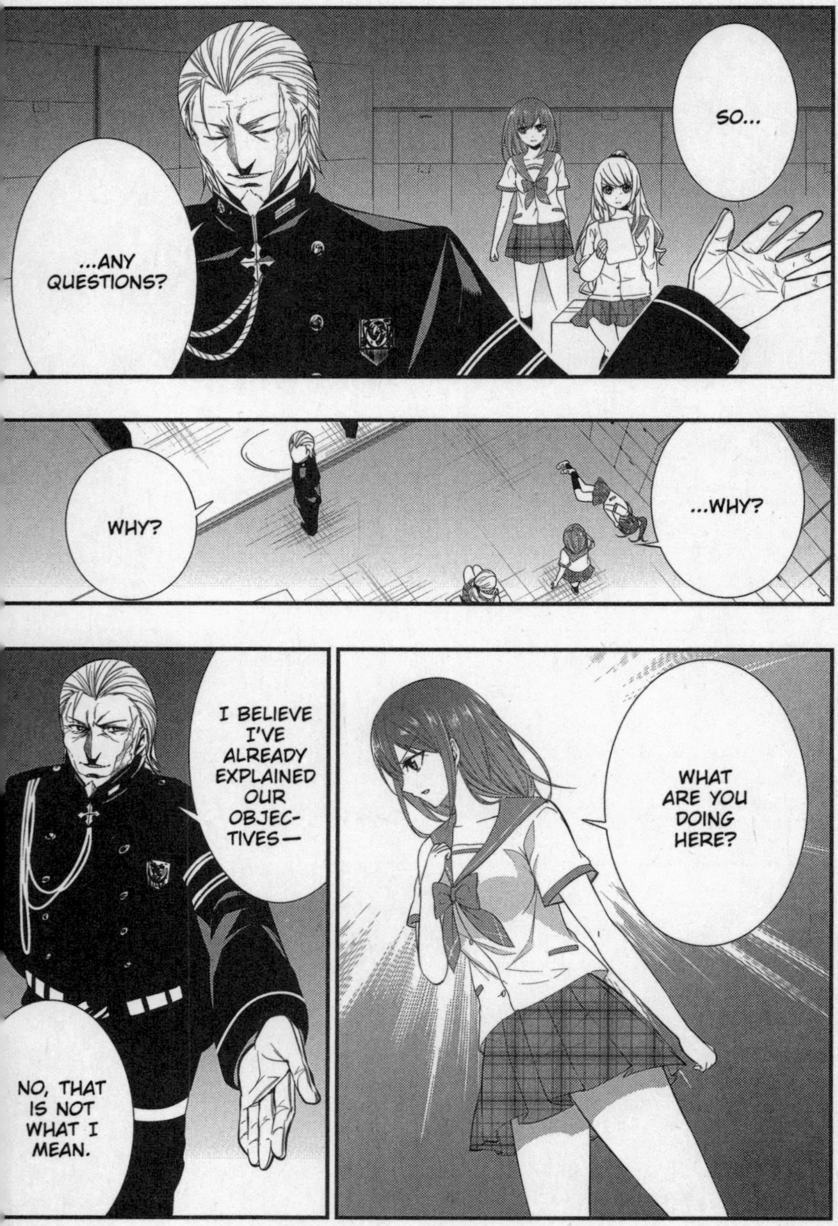
SO...
...ANY QUESTIONS?
...WHY?
WHY?
WHAT ARE YOU DOING HERE?
I BELIEVE I'VE ALREADY EXPLAINED OUR OBJECTIVES—
NO, THAT IS NOT WHAT I MEAN.

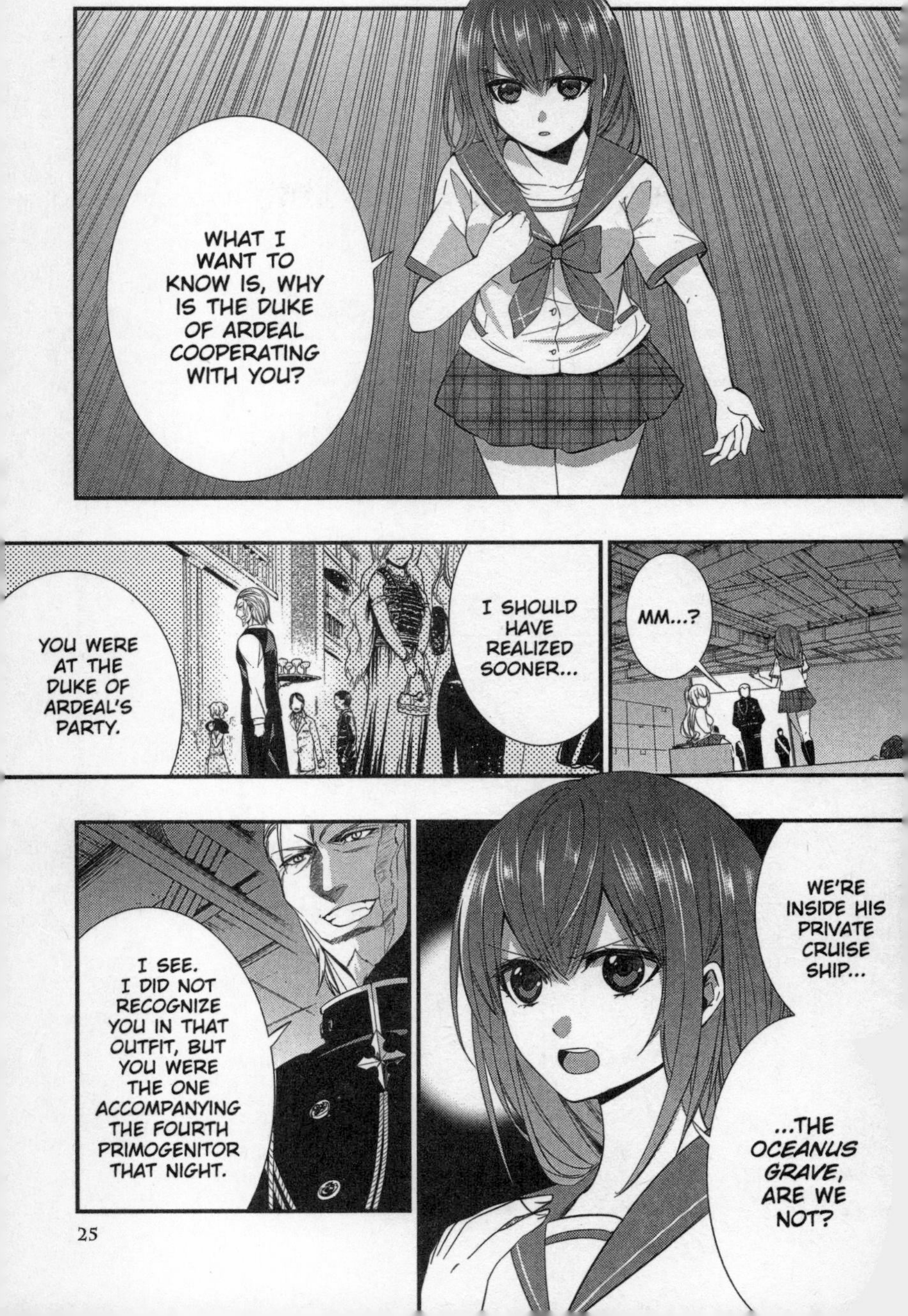
WHAT I WANT TO KNOW IS, WHY IS THE DUKE OF ARDEAL COOPERATING WITH YOU?
MM...?
I SHOULD HAVE REALIZED SOONER...
YOU WERE AT THE DUKE OF ARDEAL'S PARTY.
WE'RE INSIDE HIS PRIVATE CRUISE SHIP...
...THE *OCEANUS GRAVE*, ARE WE NOT?
I SEE. I DID NOT RECOGNIZE YOU IN THAT OUTFIT, BUT YOU WERE THE ONE ACCOMPANYING THE FOURTH PRIMOGENITOR THAT NIGHT.

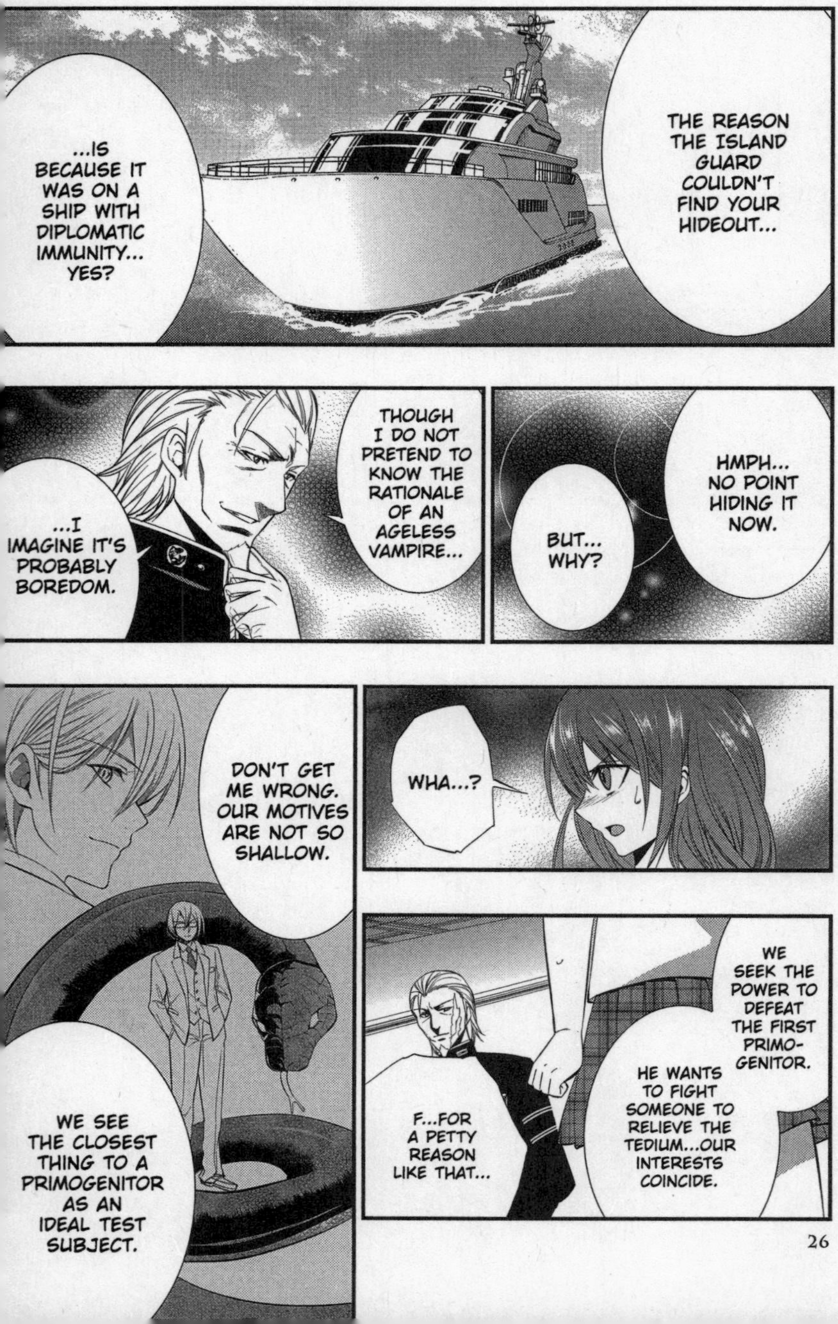
THE REASON THE ISLAND GUARD COULDN'T FIND YOUR HIDEOUT...
...IS BECAUSE IT WAS ON A SHIP WITH DIPLOMATIC IMMUNITY... YES?
HMPH... NO POINT HIDING IT NOW.
BUT... WHY?
THOUGH I DO NOT PRETEND TO KNOW THE RATIONALE OF AN AGELESS VAMPIRE...
...I IMAGINE IT'S PROBABLY BOREDOM.
WHA...?
WE SEEK THE POWER TO DEFEAT THE FIRST PRIMO-GENITOR.
HE WANTS TO FIGHT SOMEONE TO RELIEVE THE TEDIUM...OUR INTERESTS COINCIDE.
F...FOR A PETTY REASON LIKE THAT...
DON'T GET ME WRONG. OUR MOTIVES ARE NOT SO SHALLOW.
WE SEE THE CLOSEST THING TO A PRIMOGENITOR AS AN IDEAL TEST SUBJECT.

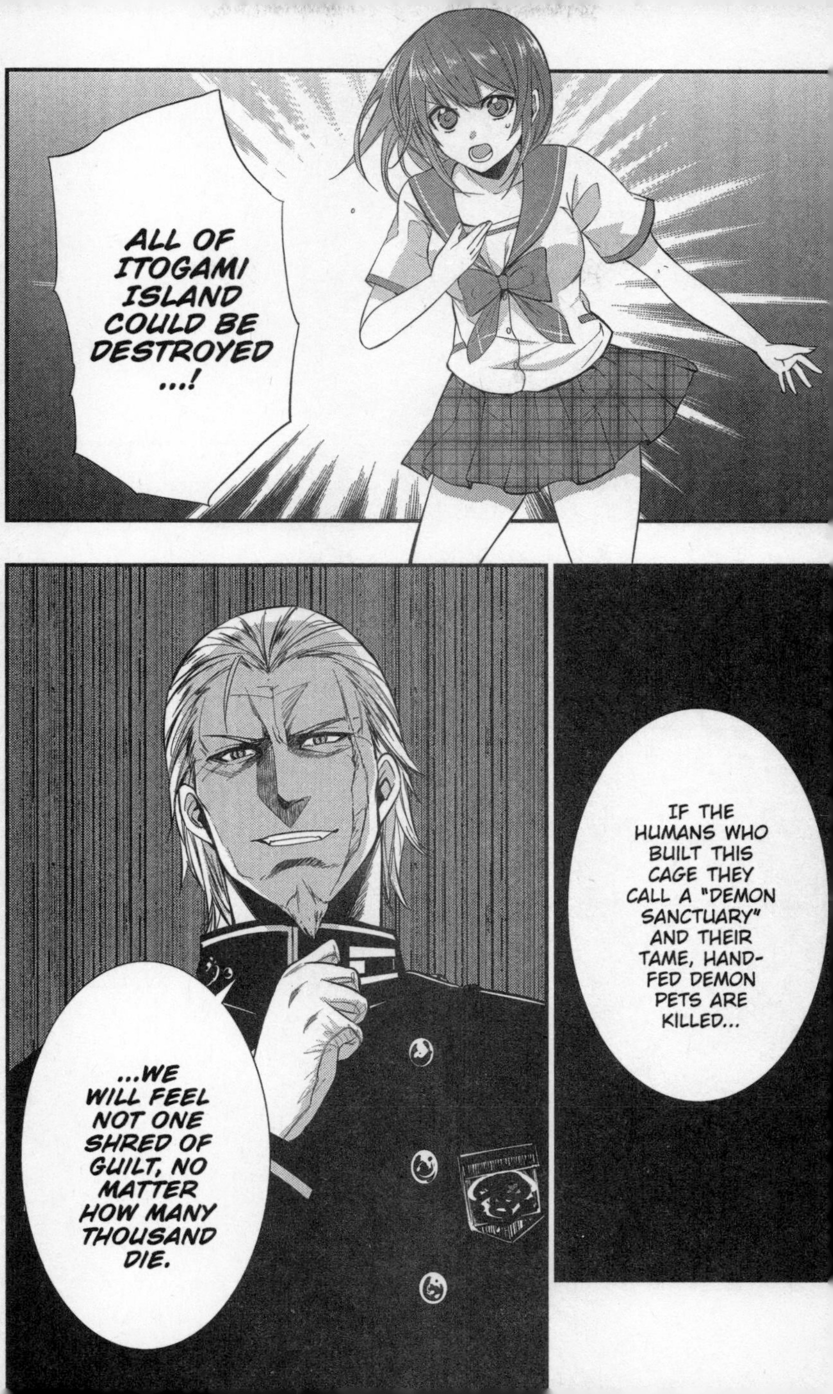
ALL OF ITOGAMI ISLAND COULD BE DESTROYED ...!
IF THE HUMANS WHO BUILT THIS CAGE THEY CALL A "DEMON SANCTUARY" AND THEIR TAME, HAND-FED DEMON PETS ARE KILLED...
...WE WILL FEEL NOT ONE SHRED OF GUILT, NO MATTER HOW MANY THOUSAND DIE.

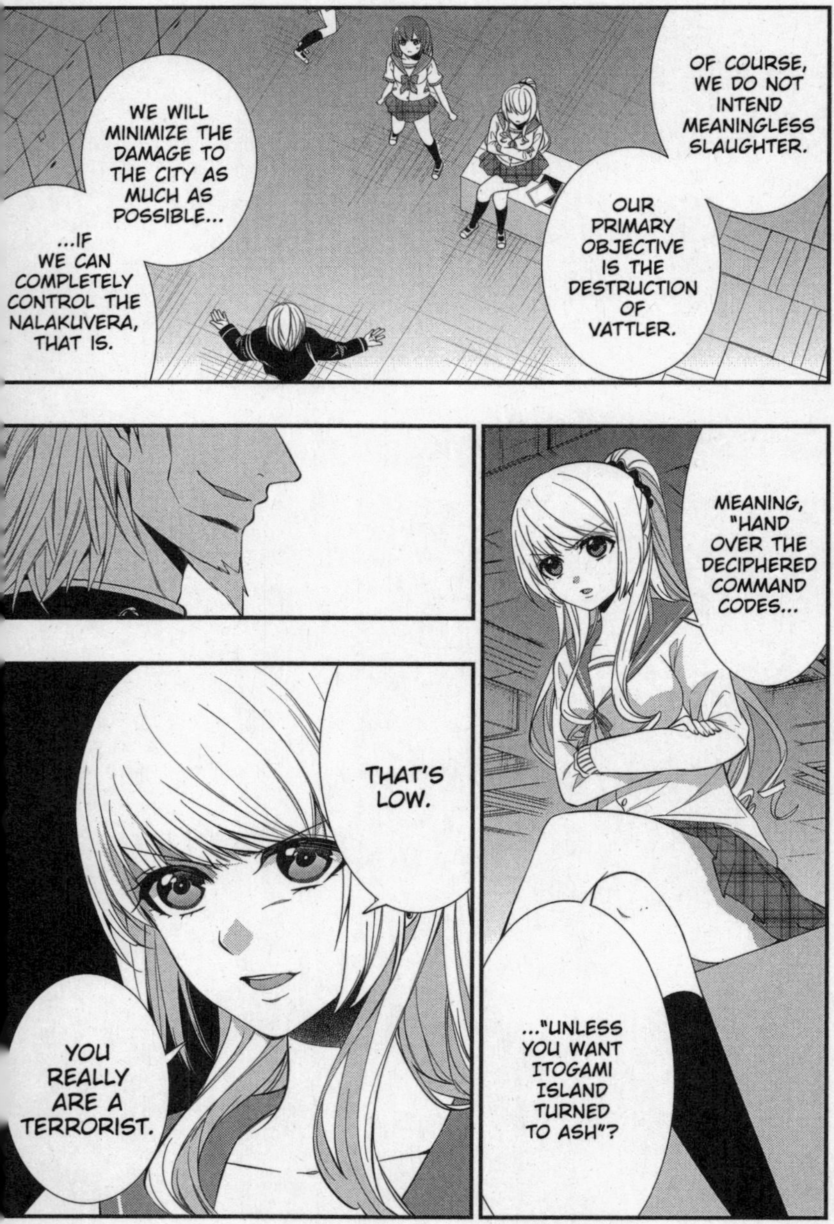
OF COURSE, WE DO NOT INTEND MEANINGLESS SLAUGHTER.
OUR PRIMARY OBJECTIVE IS THE DESTRUCTION OF VATTLER.
WE WILL MINIMIZE THE DAMAGE TO THE CITY AS MUCH AS POSSIBLE...
...IF WE CAN COMPLETELY CONTROL THE NALAKUVERA, THAT IS.
MEANING, "HAND OVER THE DECIPHERED COMMAND CODES...
..."UNLESS YOU WANT ITOGAMI ISLAND TURNED TO ASH"?
THAT'S LOW.
YOU REALLY ARE A TERRORIST.

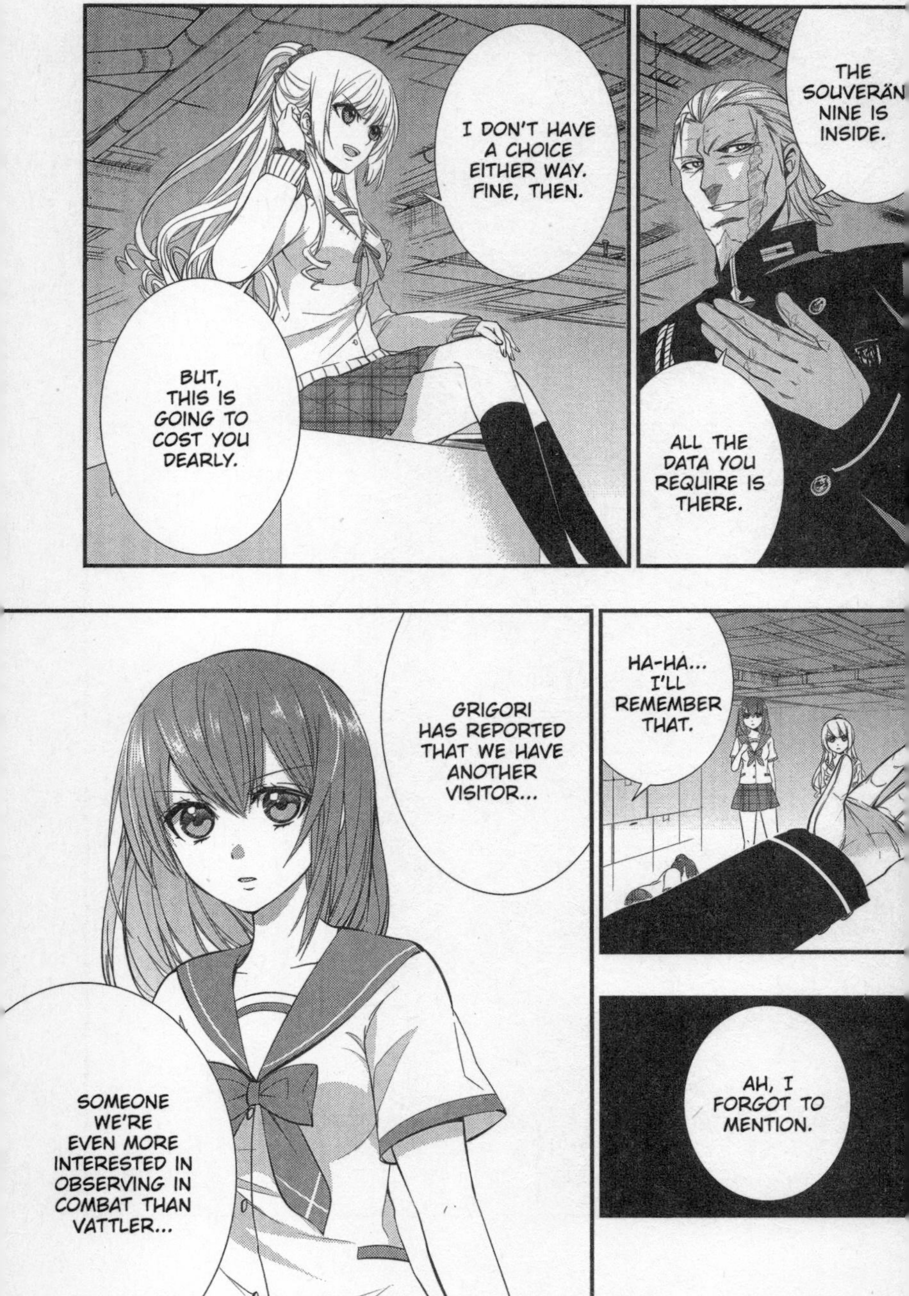
THE SOUVERÄN NINE IS INSIDE.
ALL THE DATA YOU REQUIRE IS THERE.
I DON'T HAVE A CHOICE EITHER WAY. FINE, THEN.
BUT, THIS IS GOING TO COST YOU DEARLY.
HA-HA... I'LL REMEMBER THAT.
AH, I FORGOT TO MENTION.
GRIGORI HAS REPORTED THAT WE HAVE ANOTHER VISITOR...
SOMEONE WE'RE EVEN MORE INTERESTED IN OBSERVING IN COMBAT THAN VATTLER...

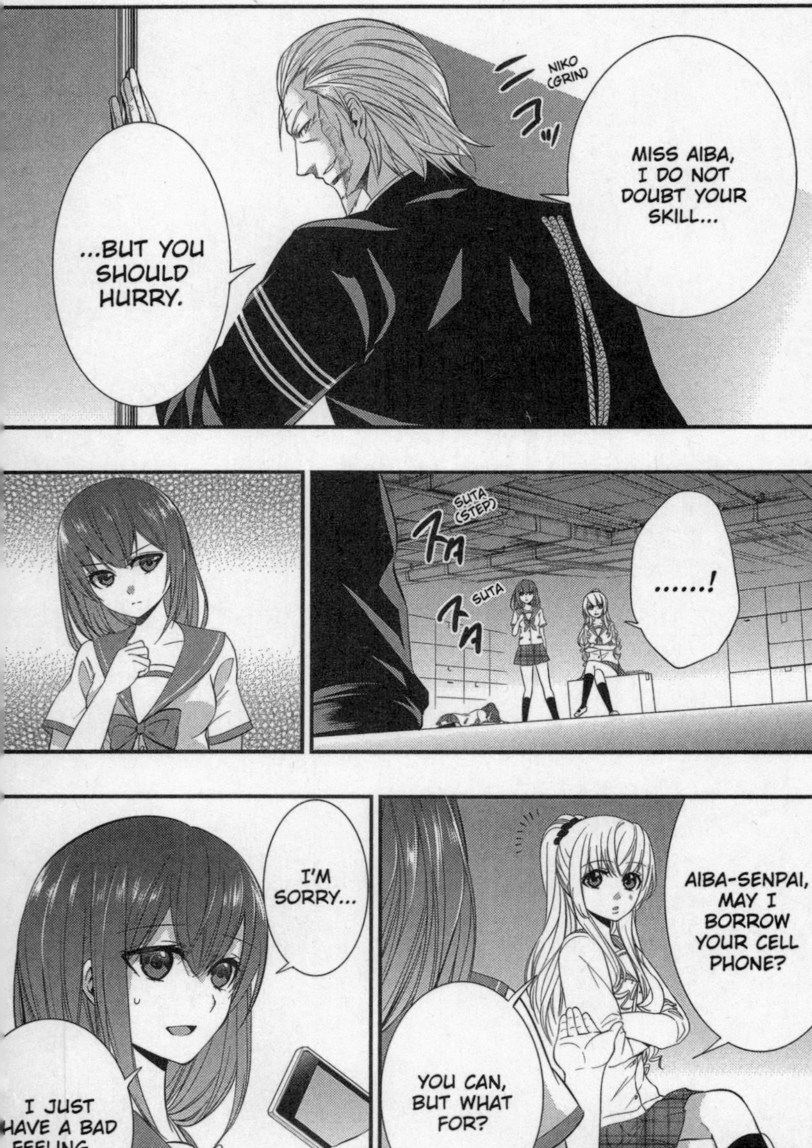
NIKO (GRIN)
MISS AIBA, I DO NOT DOUBT YOUR SKILL...
...BUT YOU SHOULD HURRY.
SUTA (STEP)
SUTA
......!
AIBA-SENPAI, MAY I BORROW YOUR CELL PHONE?
YOU CAN, BUT WHAT FOR?
I'M SORRY...
I JUST HAVE A BAD FEELING...

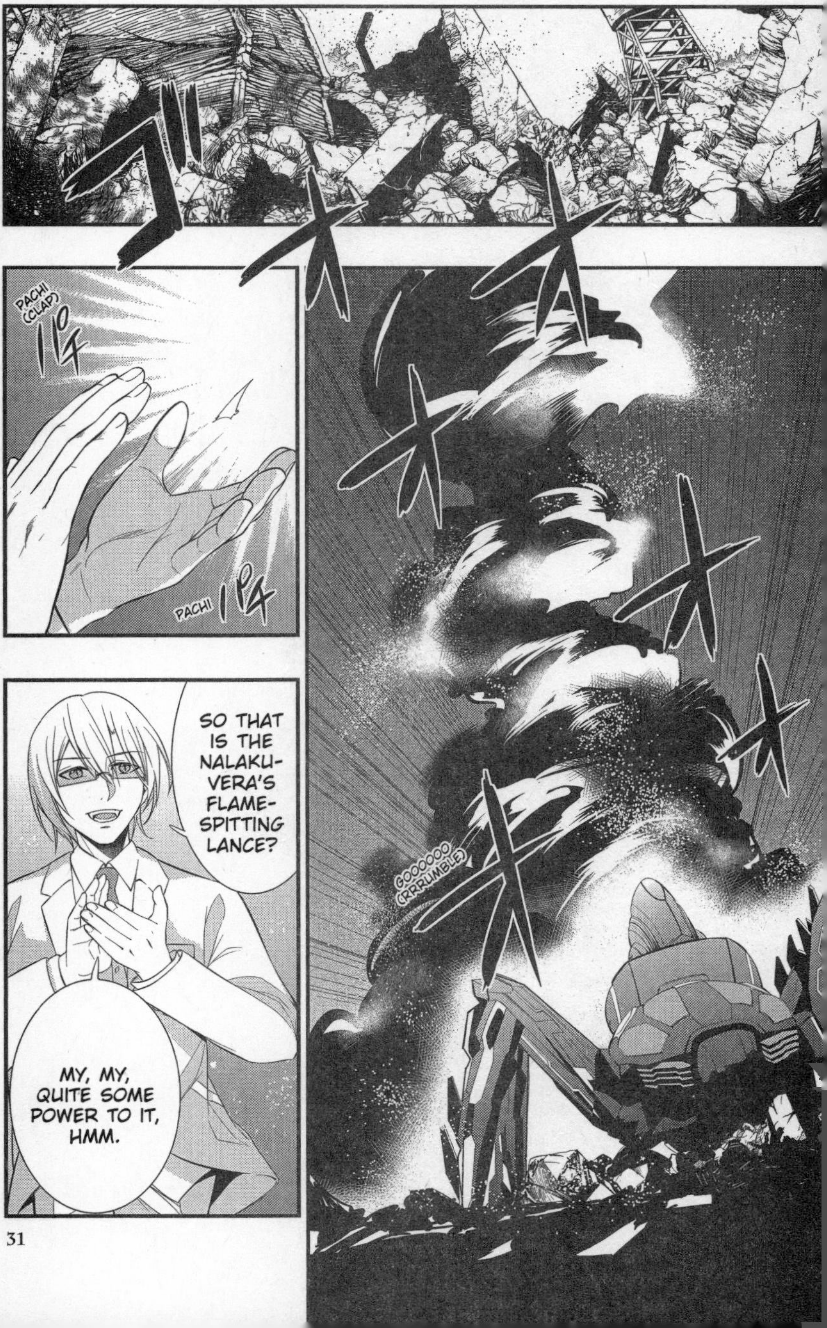
GOOOOOO (RRRUMBLE)
PACHI (CLAP)
パチ
PACHI
パチ
SO THAT IS THE NALAKU-VERA'S FLAME-SPITTING LANCE?
MY, MY, QUITE SOME POWER TO IT, HMM.

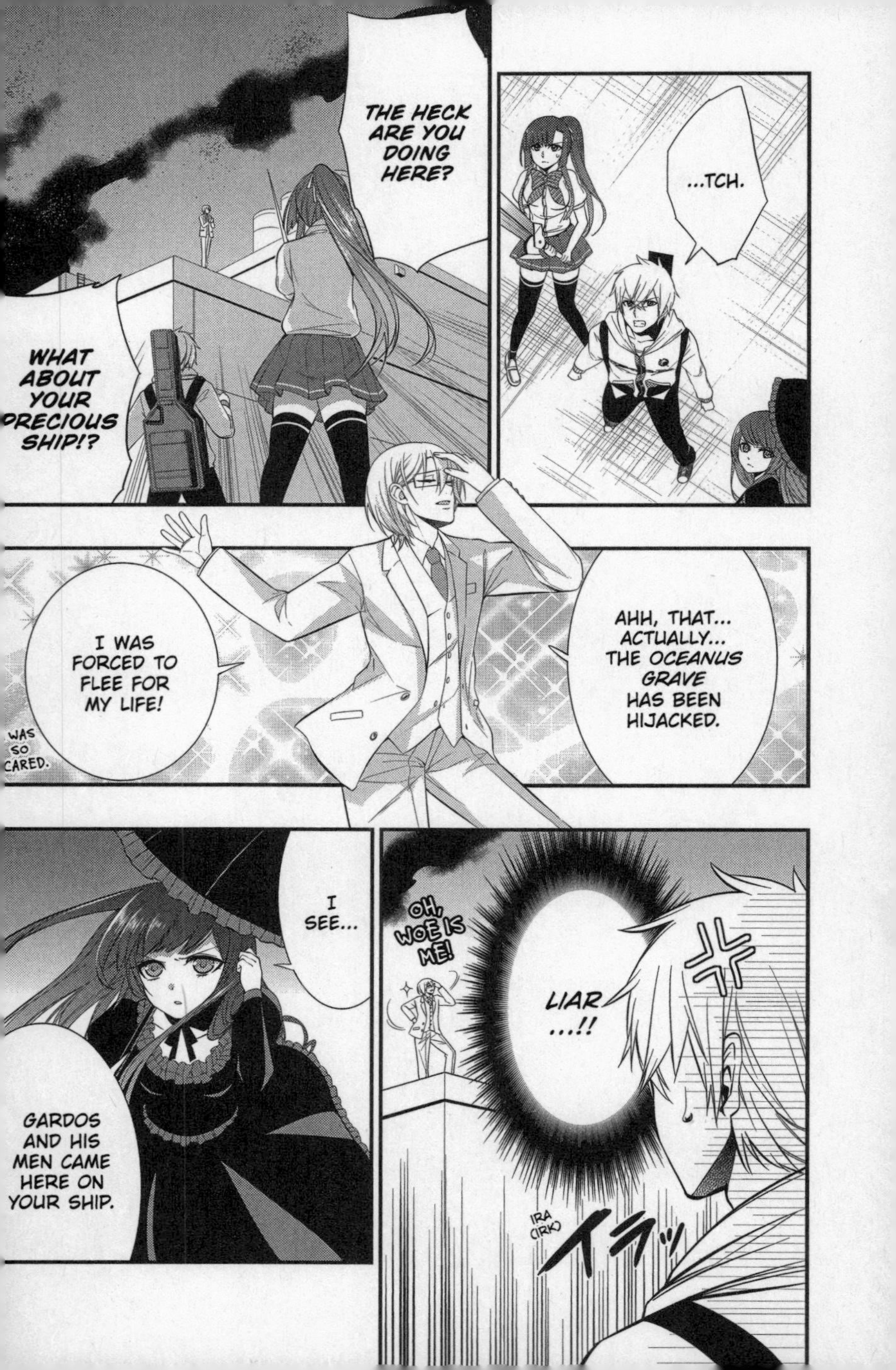
...TCH.
THE HECK ARE YOU DOING HERE?
WHAT ABOUT YOUR PRECIOUS SHIP!?
AHH, THAT... ACTUALLY... THE OCEANUS GRAVE HAS BEEN HIJACKED.
I WAS FORCED TO FLEE FOR MY LIFE!
WAS SO CARED.
OH, WOE IS ME!
LIAR ...!!
IRA (IRK)
イラッ
I SEE...
GARDOS AND HIS MEN CAME HERE ON YOUR SHIP.

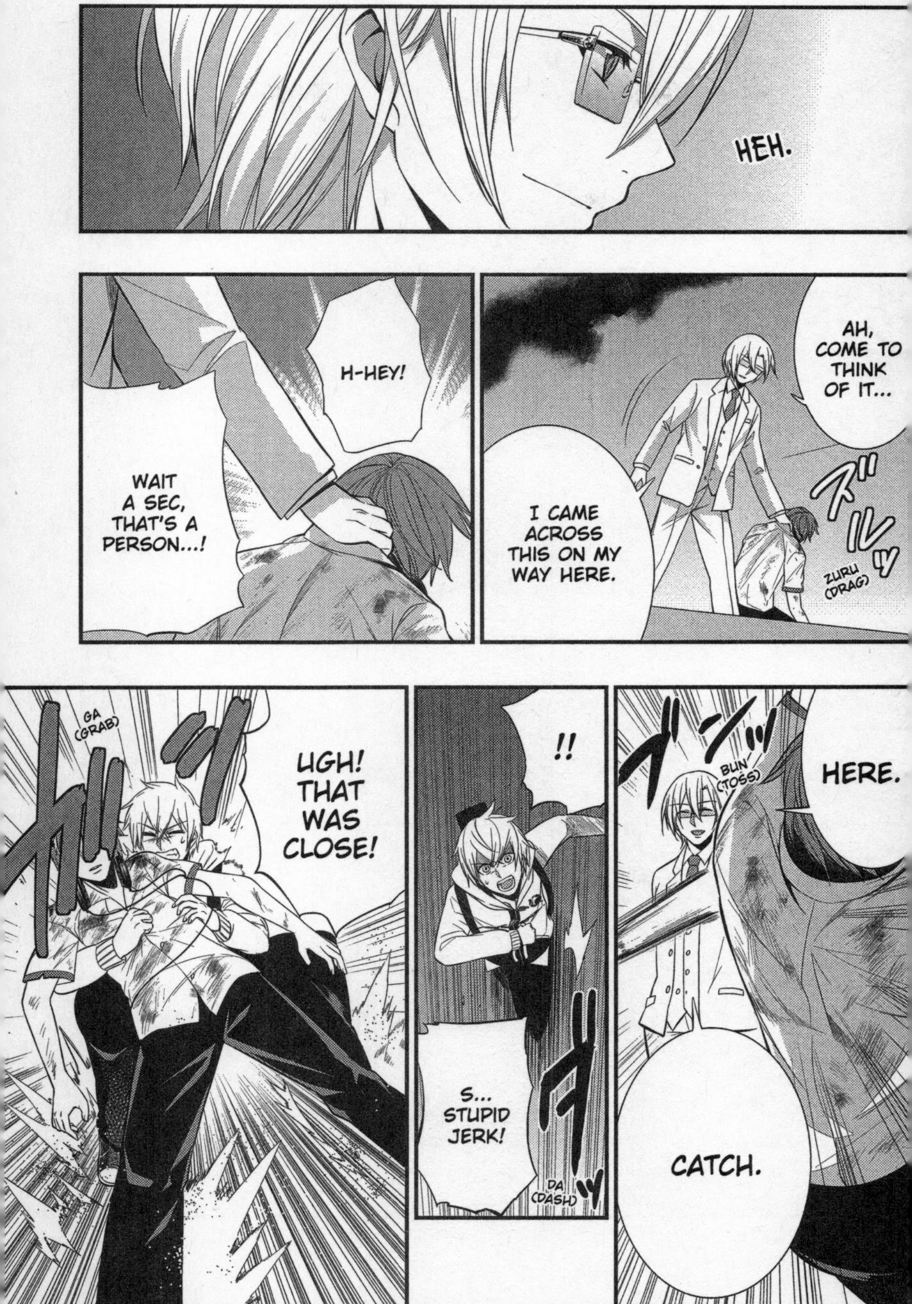
HEH.
AH, COME TO THINK OF IT...
I CAME ACROSS THIS ON MY WAY HERE.
ズルッ
ZURU (DRAG)
H-HEY!
WAIT A SEC, THAT'S A PERSON...!
ブンッ
BUN (TOSS)
HERE.
CATCH.
!!
S... STUPID JERK!
ダッ
DA (DASH)
ガッ
GA (GRAB)
UGH! THAT WAS CLOSE!

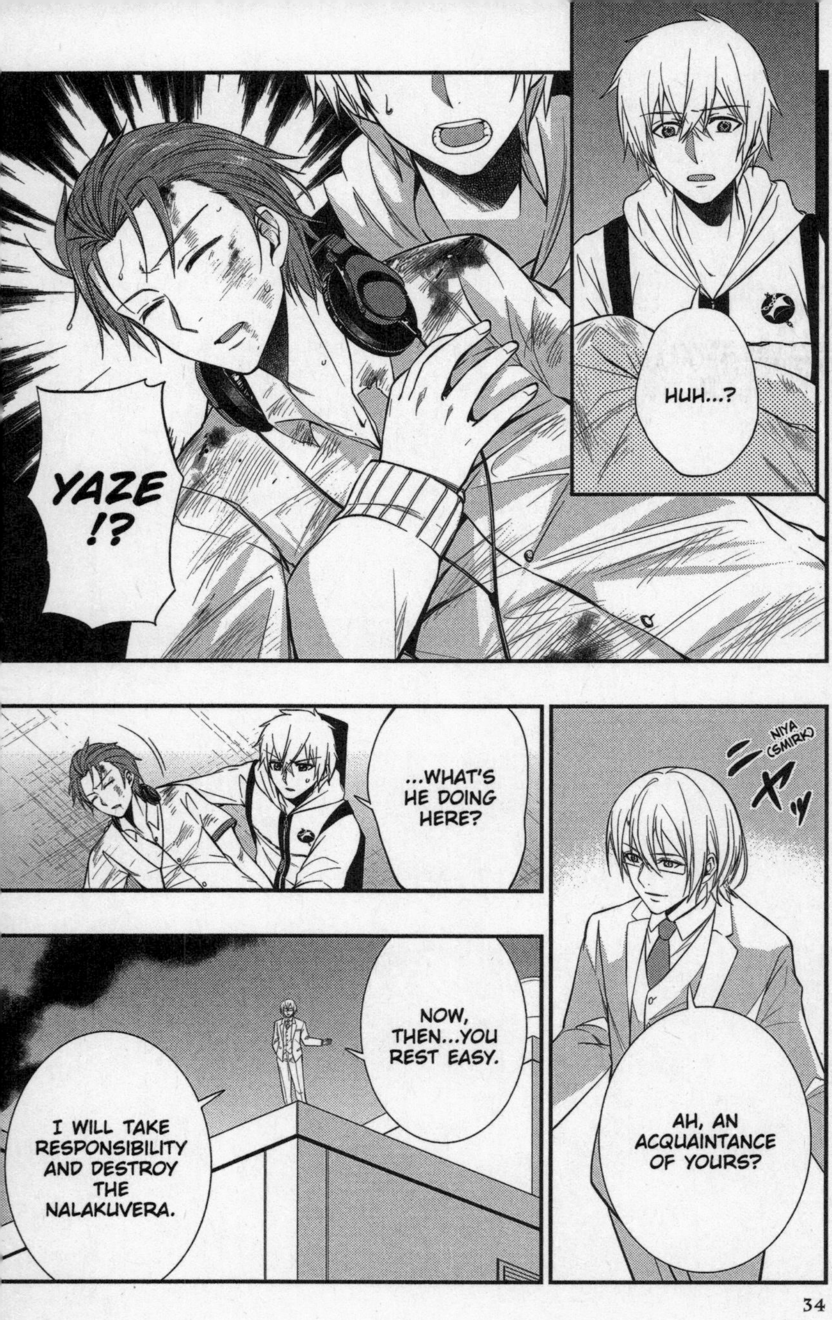
HUH...?
YAZE !?
ニヤッ
NIYA (SMIRK)
AH, AN ACQUAINTANCE OF YOURS?
...WHAT'S HE DOING HERE?
NOW, THEN...YOU REST EASY.
I WILL TAKE RESPONSIBILITY AND DESTROY THE NALAKUVERA.

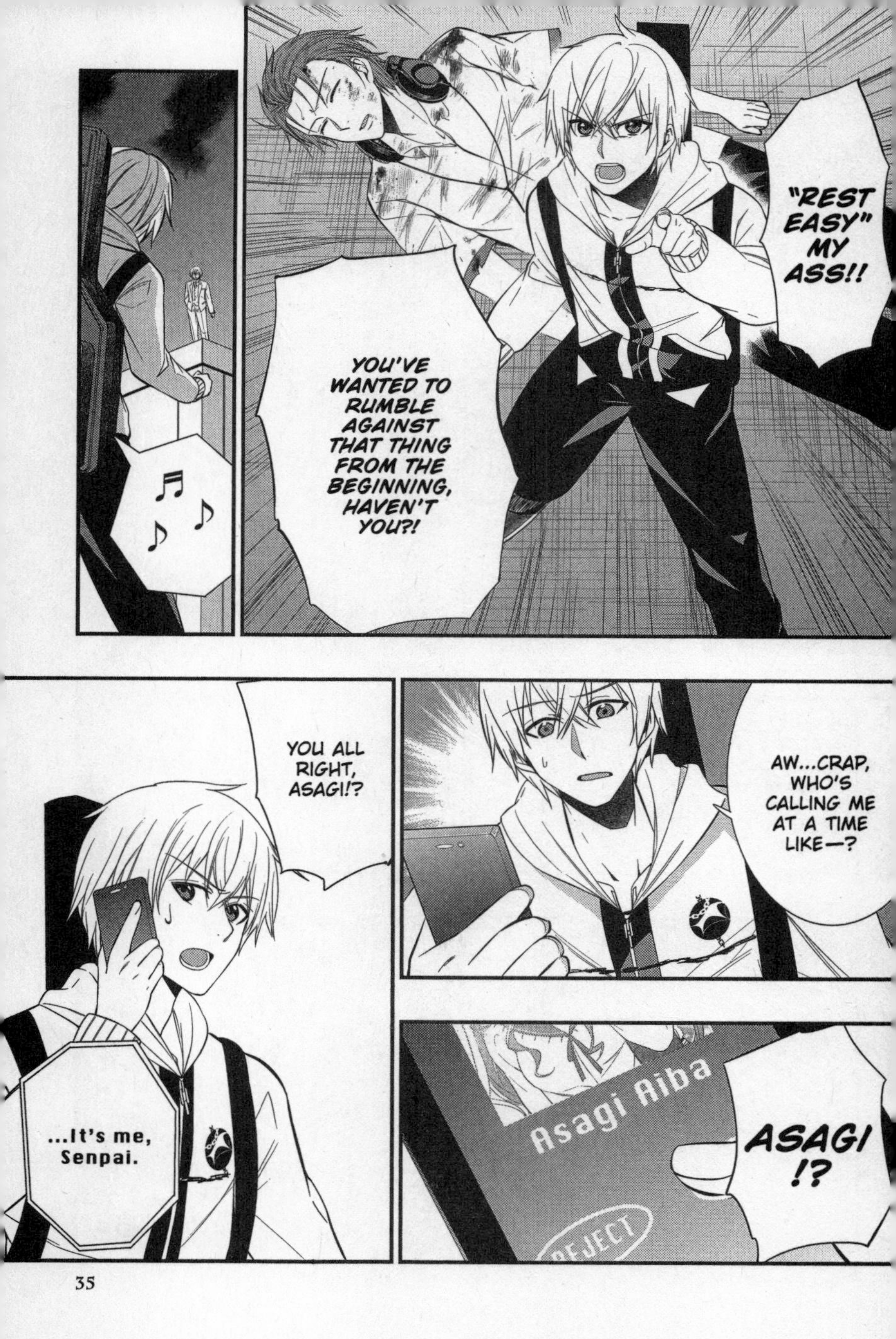
"REST EASY" MY ASS!!
YOU'VE WANTED TO RUMBLE AGAINST THAT THING FROM THE BEGINNING, HAVEN'T YOU?!
♬ ♪ ♪
AW...CRAP, WHO'S CALLING ME AT A TIME LIKE—?
Asagi Aiba
REJECT
ASAGI !?
YOU ALL RIGHT, ASAGI!?
...It's me, Senpai.

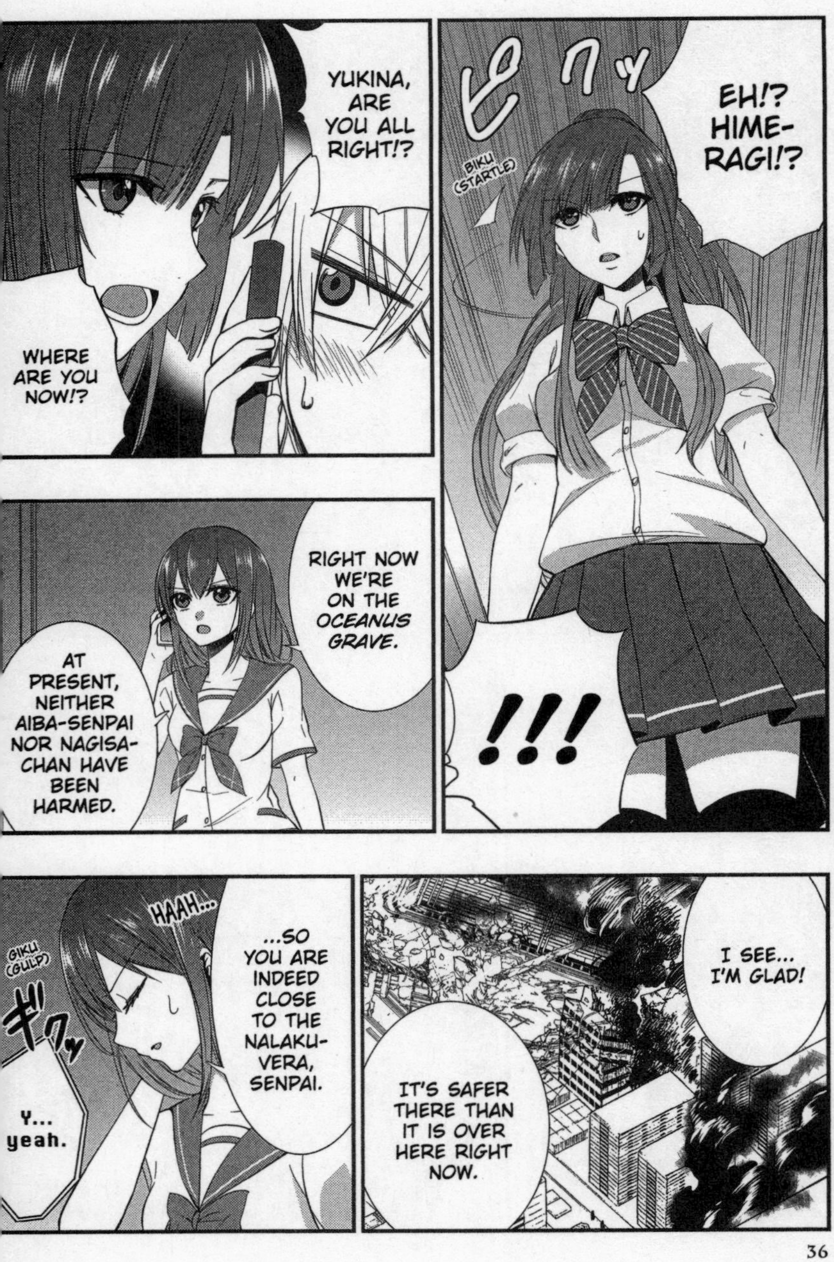
ピクッ
BIKU (STARTLE)
EH!? HIME-RAGI!?
!!!
YUKINA, ARE YOU ALL RIGHT!?
WHERE ARE YOU NOW!?
RIGHT NOW WE'RE ON THE *OCEANUS GRAVE*.
AT PRESENT, NEITHER AIBA-SENPAI NOR NAGISA-CHAN HAVE BEEN HARMED.
I SEE... I'M GLAD!
IT'S SAFER THERE THAN IT IS OVER HERE RIGHT NOW.
HAAH...
...SO YOU ARE INDEED CLOSE TO THE NALAKU-VERA, SENPAI.
GIKU (GULP)
ギクッ
Y... yeah.

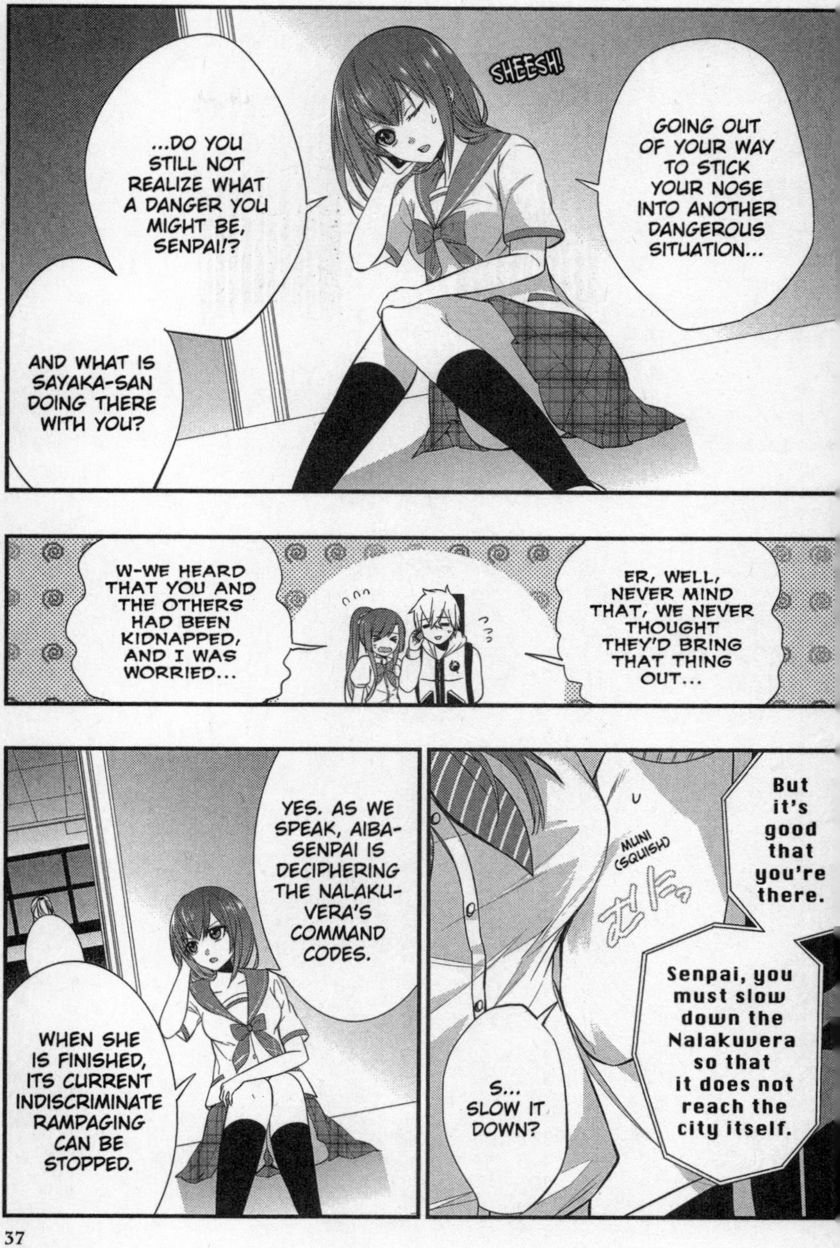
GOING OUT OF YOUR WAY TO STICK YOUR NOSE INTO ANOTHER DANGEROUS SITUATION...
SHEESH!
...DO YOU STILL NOT REALIZE WHAT A DANGER YOU MIGHT BE, SENPAI!?
AND WHAT IS SAYAKA-SAN DOING THERE WITH YOU?
ER, WELL, NEVER MIND THAT, WE NEVER THOUGHT THEY'D BRING THAT THING OUT...
W-WE HEARD THAT YOU AND THE OTHERS HAD BEEN KIDNAPPED, AND I WAS WORRIED...
But it's good that you're there.
MUNI (SQUISH)
Senpai, you must slow down the Nalakuvera so that it does not reach the city itself.
S... SLOW IT DOWN?
YES. AS WE SPEAK, AIBA-SENPAI IS DECIPHERING THE NALAKU-VERA'S COMMAND CODES.
WHEN SHE IS FINISHED, ITS CURRENT INDISCRIMINATE RAMPAGING CAN BE STOPPED.

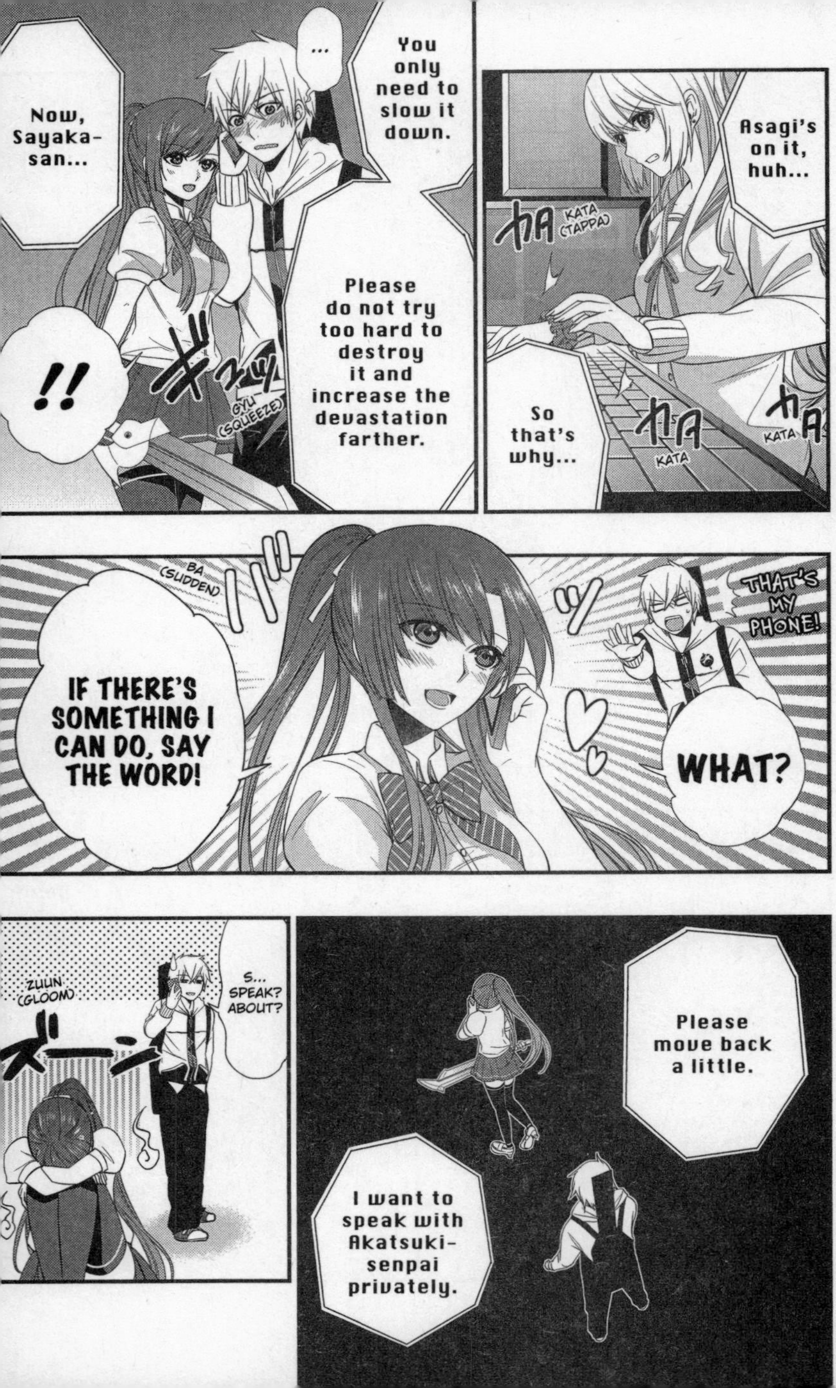
Asagi's on it, huh...
KATA (TAPPA)
So that's why...
KATA
KATA
...
You only need to slow it down.
Now, Sayaka-san...
Please do not try too hard to destroy it and increase the devastation farther.
!!
GYU (SQUEEZE)
THAT'S MY PHONE!
WHAT?
BA (SUDDEN)
IF THERE'S SOMETHING I CAN DO, SAY THE WORD!
Please move back a little.
I want to speak with Akatsuki-senpai privately.
S... SPEAK? ABOUT?
ZUUN (GLOOM)

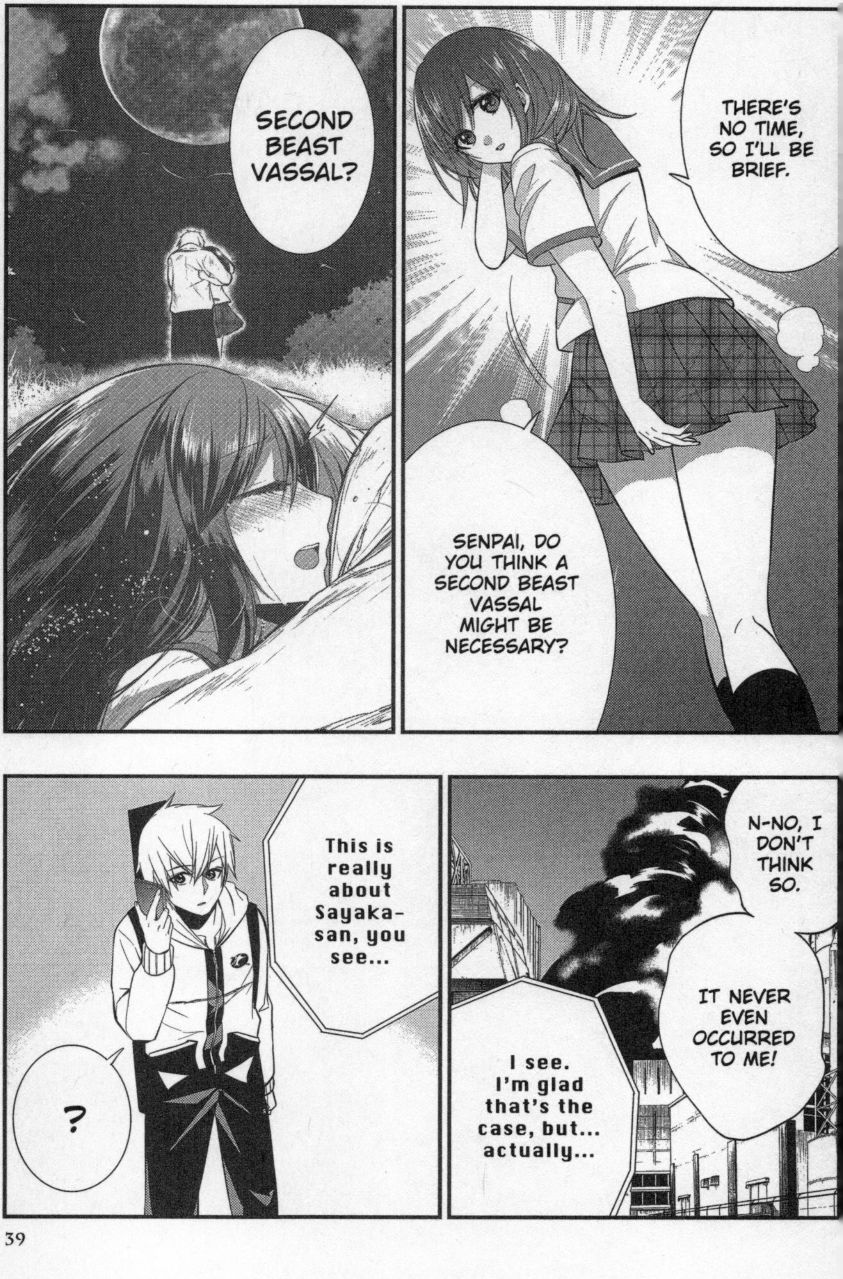
THERE'S NO TIME, SO I'LL BE BRIEF.
SENPAI, DO YOU THINK A SECOND BEAST VASSAL MIGHT BE NECESSARY?
SECOND BEAST VASSAL?
N-NO, I DON'T THINK SO.
IT NEVER EVEN OCCURRED TO ME!
I see. I'm glad that's the case, but... actually...
This is really about Sayaka-san, you see...
?

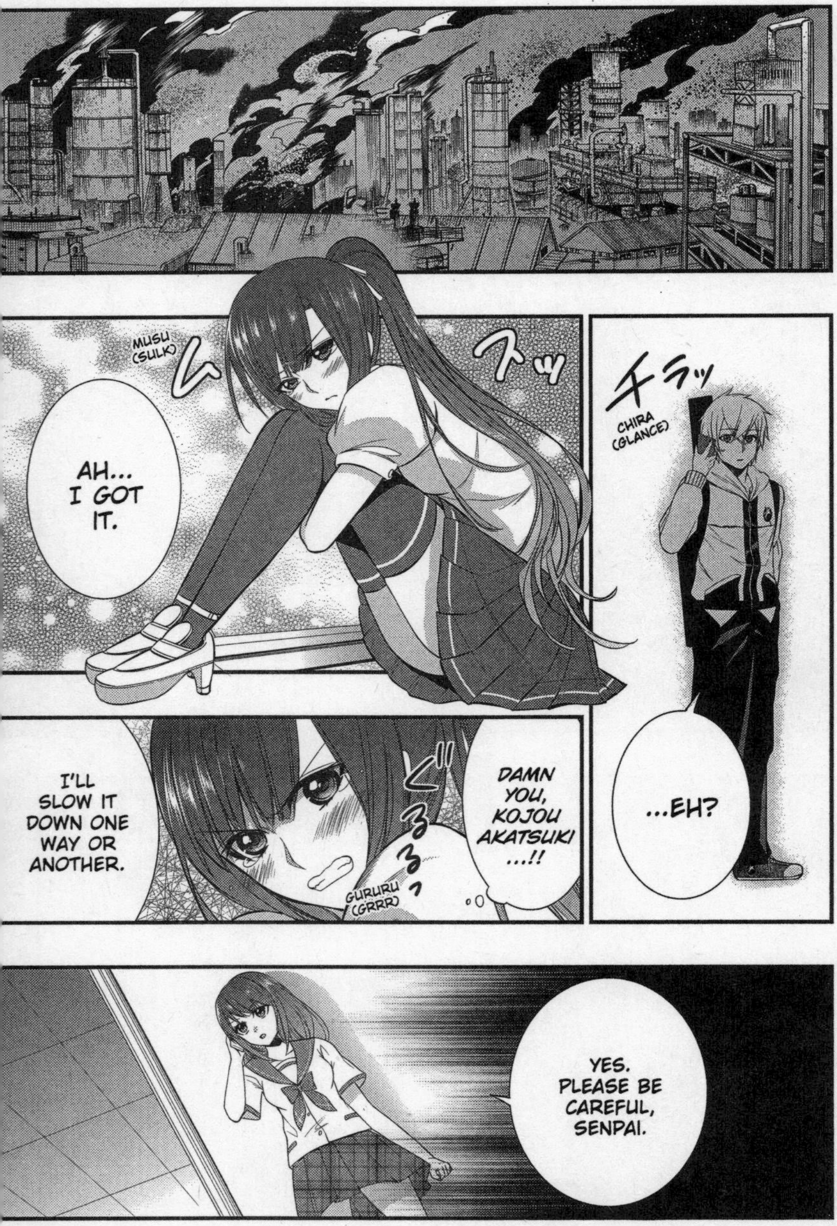
チラッ
CHIRA (GLANCE)
...EH?
ムスッ
MUSU (SULK)
AH... I GOT IT.
DAMN YOU, KOJOU AKATSUKI ...!!
ぐるるっ
GURURU (GRRR)
I'LL SLOW IT DOWN ONE WAY OR ANOTHER.
YES. PLEASE BE CAREFUL, SENPAI.

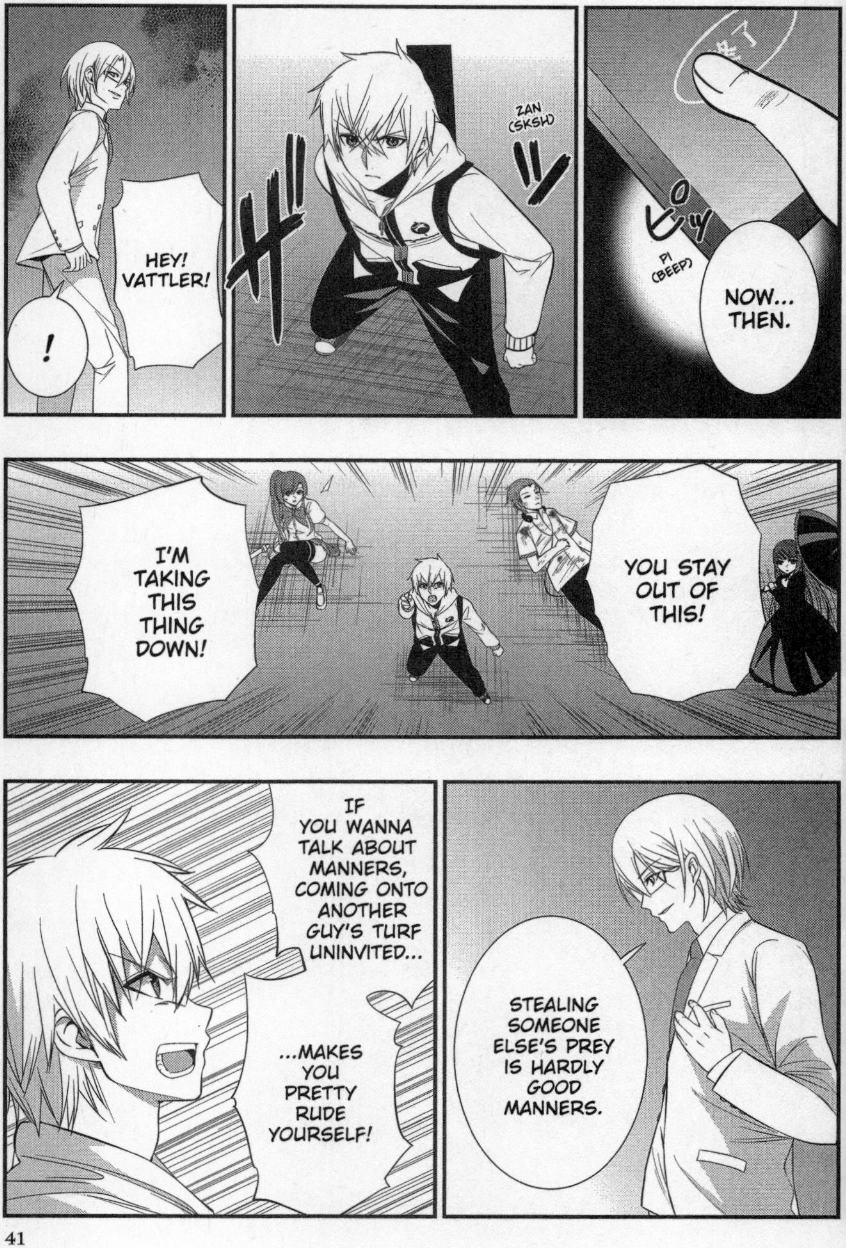
PI (BEEP)
NOW... THEN.
ZAN (SKSH)
HEY! VATTLER!
!
YOU STAY OUT OF THIS!
I'M TAKING THIS THING DOWN!
STEALING SOMEONE ELSE'S PREY IS HARDLY GOOD MANNERS.
IF YOU WANNA TALK ABOUT MANNERS, COMING ONTO ANOTHER GUY'S TURF UNINVITED...
...MAKES YOU PRETTY RUDE YOURSELF!

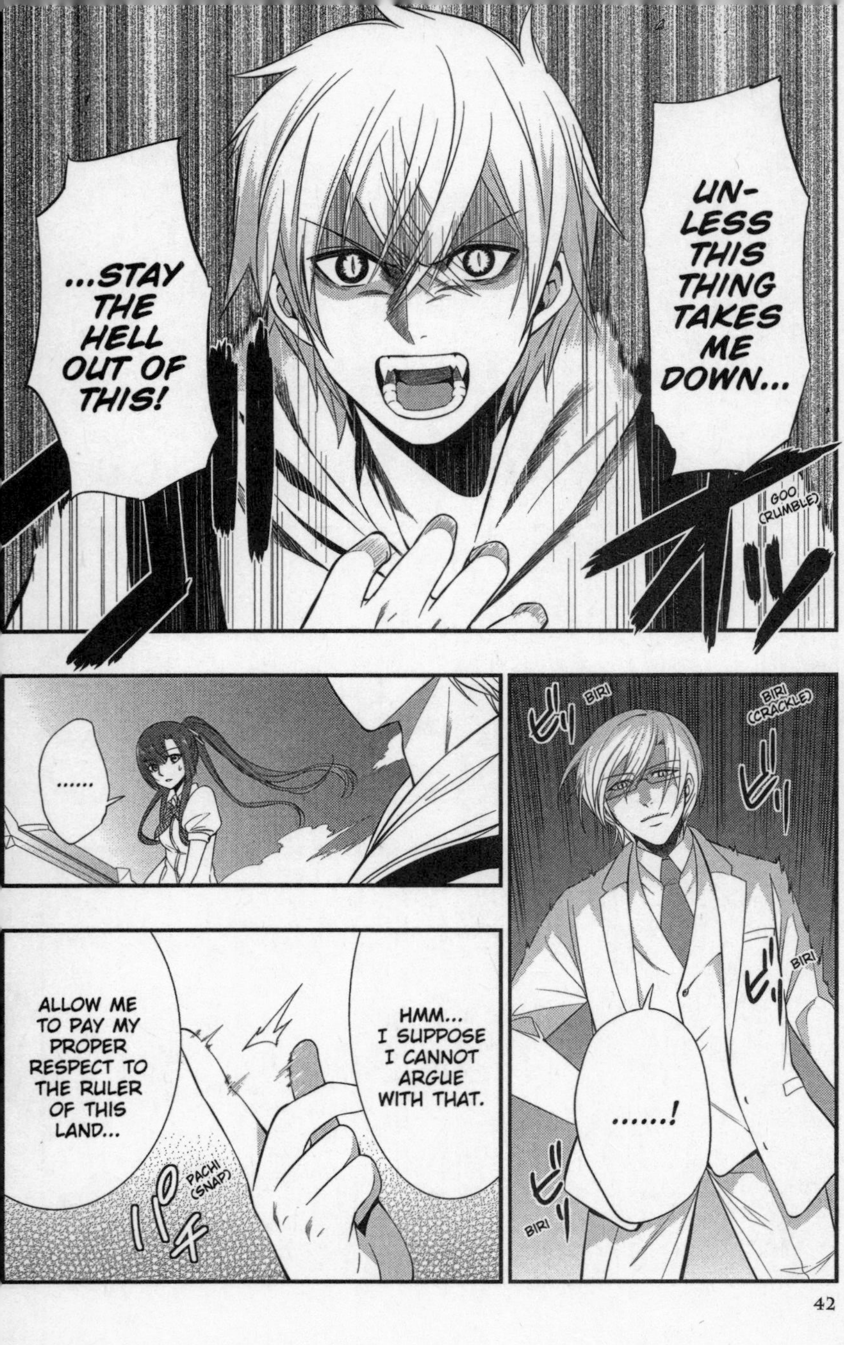
UN-LESS THIS THING TAKES ME DOWN...
...STAY THE HELL OUT OF THIS!
GOO (RUMBLE)
BIRI
BIRI (CRACKLE)
BIRI
......!
BIRI
......
HMM... I SUPPOSE I CANNOT ARGUE WITH THAT.
ALLOW ME TO PAY MY PROPER RESPECT TO THE RULER OF THIS LAND...
PACHI (SNAP)

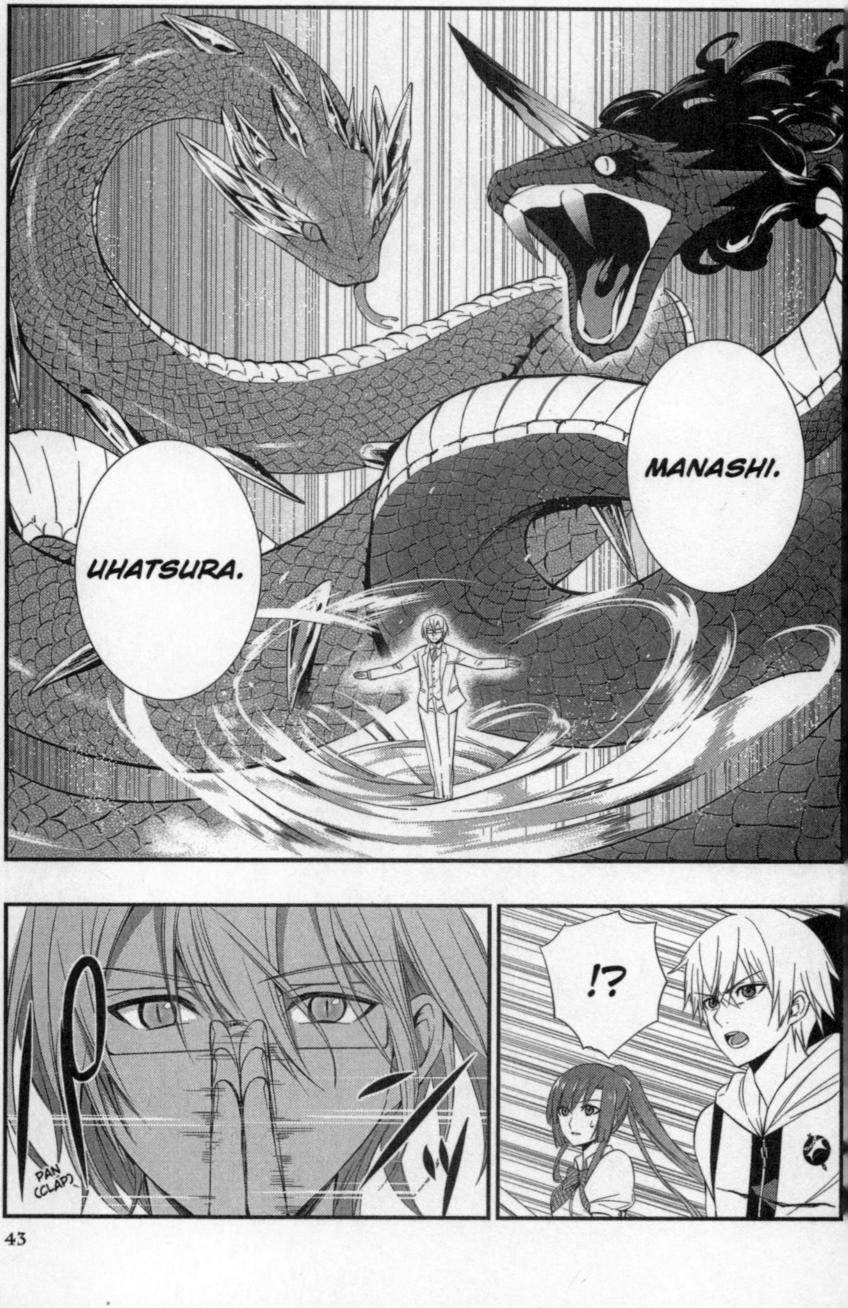
MANASHI.
UHATSURA.
!?
PAN (CLAP)

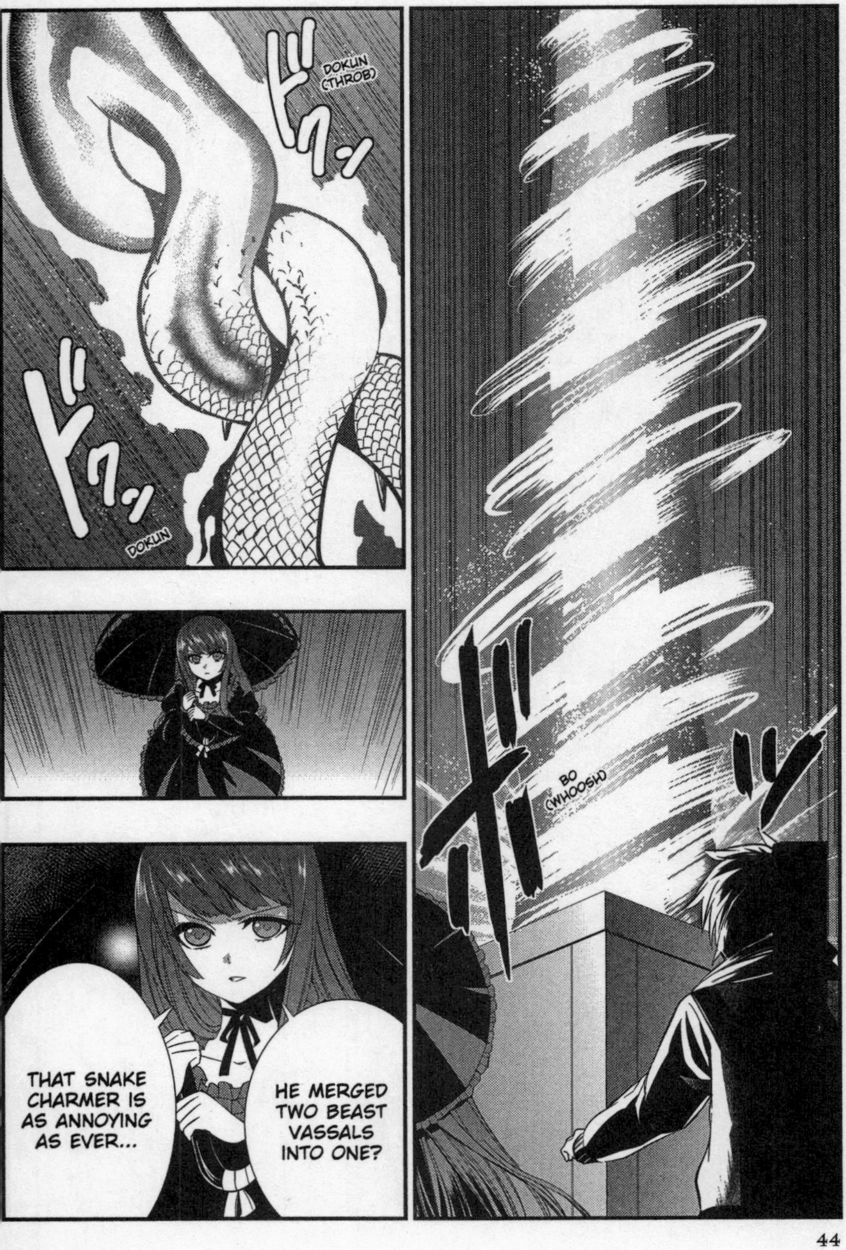
BO (WHOOSH)
DOKUN (THROB)
DOKUN
HE MERGED TWO BEAST VASSALS INTO ONE?
THAT SNAKE CHARMER IS AS ANNOYING AS EVER...

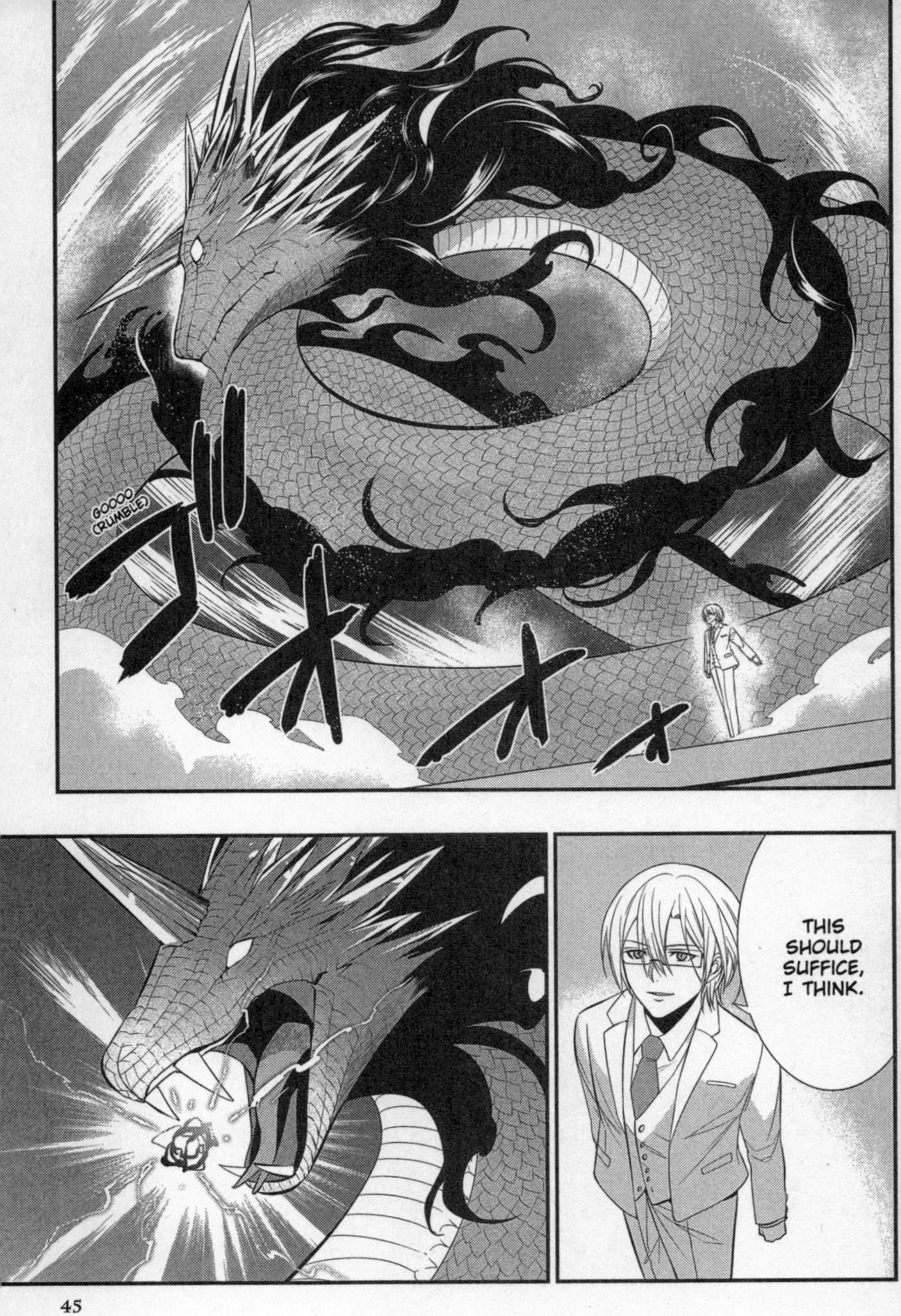
GOOOO (RUMBLE)
THIS SHOULD SUFFICE, I THINK.

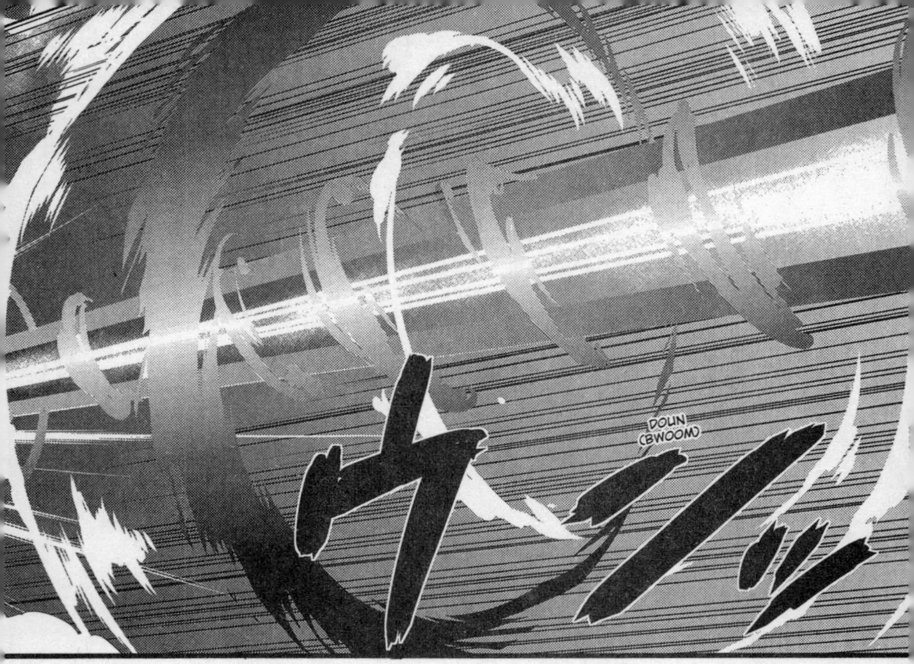
DOUN
(BWOOM)

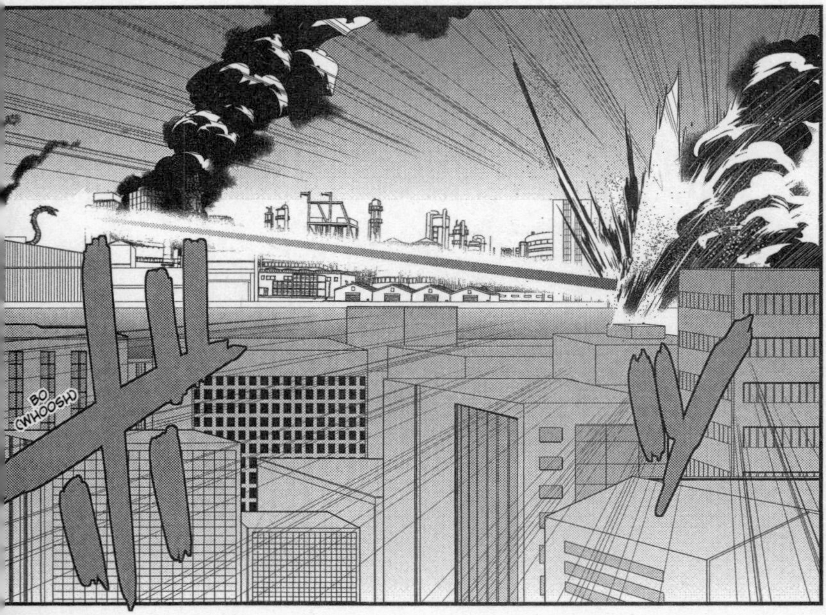
BO
(WHOOSH)

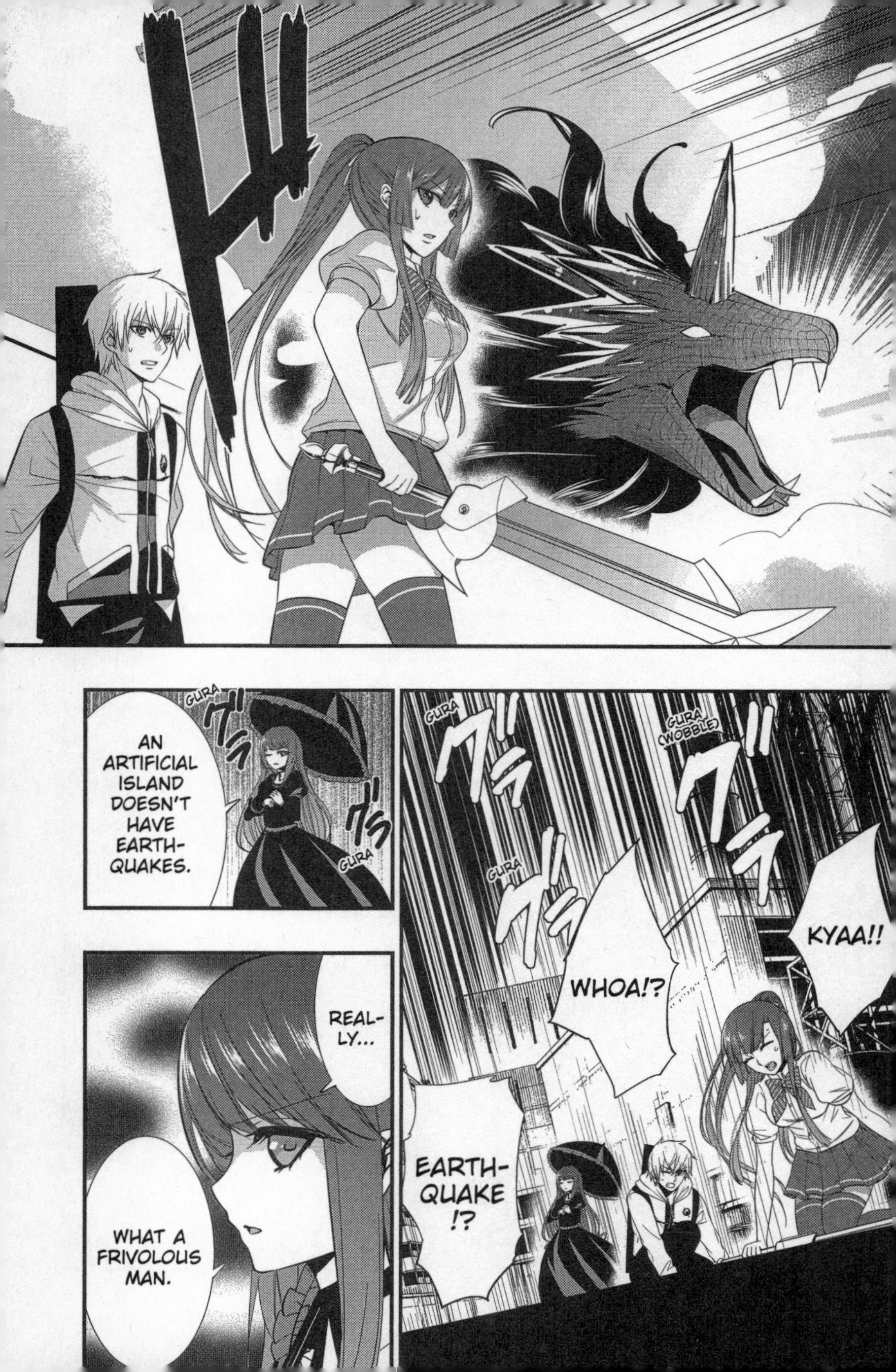
GURA (WOBBLE)
GURA
GURA
KYAA!!
WHOA!?
EARTHQUAKE!?
GURA
AN ARTIFICIAL ISLAND DOESN'T HAVE EARTHQUAKES.
GURA
REALLY...
WHAT A FRIVOLOUS MAN.

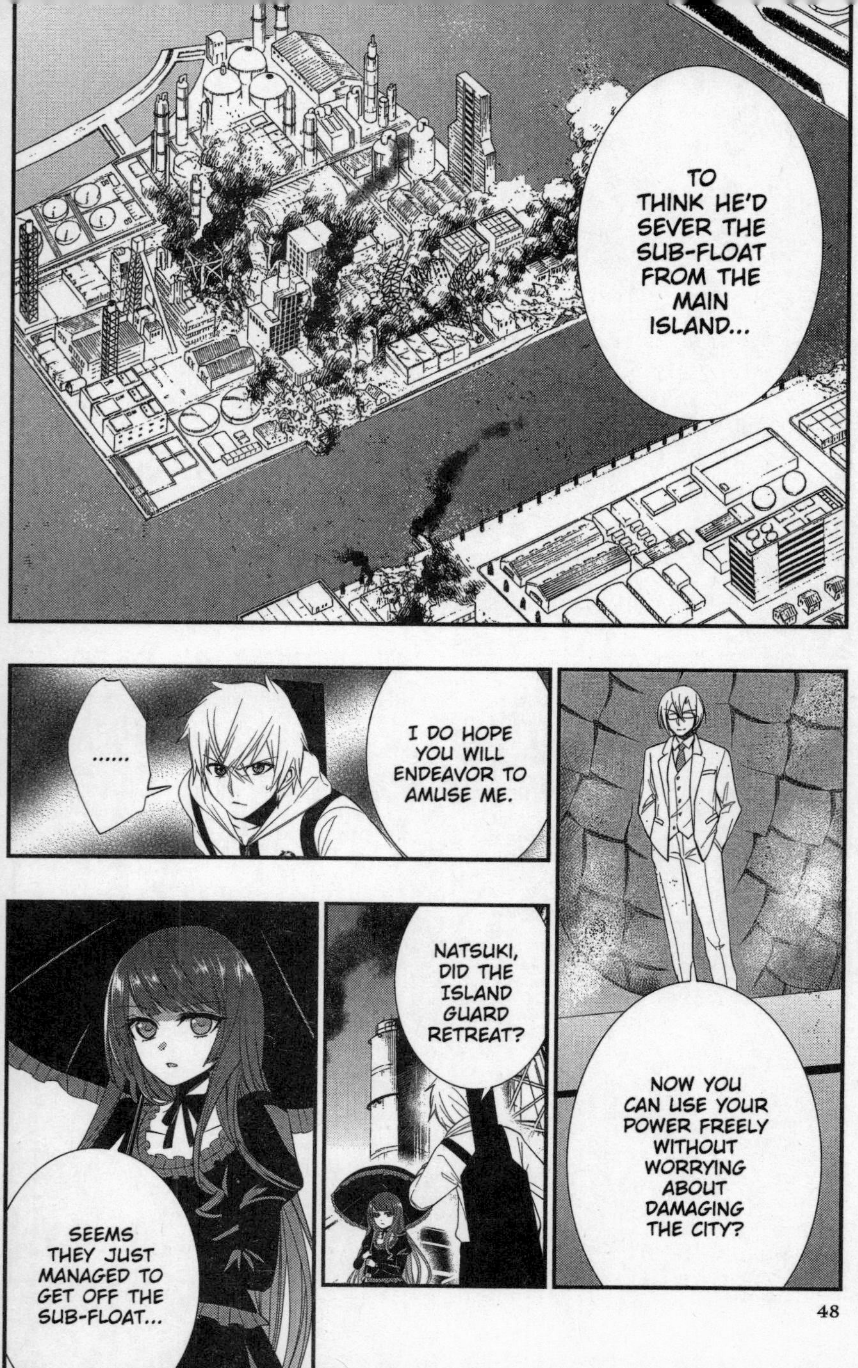
TO THINK HE'D SEVER THE SUB-FLOAT FROM THE MAIN ISLAND...
NOW YOU CAN USE YOUR POWER FREELY WITHOUT WORRYING ABOUT DAMAGING THE CITY?
I DO HOPE YOU WILL ENDEAVOR TO AMUSE ME.
......
NATSUKI, DID THE ISLAND GUARD RETREAT?
SEEMS THEY JUST MANAGED TO GET OFF THE SUB-FLOAT...

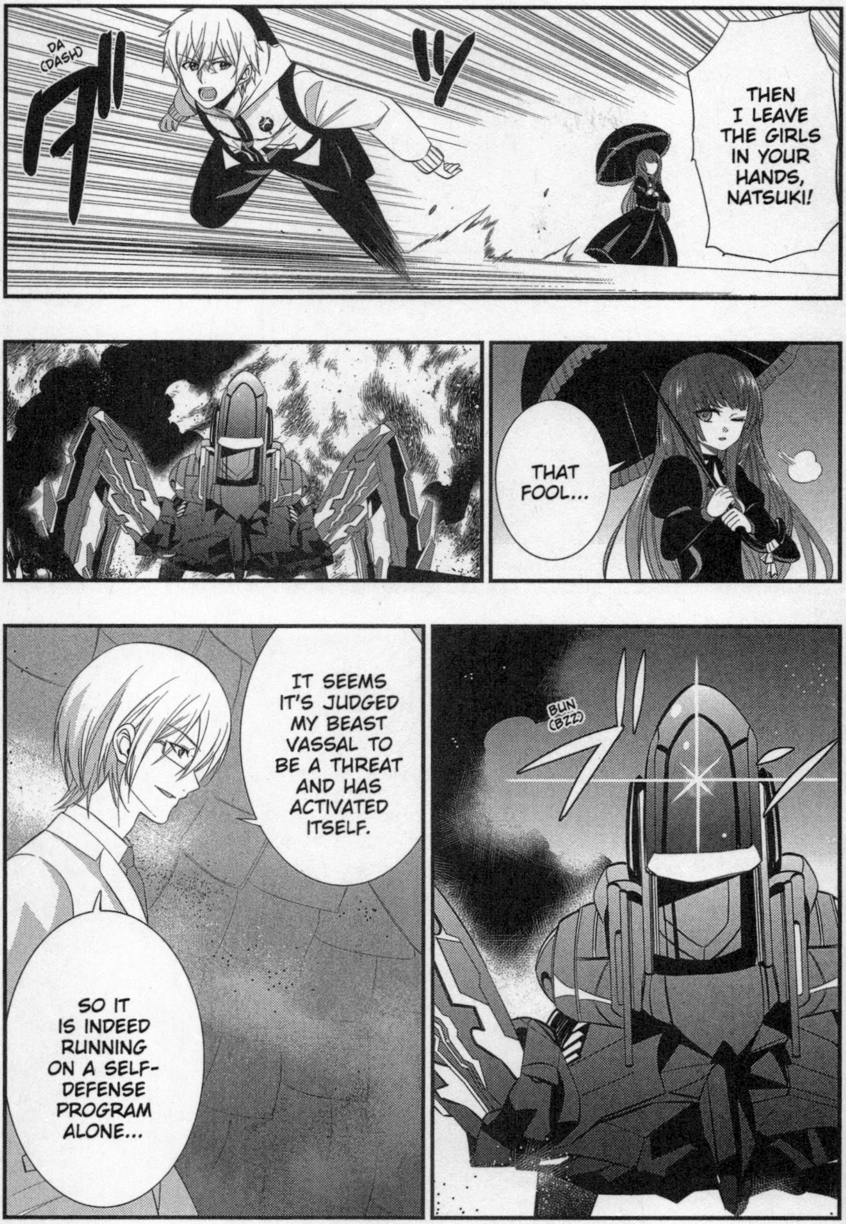
THEN I LEAVE THE GIRLS IN YOUR HANDS, NATSUKI!
DA (DASH)
THAT FOOL...
BUN (BZZ)
IT SEEMS IT'S JUDGED MY BEAST VASSAL TO BE A THREAT AND HAS ACTIVATED ITSELF.
SO IT IS INDEED RUNNING ON A SELF-DEFENSE PROGRAM ALONE...

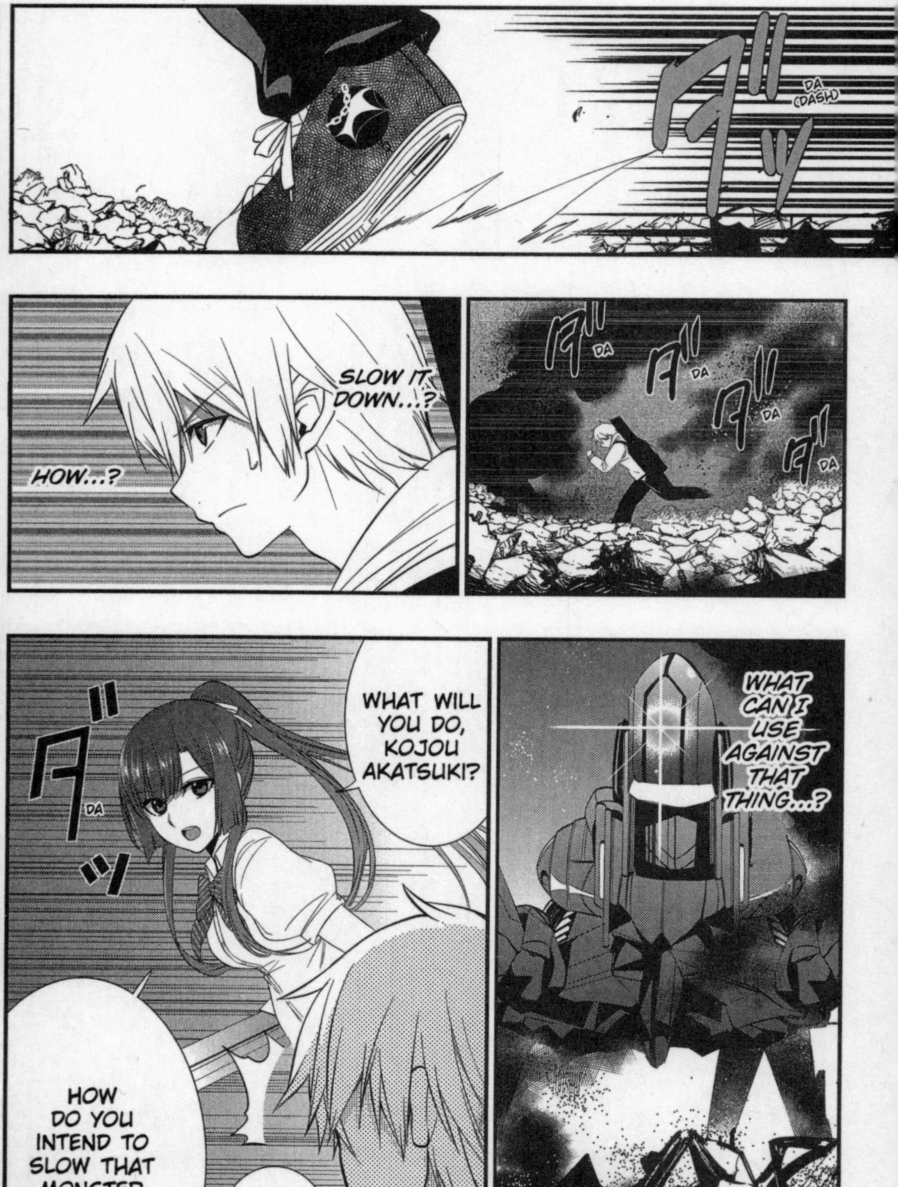
DA (DASH)
DA
DA
DA
DA
SLOW IT DOWN...?
HOW...?
WHAT CAN I USE AGAINST THAT THING...?
WHAT WILL YOU DO, KOJOU AKATSUKI?
DA
HOW DO YOU INTEND TO SLOW THAT MONSTER DOWN?
!?

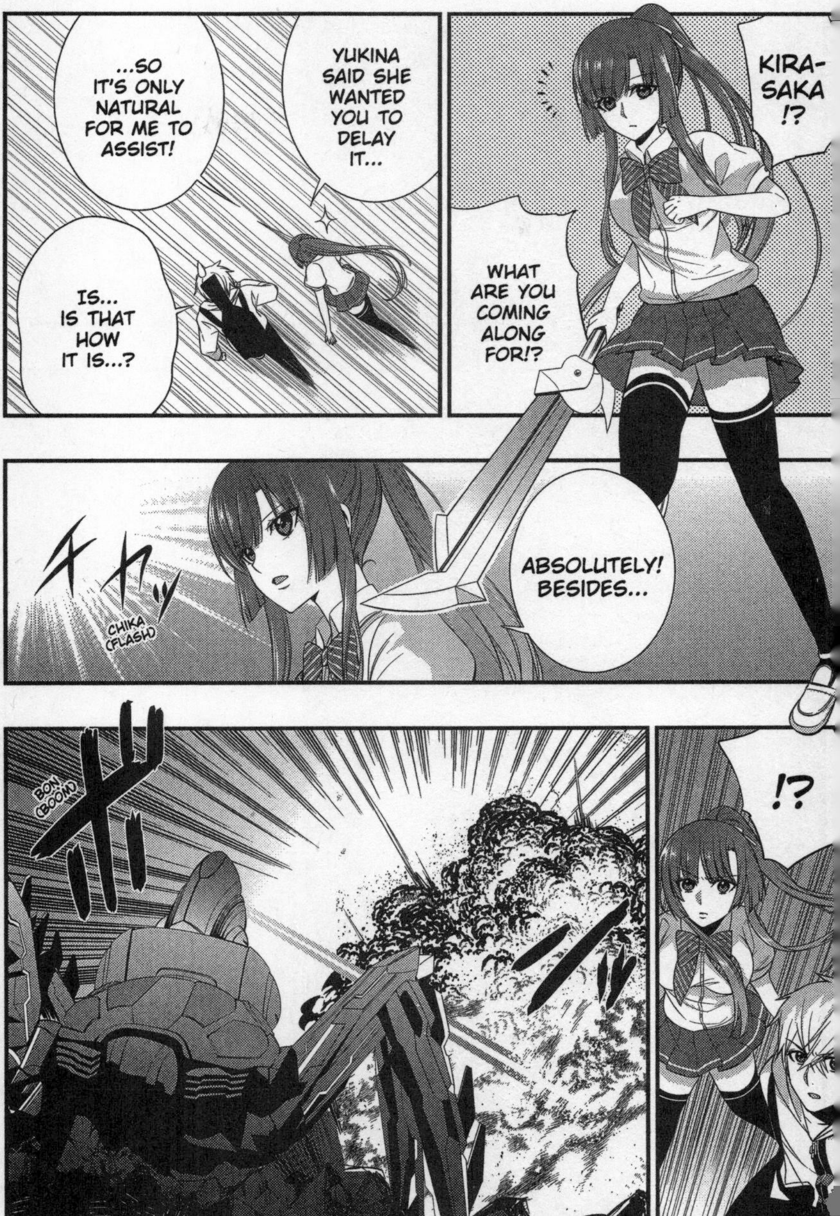
KIRA-SAKA!?
WHAT ARE YOU COMING ALONG FOR!?
YUKINA SAID SHE WANTED YOU TO DELAY IT...
...SO IT'S ONLY NATURAL FOR ME TO ASSIST!
IS... IS THAT HOW IT IS...?
ABSOLUTELY! BESIDES...
チカッ
CHIKA (FLASH)
!?
BON (BOON)

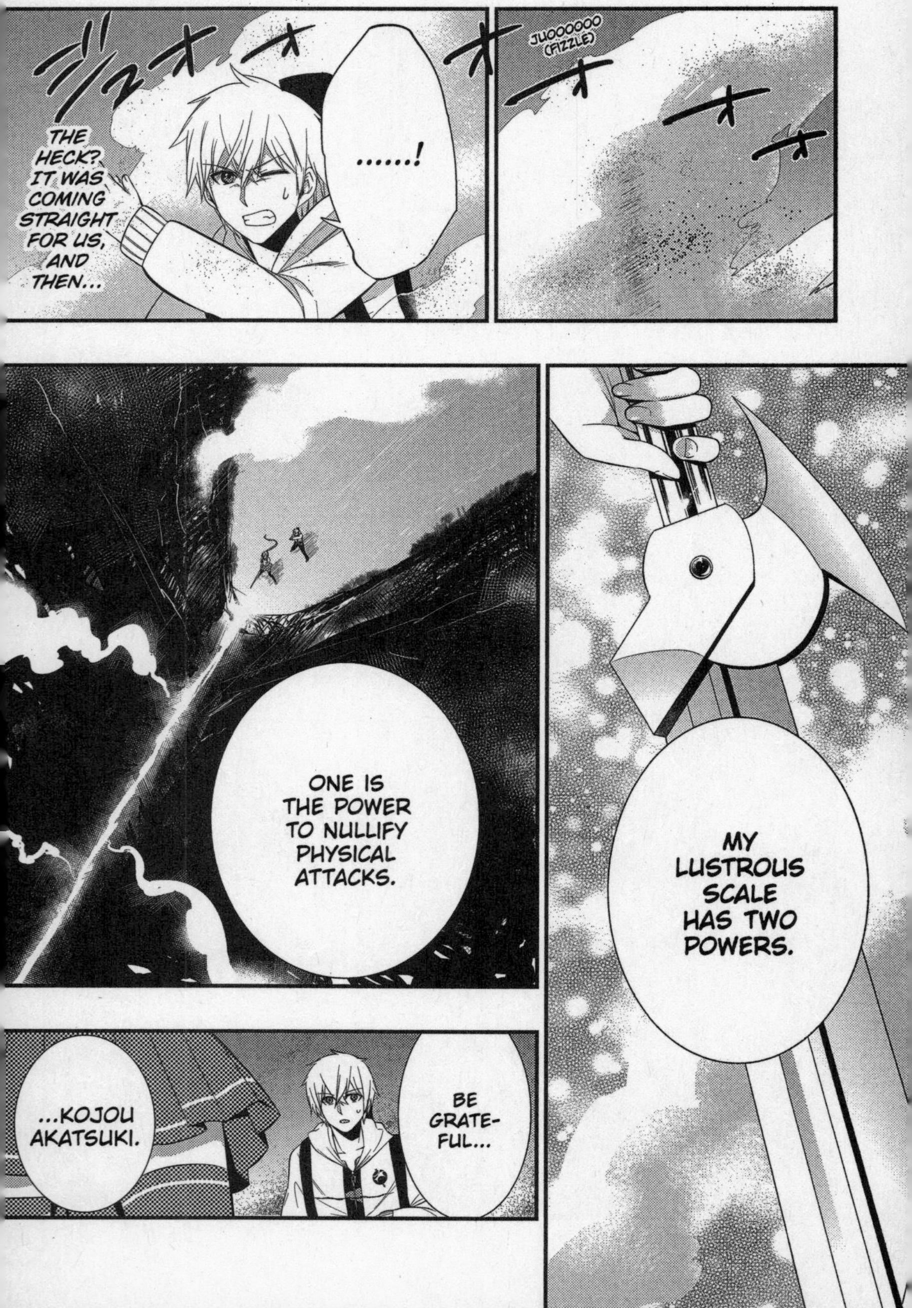

JUOOOOOO (FIZZLE)
......!
THE HECK? IT WAS COMING STRAIGHT FOR US, AND THEN...
MY LUSTROUS SCALE HAS TWO POWERS.
ONE IS THE POWER TO NULLIFY PHYSICAL ATTACKS.
BE GRATE-FUL...
...KOJOU AKATSUKI.

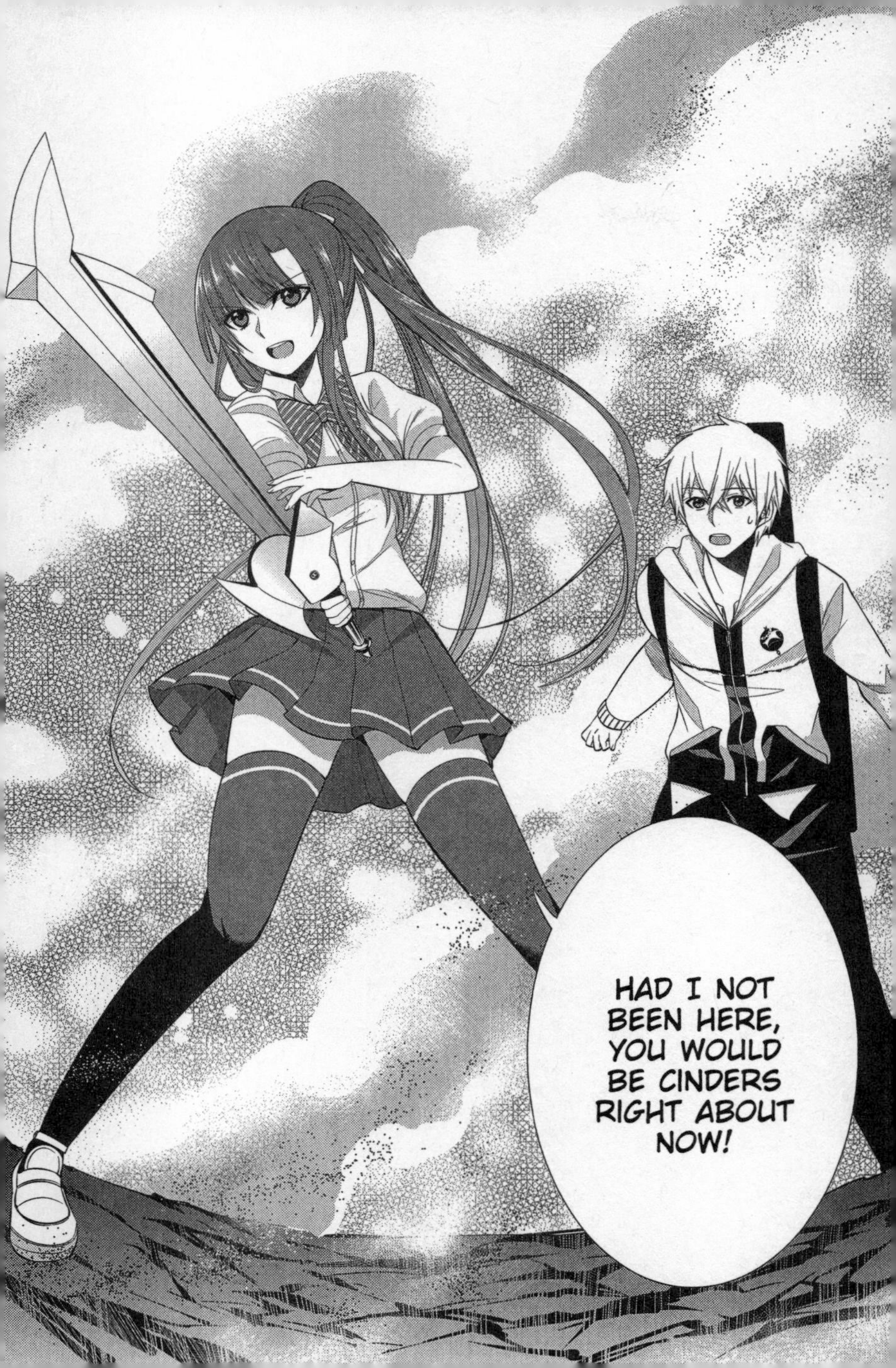
HAD I NOT BEEN HERE, YOU WOULD BE CINDERS RIGHT ABOUT NOW!

STRIKE THE BLOOD

DEFINITION

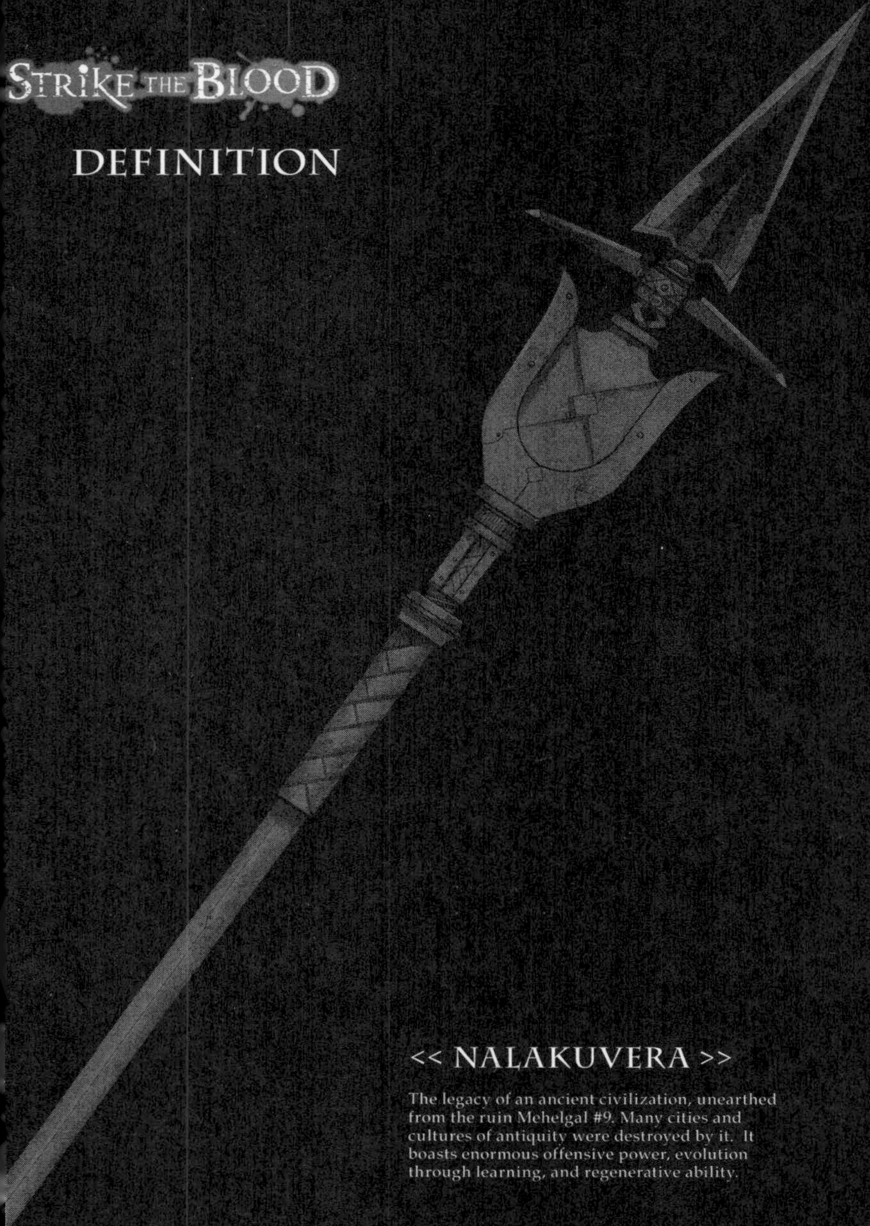

<< NALAKUVERA >>

The legacy of an ancient civilization, unearthed from the ruin Mehelgal #9. Many cities and cultures of antiquity were destroyed by it. It boasts enormous offensive power, evolution through learning, and regenerative ability.

Chapter 22: A Strange Vampire

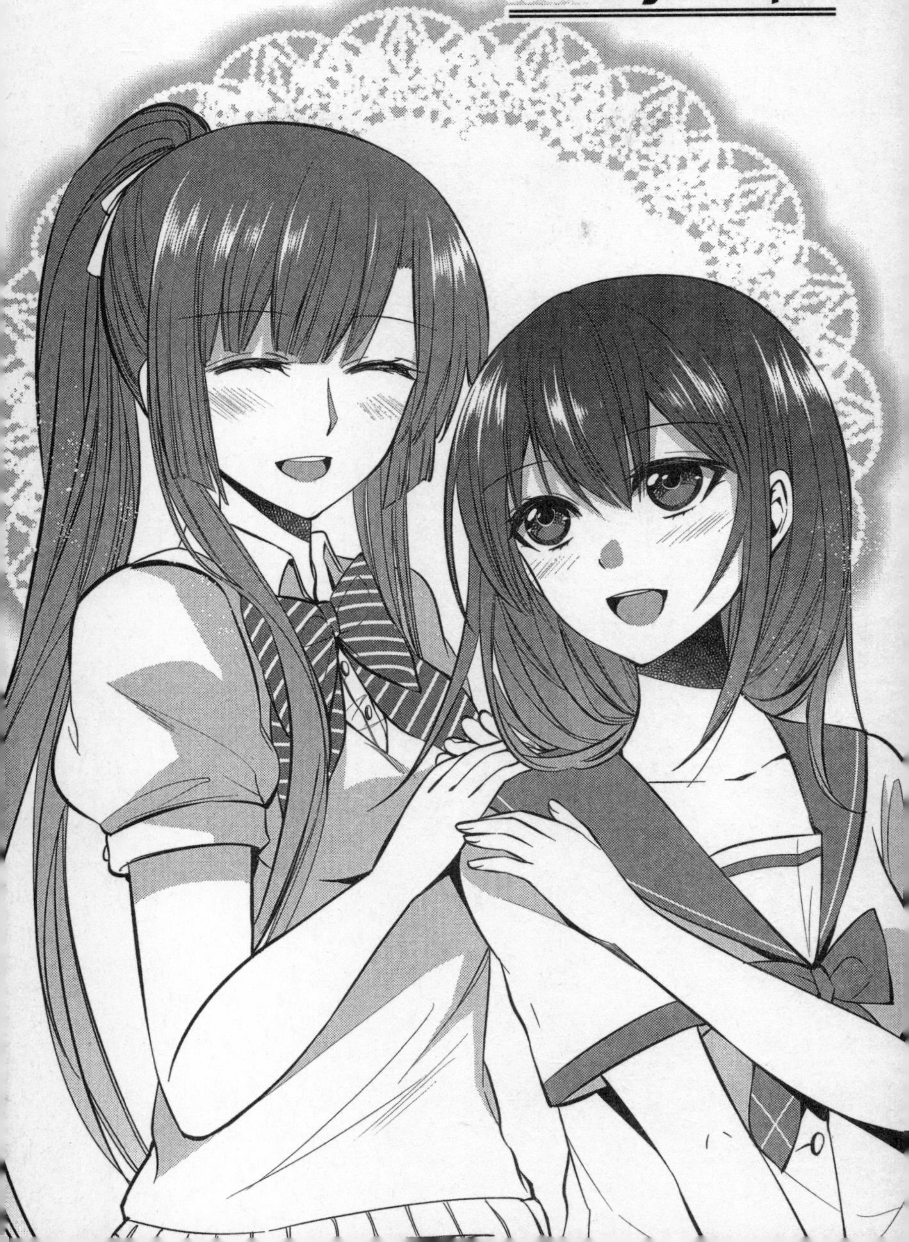

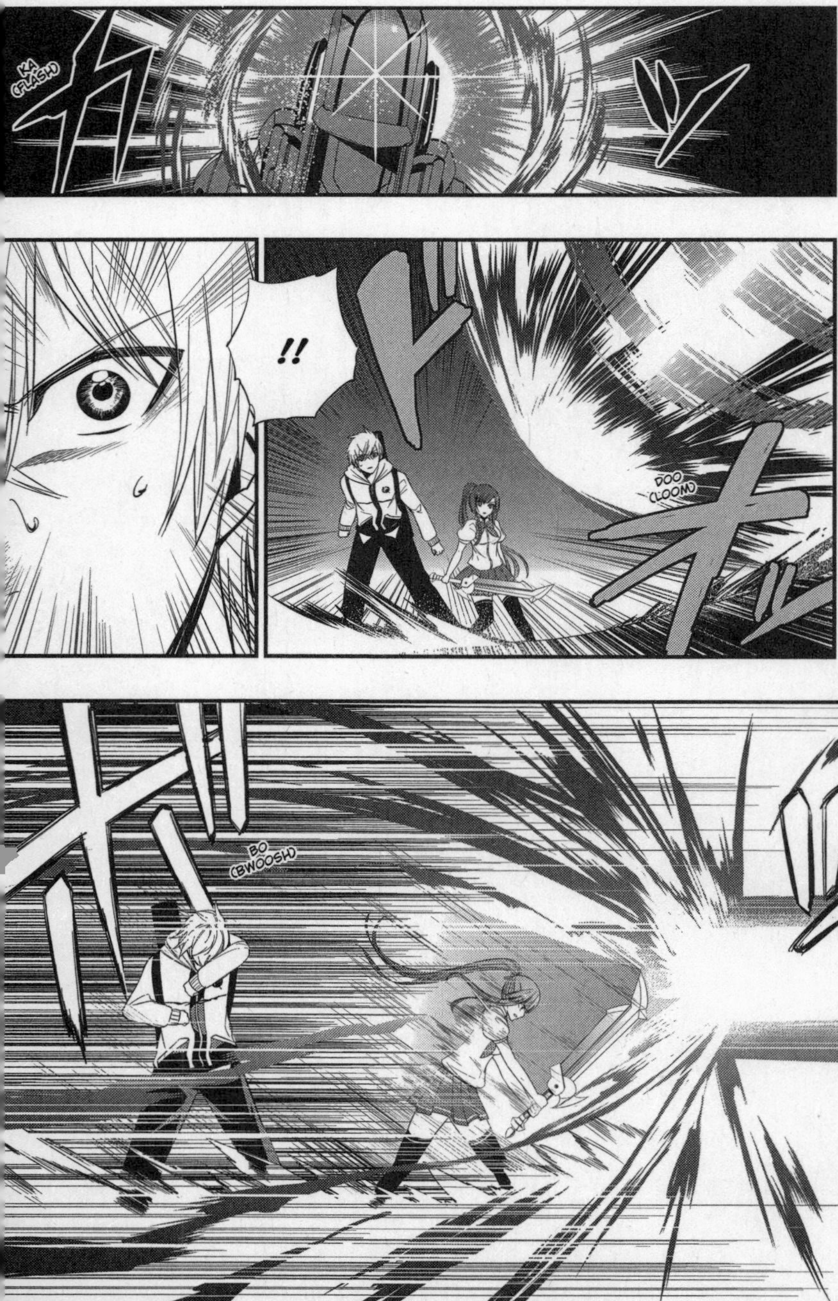
KA
(FLASH)
DOO
(LOOM)
!!
BO
(BWOOSH)

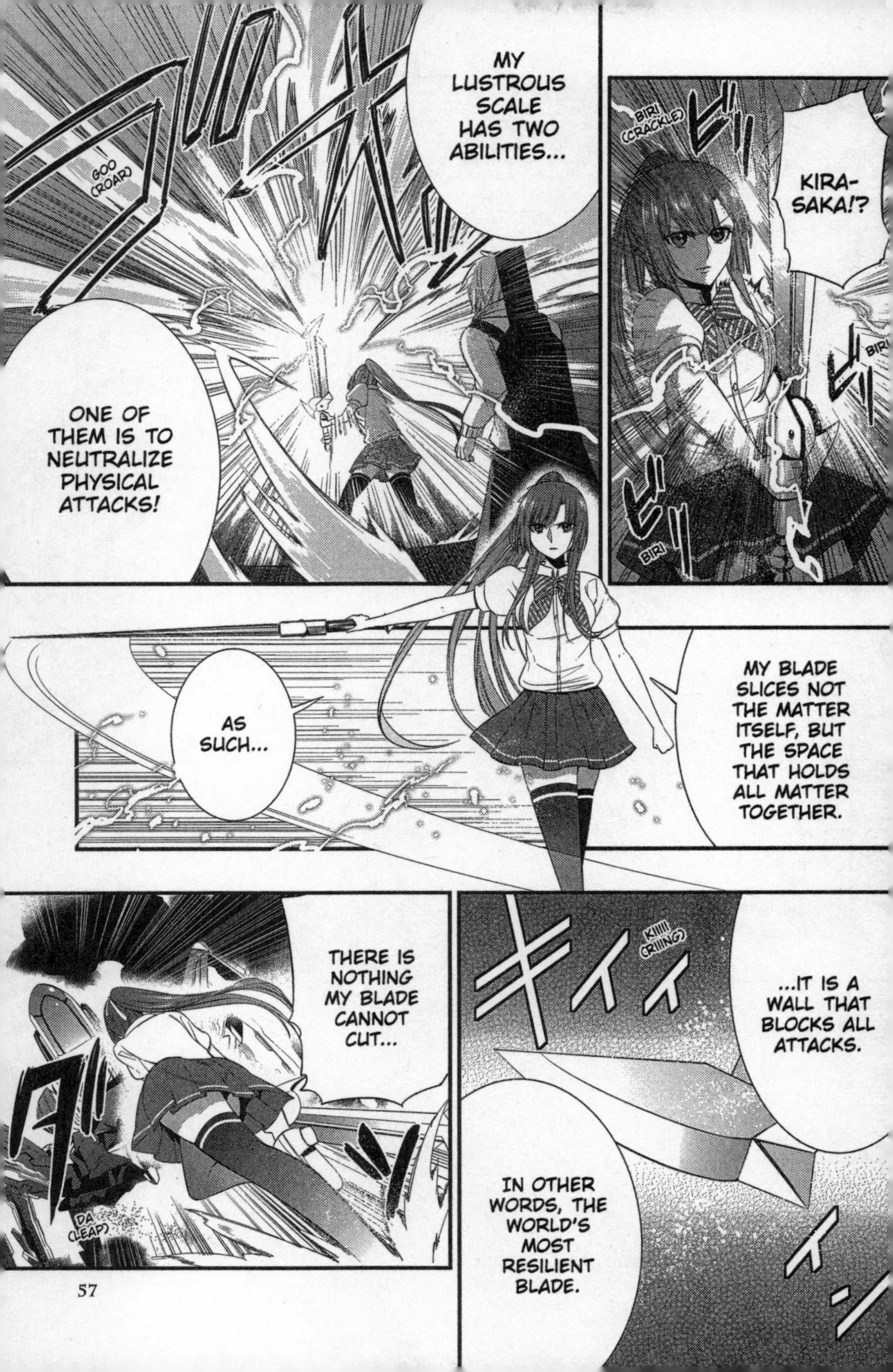
BIRI (CRACKLE)
KIRA-SAKA!?
BIRI
BIRI
MY LUSTROUS SCALE HAS TWO ABILITIES...
GOO (ROAR)
ONE OF THEM IS TO NEUTRALIZE PHYSICAL ATTACKS!
MY BLADE SLICES NOT THE MATTER ITSELF, BUT THE SPACE THAT HOLDS ALL MATTER TOGETHER.
AS SUCH...
KIIII (RIIING)
...IT IS A WALL THAT BLOCKS ALL ATTACKS.
IN OTHER WORDS, THE WORLD'S MOST RESILIENT BLADE.
THERE IS NOTHING MY BLADE CANNOT CUT...
DA (LEAP)

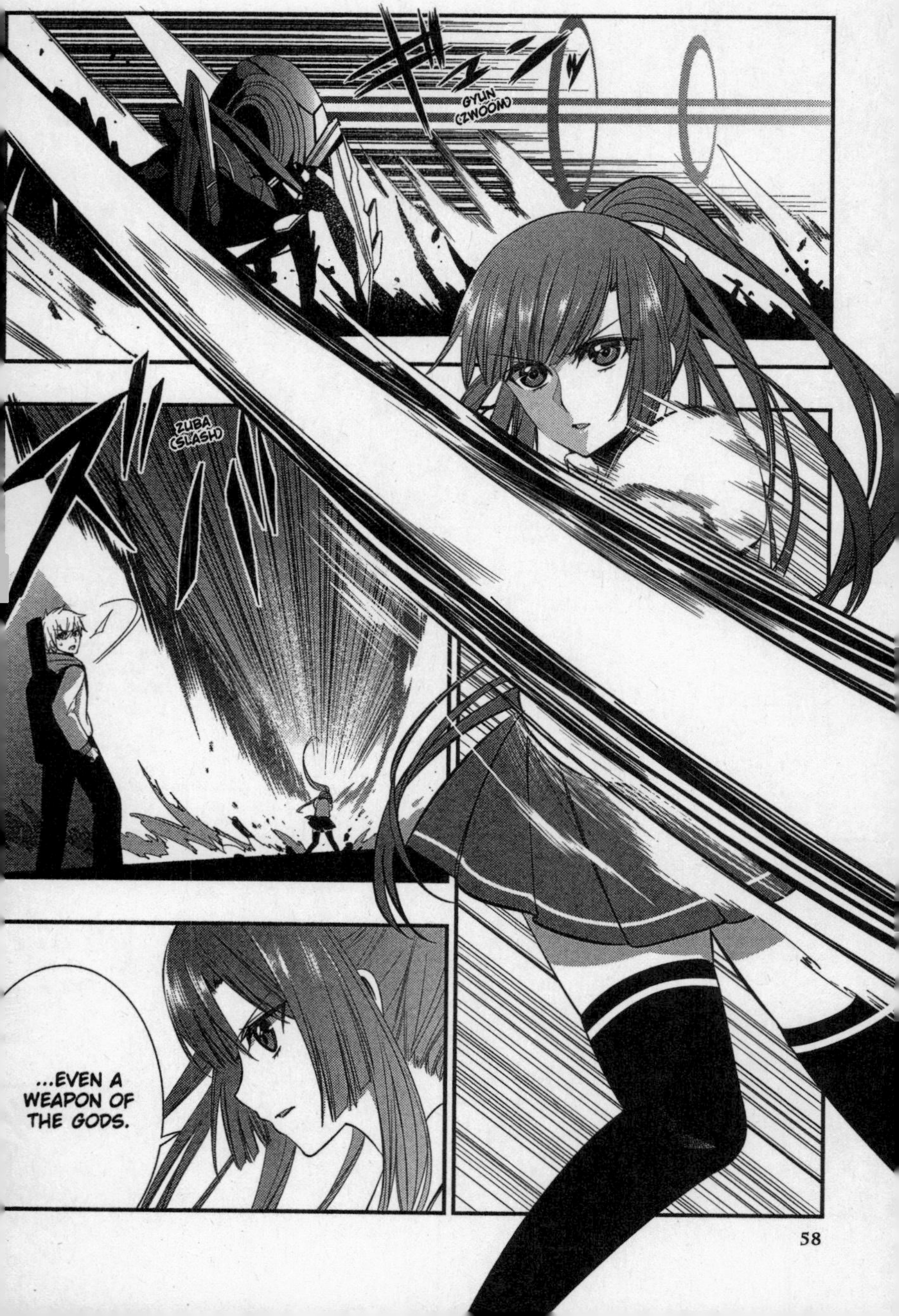
GYUN
(ZWOOM)
ZUBA
(SLASH)
...EVEN A WEAPON OF THE GODS.

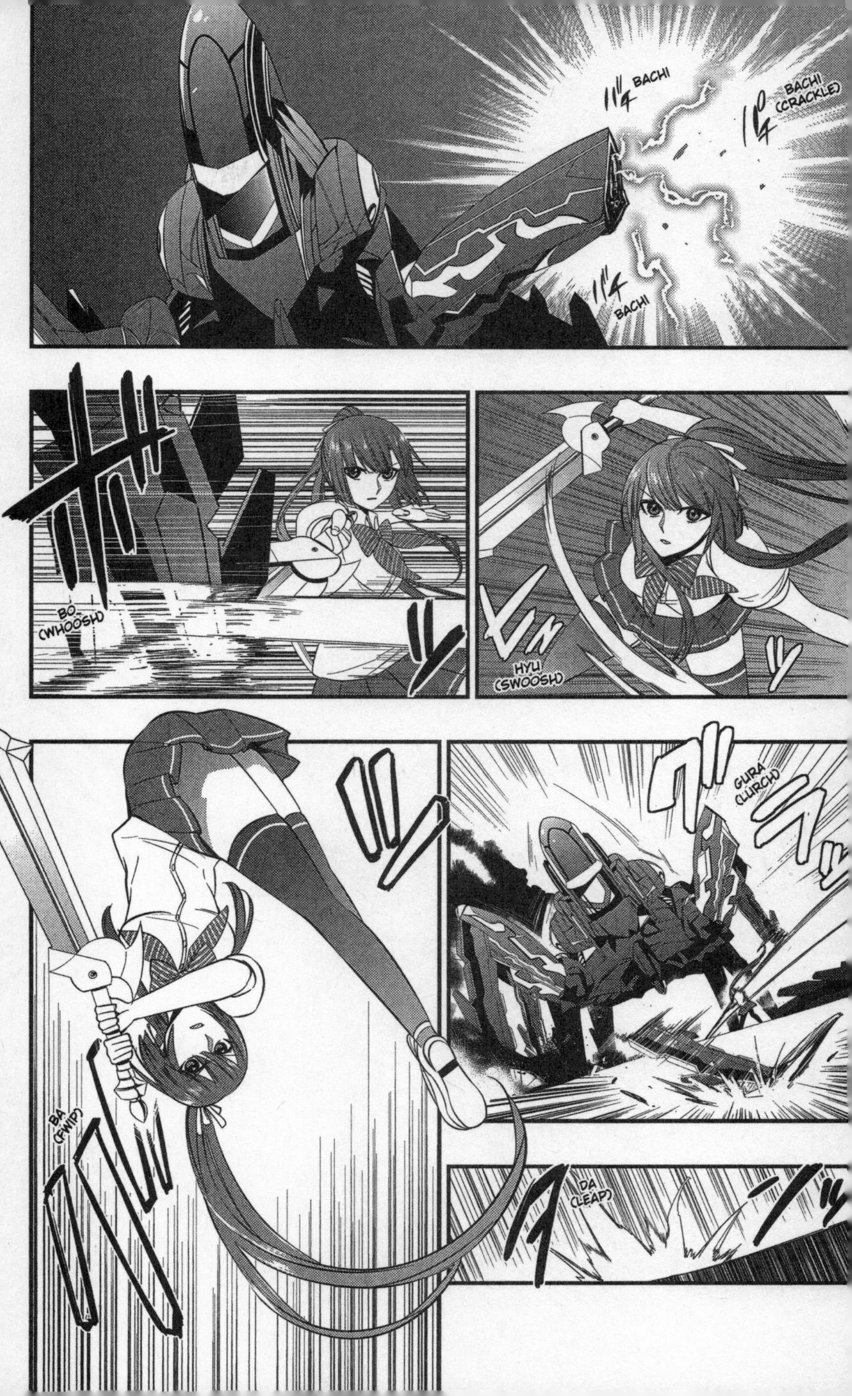
BACHI (CRACKLE)
BACHI
BACHI
HYU (SWOOSH)
BO (WHOOSH)
GURA (LURCH)
DA (LEAP)
BA (FWIP)

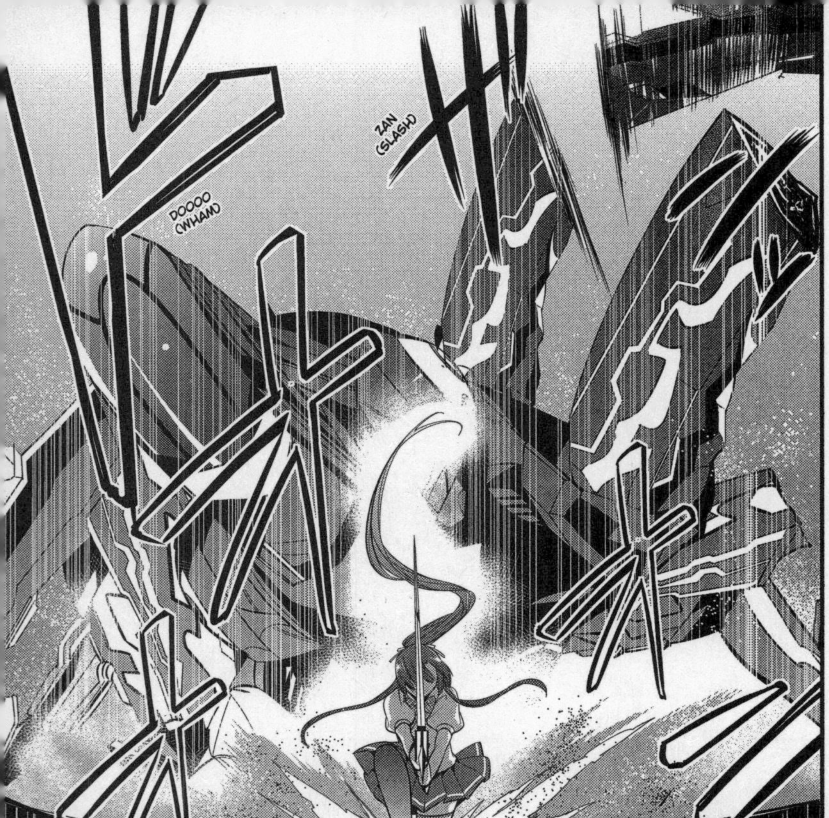
ZAN (SLASH)
DOOOO (WHAM)

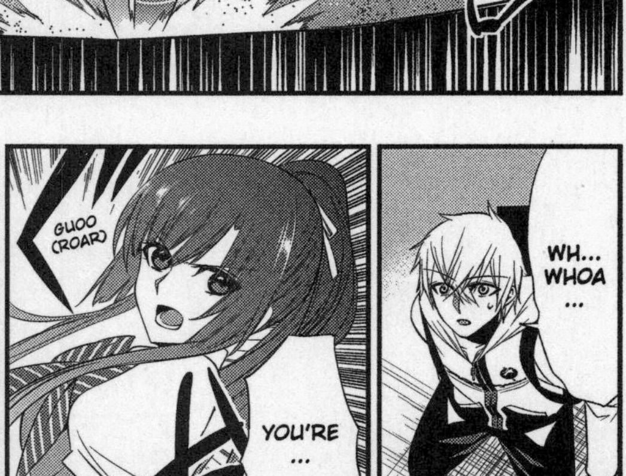
WH... WHOA ...
GUOO (ROAR)
YOU'RE ...

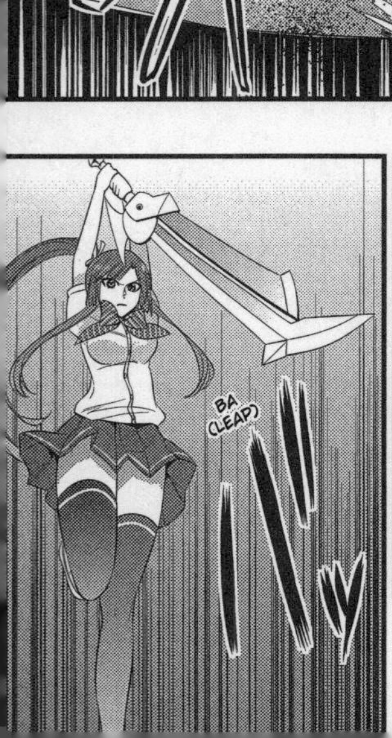
BA (LEAP)

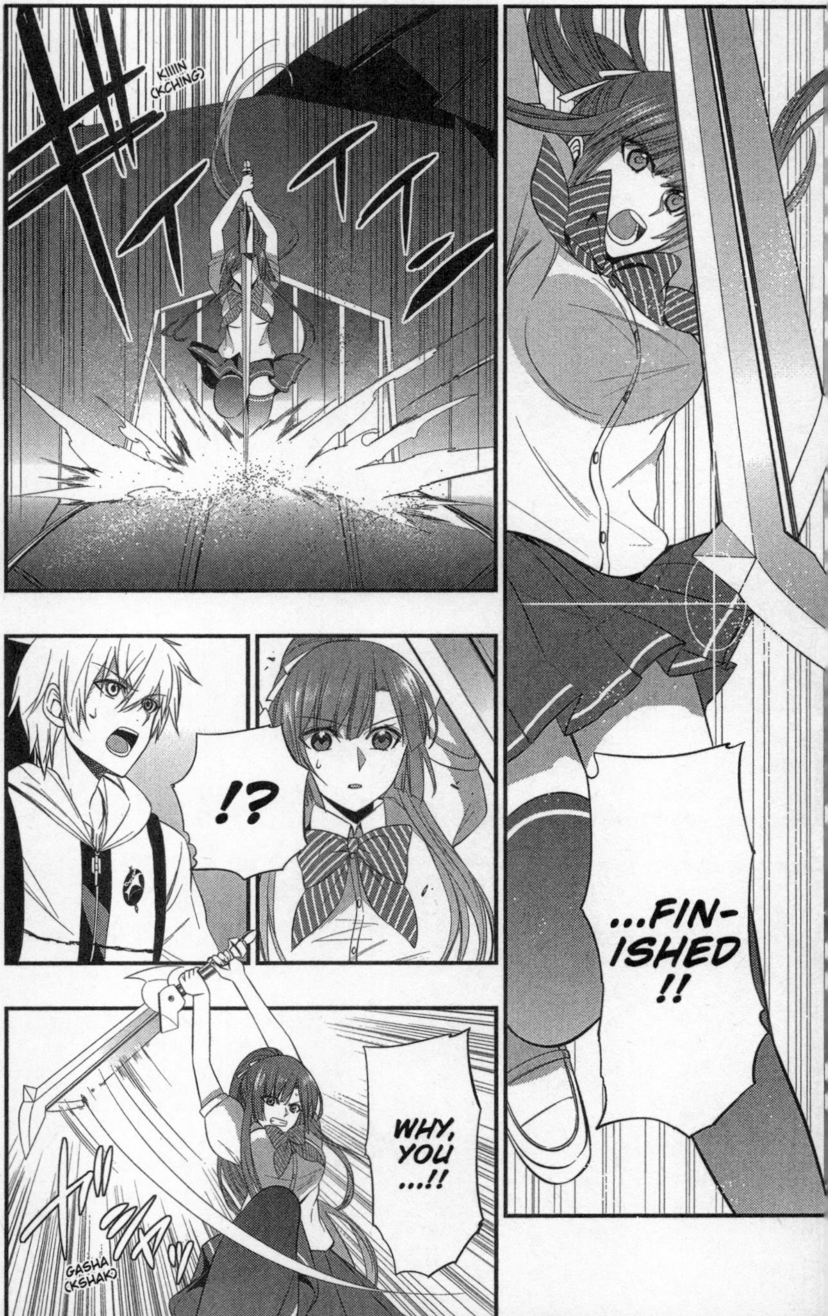
...FIN-
ISHED
!!
KIIIIN
(KCHING)
!?
WHY,
YOU
...!!
GASHA
(KSHAK)

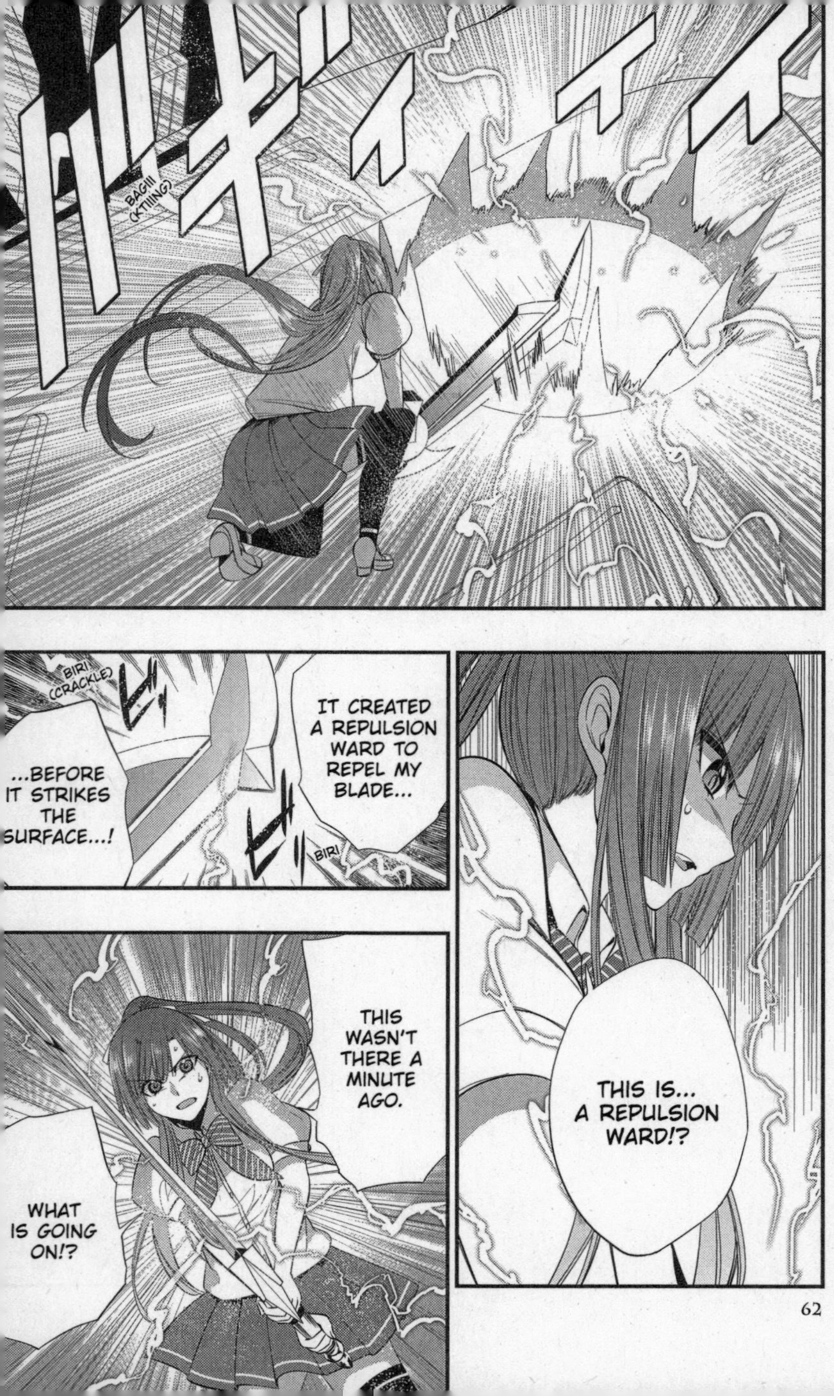
BAGIII (KTIING)
THIS IS... A REPULSION WARD!?
BIRI (CRACKLE)
IT CREATED A REPULSION WARD TO REPEL MY BLADE...
...BEFORE IT STRIKES THE SURFACE...!
BIRI
THIS WASN'T THERE A MINUTE AGO.
WHAT IS GOING ON!?

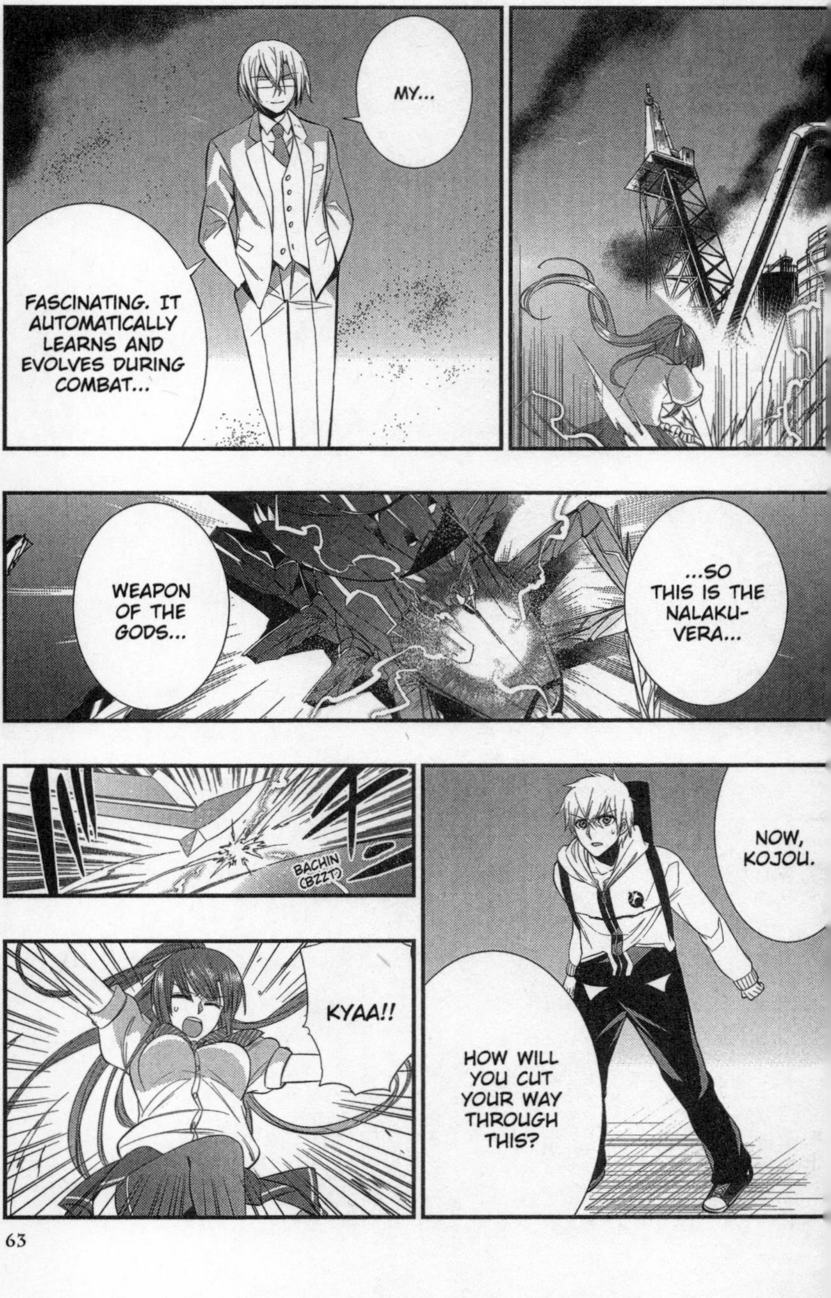
MY...
FASCINATING. IT AUTOMATICALLY LEARNS AND EVOLVES DURING COMBAT...
...SO THIS IS THE NALAKU-VERA...
WEAPON OF THE GODS...
NOW, KOJOU.
HOW WILL YOU CUT YOUR WAY THROUGH THIS?
BACHIN (BZZT)
KYAA!!

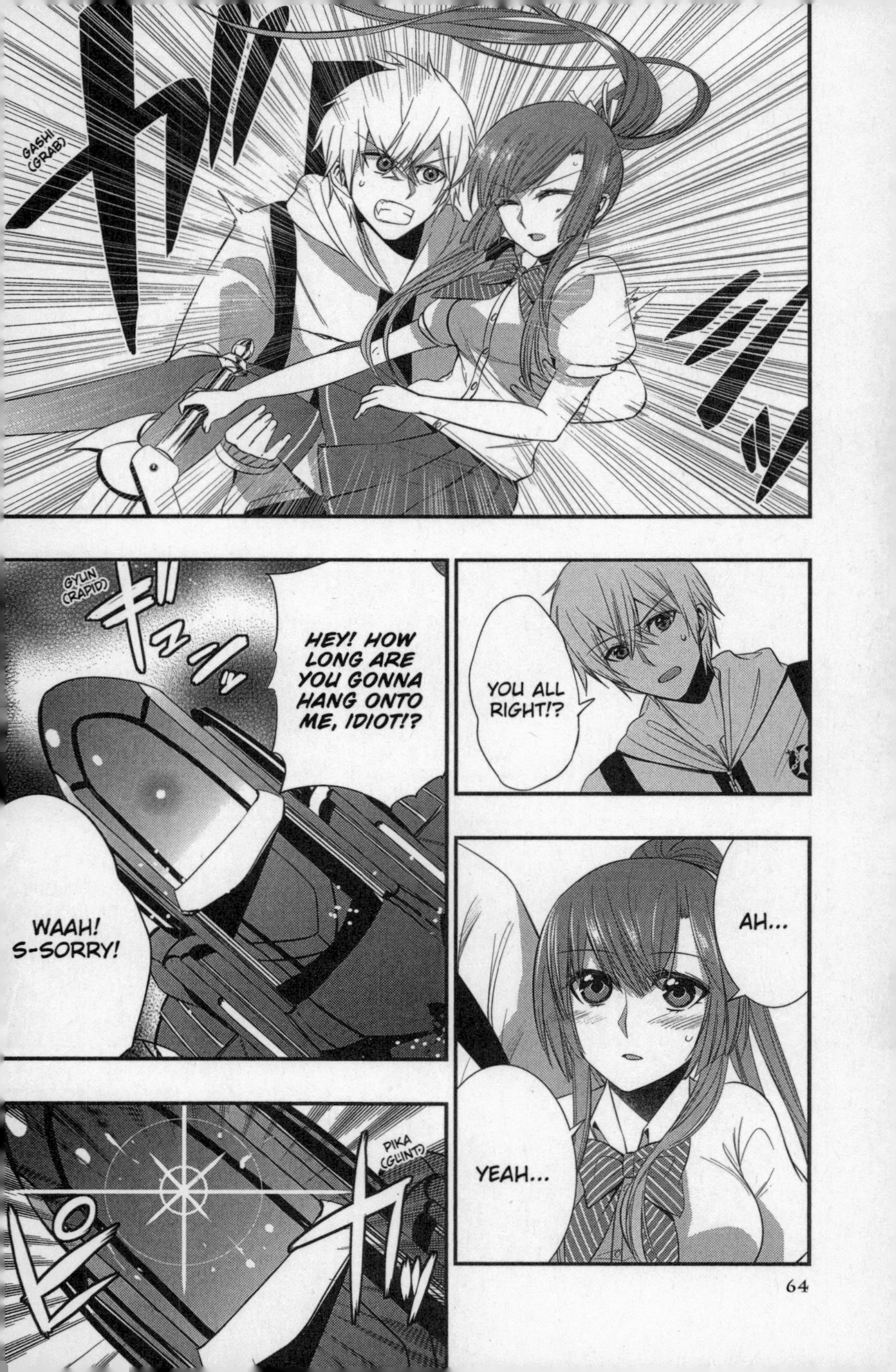
GASHI (GRAB)
YOU ALL RIGHT!?
AH...
YEAH...
GYUN (RAPID)
HEY! HOW LONG ARE YOU GONNA HANG ONTO ME, IDIOT!?
WAAH! S-SORRY!
PIKA (GLINT)

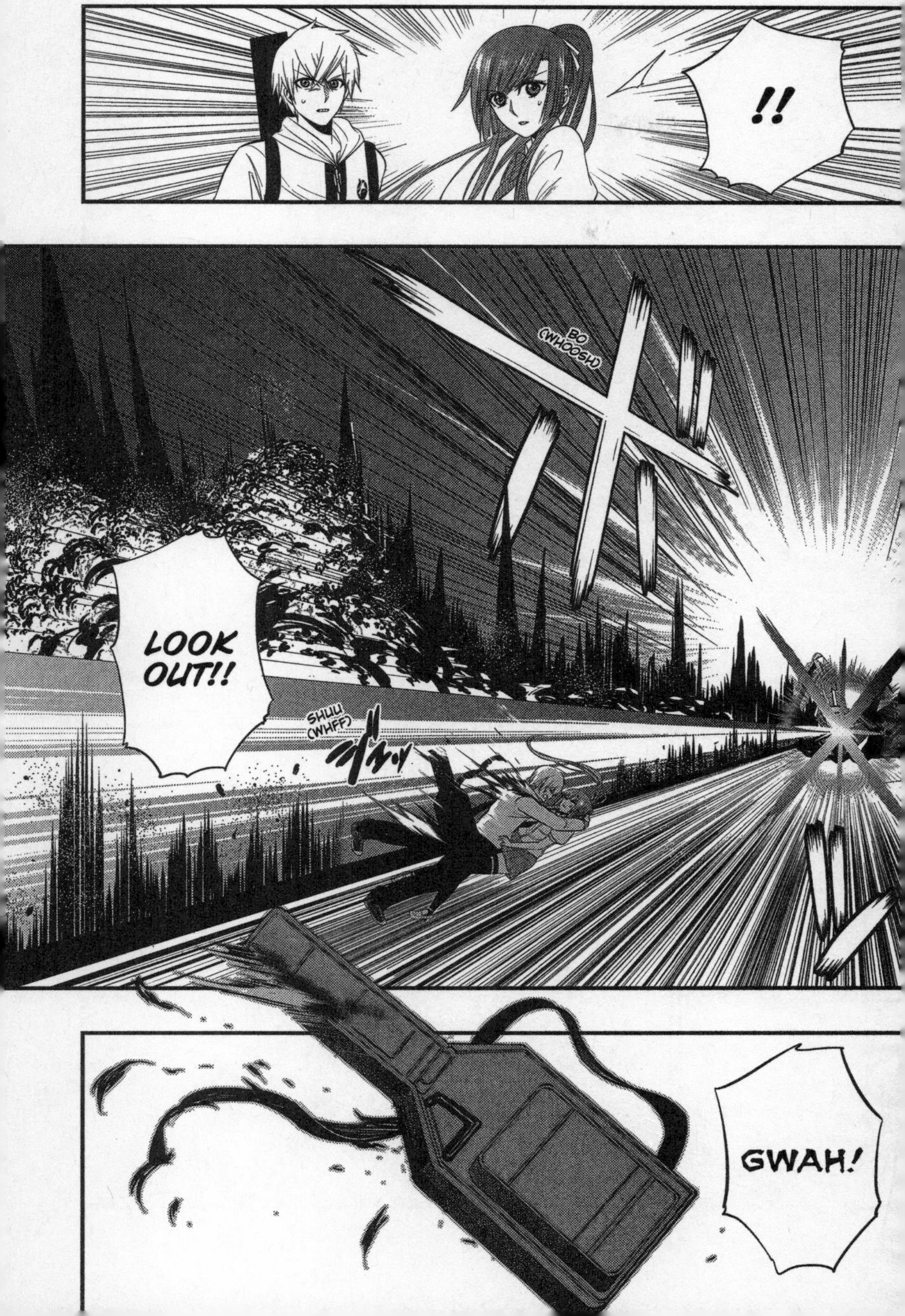
!!
BO (WHOOSH)
LOOK OUT!!
SHUU (WHFF)
GWAH!

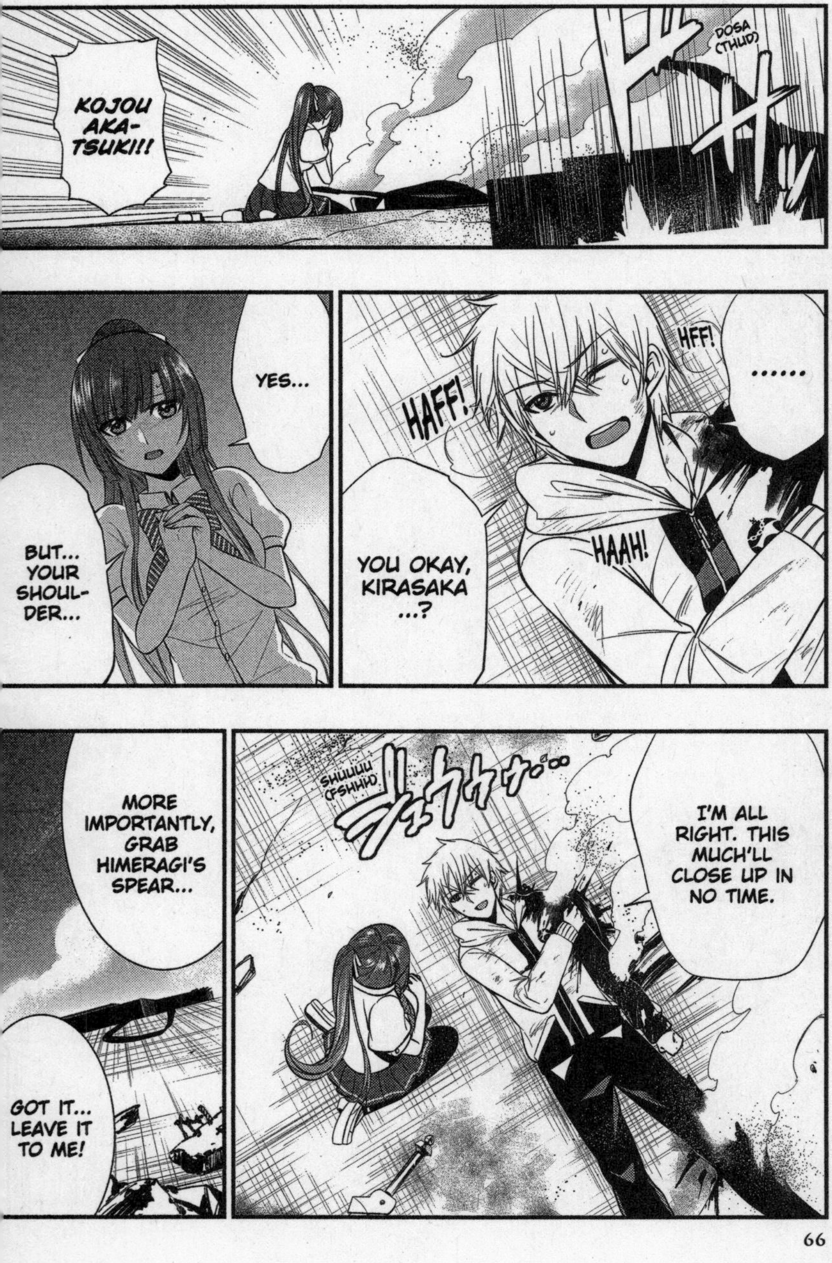
DOSA (THUD)
KOJOU AKA-TSUKI!!!
HFF!
......
HAFF!
HAAH!
YOU OKAY, KIRASAKA ...?
YES...
BUT... YOUR SHOUL-DER...
I'M ALL RIGHT. THIS MUCH'LL CLOSE UP IN NO TIME.
SHUUUU (FSHHH)
MORE IMPORTANTLY, GRAB HIMERAGI'S SPEAR...
GOT IT... LEAVE IT TO ME!

WHAT'S IT...?

GOUN

GOUN (KLUNK)

!?

GOUN

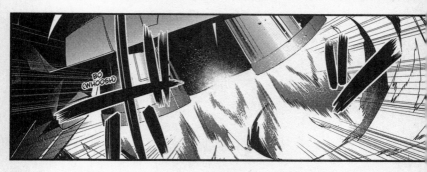

BO (WHOOSH)

IT CAN'T USE ITS LEGS, SO IT'S TRYIN' TO FLY!?

GOOOOO (RRRUMBLE)

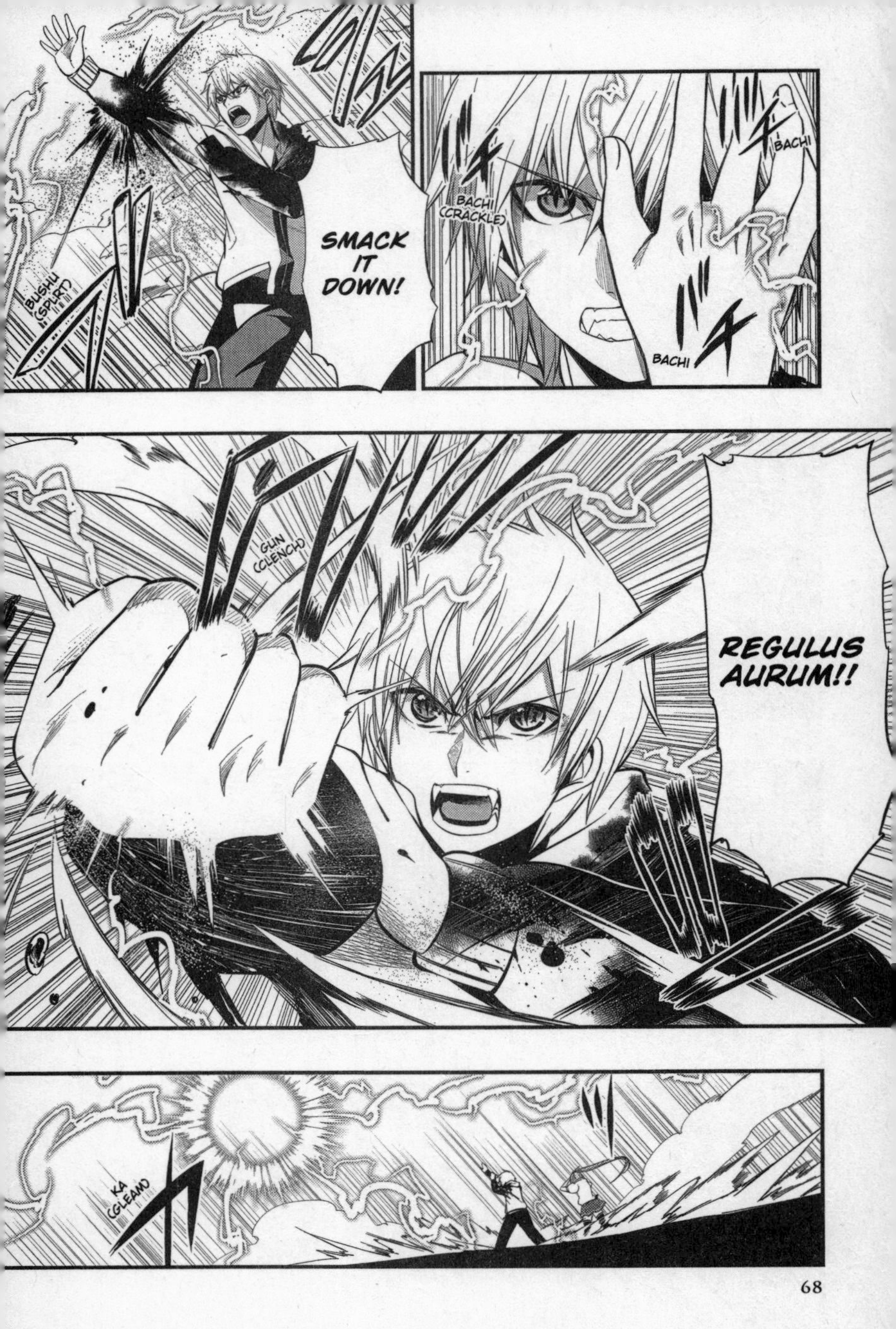
BACHI
BACHI (CRACKLE)
BACHI
SMACK IT DOWN!
BUSHU (SPLRT)
REGULUS AURUM!!
GUN (CLENCH)
KA (GLEAM)

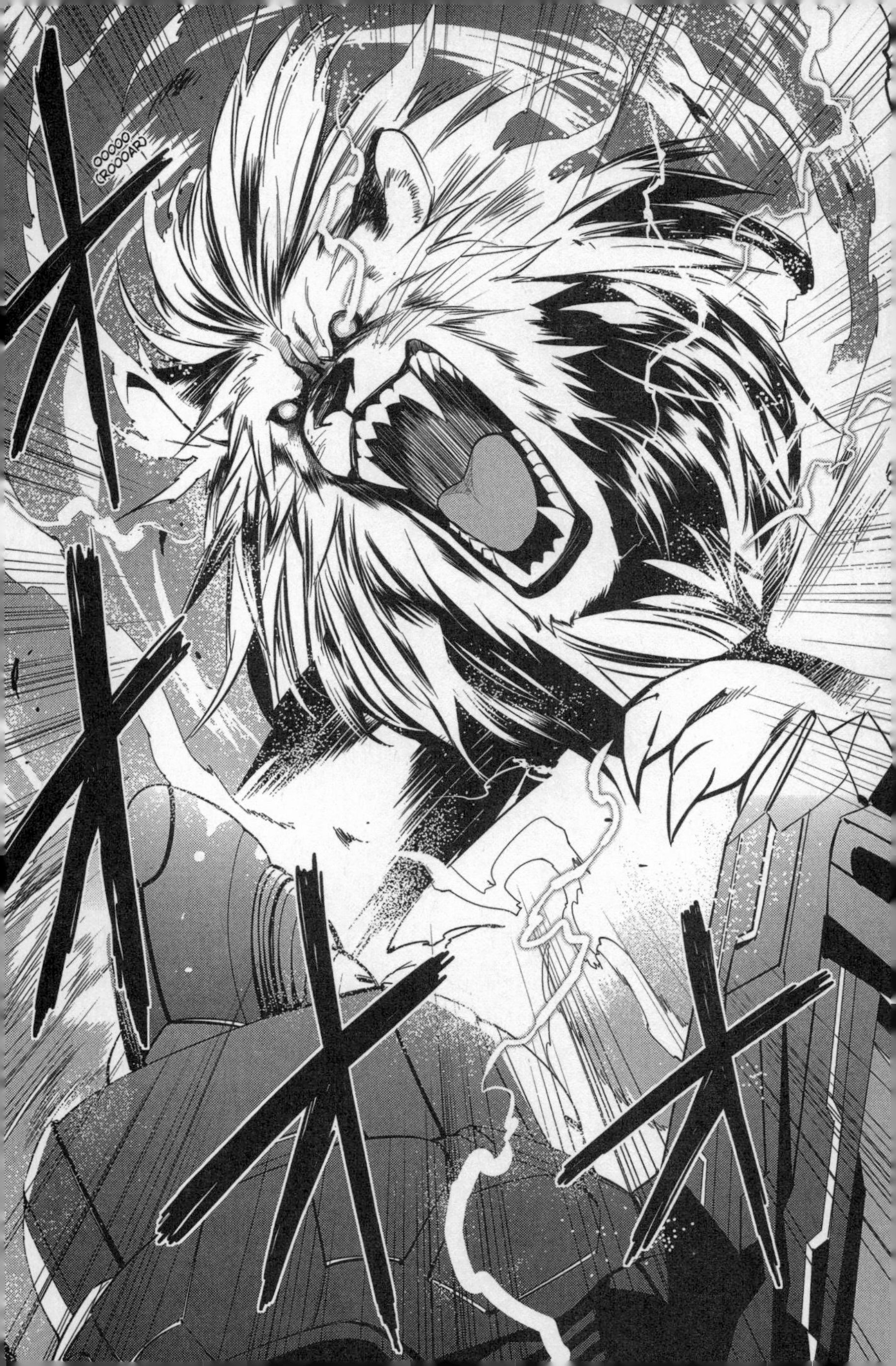
OOOOO
(ROOOAR)

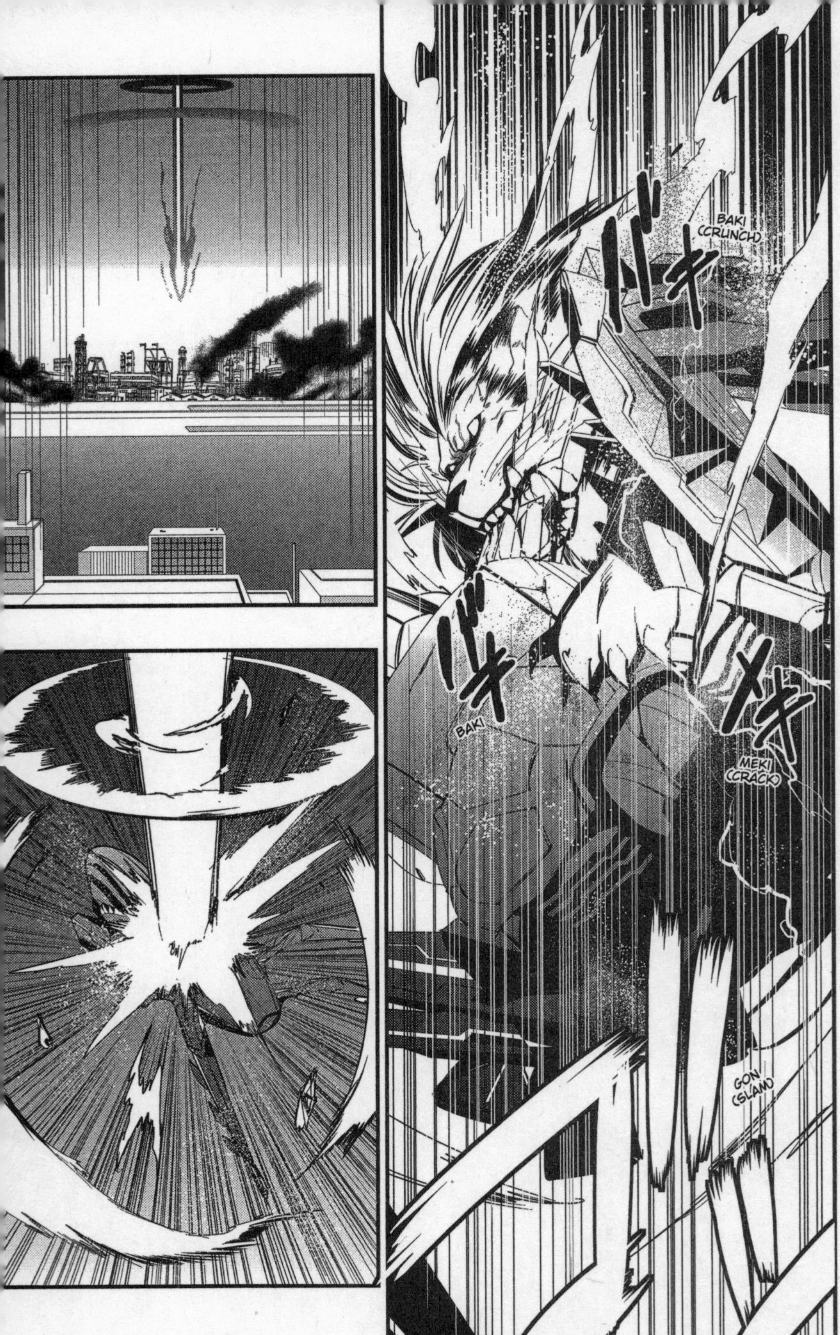
BAKI
(CRUNCH)
MEKI
(CRACK)
BAKI
GON
(SLAM)

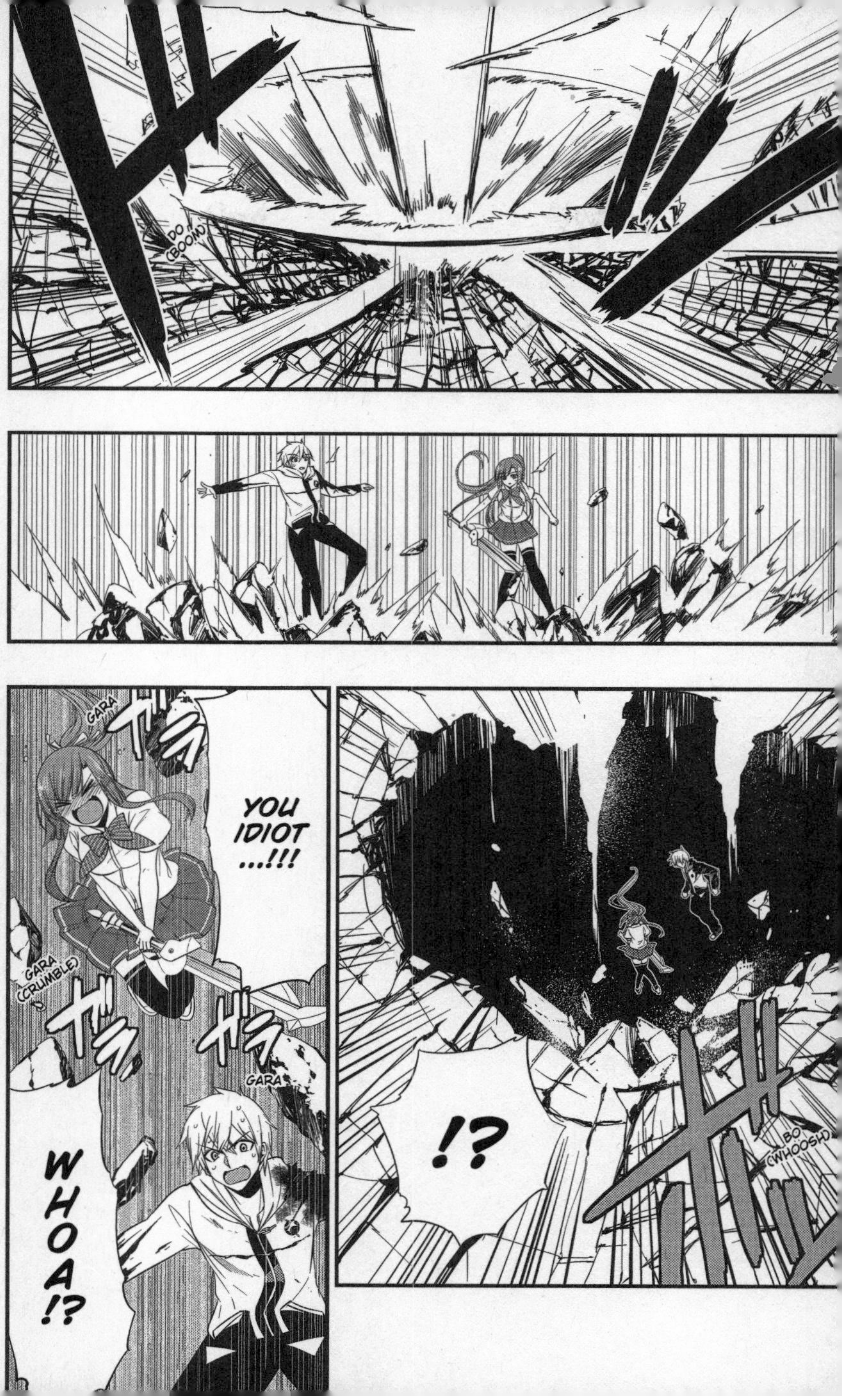
DO (BOOM)
!?
BO (WHOOSH)
GARA
YOU IDIOT ...!!!
GARA (CRUMBLE)
GARA
WHOA!?

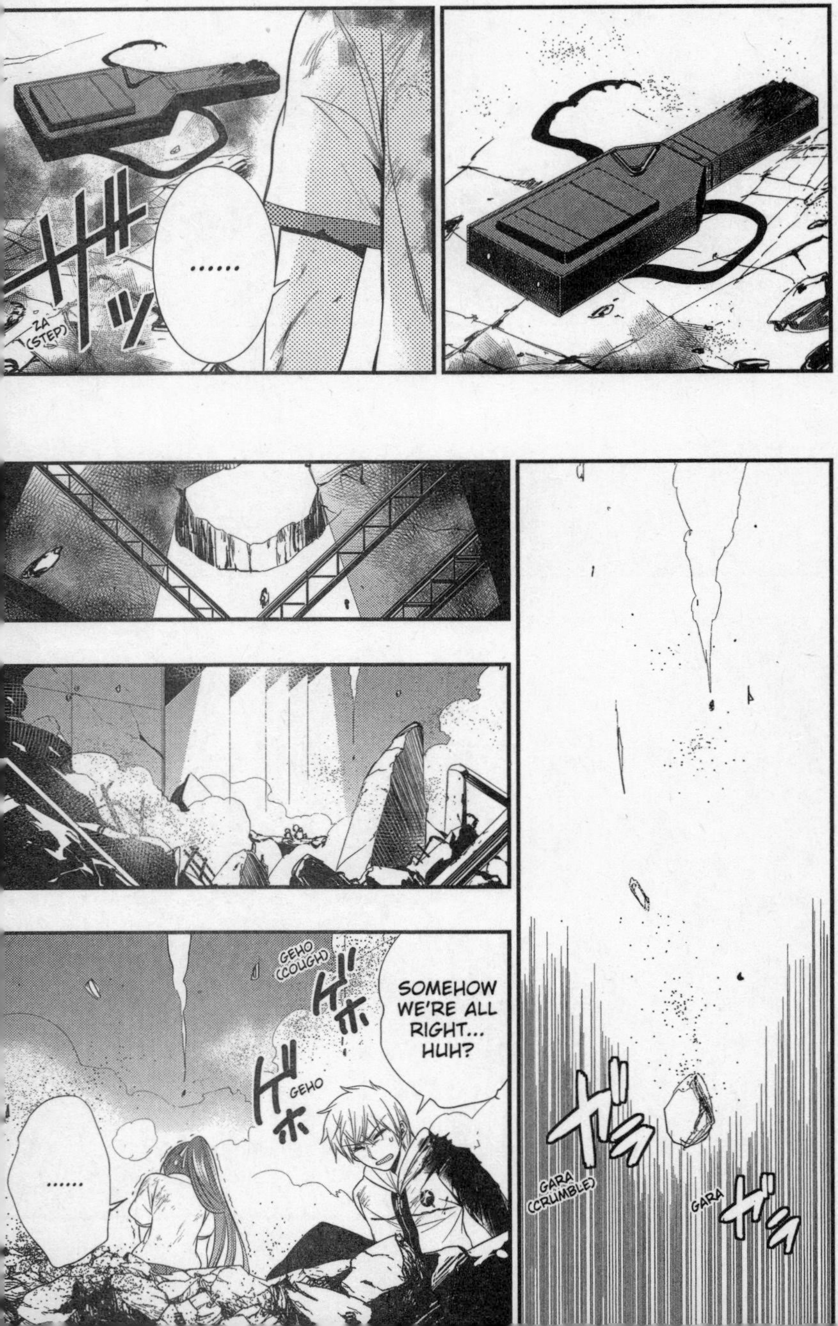
......
ZA (STEP)
GARA (CRUMBLE)
GARA
SOMEHOW WE'RE ALL RIGHT... HUH?
GEHO (COUGH)
GEHO
......

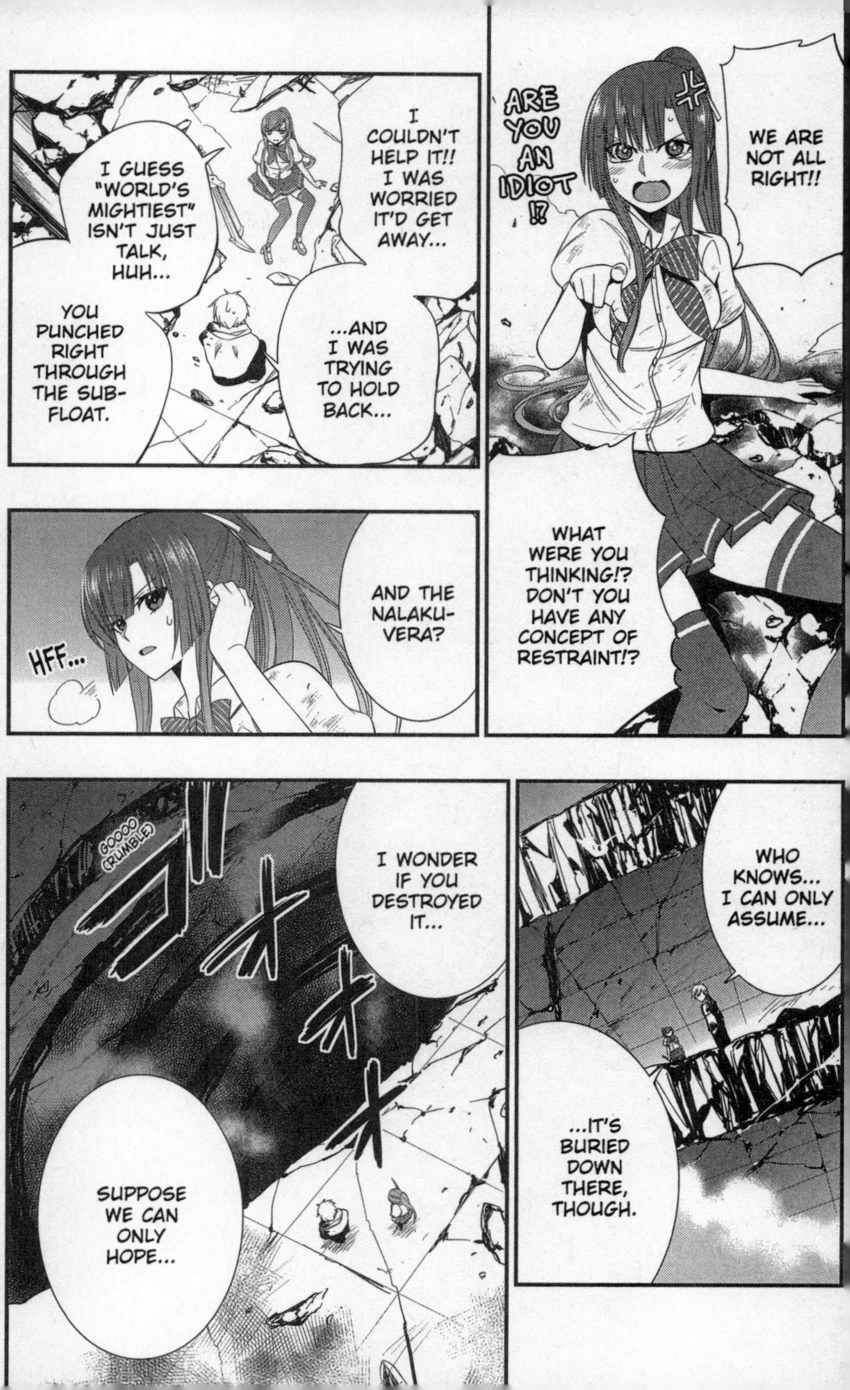
WE ARE NOT ALL RIGHT!!
ARE YOU AN IDIOT!?
WHAT WERE YOU THINKING!? DON'T YOU HAVE ANY CONCEPT OF RESTRAINT!?
I COULDN'T HELP IT!! I WAS WORRIED IT'D GET AWAY...
...AND I WAS TRYING TO HOLD BACK...
I GUESS "WORLD'S MIGHTIEST" ISN'T JUST TALK, HUH...
YOU PUNCHED RIGHT THROUGH THE SUB-FLOAT.
AND THE NALAKU-VERA?
HFF...
WHO KNOWS... I CAN ONLY ASSUME...
...IT'S BURIED DOWN THERE, THOUGH.
I WONDER IF YOU DESTROYED IT...
GOOOO (RUMBLE)
SUPPOSE WE CAN ONLY HOPE...

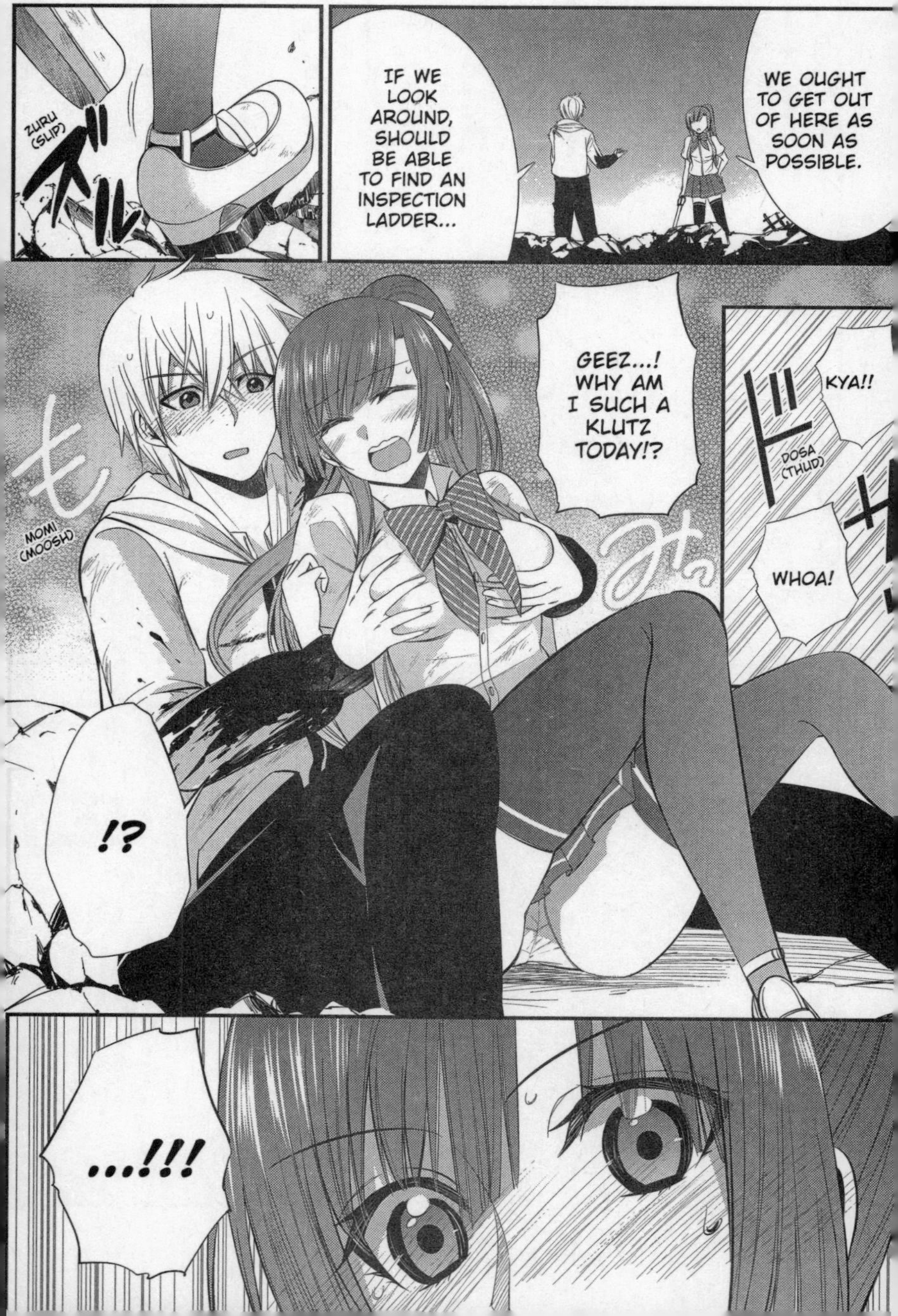
WE OUGHT TO GET OUT OF HERE AS SOON AS POSSIBLE.
IF WE LOOK AROUND, SHOULD BE ABLE TO FIND AN INSPECTION LADDER...
ZURU (SLIP)
KYA!!
DOSA (THUD)
WHOA!
GEEZ...! WHY AM I SUCH A KLUTZ TODAY!?
MOMI (MOOSH)
!?
...!!!

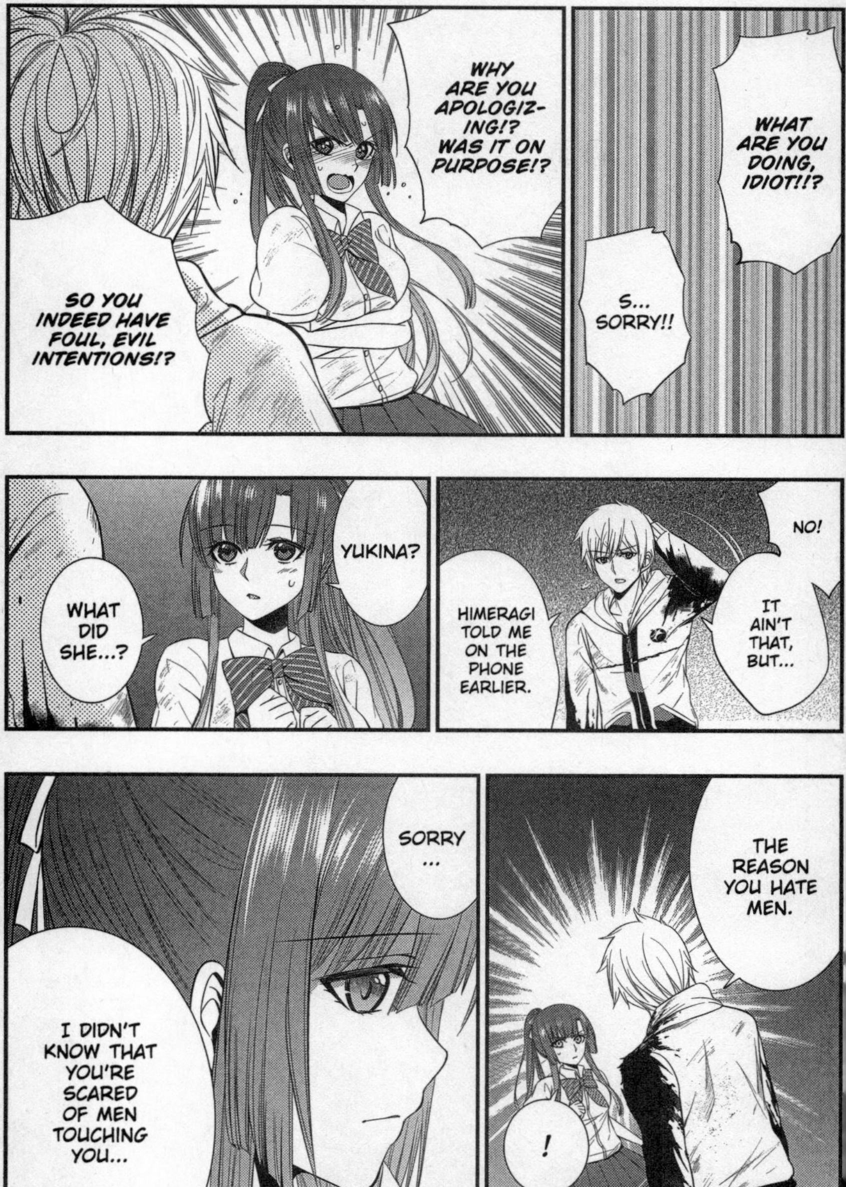

WHAT ARE YOU DOING, IDIOT!!?
S... SORRY!!
WHY ARE YOU APOLOGIZING!? WAS IT ON PURPOSE!?
SO YOU INDEED HAVE FOUL, EVIL INTENTIONS!?
NO!
IT AIN'T THAT, BUT...
HIMERAGI TOLD ME ON THE PHONE EARLIER.
YUKINA?
WHAT DID SHE...?
THE REASON YOU HATE MEN.
!
SORRY...
I DIDN'T KNOW THAT YOU'RE SCARED OF MEN TOUCHING YOU...

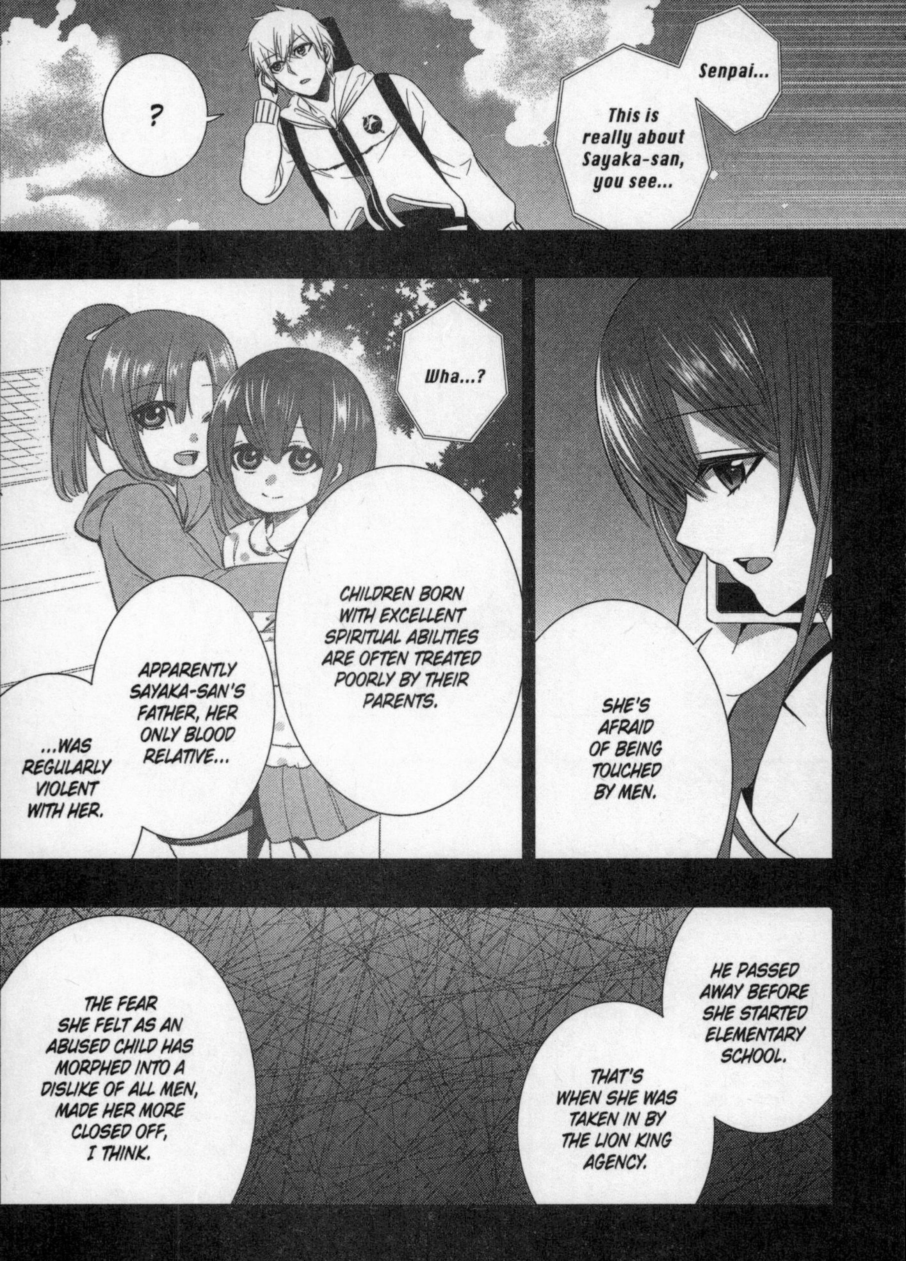
Senpai... This is really about Sayaka-san, you see...
?
SHE'S AFRAID OF BEING TOUCHED BY MEN.
Wha...?
CHILDREN BORN WITH EXCELLENT SPIRITUAL ABILITIES ARE OFTEN TREATED POORLY BY THEIR PARENTS.
APPARENTLY SAYAKA-SAN'S FATHER, HER ONLY BLOOD RELATIVE...
...WAS REGULARLY VIOLENT WITH HER.
HE PASSED AWAY BEFORE SHE STARTED ELEMENTARY SCHOOL.
THAT'S WHEN SHE WAS TAKEN IN BY THE LION KING AGENCY.
THE FEAR SHE FELT AS AN ABUSED CHILD HAS MORPHED INTO A DISLIKE OF ALL MEN, MADE HER MORE CLOSED OFF, I THINK.

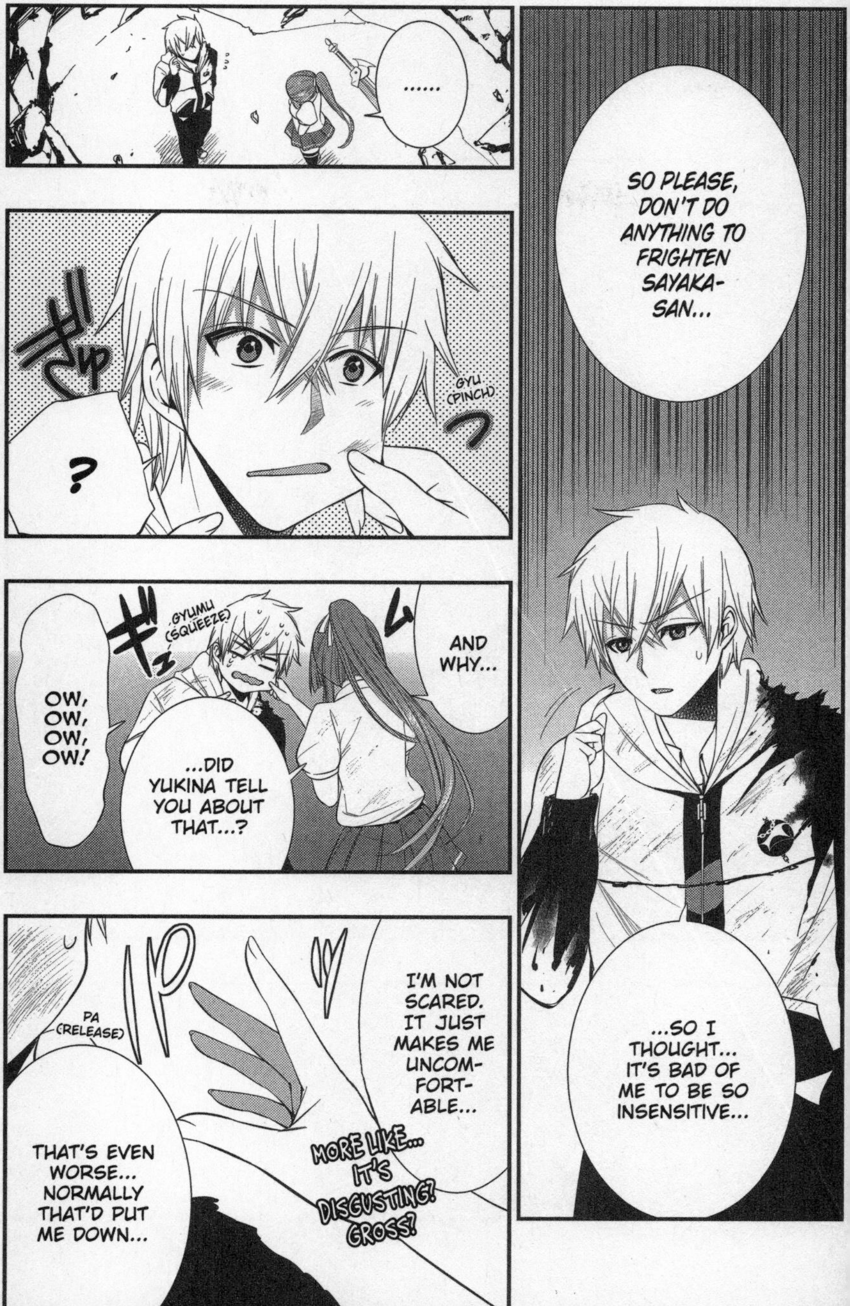

SO PLEASE, DON'T DO ANYTHING TO FRIGHTEN SAYAKA-SAN...
...SO I THOUGHT... IT'S BAD OF ME TO BE SO INSENSITIVE...
......
GYU (PINCH)
?
AND WHY...
...DID YUKINA TELL YOU ABOUT THAT...?
GYUMU (SQUEEZE)
OW, OW, OW, OW!
I'M NOT SCARED. IT JUST MAKES ME UNCOM-FORT-ABLE...
MORE LIKE... IT'S DISGUSTING! GROSS?
PA (RELEASE)
THAT'S EVEN WORSE... NORMALLY THAT'D PUT ME DOWN...

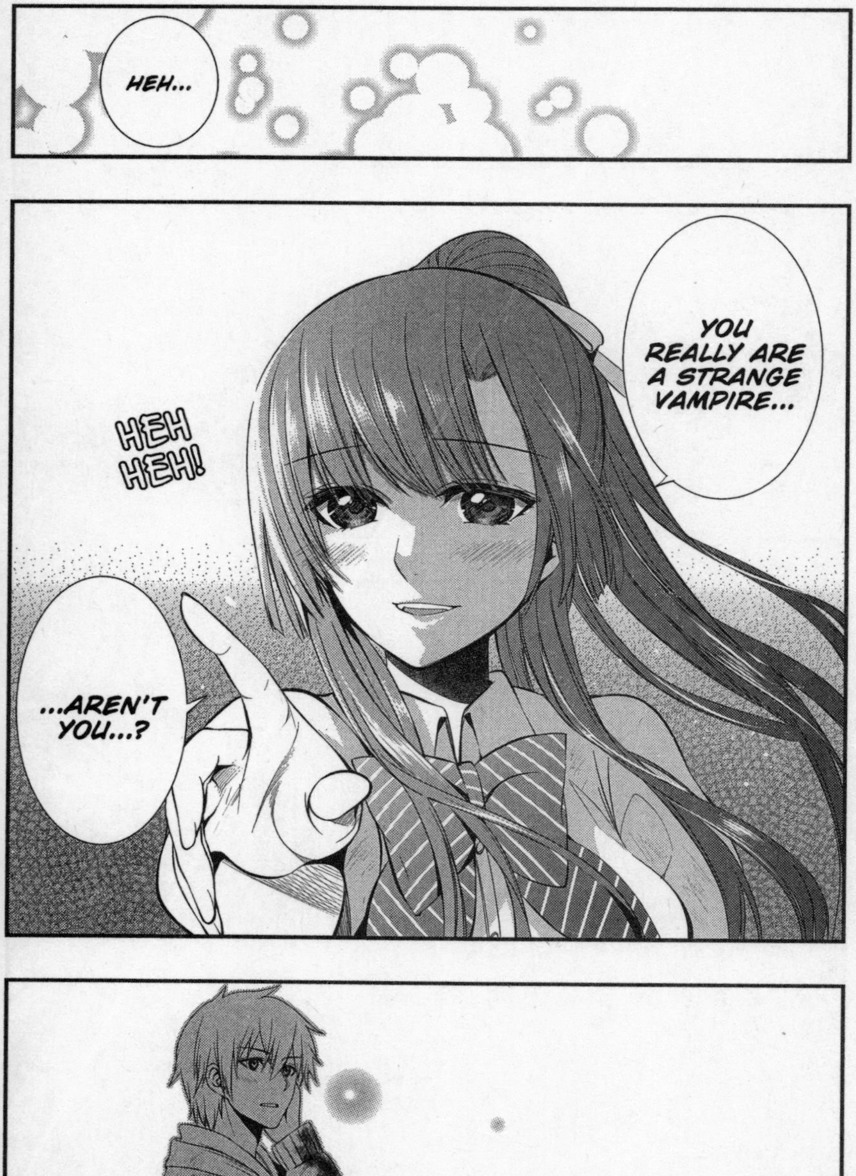
HEH...
YOU REALLY ARE A STRANGE VAMPIRE...
HEH HEH!
...AREN'T YOU...?

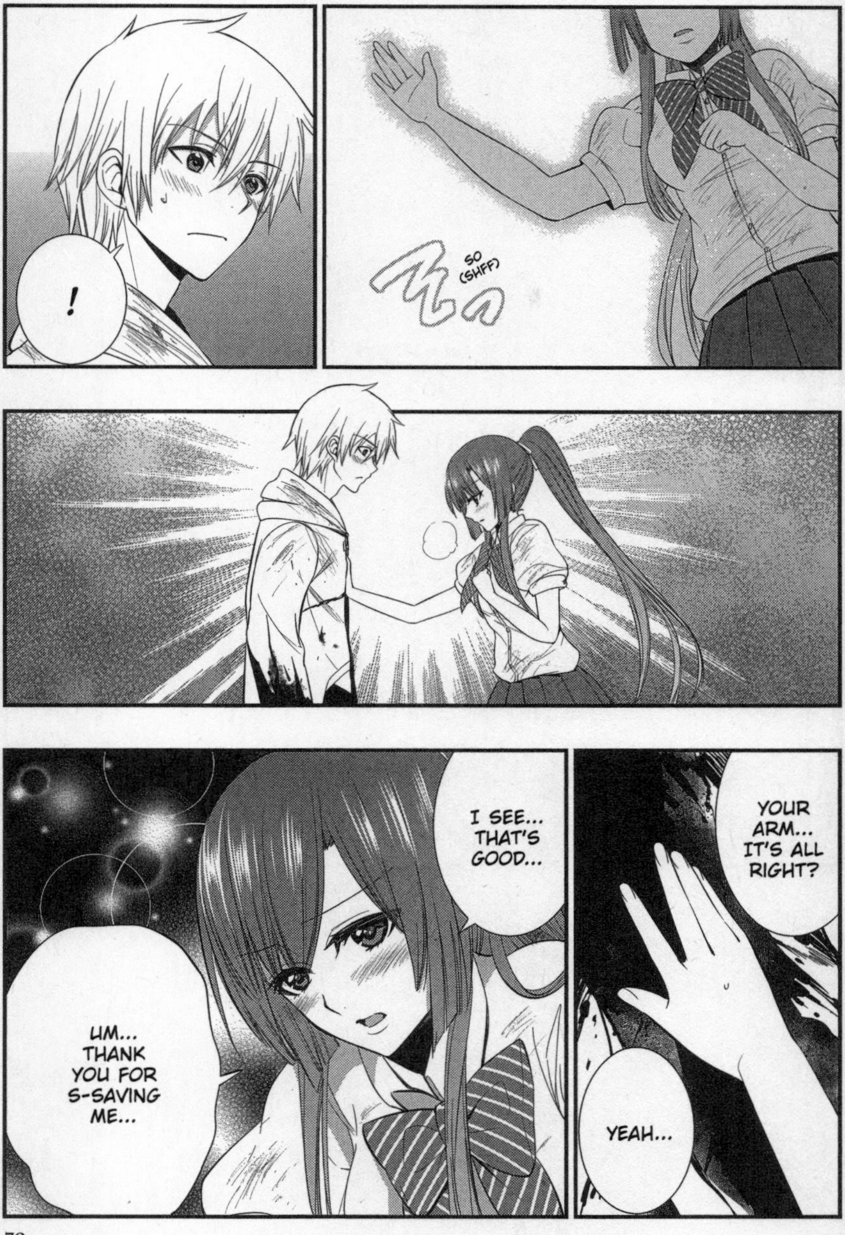
SO (SHFF)
!
YOUR ARM... IT'S ALL RIGHT?
YEAH...
I SEE... THAT'S GOOD...
UM... THANK YOU FOR S-SAVING ME...

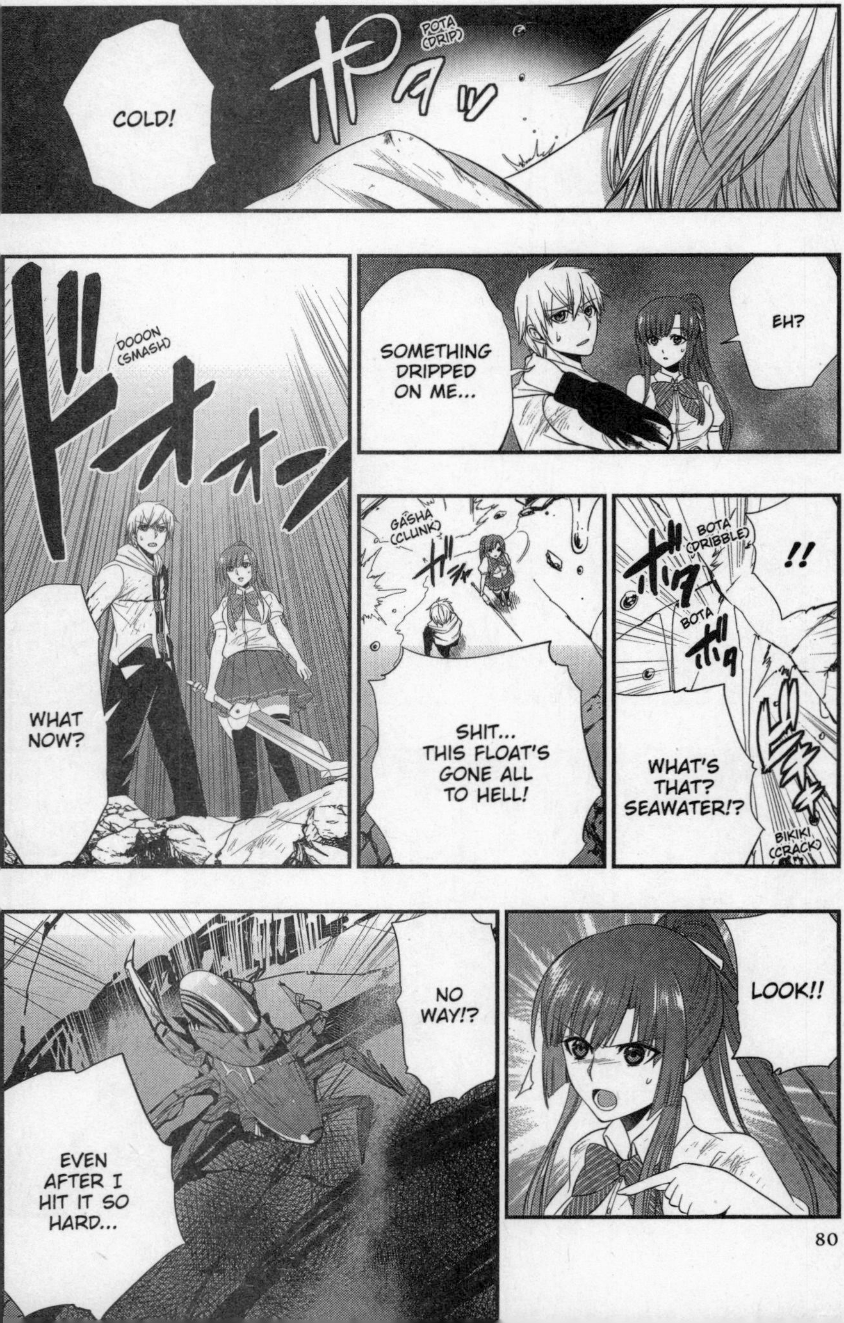
POTA (DRIP)
COLD!
EH?
SOMETHING DRIPPED ON ME...
BOTA (DRIBBLE)
!!
BOTA
WHAT'S THAT? SEAWATER!?
BIKIKI (CRACK)
GASHA (CLUNK)
SHIT... THIS FLOAT'S GONE ALL TO HELL!
DOOON (SMASH)
WHAT NOW?
LOOK!!
NO WAY!?
EVEN AFTER I HIT IT SO HARD...

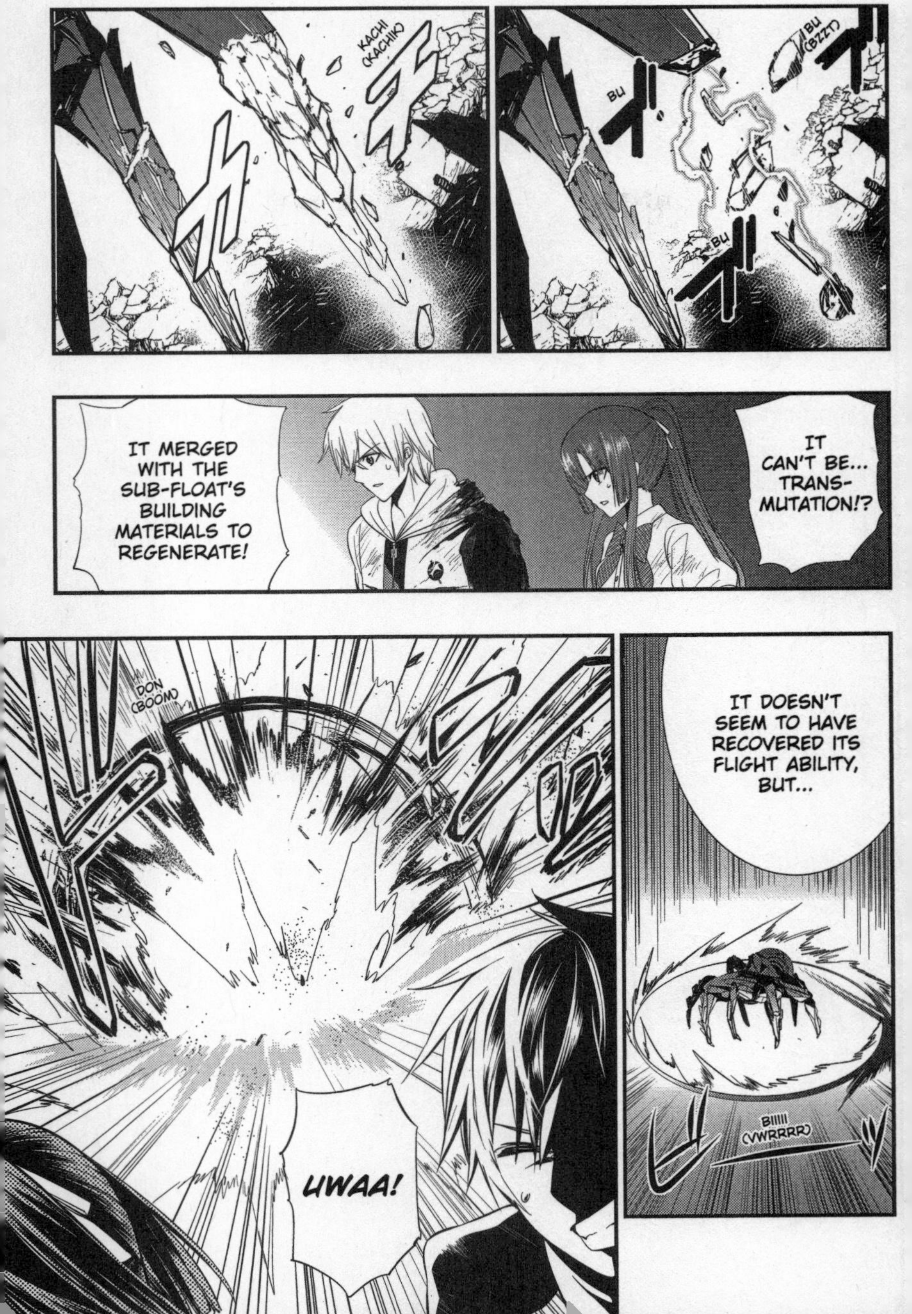
BU (BZZT)
BU
BU
KACHI (KACHIK)
IT CAN'T BE... TRANSMUTATION!?
IT MERGED WITH THE SUB-FLOAT'S BUILDING MATERIALS TO REGENERATE!
IT DOESN'T SEEM TO HAVE RECOVERED ITS FLIGHT ABILITY, BUT...
BIIIII (VWRRRR)
DON (BOOM)
UWAA!

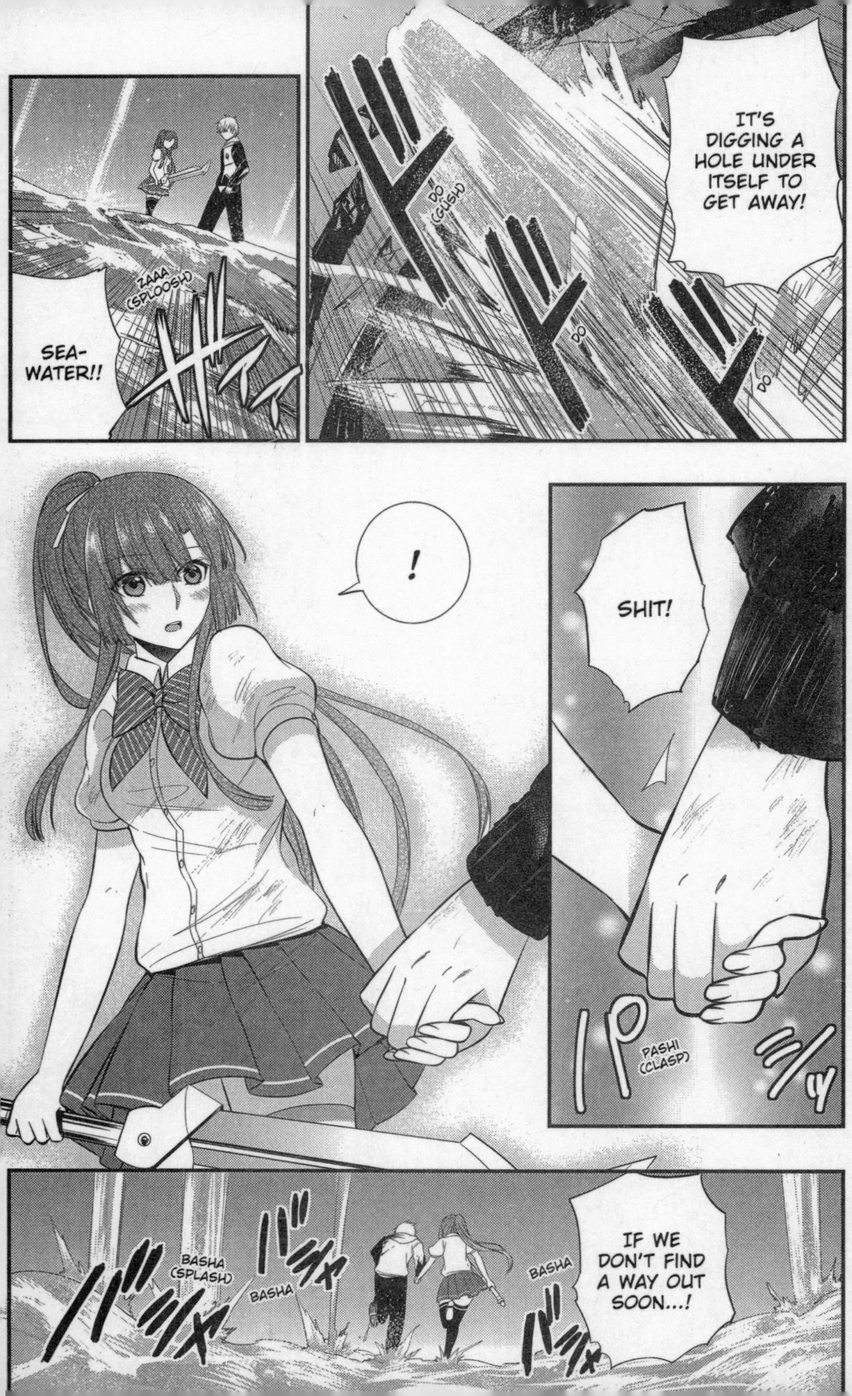
IT'S DIGGING A HOLE UNDER ITSELF TO GET AWAY!
DO (GUSH)
DO
DO
ZAAA (SPLOOSH)
SEA-WATER!!
SHIT!
PASHI (CLASP)
!
IF WE DON'T FIND A WAY OUT SOON...!
BASHA
BASHA (SPLASH)
BASHA

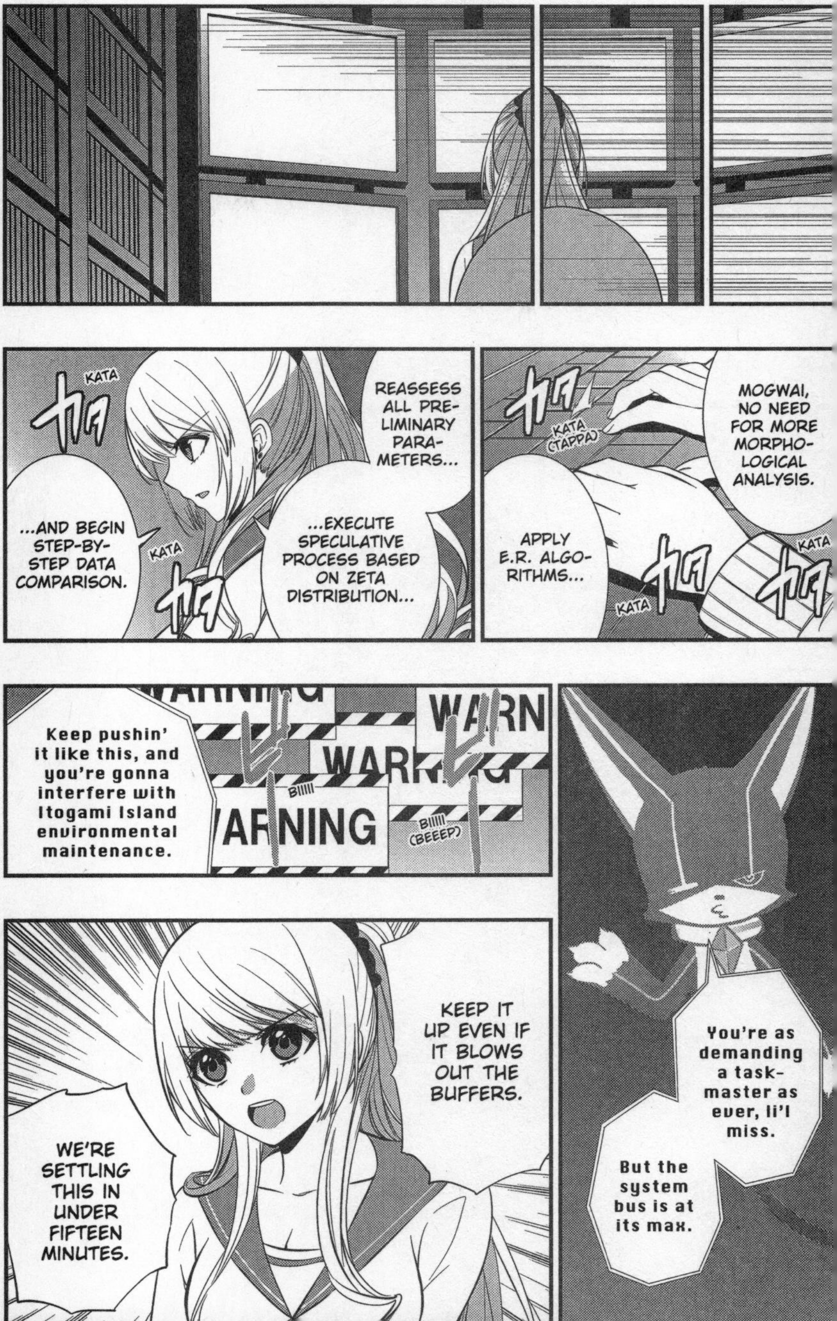
MOGWAI, NO NEED FOR MORE MORPHOLOGICAL ANALYSIS.
KATA (TAPPA)
APPLY E.R. ALGORITHMS...
KATA
KATA
REASSESS ALL PRELIMINARY PARAMETERS...
KATA
...EXECUTE SPECULATIVE PROCESS BASED ON ZETA DISTRIBUTION...
KATA
...AND BEGIN STEP-BY-STEP DATA COMPARISON.
You're as demanding a taskmaster as ever, li'l miss.
But the system bus is at its max.
WARN
WARNING
WARNING
BIIIII (BEEEP)
BIIIII
Keep pushin' it like this, and you're gonna interfere with Itogami Island environmental maintenance.
KEEP IT UP EVEN IF IT BLOWS OUT THE BUFFERS.
WE'RE SETTLING THIS IN UNDER FIFTEEN MINUTES.

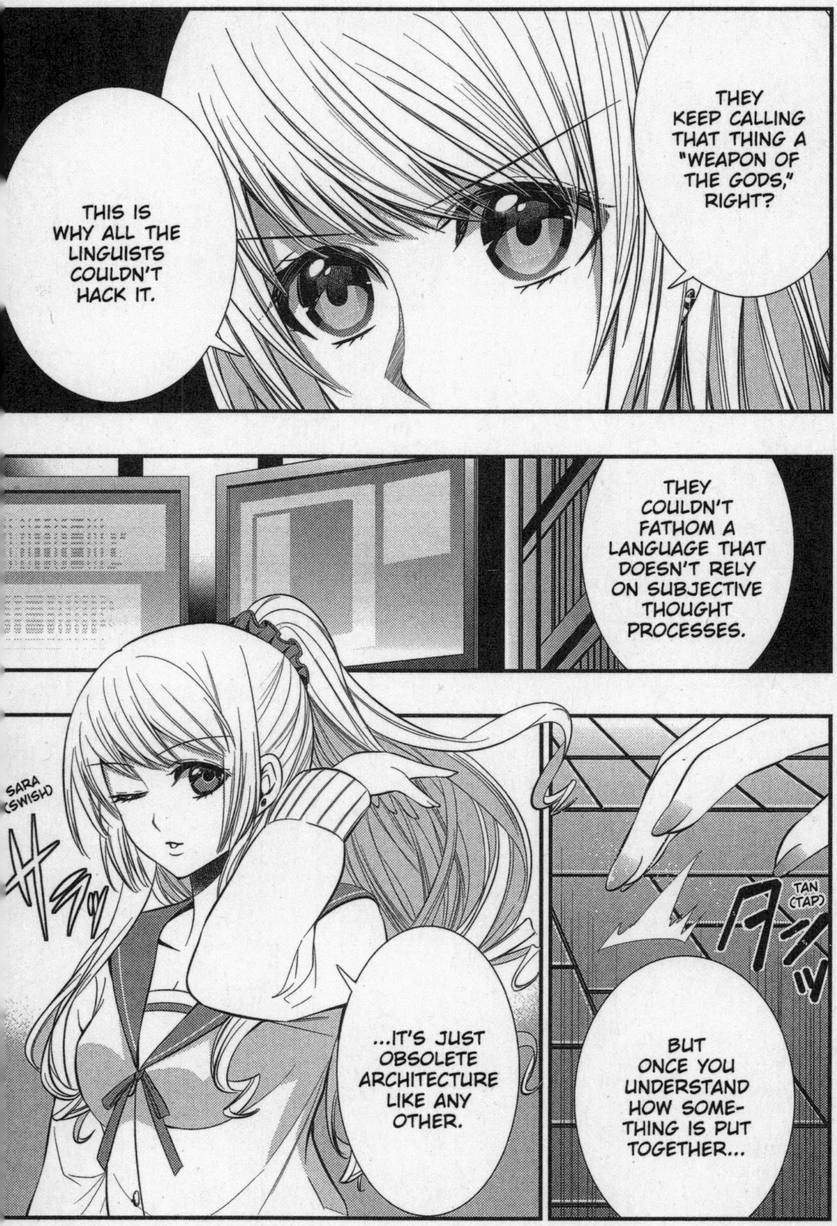
THEY KEEP CALLING THAT THING A "WEAPON OF THE GODS," RIGHT?
THIS IS WHY ALL THE LINGUISTS COULDN'T HACK IT.
THEY COULDN'T FATHOM A LANGUAGE THAT DOESN'T RELY ON SUBJECTIVE THOUGHT PROCESSES.
TAN (TAP)
BUT ONCE YOU UNDERSTAND HOW SOME-THING IS PUT TOGETHER...
SARA (SWISH)
...IT'S JUST OBSOLETE ARCHITECTURE LIKE ANY OTHER.

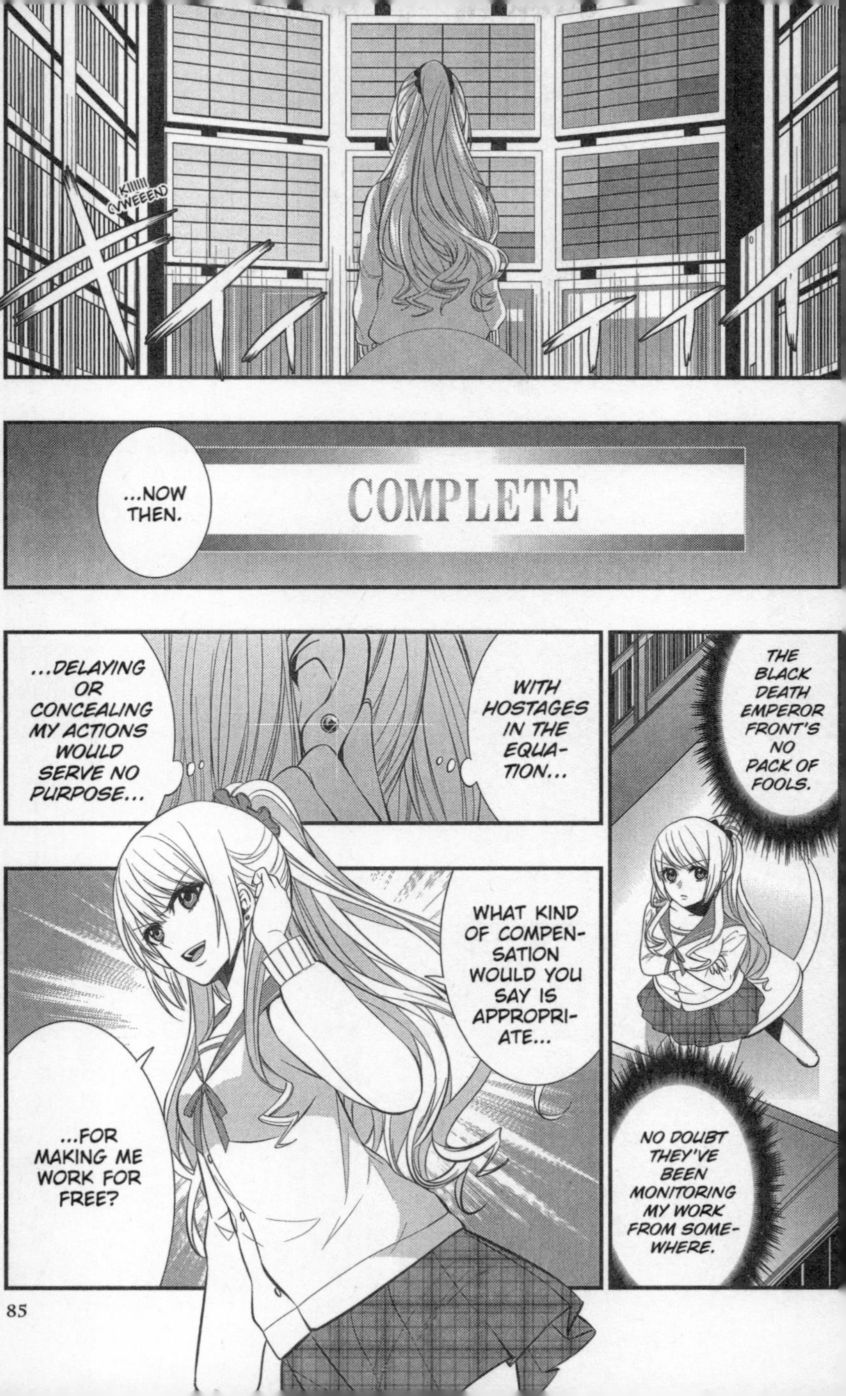
KIIIIII
(VWEEEN)
COMPLETE
...NOW THEN.
THE BLACK DEATH EMPEROR FRONT'S NO PACK OF FOOLS.
NO DOUBT THEY'VE BEEN MONITORING MY WORK FROM SOMEWHERE.
WITH HOSTAGES IN THE EQUATION...
...DELAYING OR CONCEALING MY ACTIONS WOULD SERVE NO PURPOSE...
WHAT KIND OF COMPENSATION WOULD YOU SAY IS APPROPRIATE...
...FOR MAKING ME WORK FOR FREE?

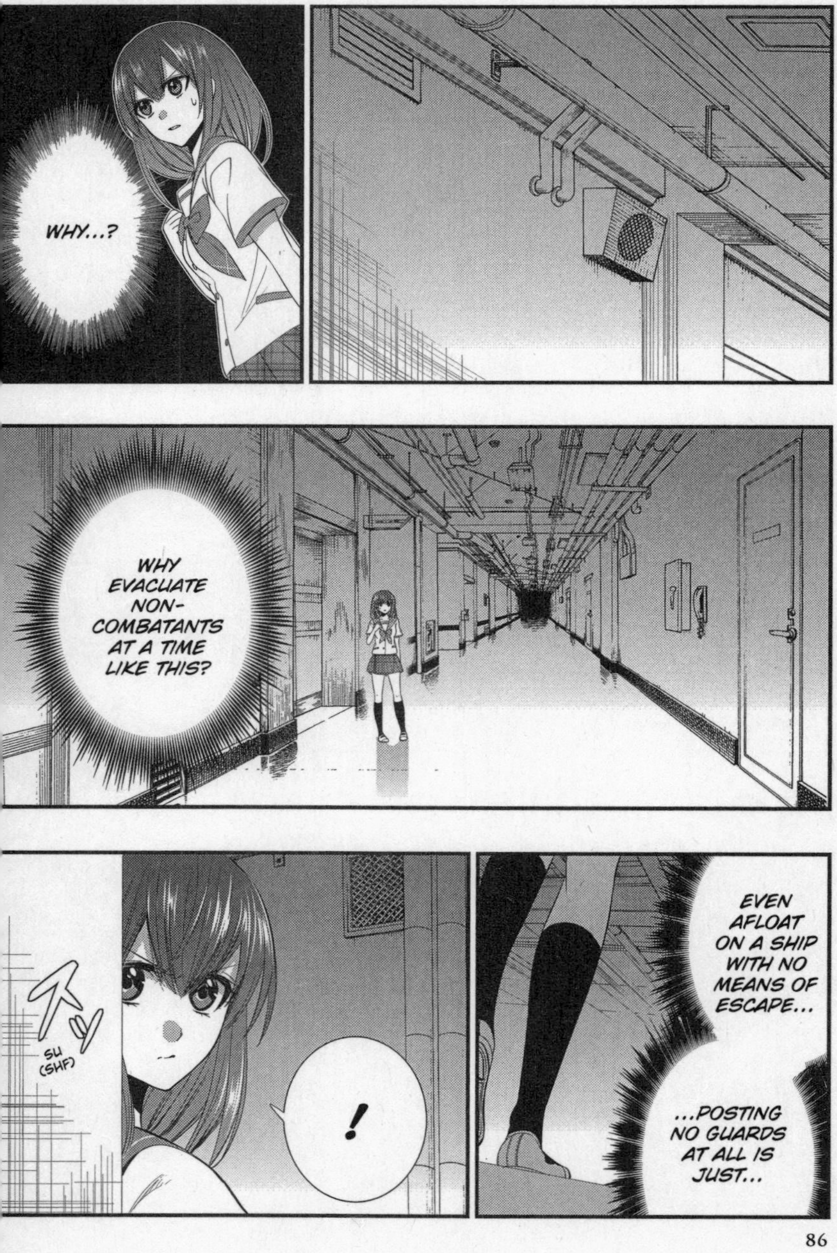
WHY...?
WHY EVACUATE NON-COMBATANTS AT A TIME LIKE THIS?
EVEN AFLOAT ON A SHIP WITH NO MEANS OF ESCAPE...
...POSTING NO GUARDS AT ALL IS JUST...
!
スッ
SU (SHF)

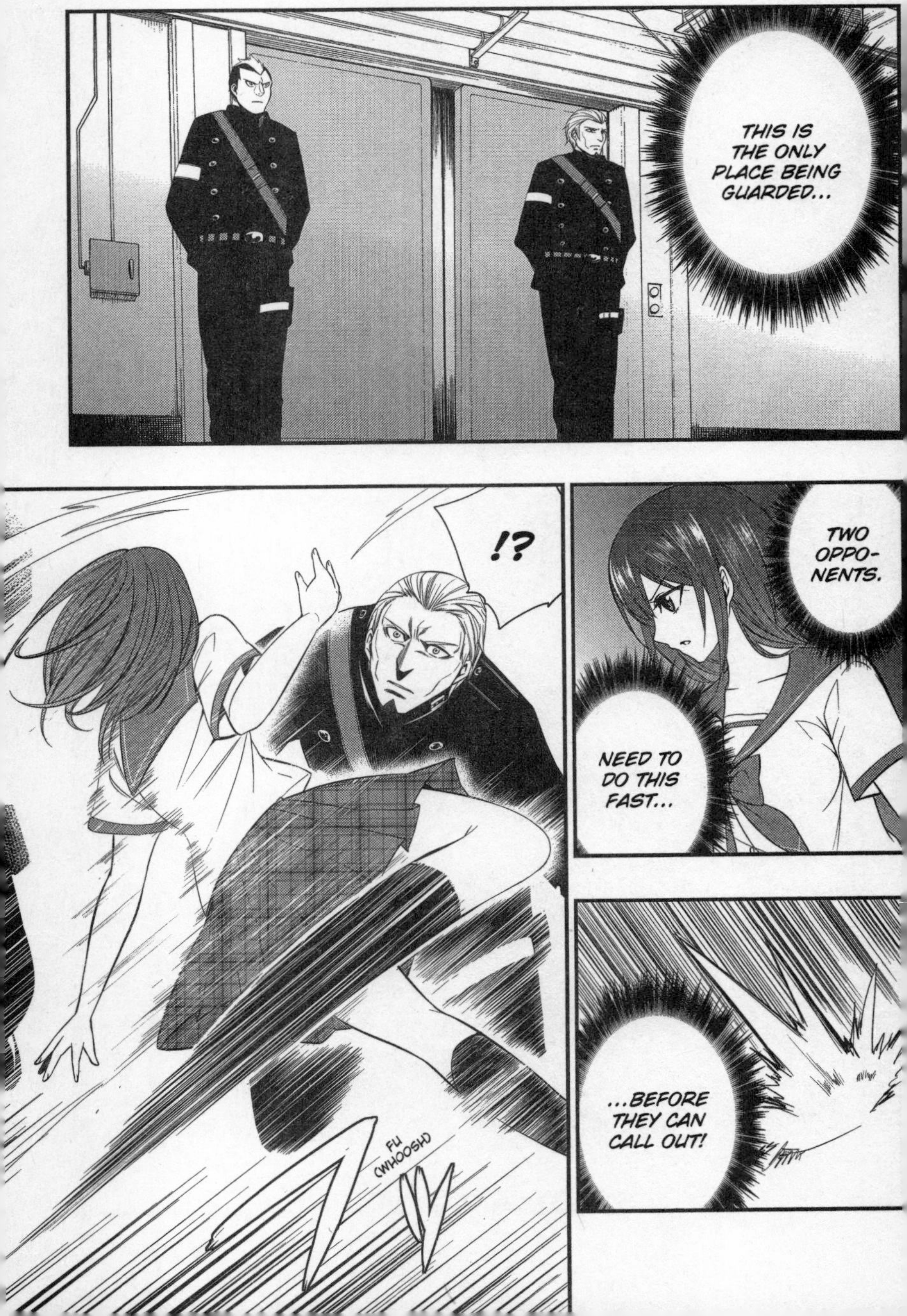
THIS IS THE ONLY PLACE BEING GUARDED...
TWO OPPO-NENTS.
NEED TO DO THIS FAST...
...BEFORE THEY CAN CALL OUT!
!?
FU (WHOOSH)

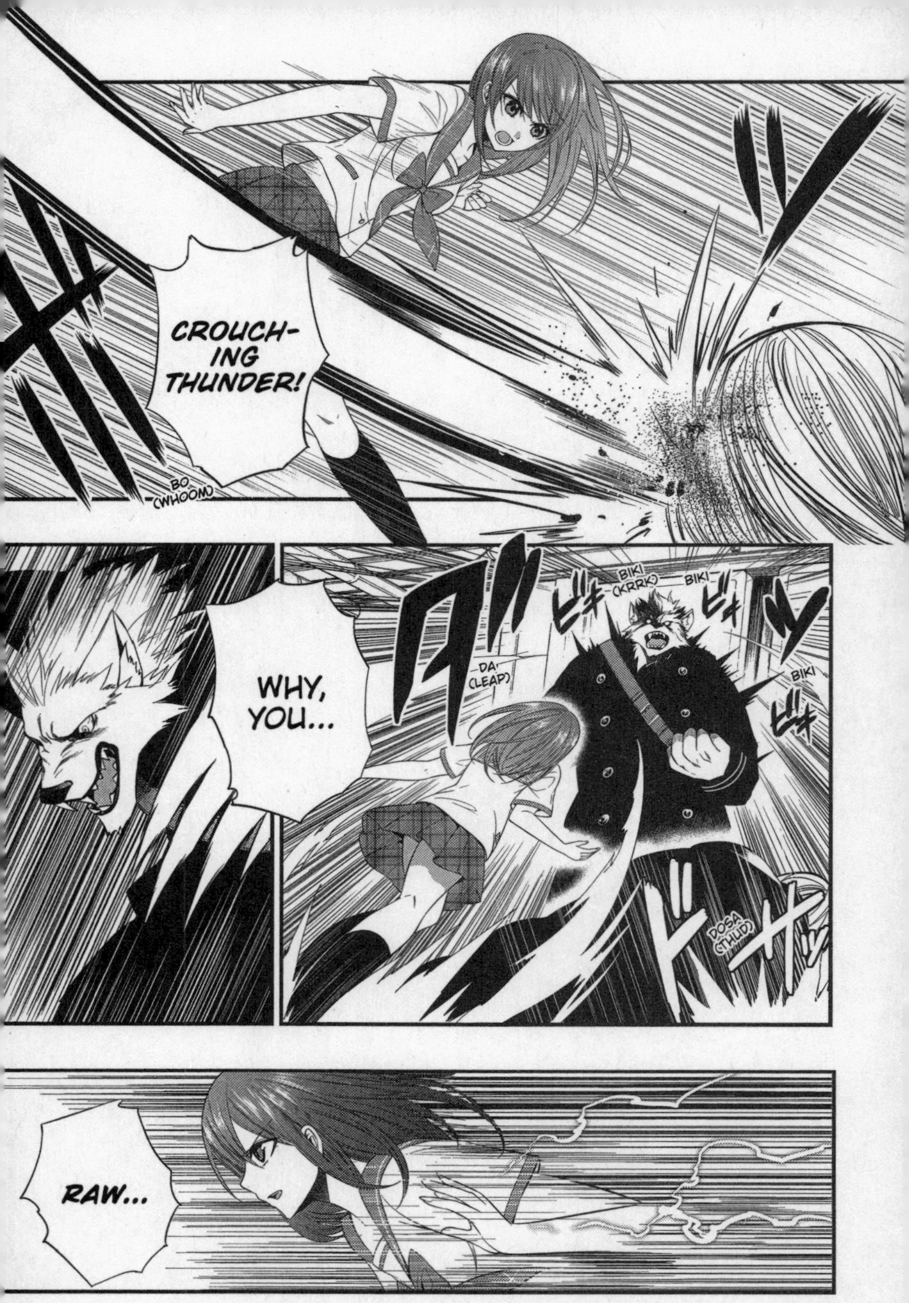
CROUCHING THUNDER!
BO (WHOOM)
BIKI
BIKI (KRRK)
BIKI
DA (LEAP)
DOSA (THUD)
WHY, YOU...
RAW...

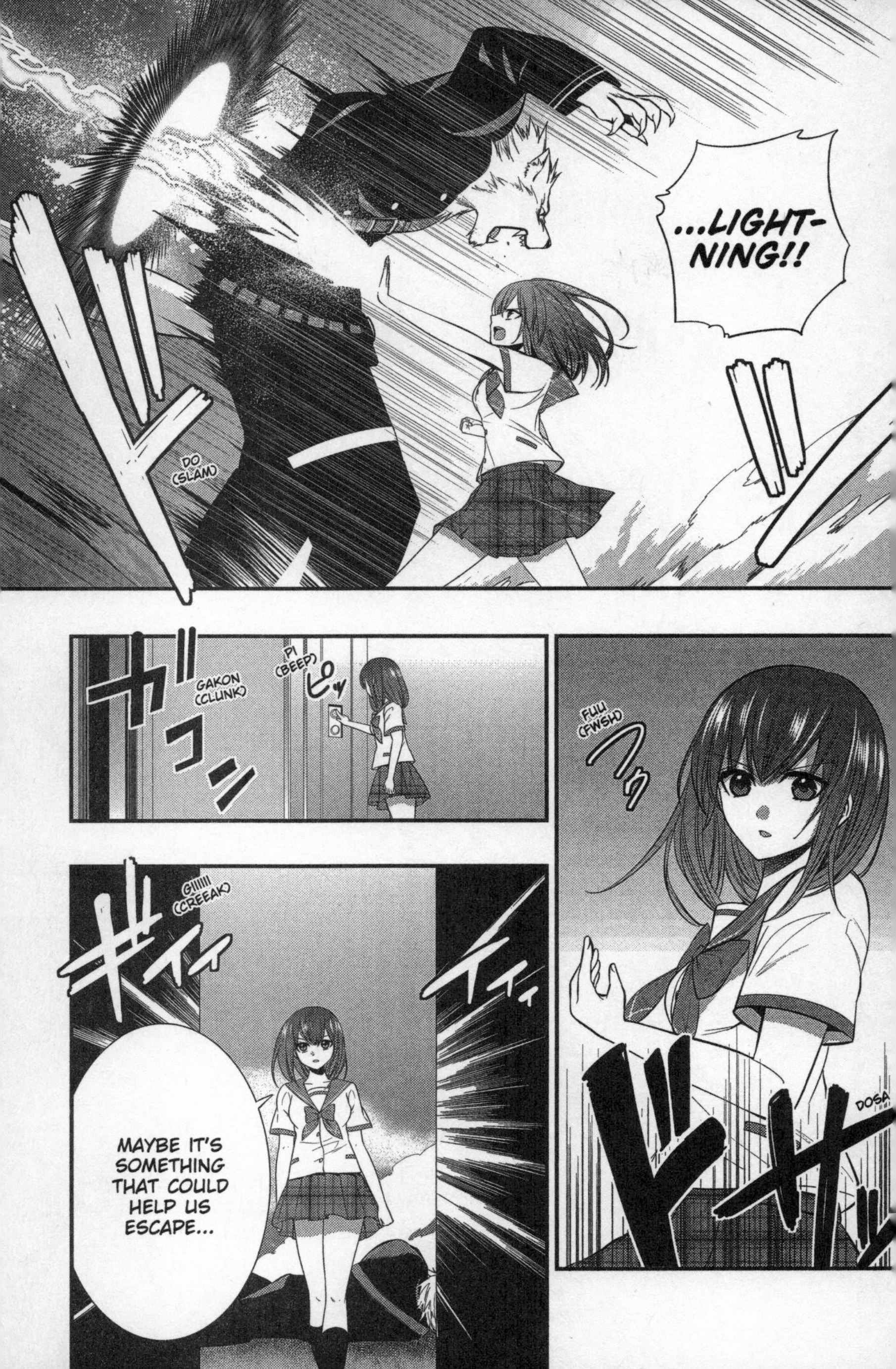
...LIGHT-NING!!
DO (SLAM)
FUU (FWSH)
DOSA
PI (BEEP)
ピッ
GAKON (CLUNK)
GIIIII (CREEAK)
MAYBE IT'S SOMETHING THAT COULD HELP US ESCAPE...

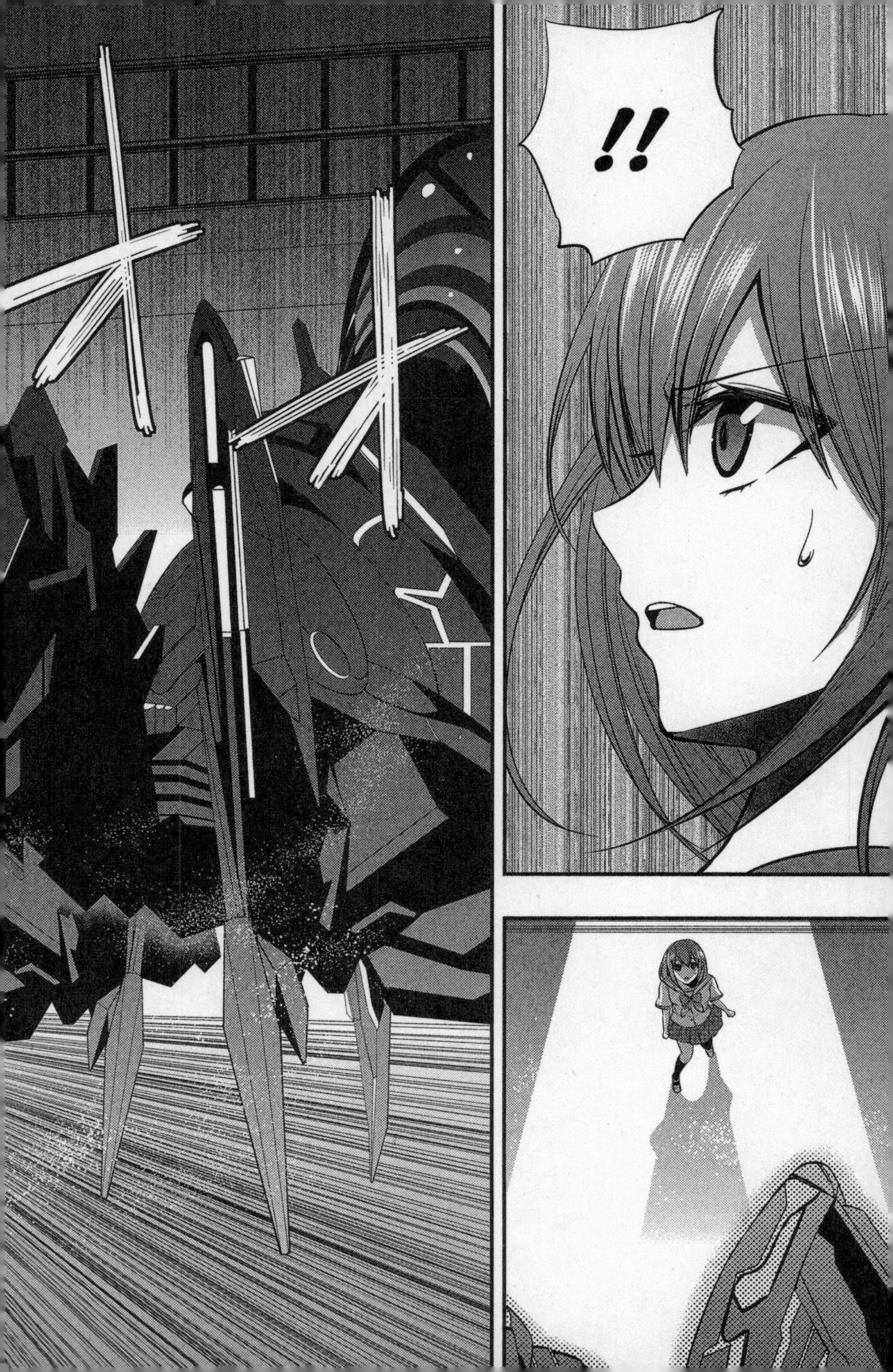
!!

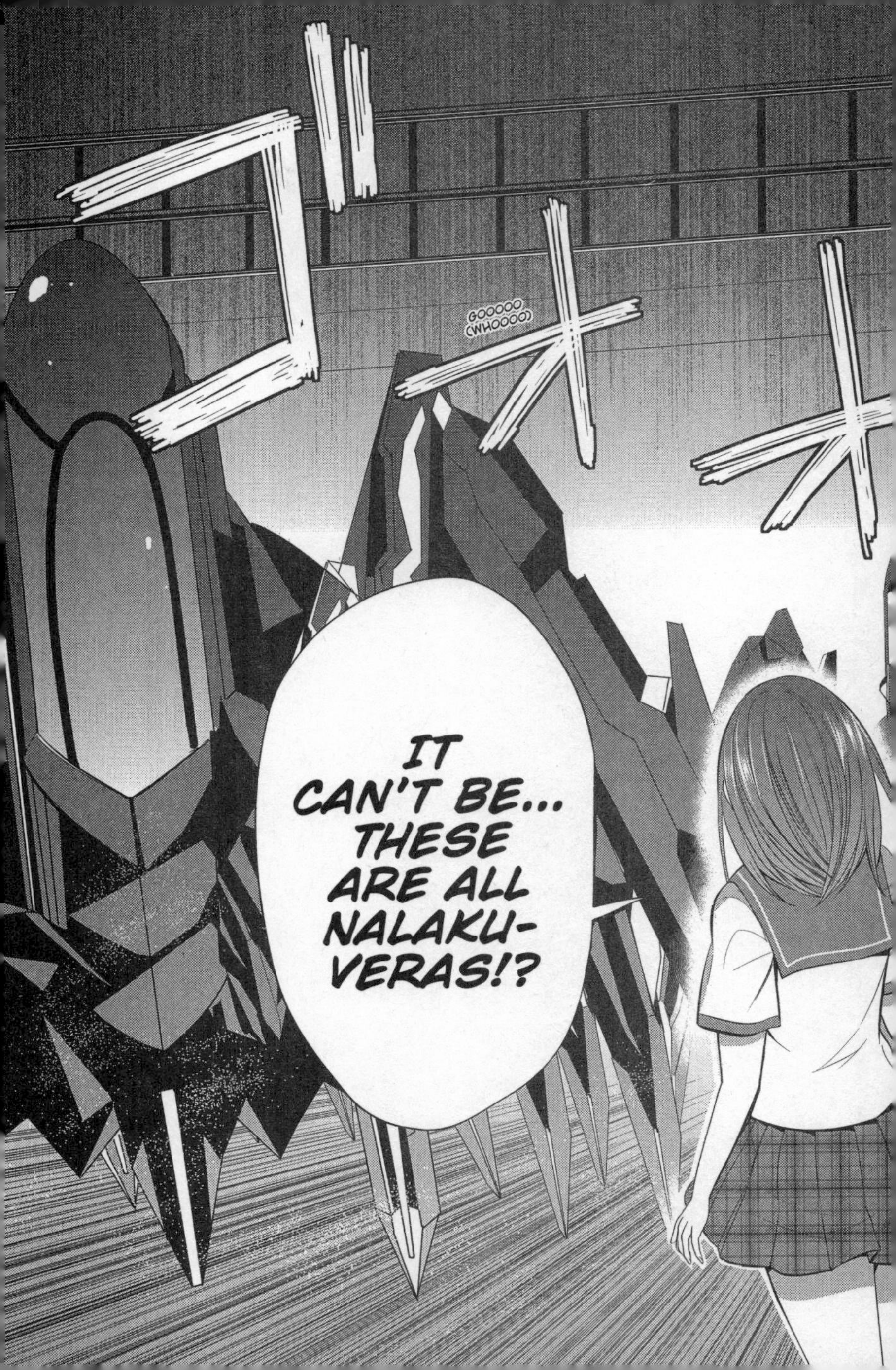
GOOOOO (WHOOOO)
IT CAN'T BE... THESE ARE ALL NALAKU-VERAS!?

STRIKE THE BLOOD

DEFINITION

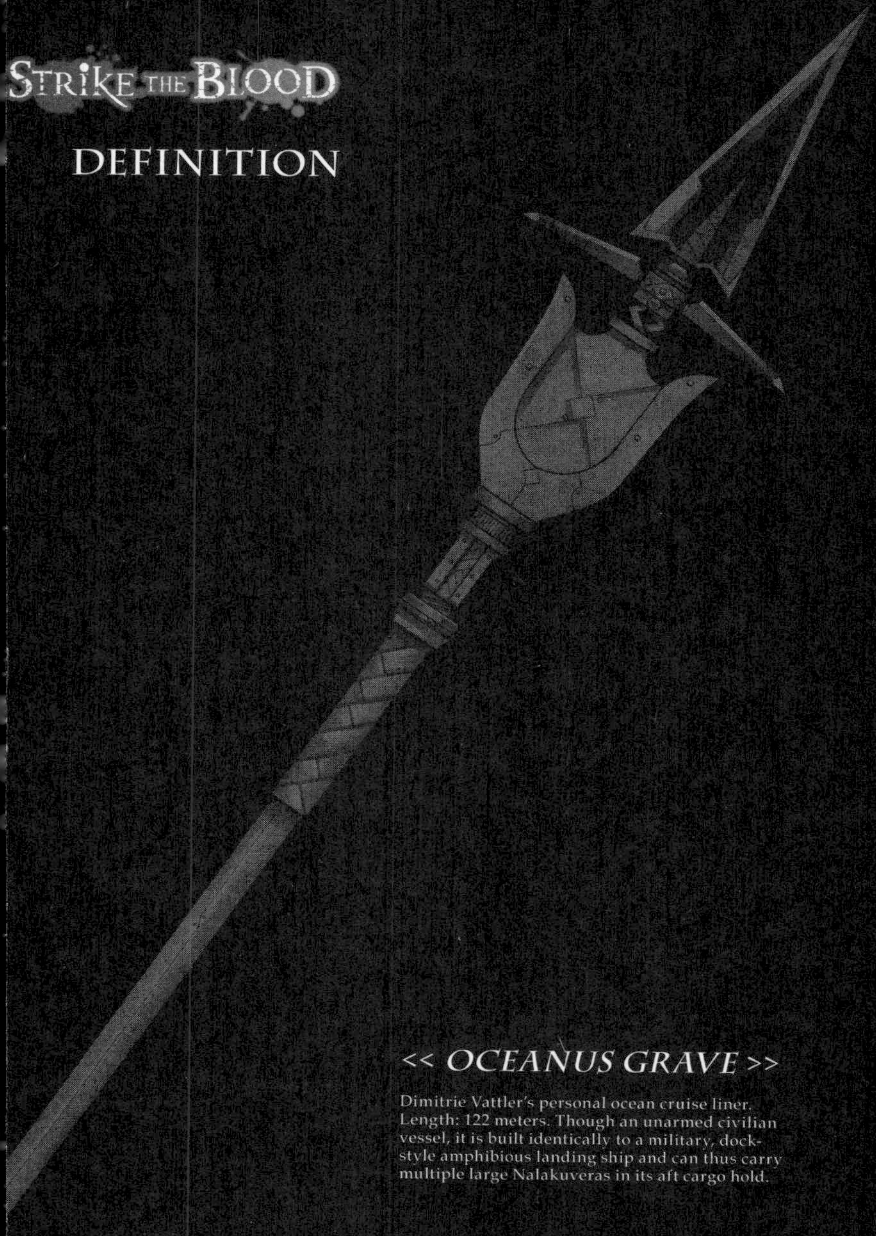

<< *OCEANUS GRAVE* >>

Dimitrie Vattler's personal ocean cruise liner. Length: 122 meters. Though an unarmed civilian vessel, it is built identically to a military, dock-style amphibious landing ship and can thus carry multiple large Nalakuveras in its aft cargo hold.

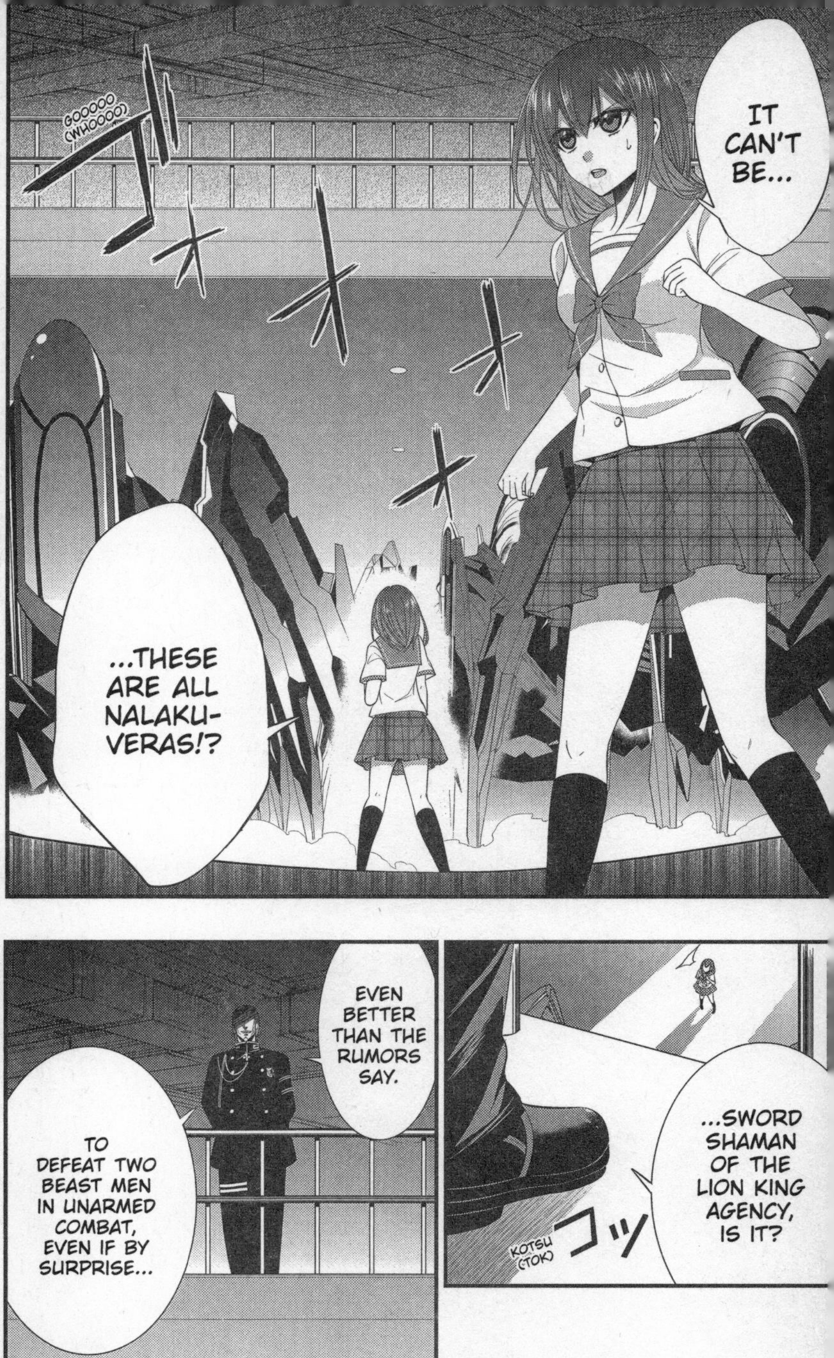
IT CAN'T BE...
GOOOOO (WHOOOO)
...THESE ARE ALL NALAKU-VERAS!?
...SWORD SHAMAN OF THE LION KING AGENCY, IS IT?
KOTSU (TOK)
EVEN BETTER THAN THE RUMORS SAY.
TO DEFEAT TWO BEAST MEN IN UNARMED COMBAT, EVEN IF BY SURPRISE...

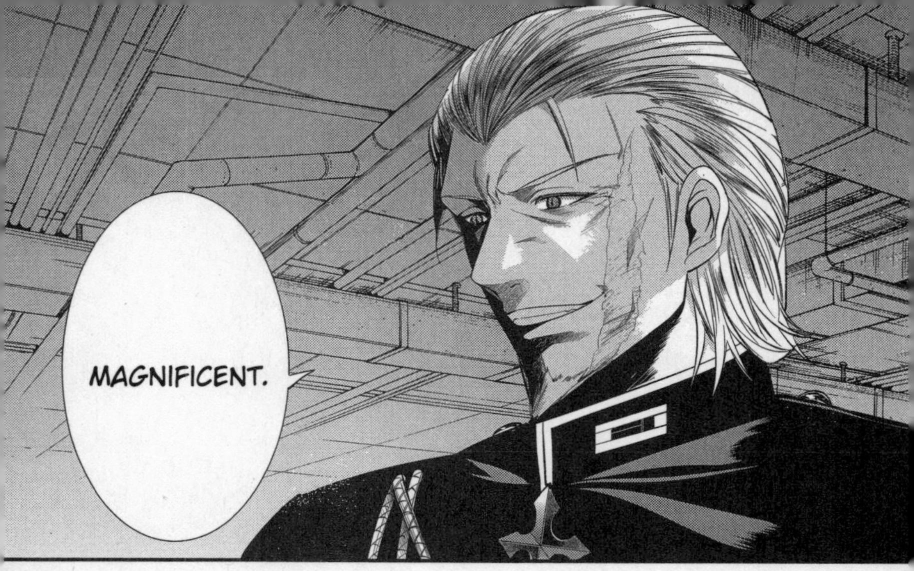
MAGNIFICENT.

Chapter 23:
Shake the Very Sea

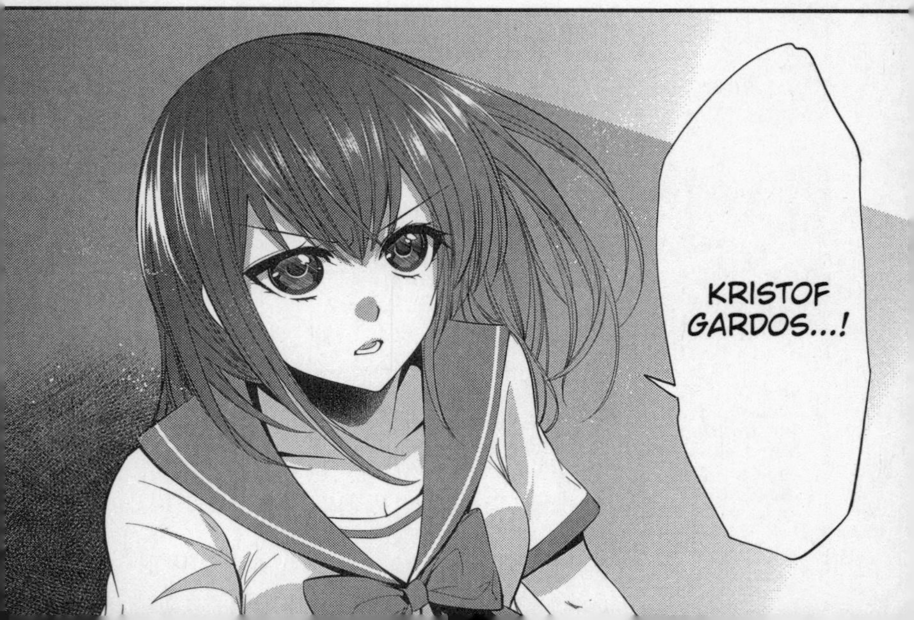
KRISTOF GARDOS...!

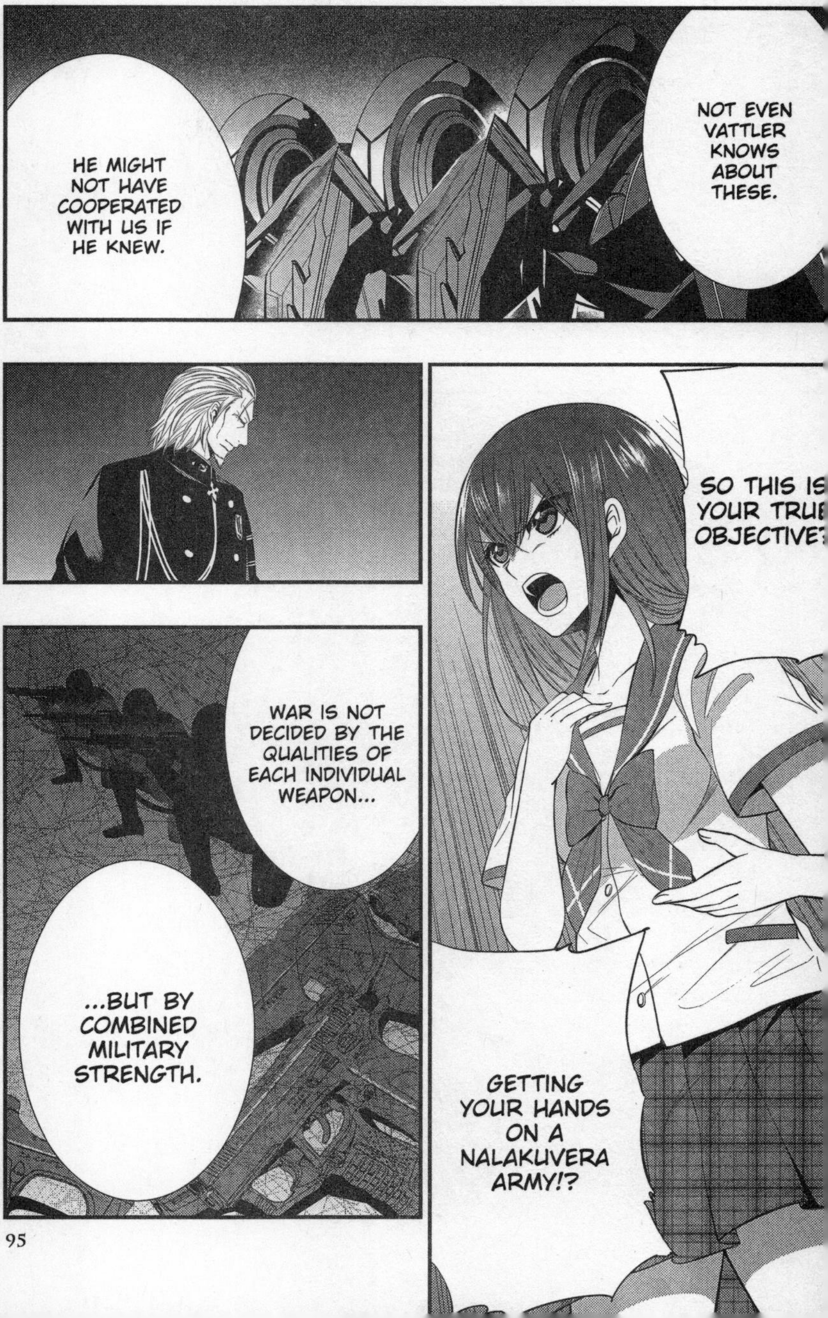
NOT EVEN VATTLER KNOWS ABOUT THESE.
HE MIGHT NOT HAVE COOPERATED WITH US IF HE KNEW.
SO THIS IS YOUR TRUE OBJECTIVE
GETTING YOUR HANDS ON A NALAKUVERA ARMY!?
WAR IS NOT DECIDED BY THE QUALITIES OF EACH INDIVIDUAL WEAPON...
...BUT BY COMBINED MILITARY STRENGTH.

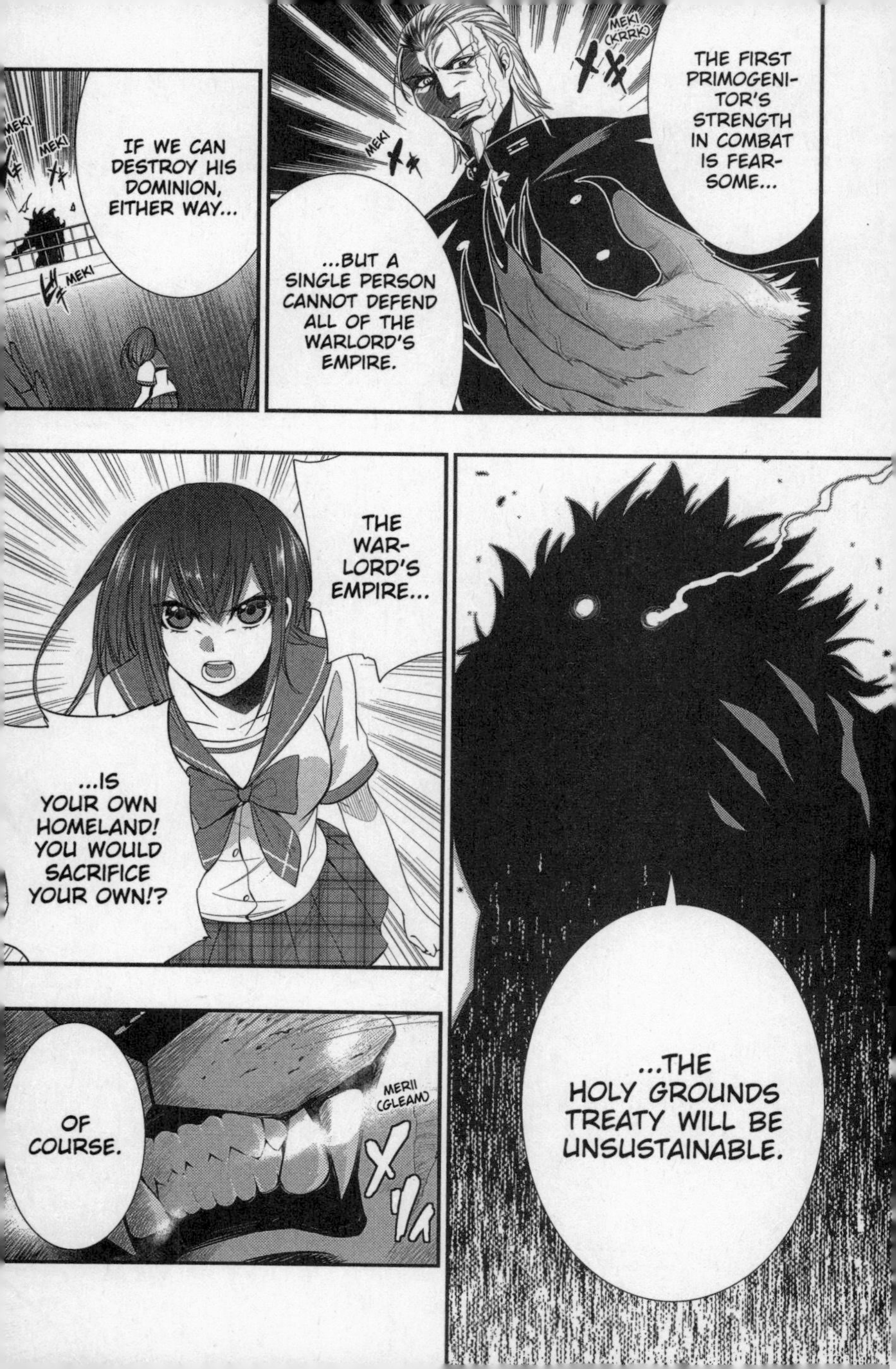
MEKI (KRRK)
THE FIRST PRIMOGENITOR'S STRENGTH IN COMBAT IS FEARSOME...
MEKI
...BUT A SINGLE PERSON CANNOT DEFEND ALL OF THE WARLORD'S EMPIRE.
MEKI
MEKI
IF WE CAN DESTROY HIS DOMINION, EITHER WAY...
MEKI
...THE HOLY GROUNDS TREATY WILL BE UNSUSTAINABLE.
THE WARLORD'S EMPIRE...
...IS YOUR OWN HOMELAND! YOU WOULD SACRIFICE YOUR OWN!?
MERII (GLEAM)
OF COURSE.

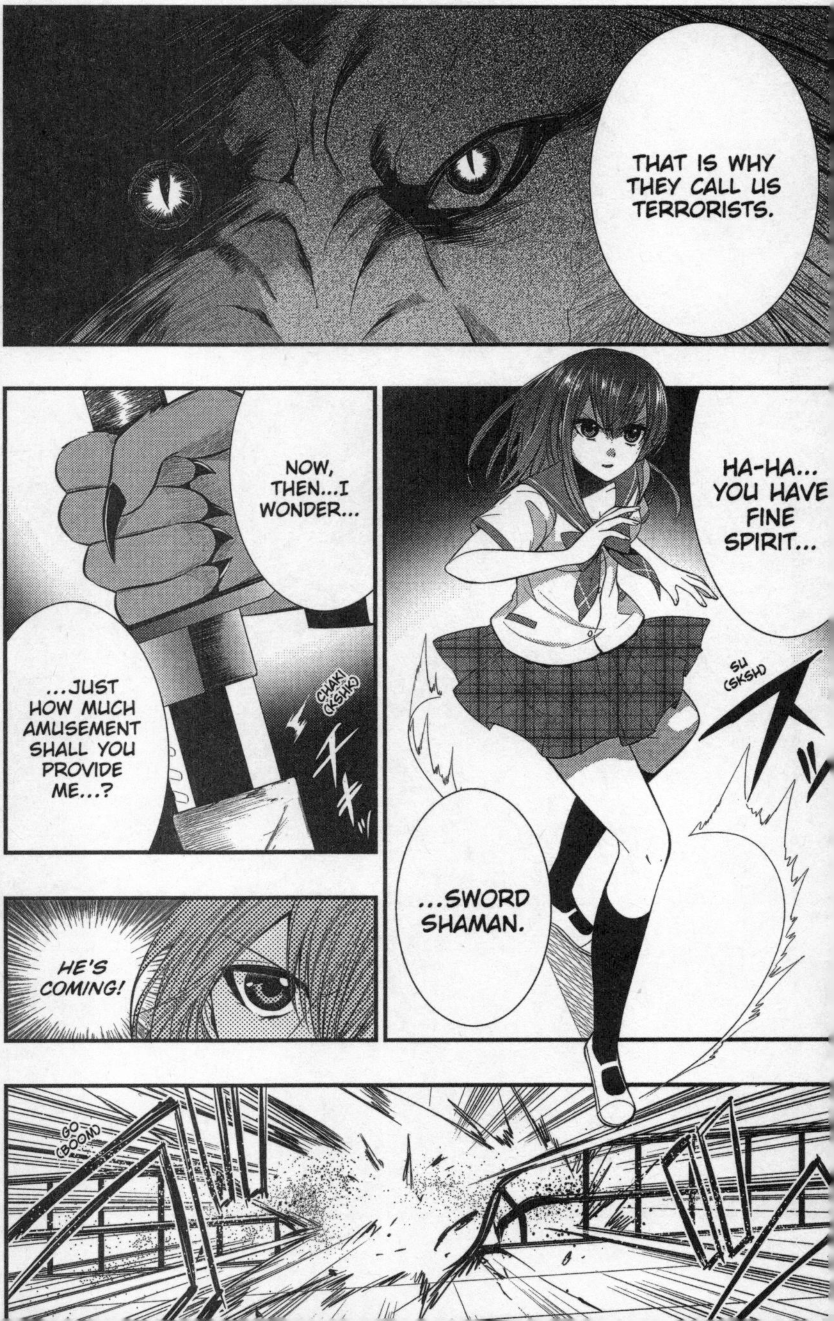
THAT IS WHY THEY CALL US TERRORISTS.
HA-HA... YOU HAVE FINE SPIRIT...
SU (SKSH)
...SWORD SHAMAN.
NOW, THEN...I WONDER...
...JUST HOW MUCH AMUSEMENT SHALL YOU PROVIDE ME...?
CHAKI (KSHK)
HE'S COMING!
GO (BOOM)

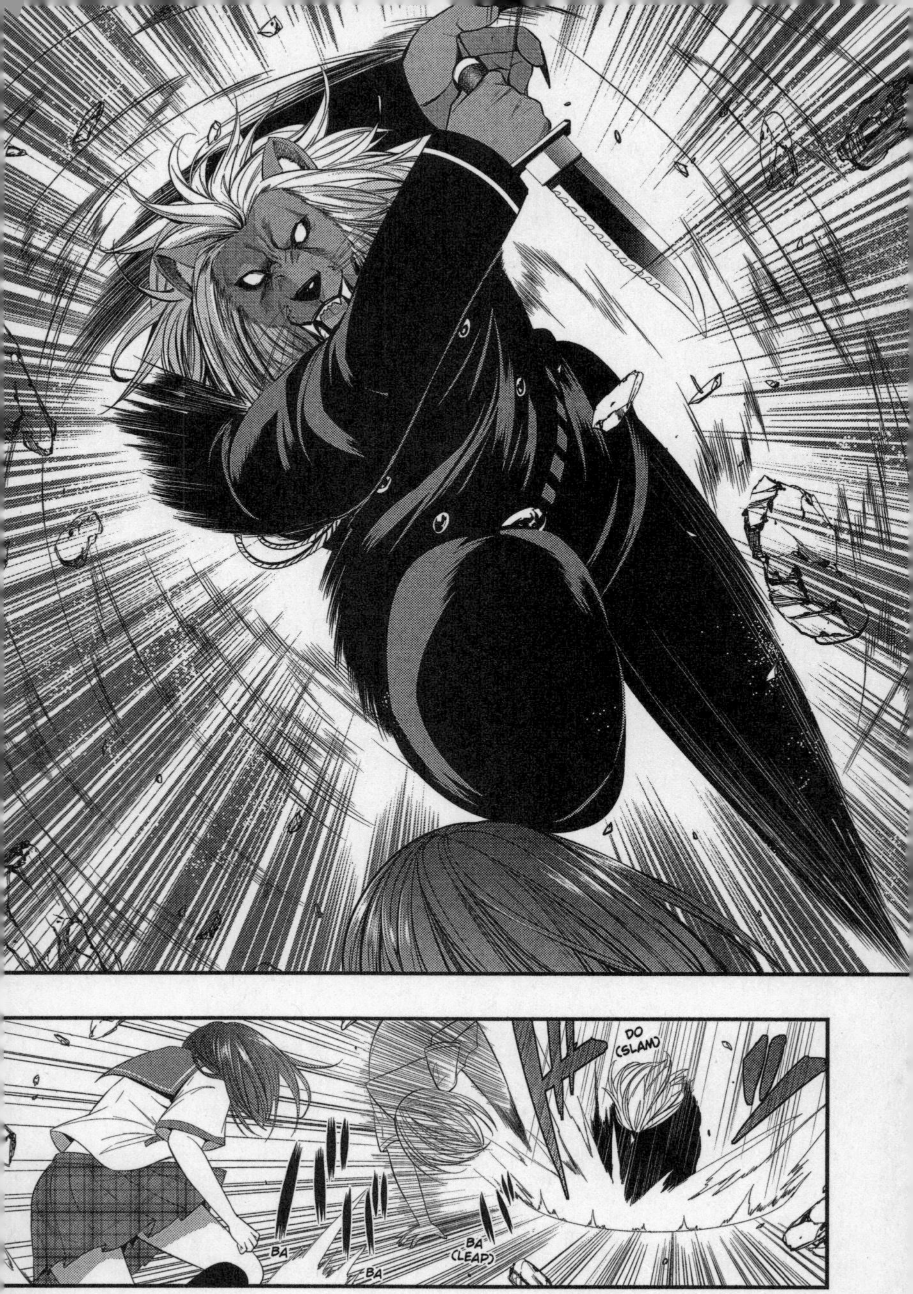
DO
(SLAM)
BA
(LEAP)
BA
BA

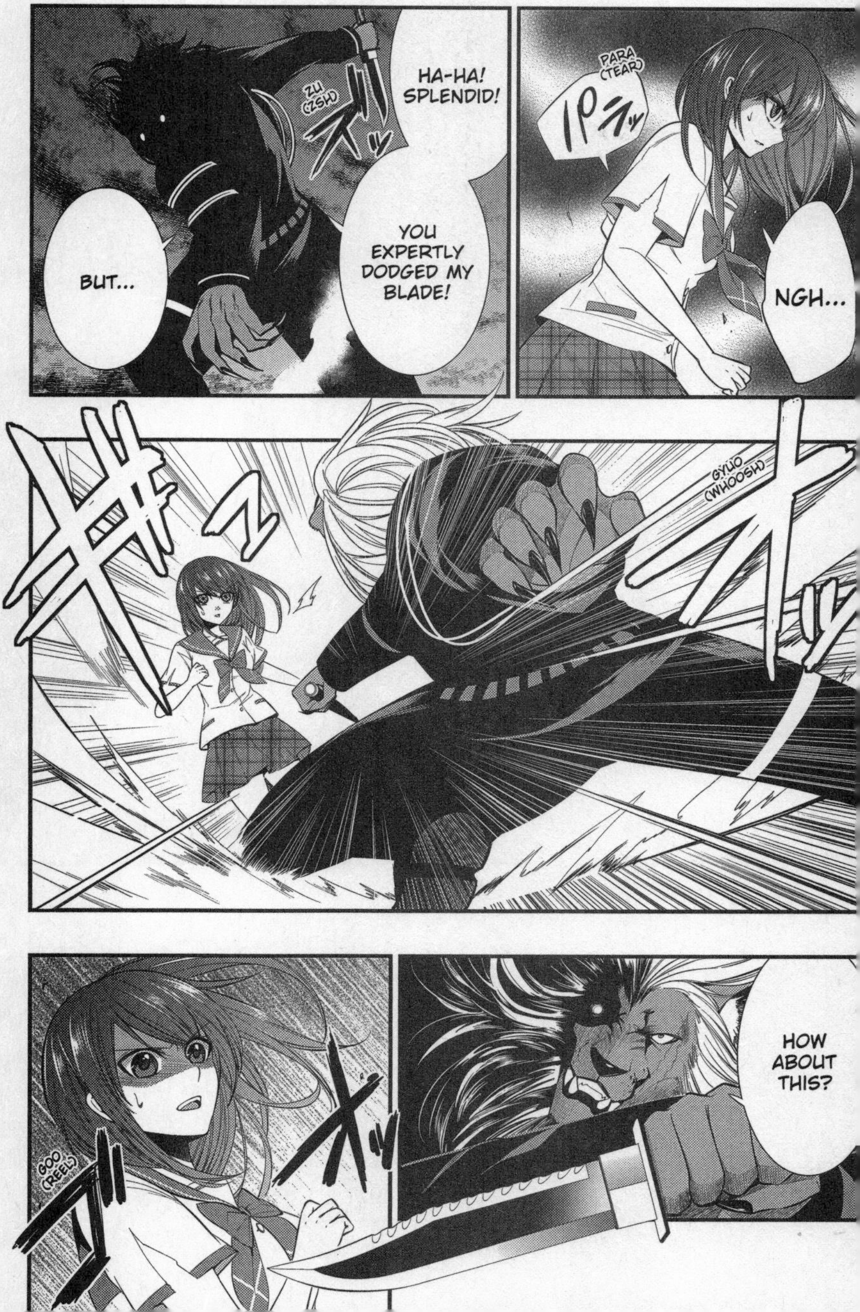
PARA (TEAR)
パラッ
NGH...
HA-HA! SPLENDID!
ZU (ZSH)
YOU EXPERTLY DODGED MY BLADE!
BUT...
GYUO (WHOOSH)
HOW ABOUT THIS?
GOO (REEL)

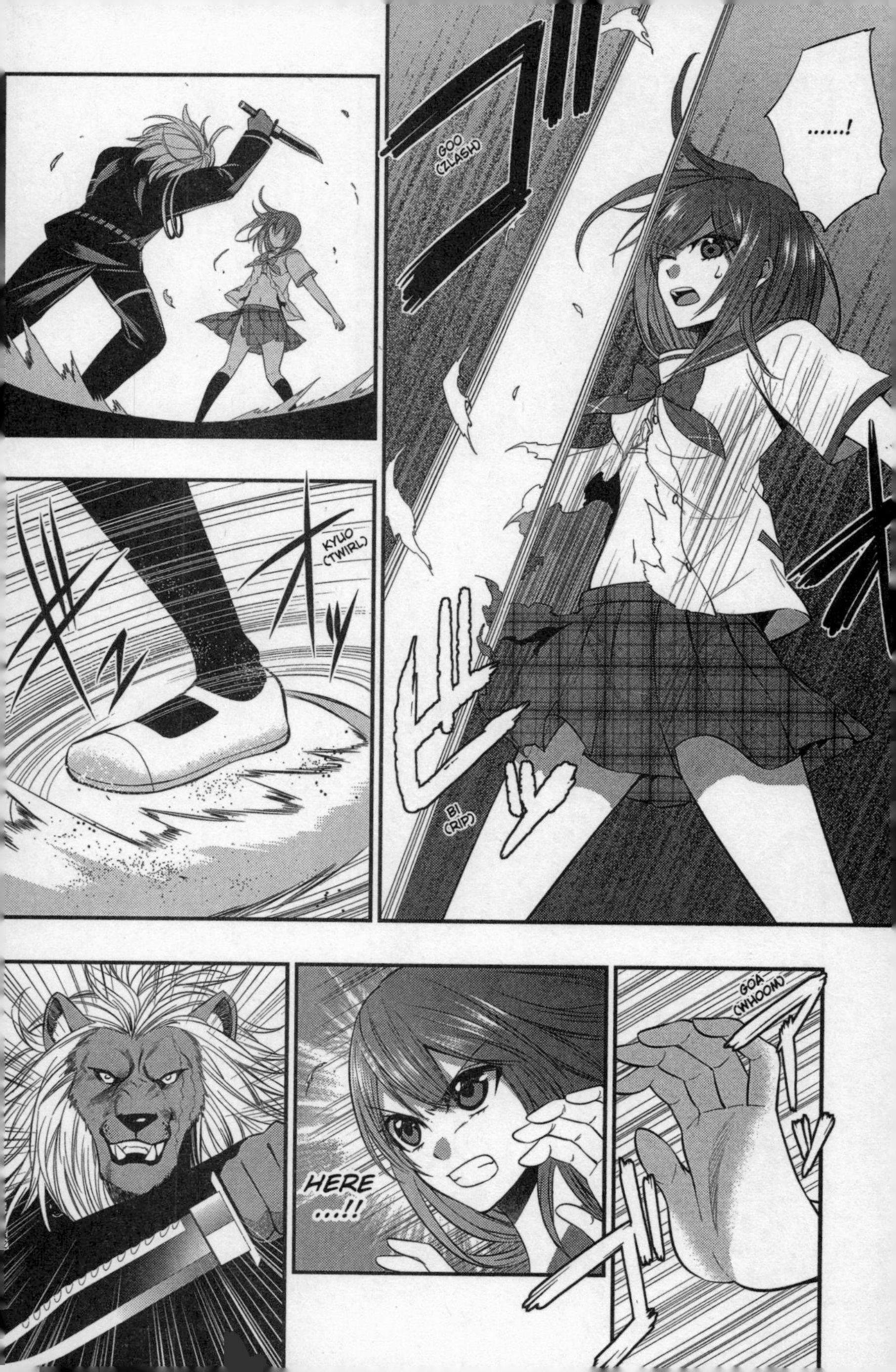

......!
GOO (ZLASH)
BI (RIP)
KYUO (TWIRL)
GOA (WHOOM)
HERE ...!!

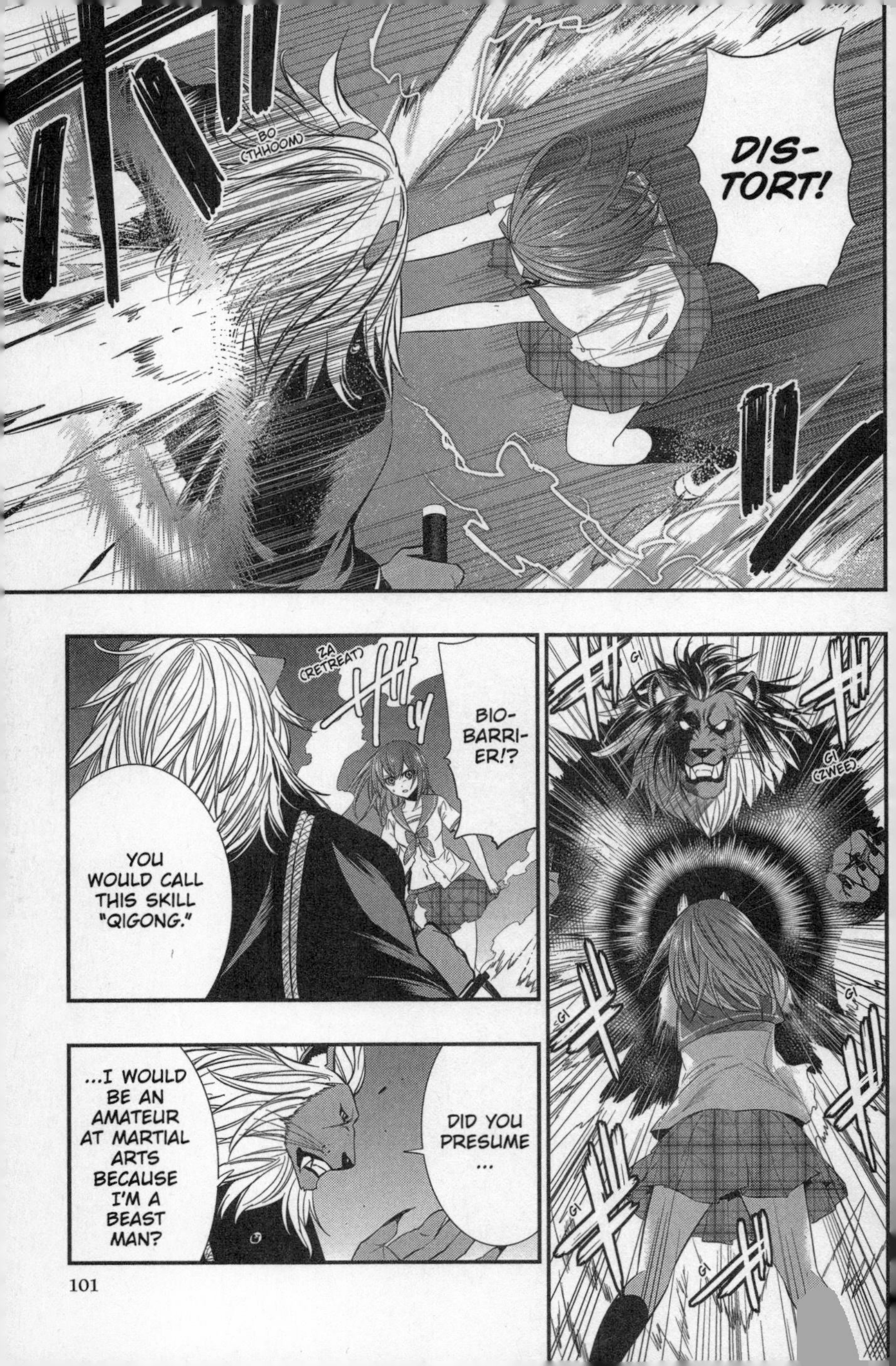
DIS-TORT!
BO (THHOOM)
GI
GI (ZWEE)
GI
GI
GI
GI
ZA (RETREAT)
BIO-BARRIER!?
YOU WOULD CALL THIS SKILL "QIGONG."
DID YOU PRESUME ...
...I WOULD BE AN AMATEUR AT MARTIAL ARTS BECAUSE I'M A BEAST MAN?

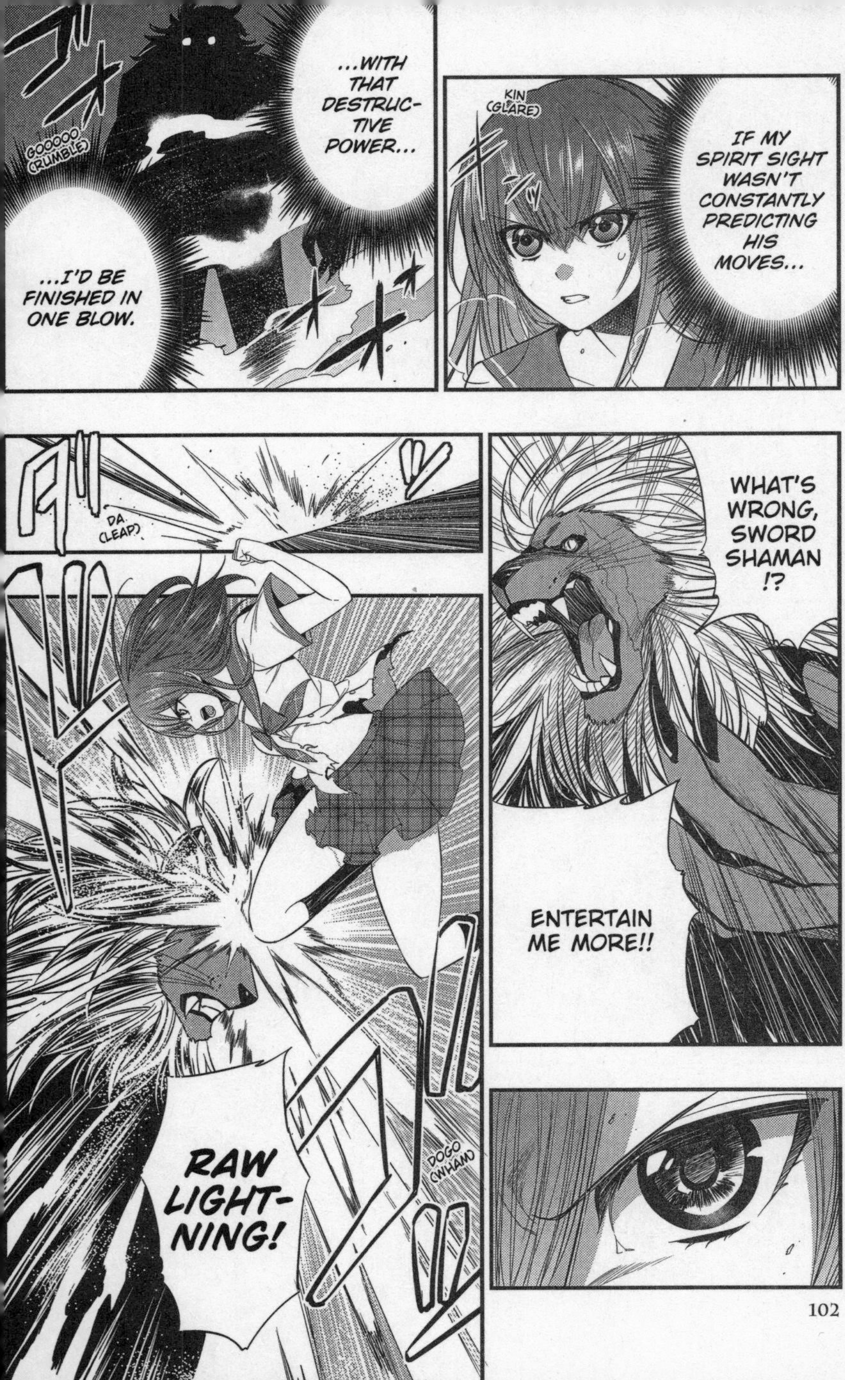
KIN (GLARE)
IF MY SPIRIT SIGHT WASN'T CONSTANTLY PREDICTING HIS MOVES...
...WITH THAT DESTRUC-TIVE POWER...
GOOOOO (RUMBLE)
...I'D BE FINISHED IN ONE BLOW.
WHAT'S WRONG, SWORD SHAMAN!?
ENTERTAIN ME MORE!!
DA (LEAP)
DOGO (WHAM)
RAW LIGHT-NING!

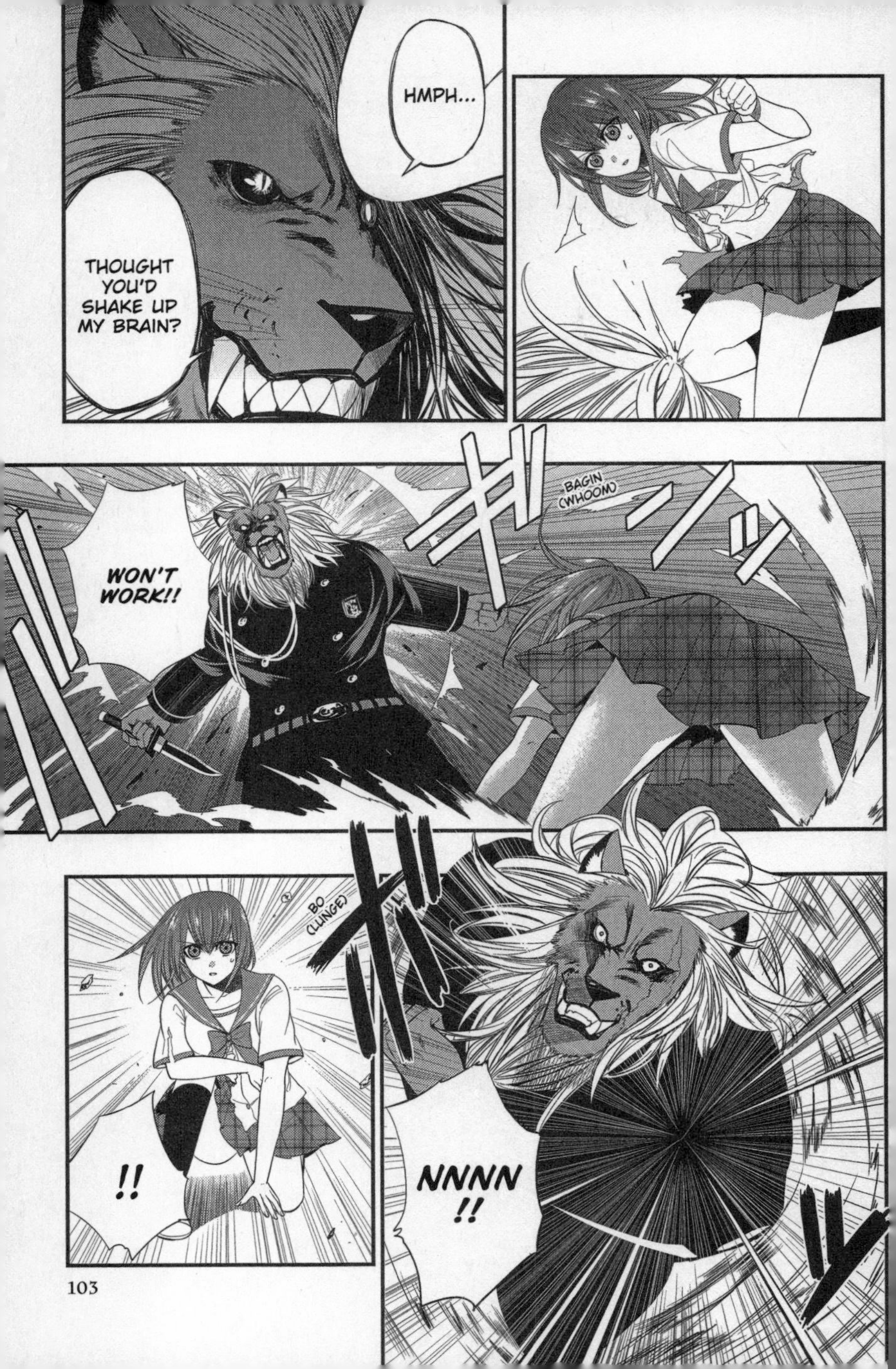

HMPH...
THOUGHT YOU'D SHAKE UP MY BRAIN?
BAGIN (WHOOM)
WON'T WORK!!
BO (LUNGE)
NNNN!!
!!

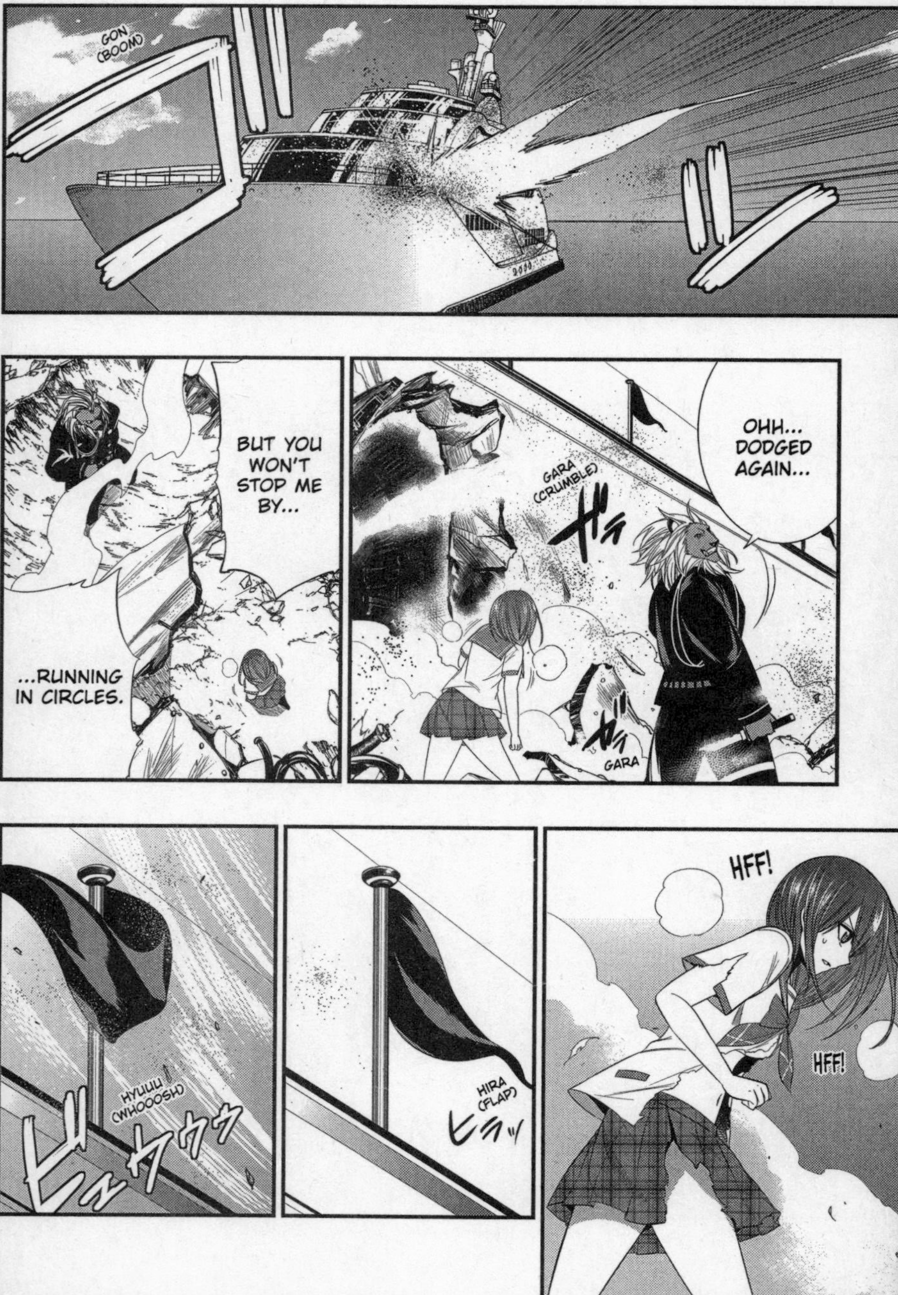
GON (BOOM)
GARA (CRUMBLE)
OHH... DODGED AGAIN...
GARA
BUT YOU WON'T STOP ME BY...
...RUNNING IN CIRCLES.
HFF!
HFF!
HIRA (FLAP)
HYUUU (WHOOOSH)

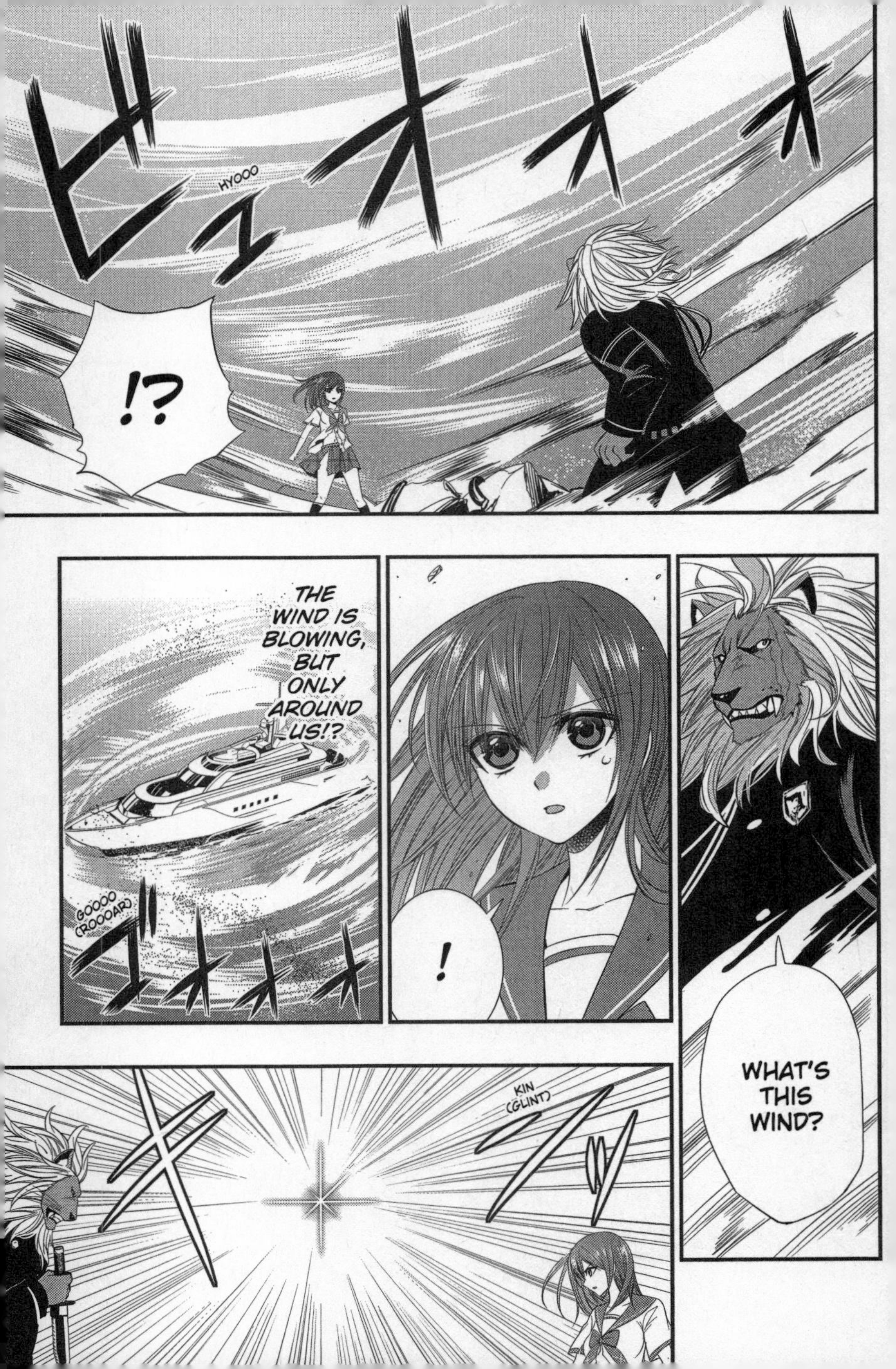
HYOOO
!?
WHAT'S THIS WIND?
!
THE WIND IS BLOWING, BUT ONLY AROUND US!?
GOOOO (ROOOAR)
KIN (GLINT)

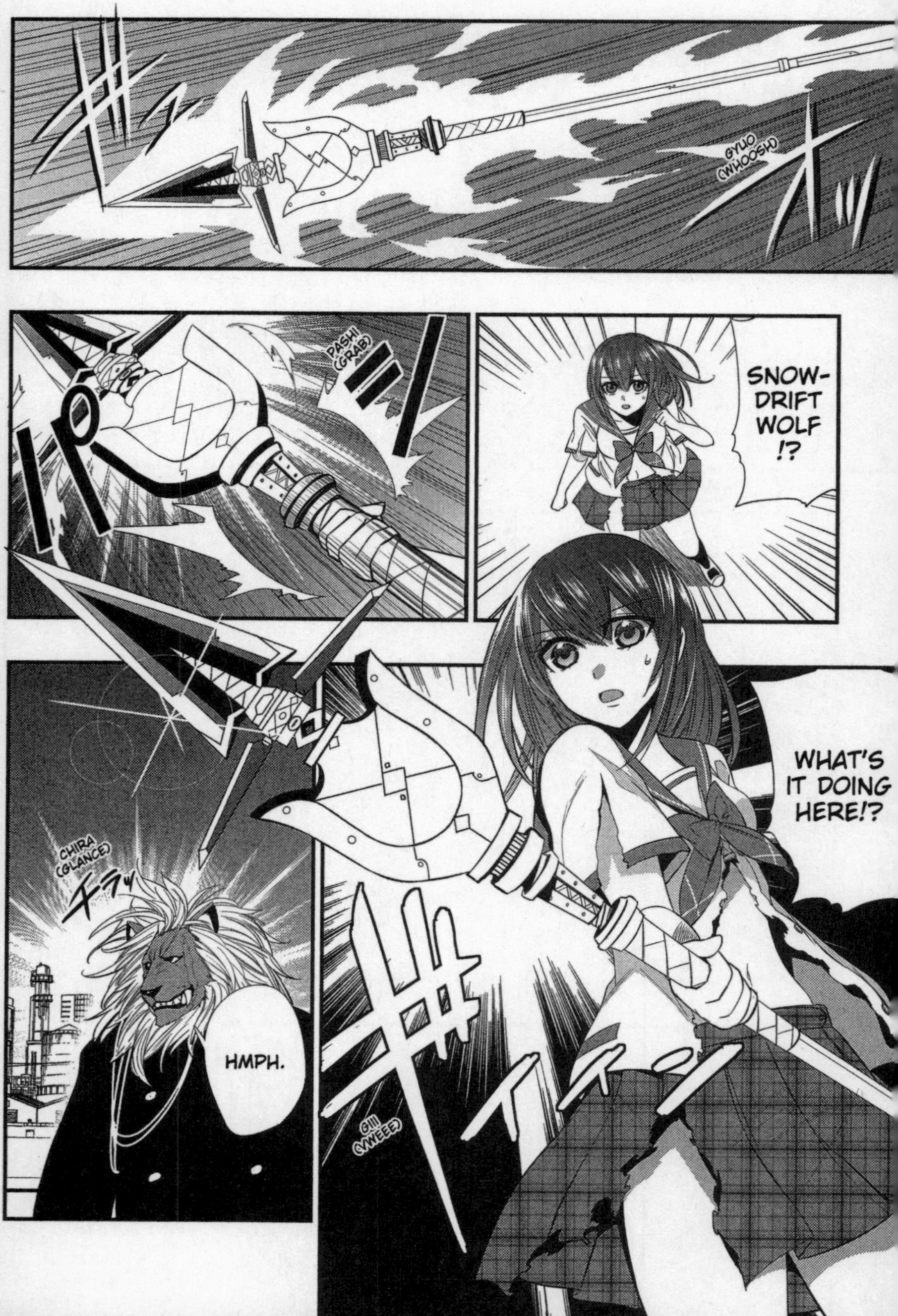
GYUO (WHOOSH)
SNOW-DRIFT WOLF !?
PASHI (GRAB)
WHAT'S IT DOING HERE!?
GIII (VWEEE)
CHIRA (GLANCE)
HMPH.

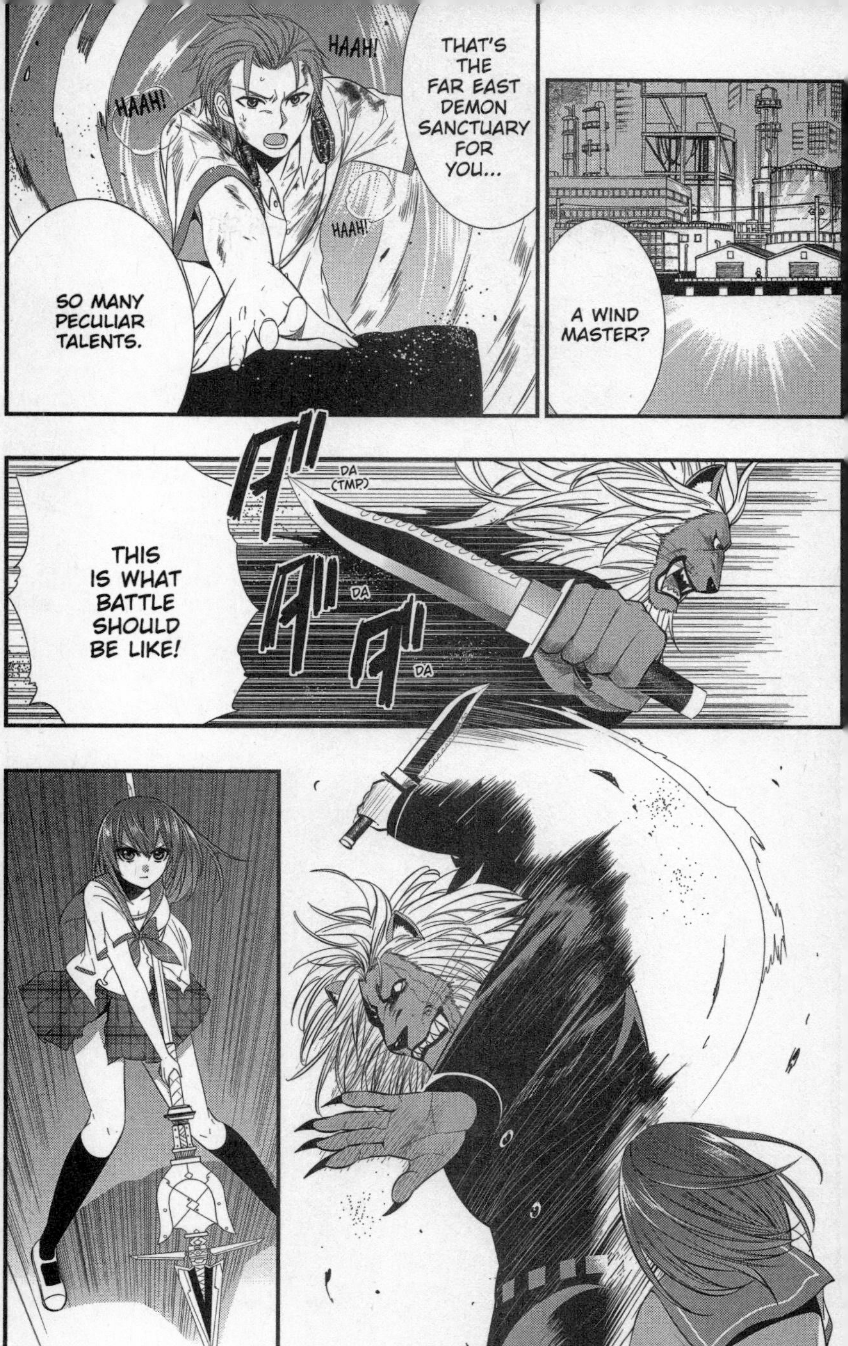
A WIND MASTER?
THAT'S THE FAR EAST DEMON SANCTUARY FOR YOU...
HAAH!
HAAH!
HAAH!
SO MANY PECULIAR TALENTS.
ダ
DA (TMP)
ダ
DA
ダ
DA
THIS IS WHAT BATTLE SHOULD BE LIKE!

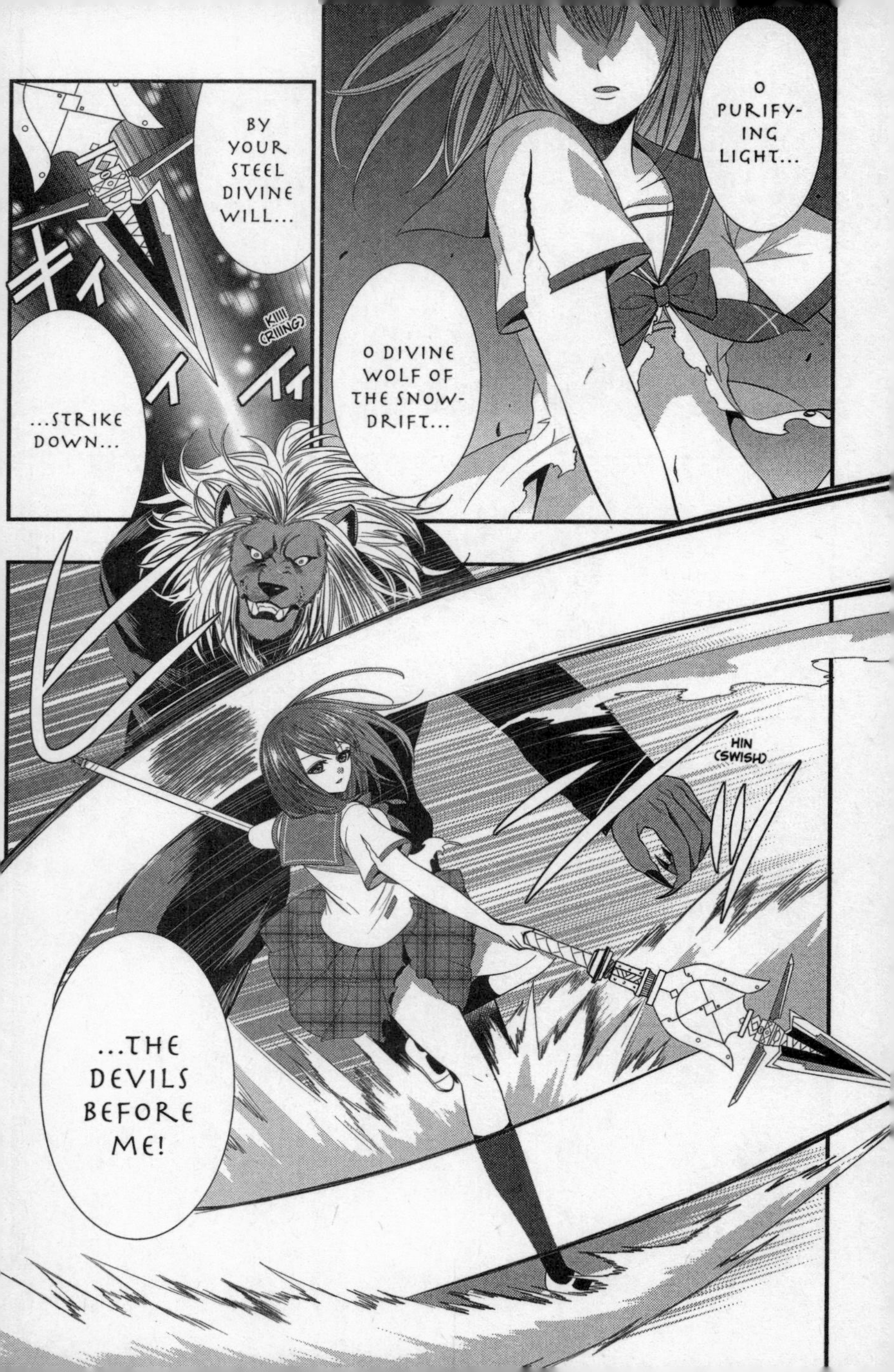
O PURIFY-ING LIGHT...
O DIVINE WOLF OF THE SNOW-DRIFT...
BY YOUR STEEL DIVINE WILL...
KIIII (CRIIING)
...STRIKE DOWN...
HIN (SWISH)
...THE DEVILS BEFORE ME!

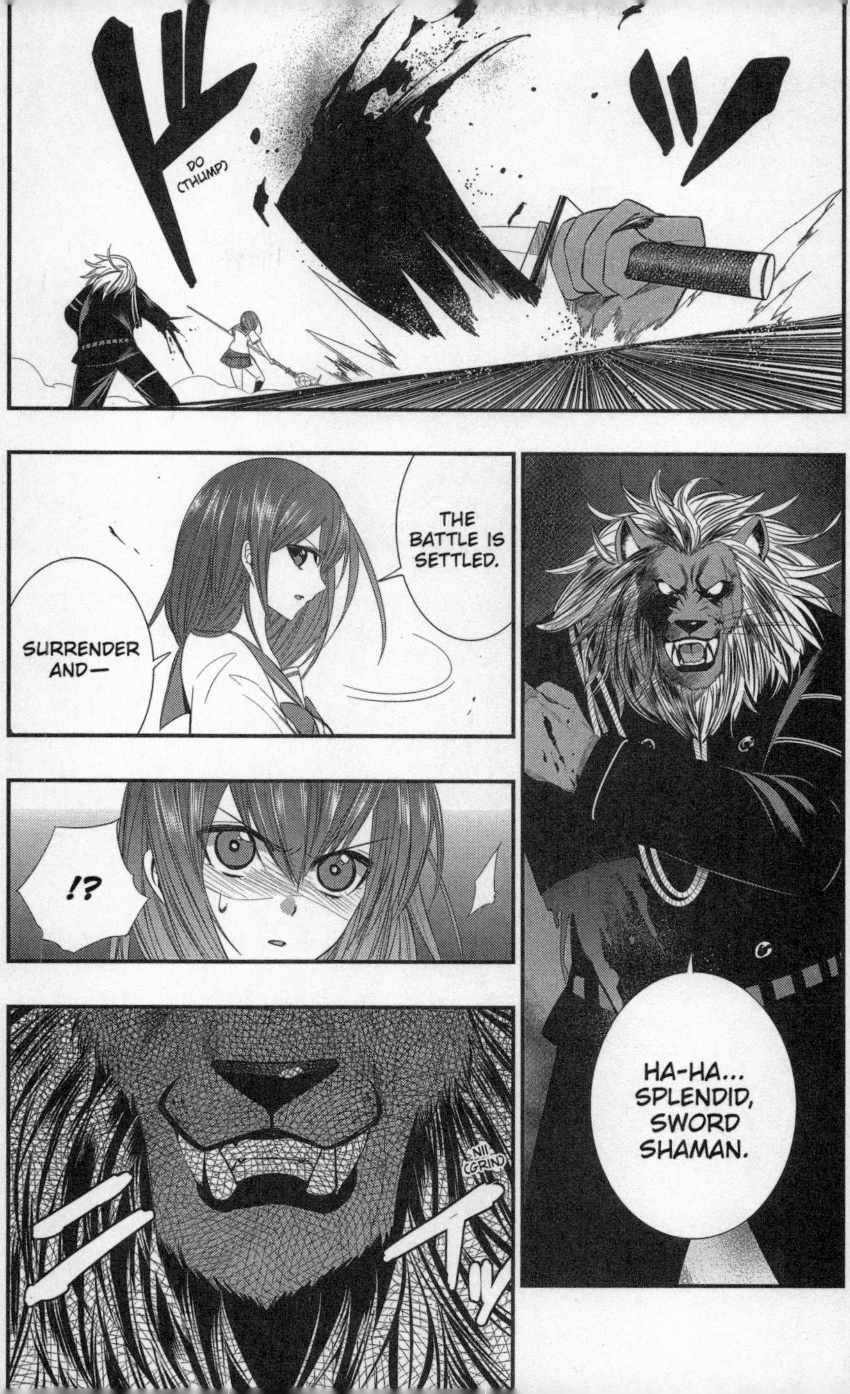
DO
(THUMP)
HA-HA... SPLENDID, SWORD SHAMAN.
THE BATTLE IS SETTLED.
SURRENDER AND—
!?
NII
(GRIND)

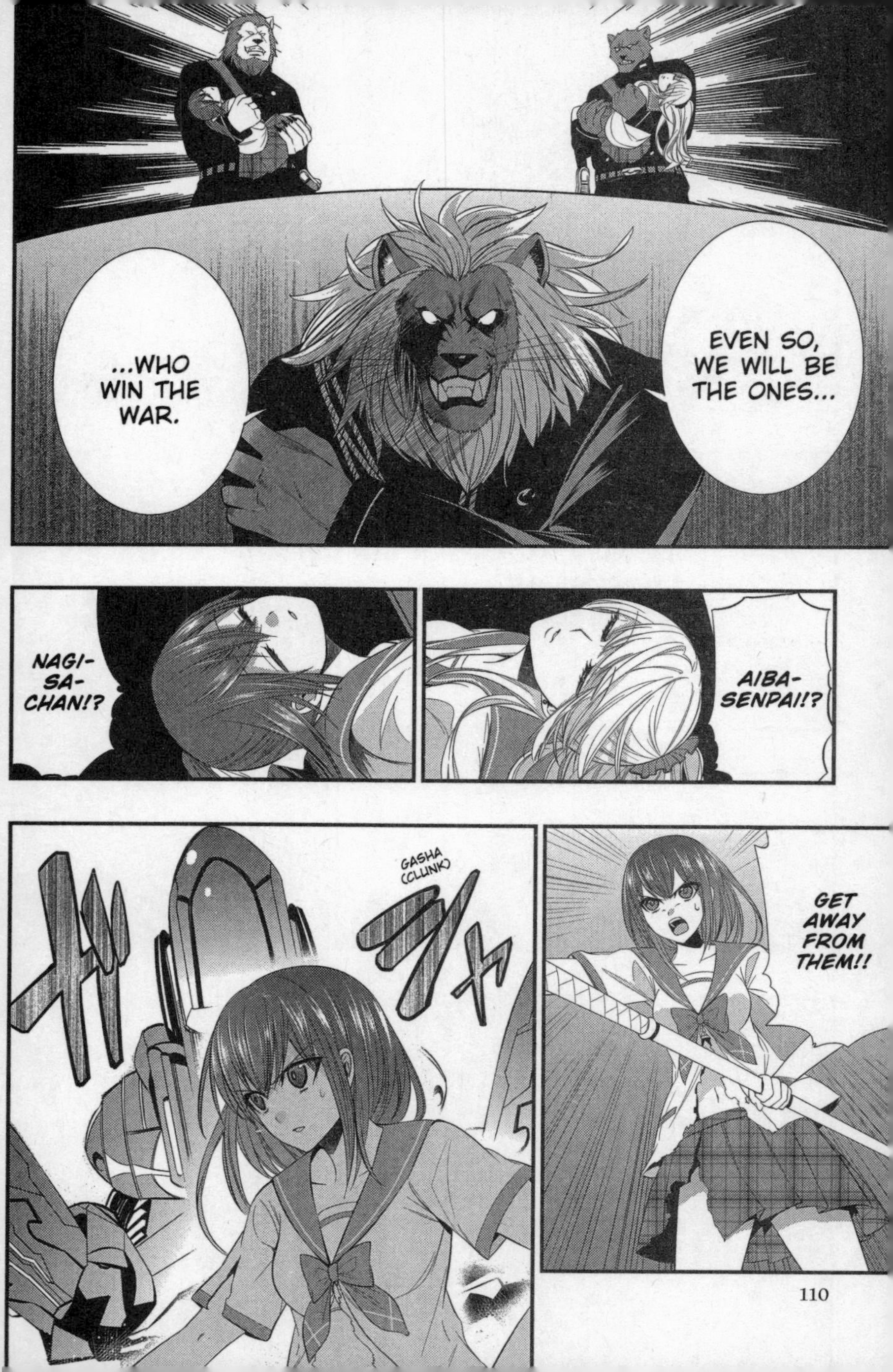
EVEN SO, WE WILL BE THE ONES...
...WHO WIN THE WAR.
AIBA-SENPAI!?
NAGI-SA-CHAN!?
GET AWAY FROM THEM!!
GASHA (CLUNK)

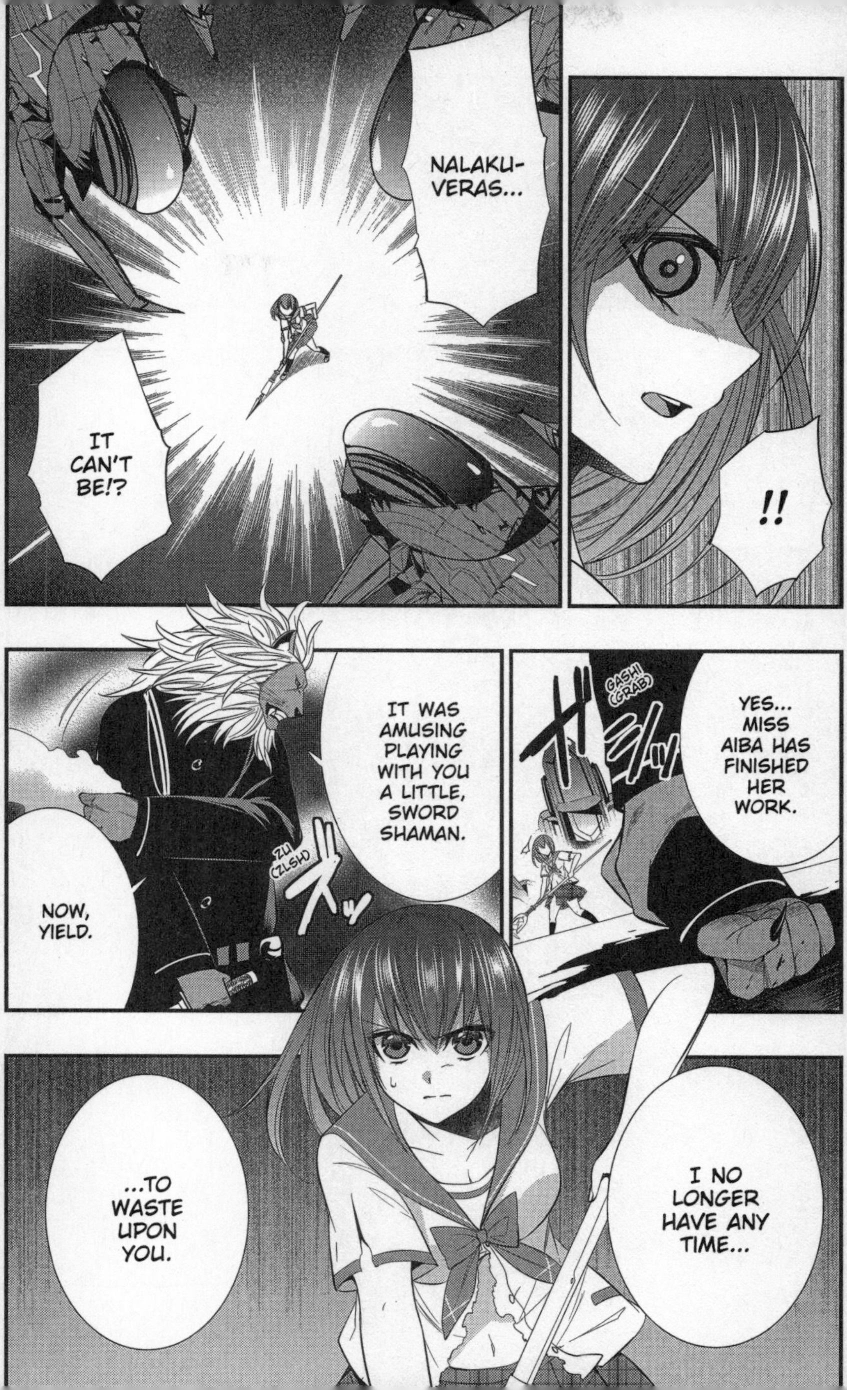
!!
NALAKU-
VERAS...
IT CAN'T BE!?
GASHI (GRAB)
YES... MISS AIBA HAS FINISHED HER WORK.
IT WAS AMUSING PLAYING WITH YOU A LITTLE, SWORD SHAMAN.
ZU (ZLSH)
NOW, YIELD.
I NO LONGER HAVE ANY TIME...
...TO WASTE UPON YOU.

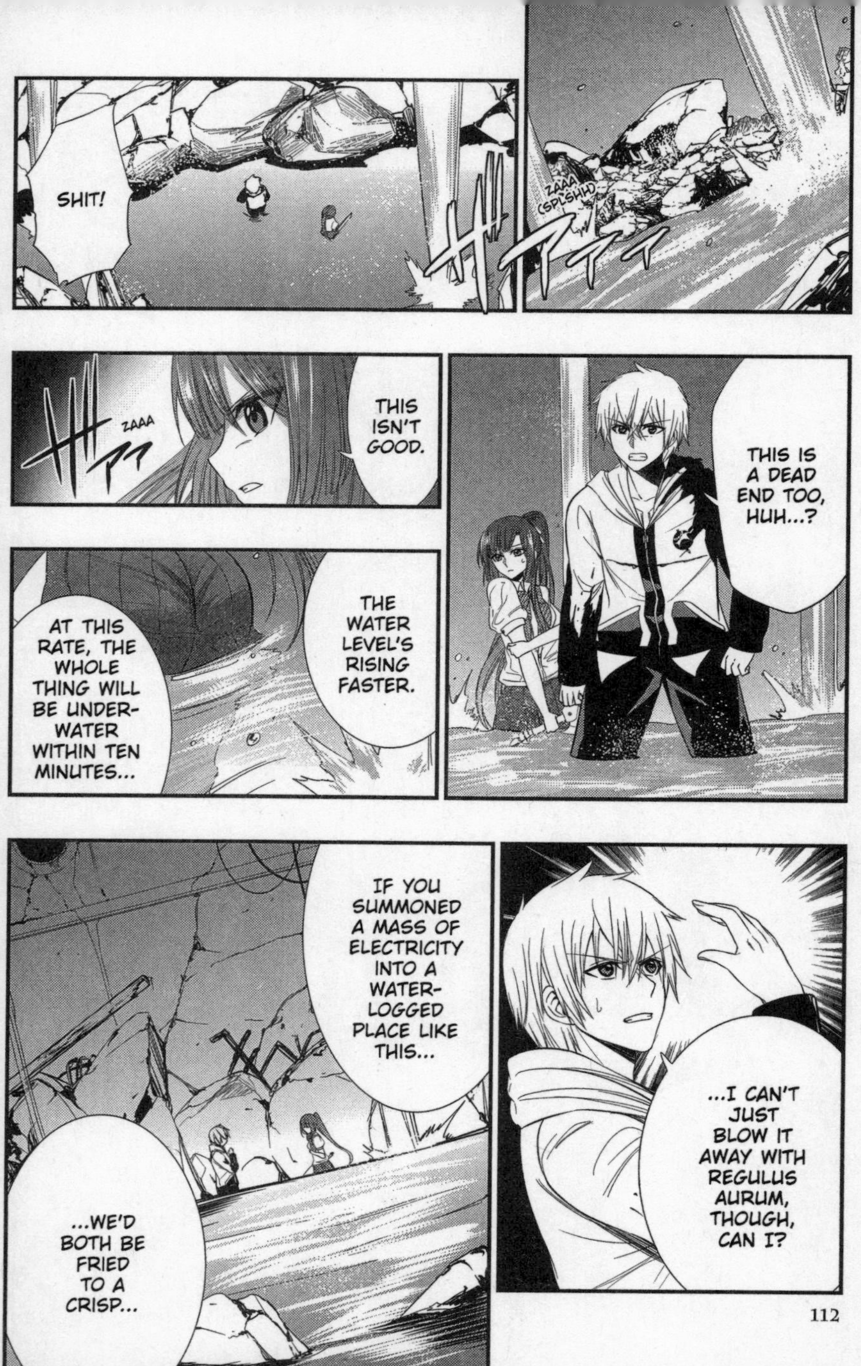
ZAAA (SPLSHH)
SHIT!
THIS IS A DEAD END TOO, HUH...?
THIS ISN'T GOOD.
ZAAA
THE WATER LEVEL'S RISING FASTER.
AT THIS RATE, THE WHOLE THING WILL BE UNDER-WATER WITHIN TEN MINUTES...
...I CAN'T JUST BLOW IT AWAY WITH REGULUS AURUM, THOUGH, CAN I?
IF YOU SUMMONED A MASS OF ELECTRICITY INTO A WATER-LOGGED PLACE LIKE THIS...
...WE'D BOTH BE FRIED TO A CRISP...

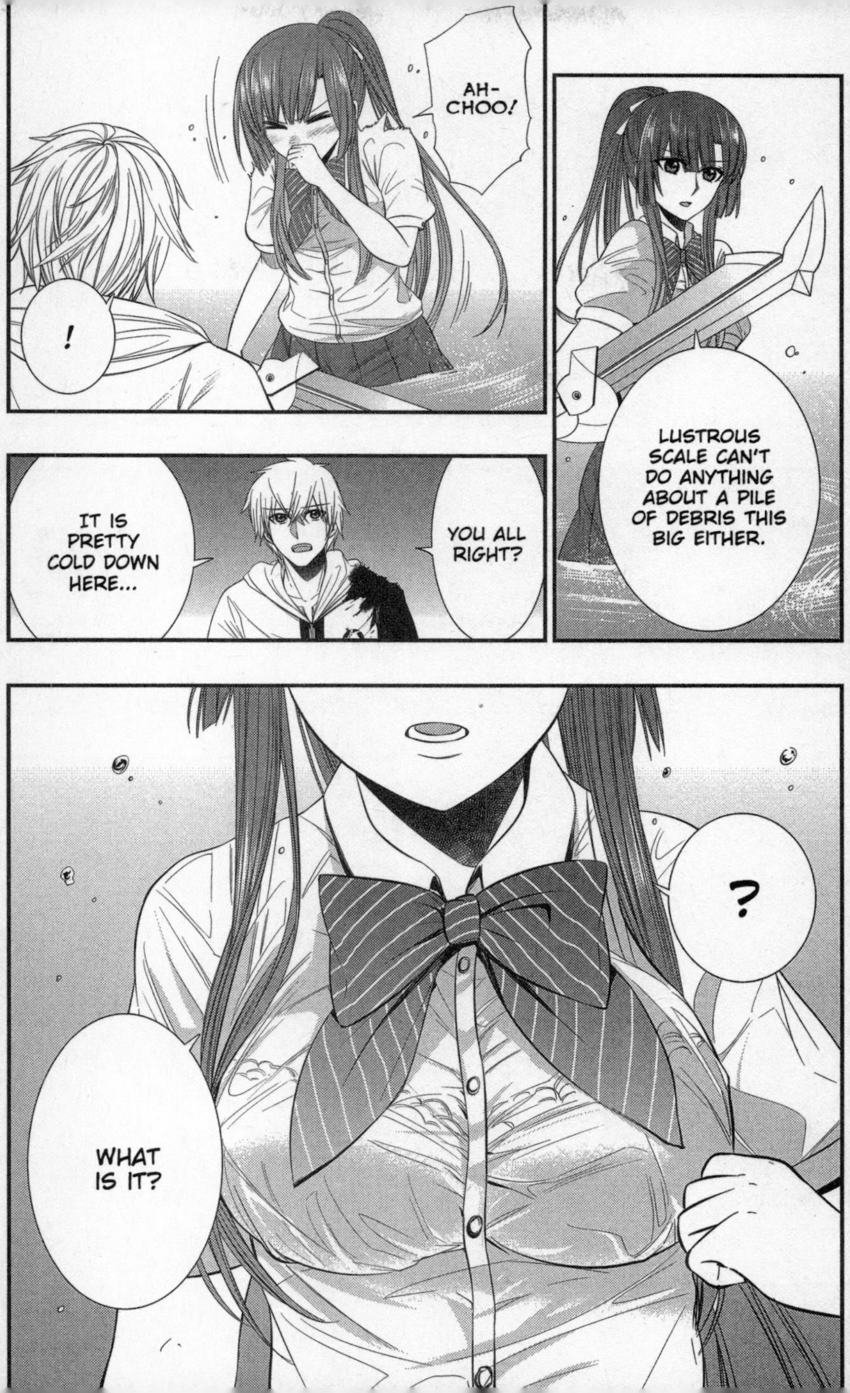
LUSTROUS SCALE CAN'T DO ANYTHING ABOUT A PILE OF DEBRIS THIS BIG EITHER.
AH-CHOO!
!
YOU ALL RIGHT?
IT IS PRETTY COLD DOWN HERE...
?
WHAT IS IT?

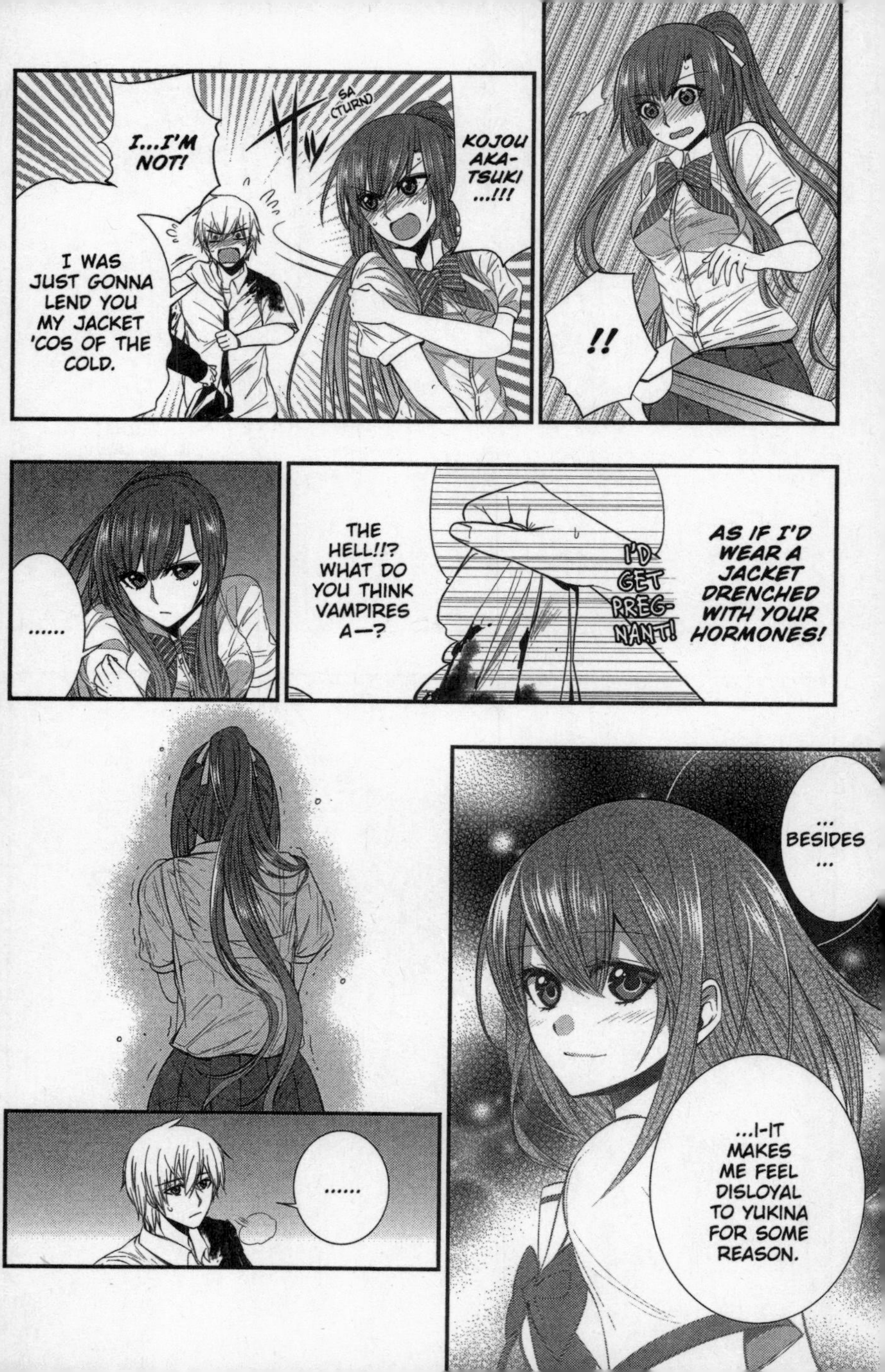
!!
KOJOU AKATSUKI ...!!!
SA (TURN)
I...I'M NOT!
I WAS JUST GONNA LEND YOU MY JACKET 'COS OF THE COLD.
AS IF I'D WEAR A JACKET DRENCHED WITH YOUR HORMONES!
I'D GET PREG-NANT!
THE HELL!!? WHAT DO YOU THINK VAMPIRES A—?
......
... BESIDES ...
...I-IT MAKES ME FEEL DISLOYAL TO YUKINA FOR SOME REASON.
......

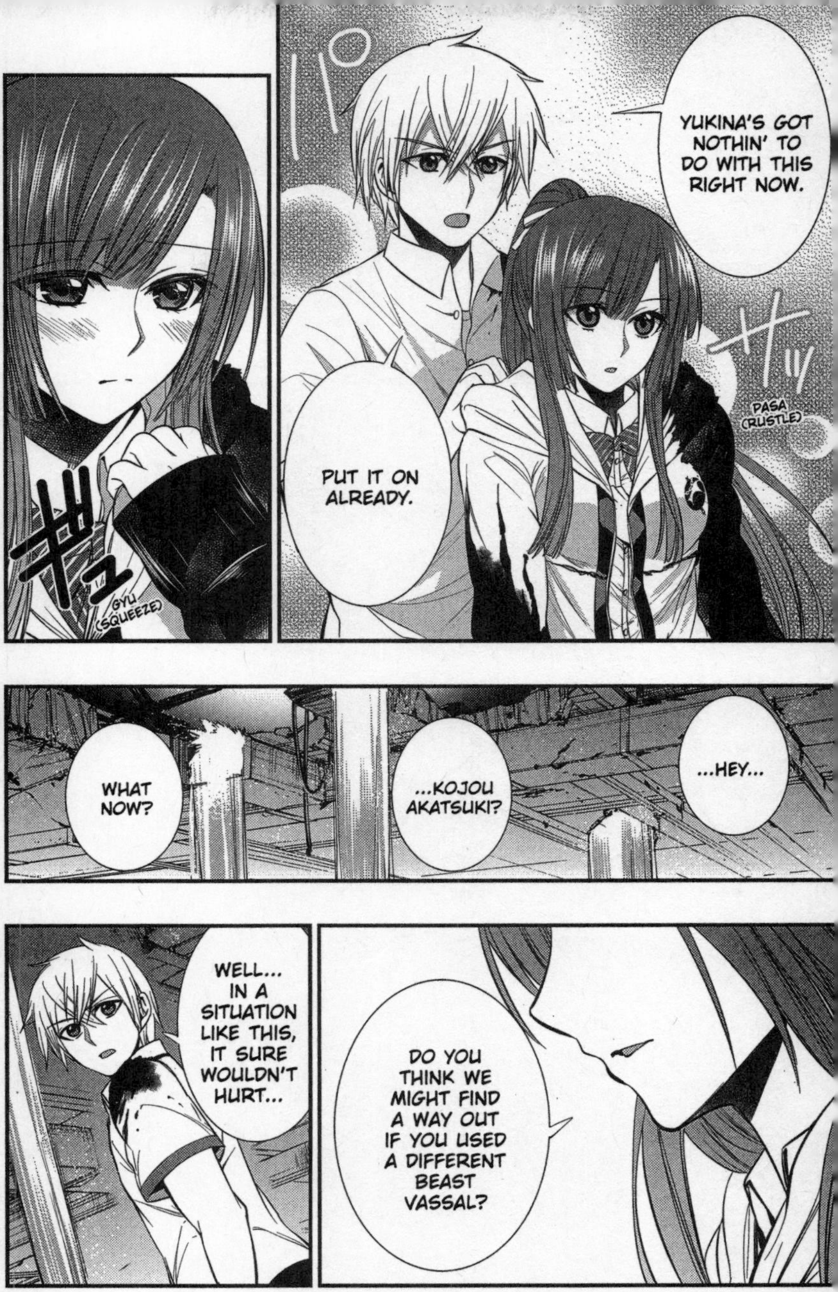
YUKINA'S GOT NOTHIN' TO DO WITH THIS RIGHT NOW.
PASA (RUSTLE)
PUT IT ON ALREADY.
ギュ
GYU (SQUEEZE)
...HEY...
...KOJOU AKATSUKI?
WHAT NOW?
DO YOU THINK WE MIGHT FIND A WAY OUT IF YOU USED A DIFFERENT BEAST VASSAL?
WELL... IN A SITUATION LIKE THIS, IT SURE WOULDN'T HURT...

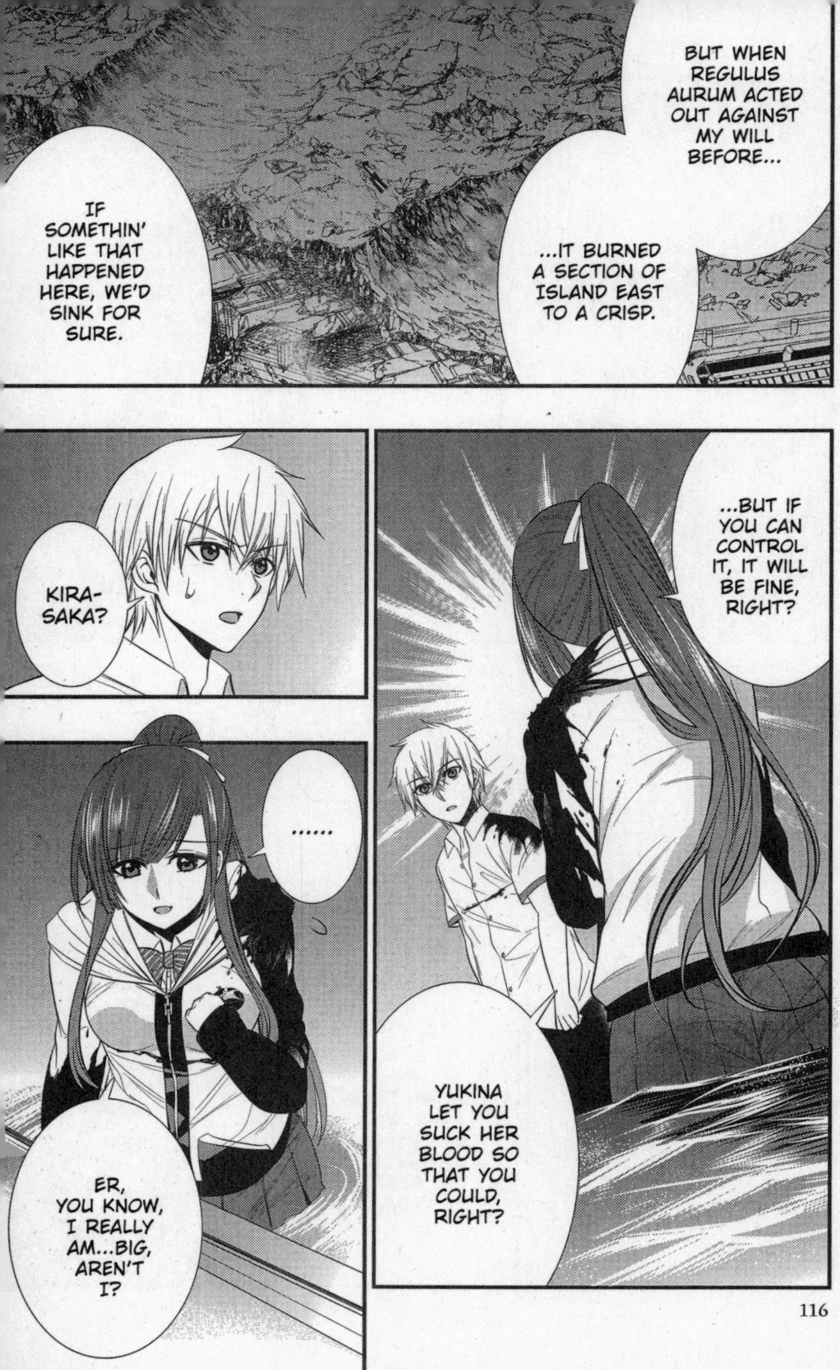
BUT WHEN REGULUS AURUM ACTED OUT AGAINST MY WILL BEFORE...
...IT BURNED A SECTION OF ISLAND EAST TO A CRISP.
IF SOMETHIN' LIKE THAT HAPPENED HERE, WE'D SINK FOR SURE.
...BUT IF YOU CAN CONTROL IT, IT WILL BE FINE, RIGHT?
YUKINA LET YOU SUCK HER BLOOD SO THAT YOU COULD, RIGHT?
KIRA-SAKA?
......
ER, YOU KNOW, I REALLY AM...BIG, AREN'T I?

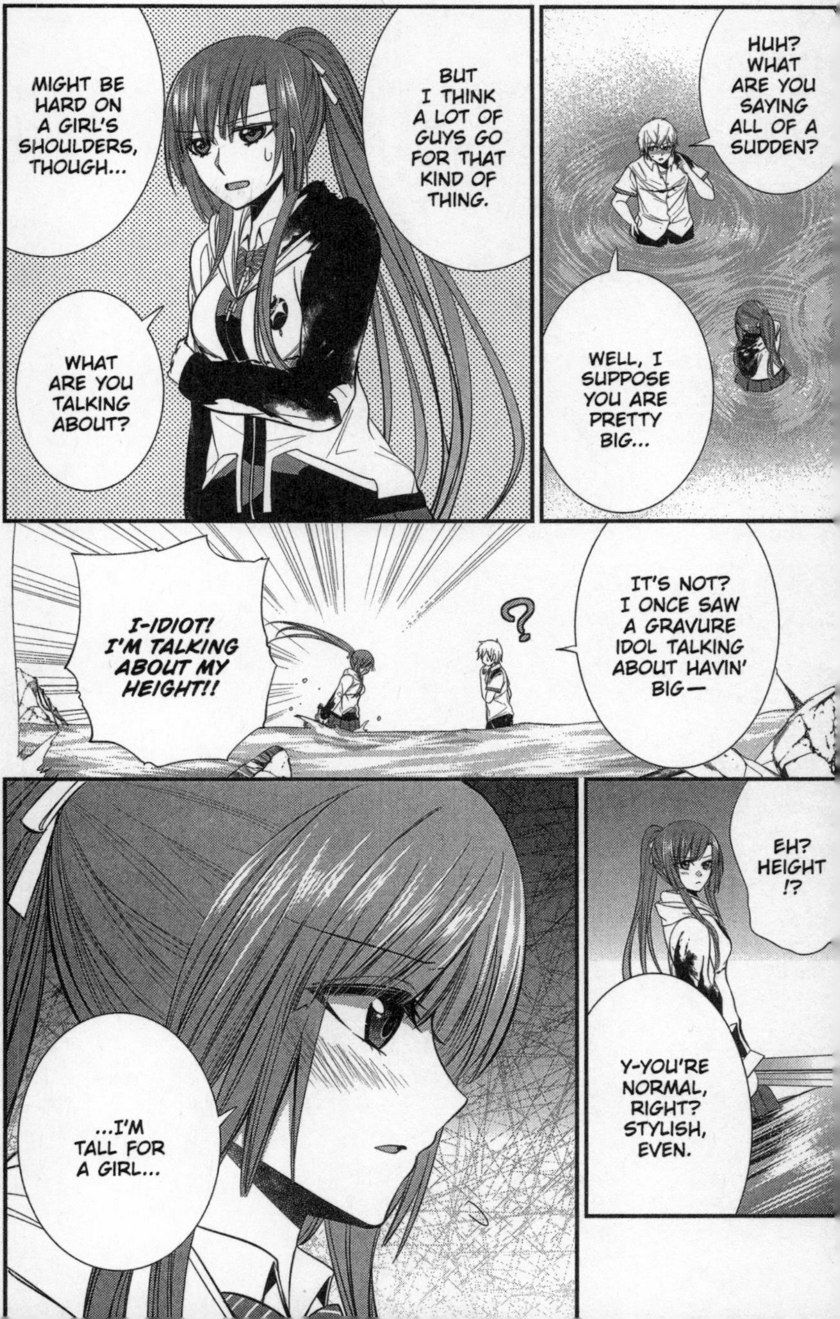
HUH? WHAT ARE YOU SAYING ALL OF A SUDDEN?
WELL, I SUPPOSE YOU ARE PRETTY BIG...
BUT I THINK A LOT OF GUYS GO FOR THAT KIND OF THING.
MIGHT BE HARD ON A GIRL'S SHOULDERS, THOUGH...
WHAT ARE YOU TALKING ABOUT?
IT'S NOT? I ONCE SAW A GRAVURE IDOL TALKING ABOUT HAVIN' BIG—
I-IDIOT! I'M TALKING ABOUT MY HEIGHT!!
EH? HEIGHT !?
Y-YOU'RE NORMAL, RIGHT? STYLISH, EVEN.
...I'M TALL FOR A GIRL...

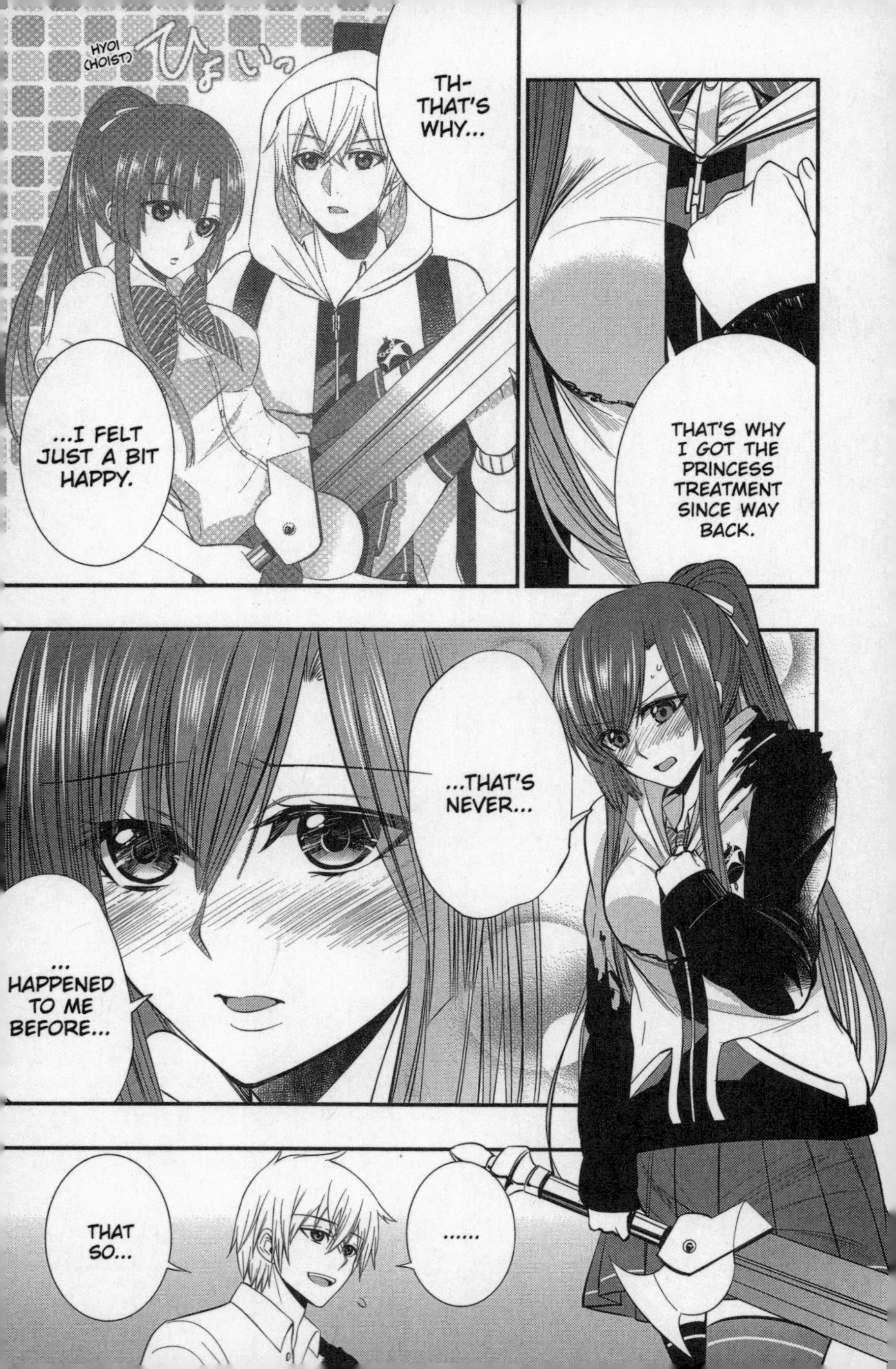
THAT'S WHY I GOT THE PRINCESS TREATMENT SINCE WAY BACK.
HYOI (HOIST)
ひょいっ
TH- THAT'S WHY...
...I FELT JUST A BIT HAPPY.
...THAT'S NEVER...
...HAPPENED TO ME BEFORE...
......
THAT SO...

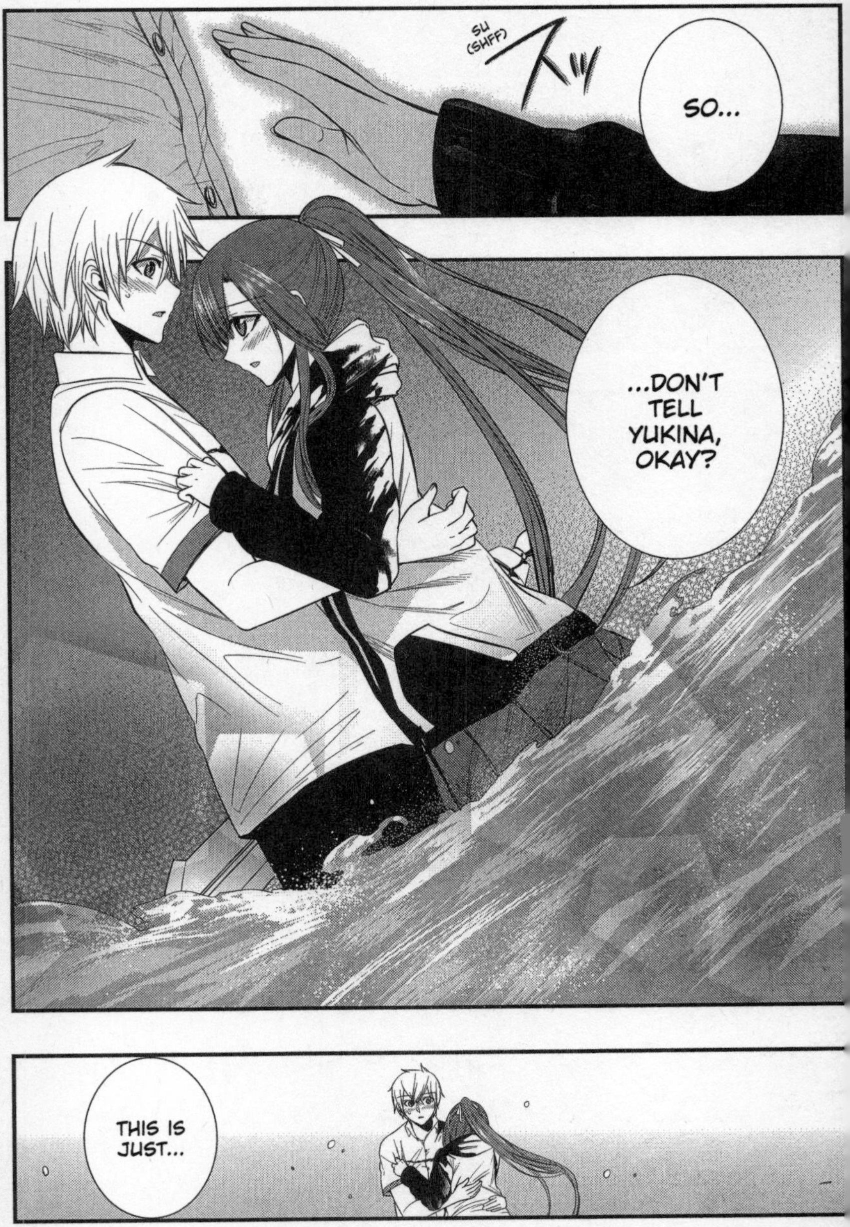
SO...
SU (SHFF) スッ
...DON'T TELL YUKINA, OKAY?
THIS IS JUST...

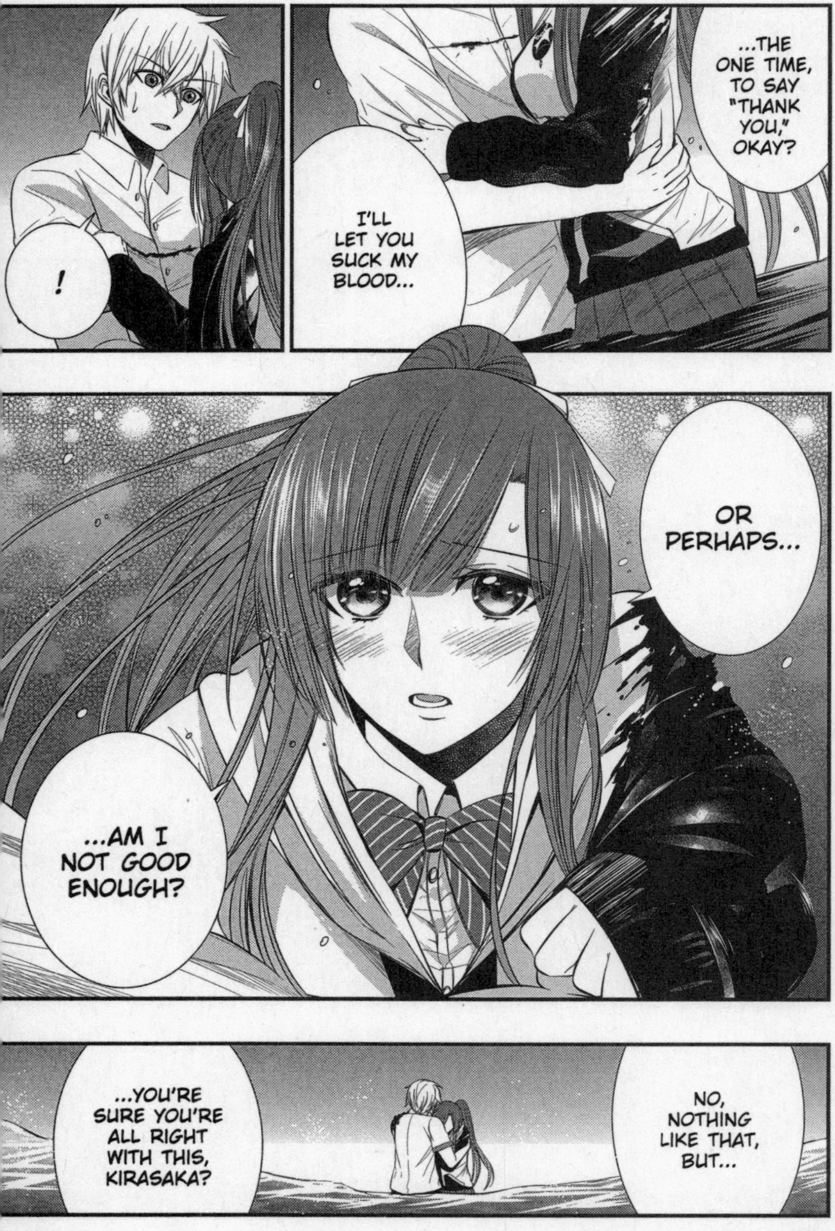
...THE ONE TIME, TO SAY "THANK YOU," OKAY?
I'LL LET YOU SUCK MY BLOOD...
!
OR PERHAPS...
...AM I NOT GOOD ENOUGH?
NO, NOTHING LIKE THAT, BUT...
...YOU'RE SURE YOU'RE ALL RIGHT WITH THIS, KIRASAKA?

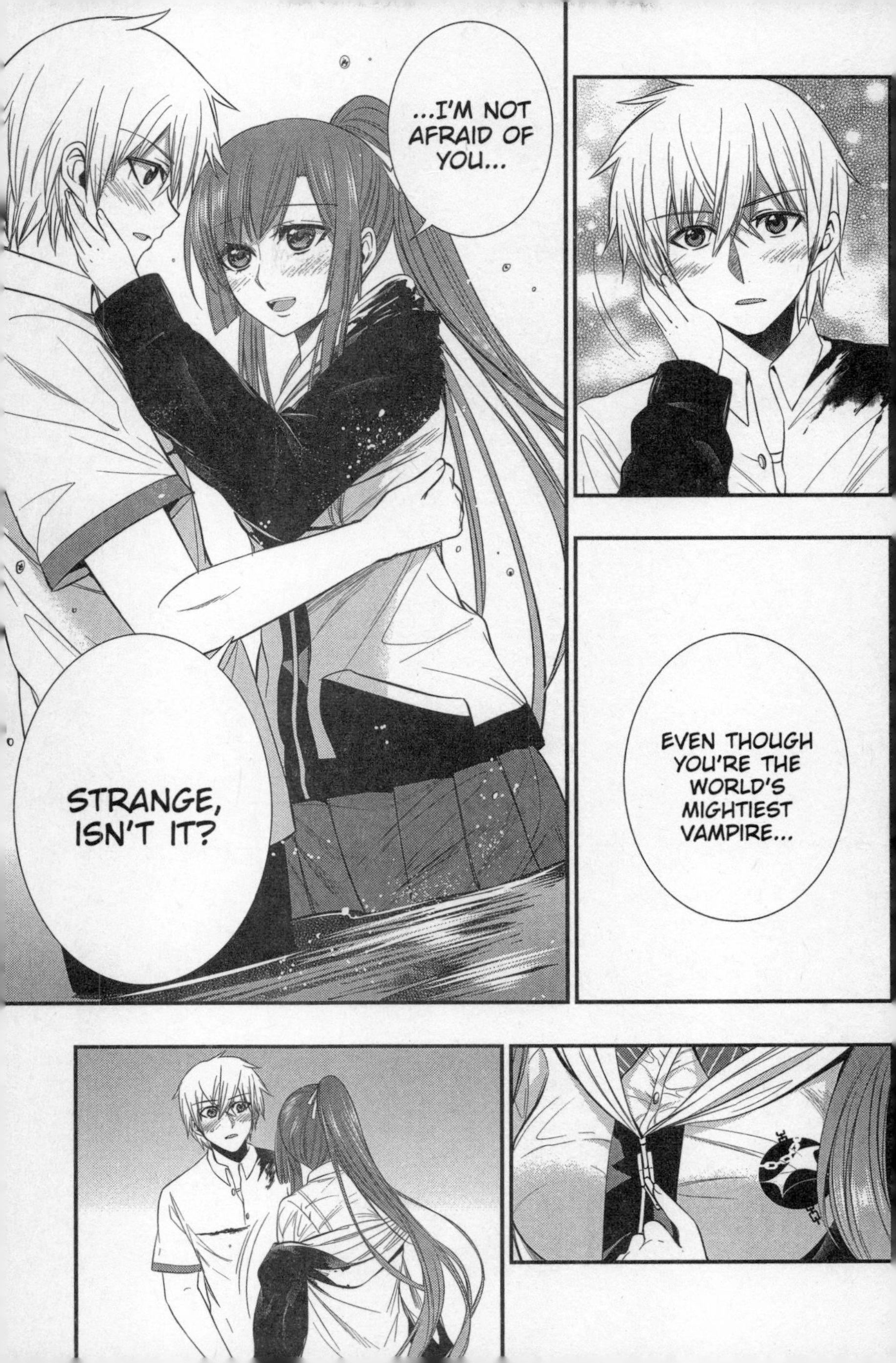
EVEN THOUGH YOU'RE THE WORLD'S MIGHTIEST VAMPIRE...
...I'M NOT AFRAID OF YOU...
STRANGE, ISN'T IT?

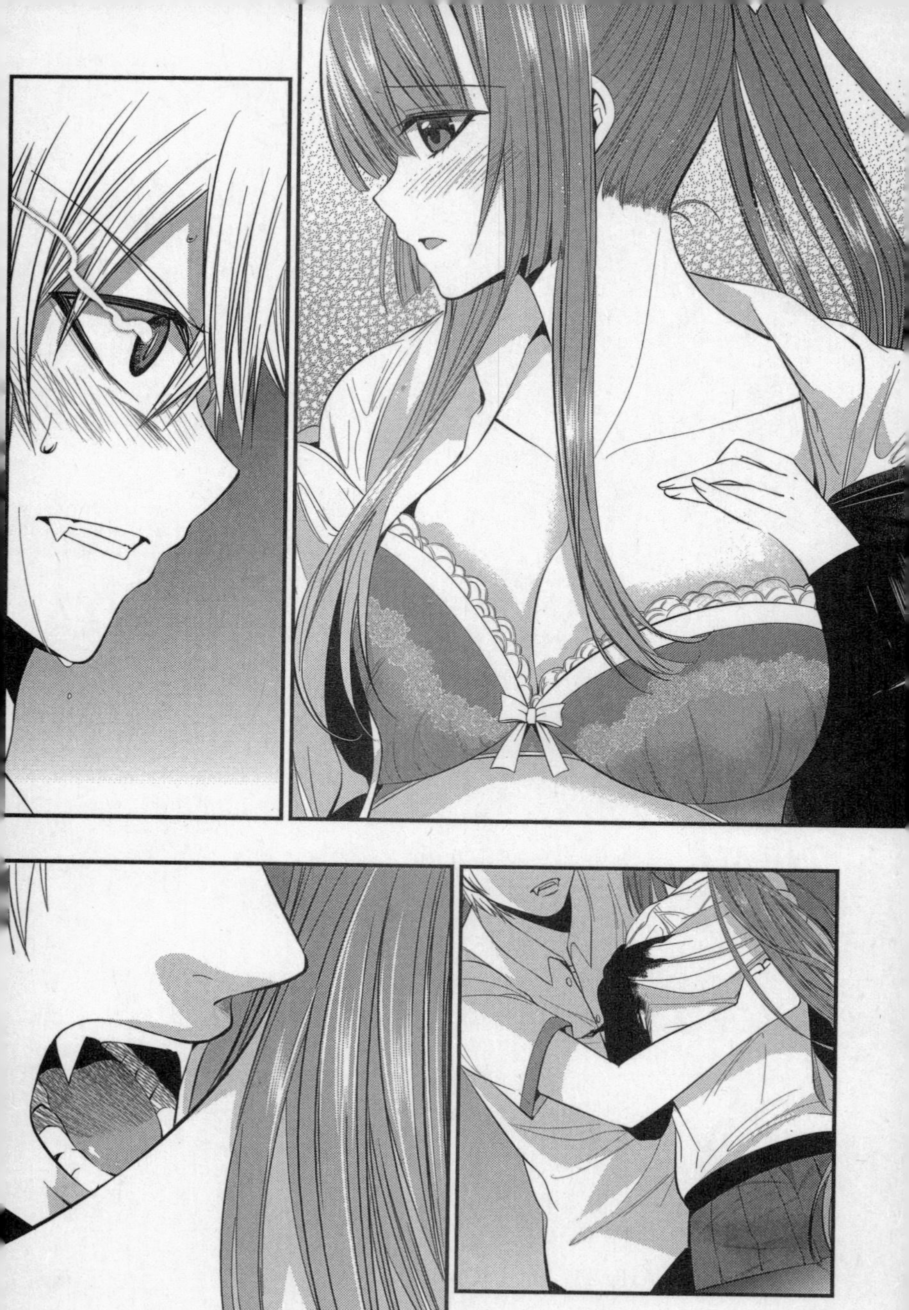

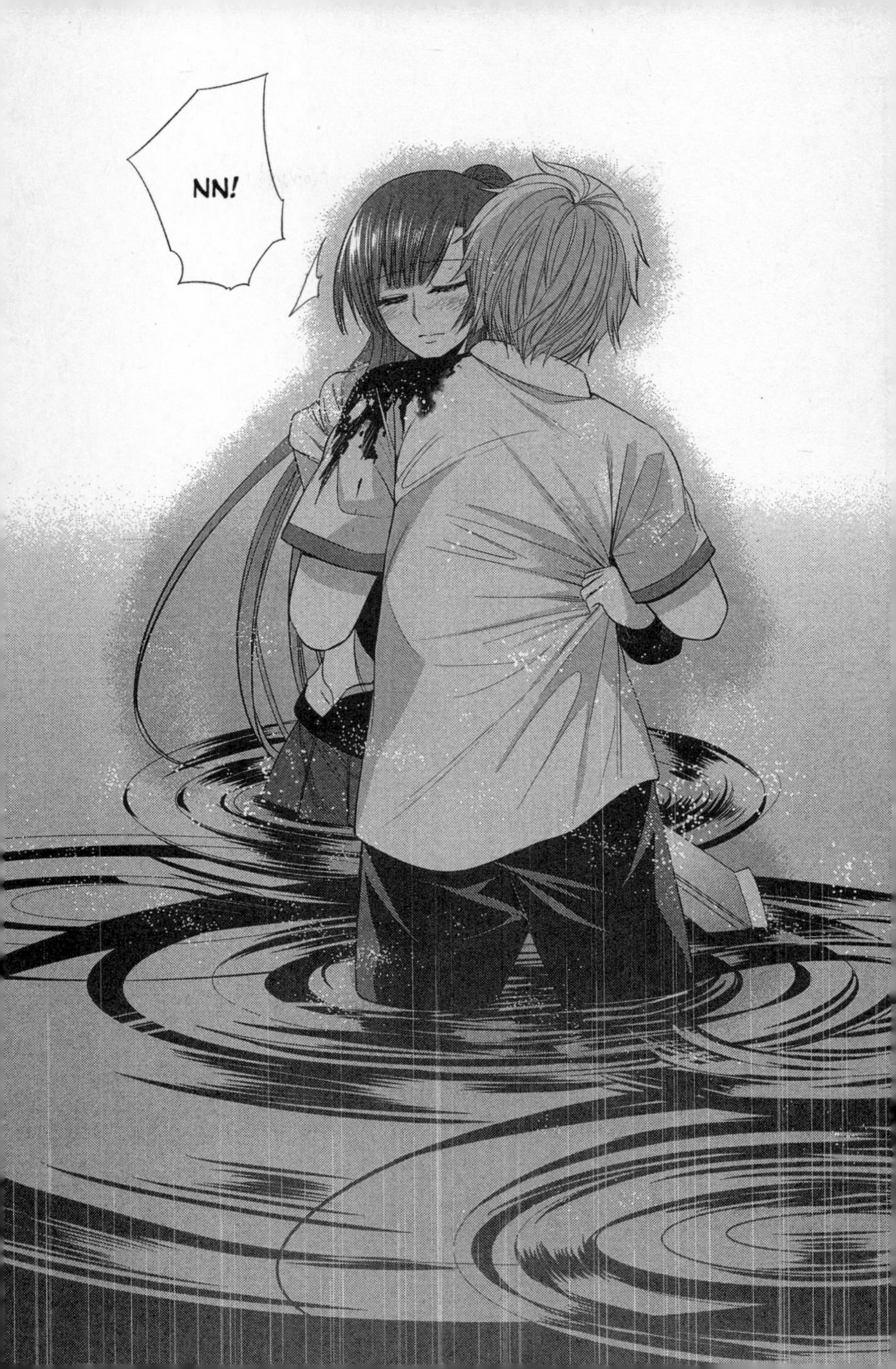
NN!

STRIKE THE BLOOD DEFINITION

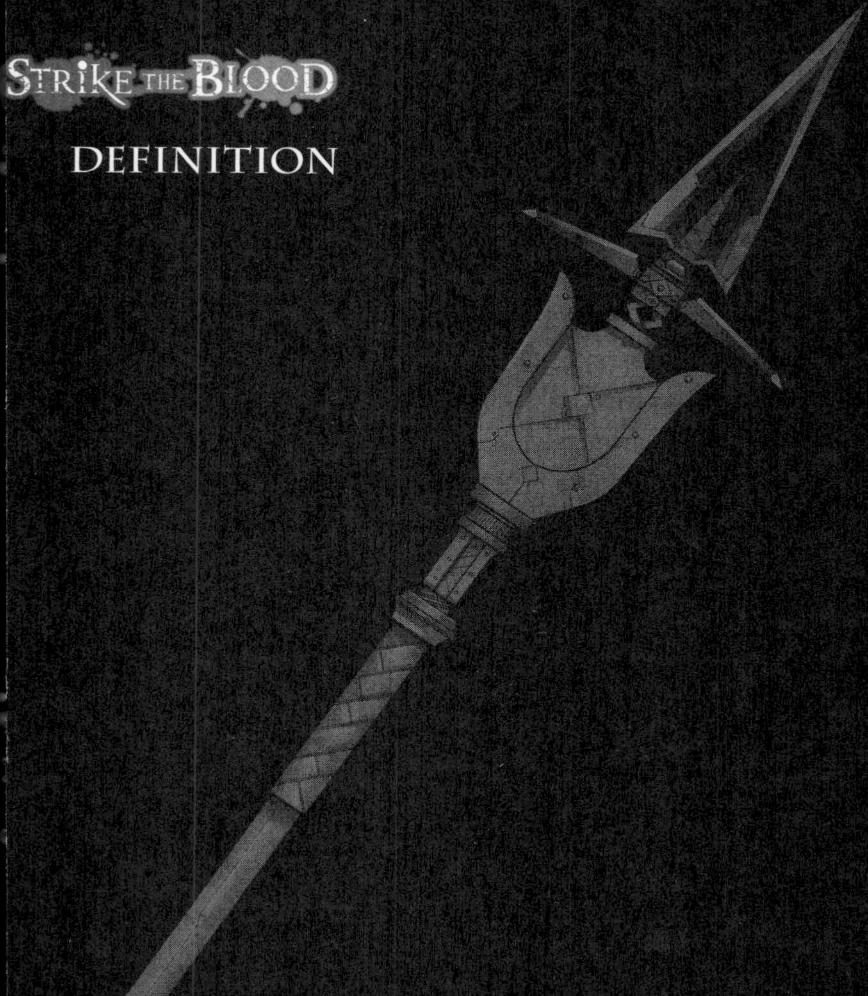

<< AERO DYNE >>

A projection that Yaze Motoki, Hyper-Adapter, produces using his control of the air. As it resembles a spirit with physical substance, he is able to remotely control it tens of meters away, provided it is in an open space. He used this skill to deliver Snowdrift Wolf to Yukina.

ドグ
(SLUMP)

SHIT!

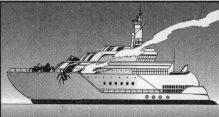

THEY ALREADY DECIPHERED THE CODES!?

HFF!

HFF!

ASAGI DID HER PART A LITTLE TOO WELL...

コツ
(STEP)

コツ
KO

I SEE.

!

I'M GONNA GET IN TROUBLE FOR THIS TOO...

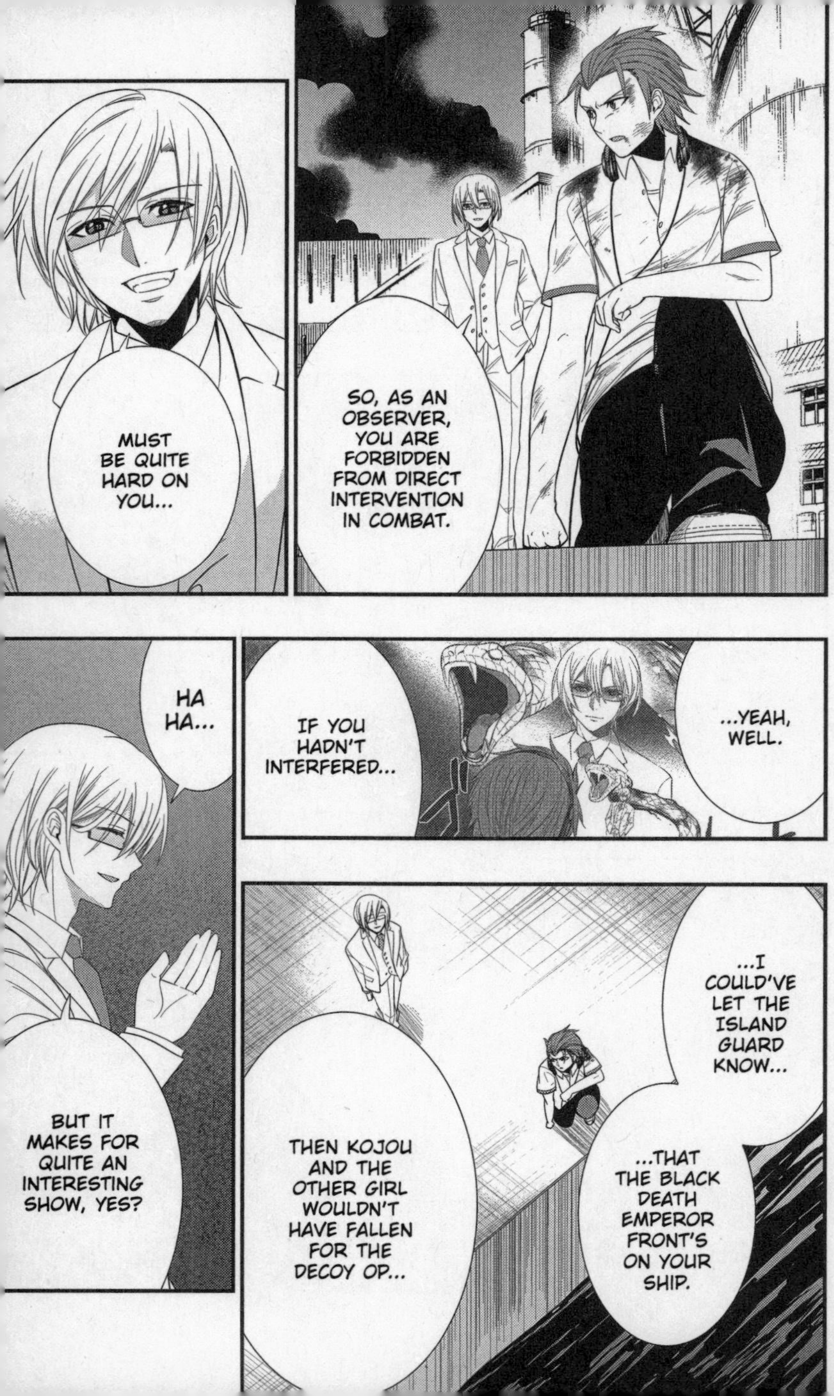
SO, AS AN OBSERVER, YOU ARE FORBIDDEN FROM DIRECT INTERVENTION IN COMBAT.
MUST BE QUITE HARD ON YOU...
...YEAH, WELL.
IF YOU HADN'T INTERFERED...
...I COULD'VE LET THE ISLAND GUARD KNOW...
...THAT THE BLACK DEATH EMPEROR FRONT'S ON YOUR SHIP.
THEN KOJOU AND THE OTHER GIRL WOULDN'T HAVE FALLEN FOR THE DECOY OP...
HA HA...
BUT IT MAKES FOR QUITE AN INTERESTING SHOW, YES?

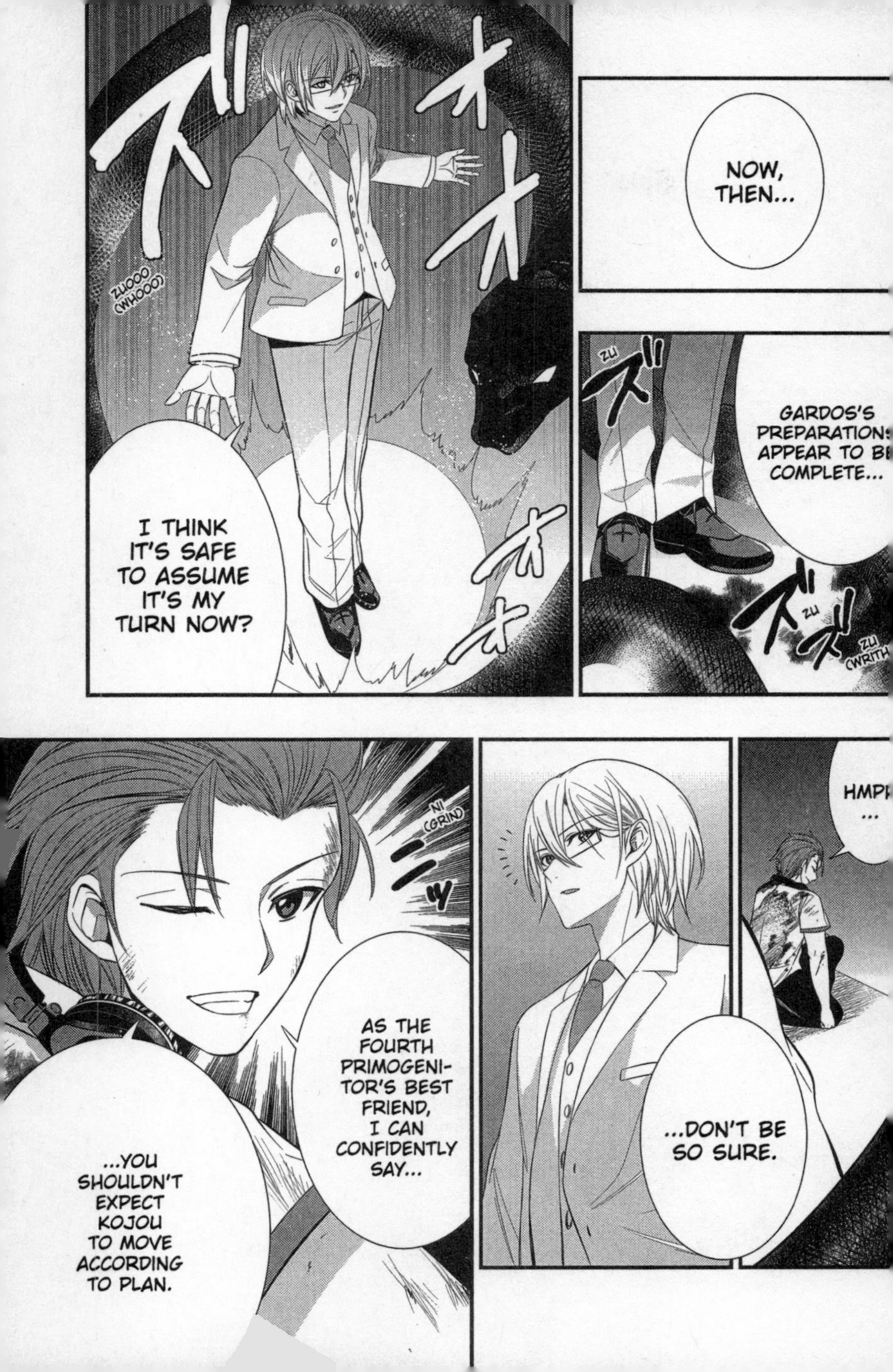
NOW, THEN...
GARDOS'S PREPARATION APPEAR TO B COMPLETE...
ZU
ZU
ZU (WRITH
ZUOOO (WHOOO)
I THINK IT'S SAFE TO ASSUME IT'S MY TURN NOW?
HMP ...
...DON'T BE SO SURE.
NI (GRIN)
AS THE FOURTH PRIMOGENI-TOR'S BEST FRIEND, I CAN CONFIDENTLY SAY...
...YOU SHOULDN'T EXPECT KOJOU TO MOVE ACCORDING TO PLAN.

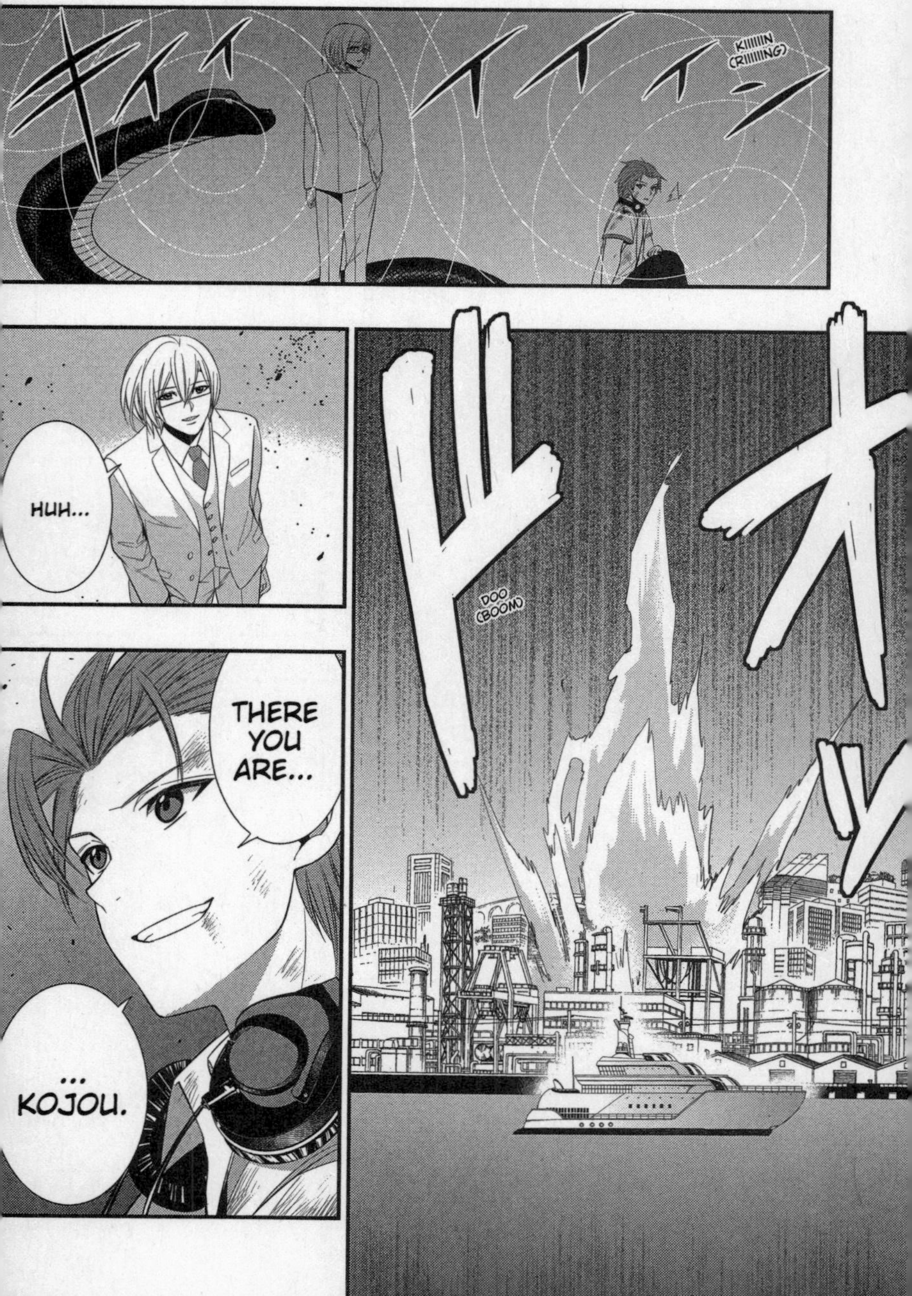
KIIIIIN (RIIIIING)
DOO (BOOM)
HUH...
THERE YOU ARE...
... KOJOU.

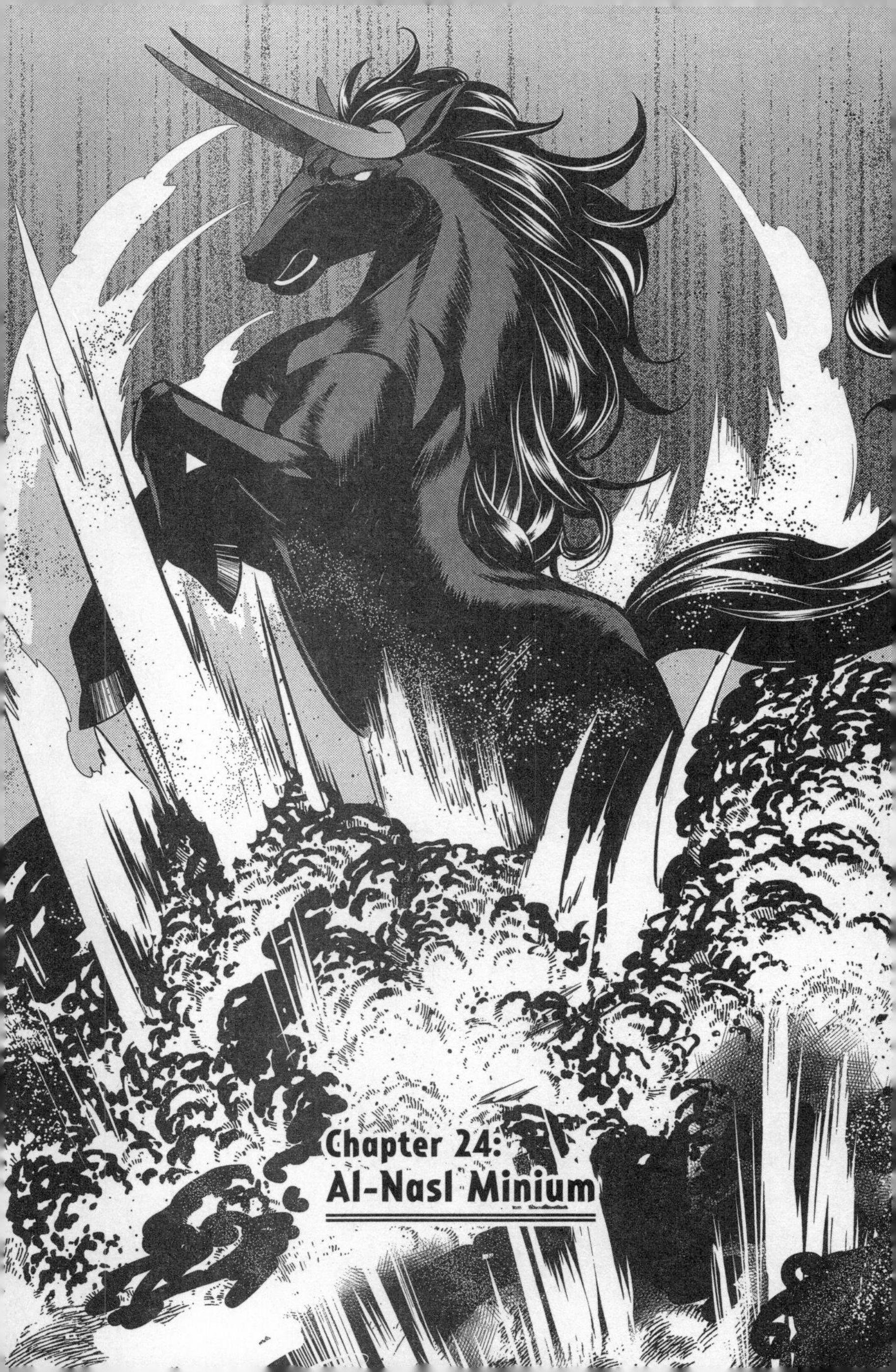
Chapter 24:
Al-Nasl Minium

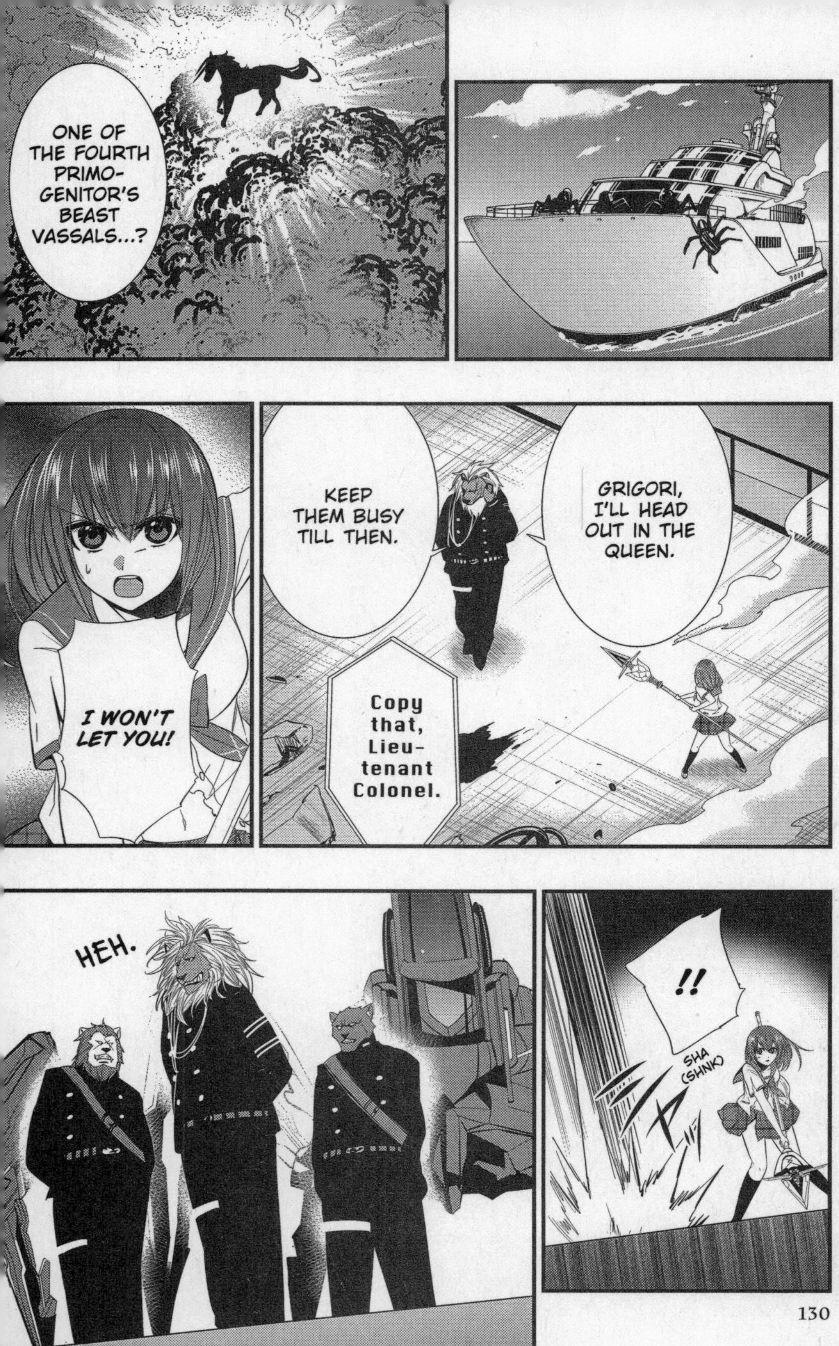
ONE OF THE FOURTH PRIMO-GENITOR'S BEAST VASSALS...?
GRIGORI, I'LL HEAD OUT IN THE QUEEN.
KEEP THEM BUSY TILL THEN.
Copy that, Lieu-tenant Colonel.
I WON'T LET YOU!
!!
SHA (SHNK)
HEH.

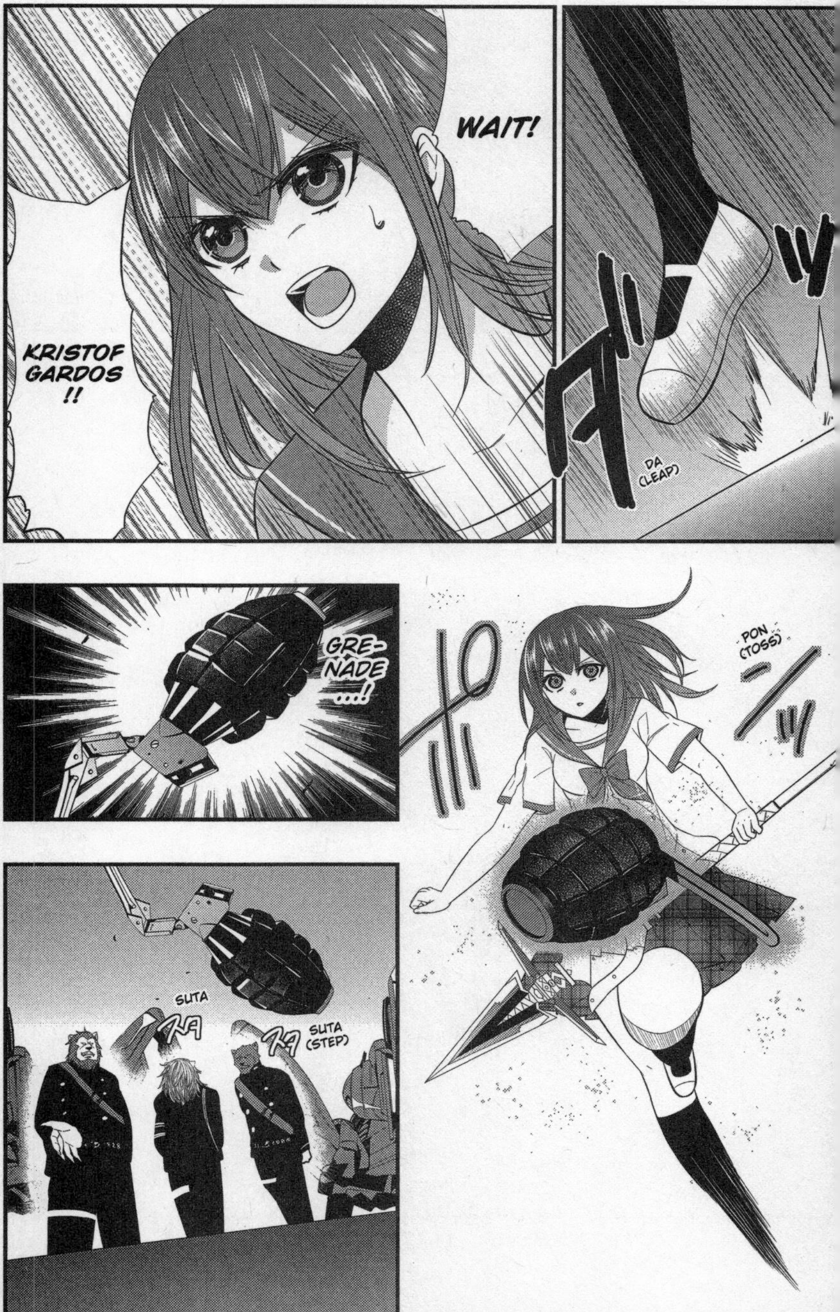
DA (LEAP)
WAIT!
KRISTOF GARDOS !!
PON (TOSS)
GRE-NADE ...!
SUTA (STEP)
SUTA

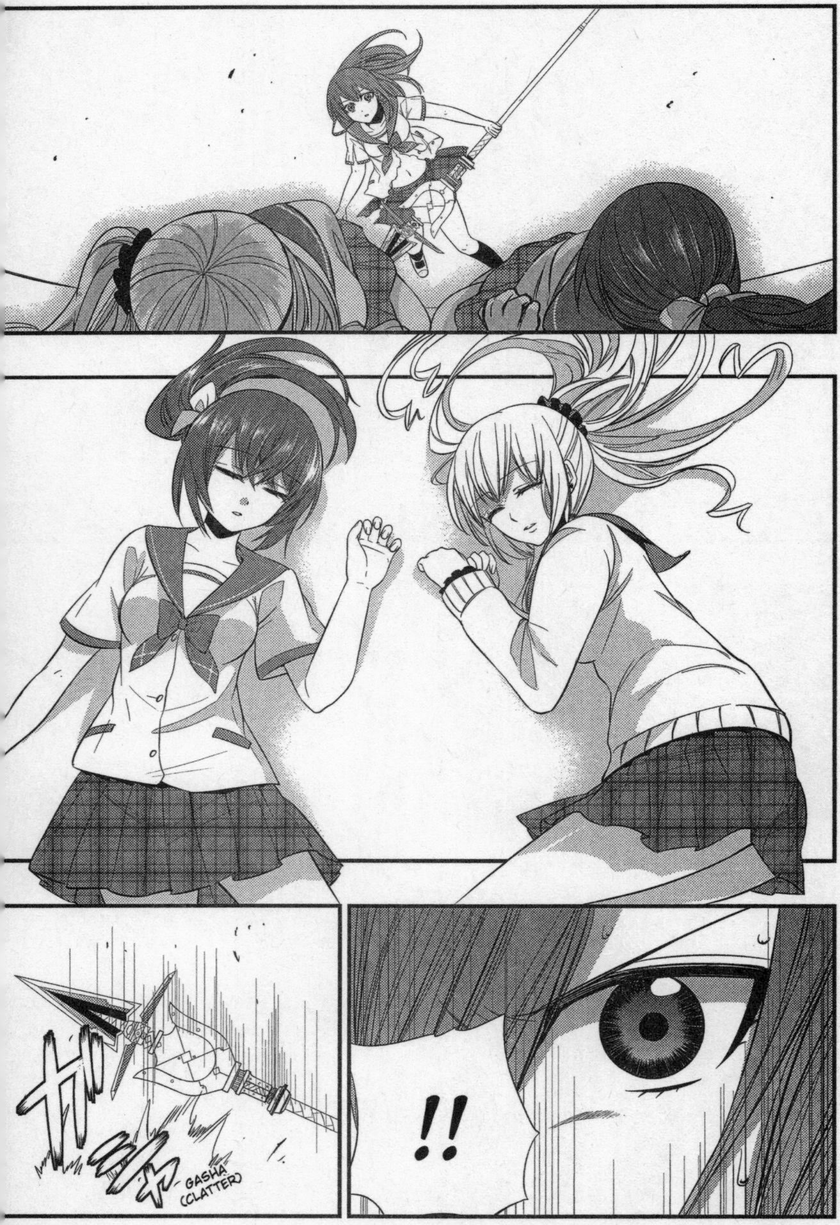
!!
GASHA (CLATTER)

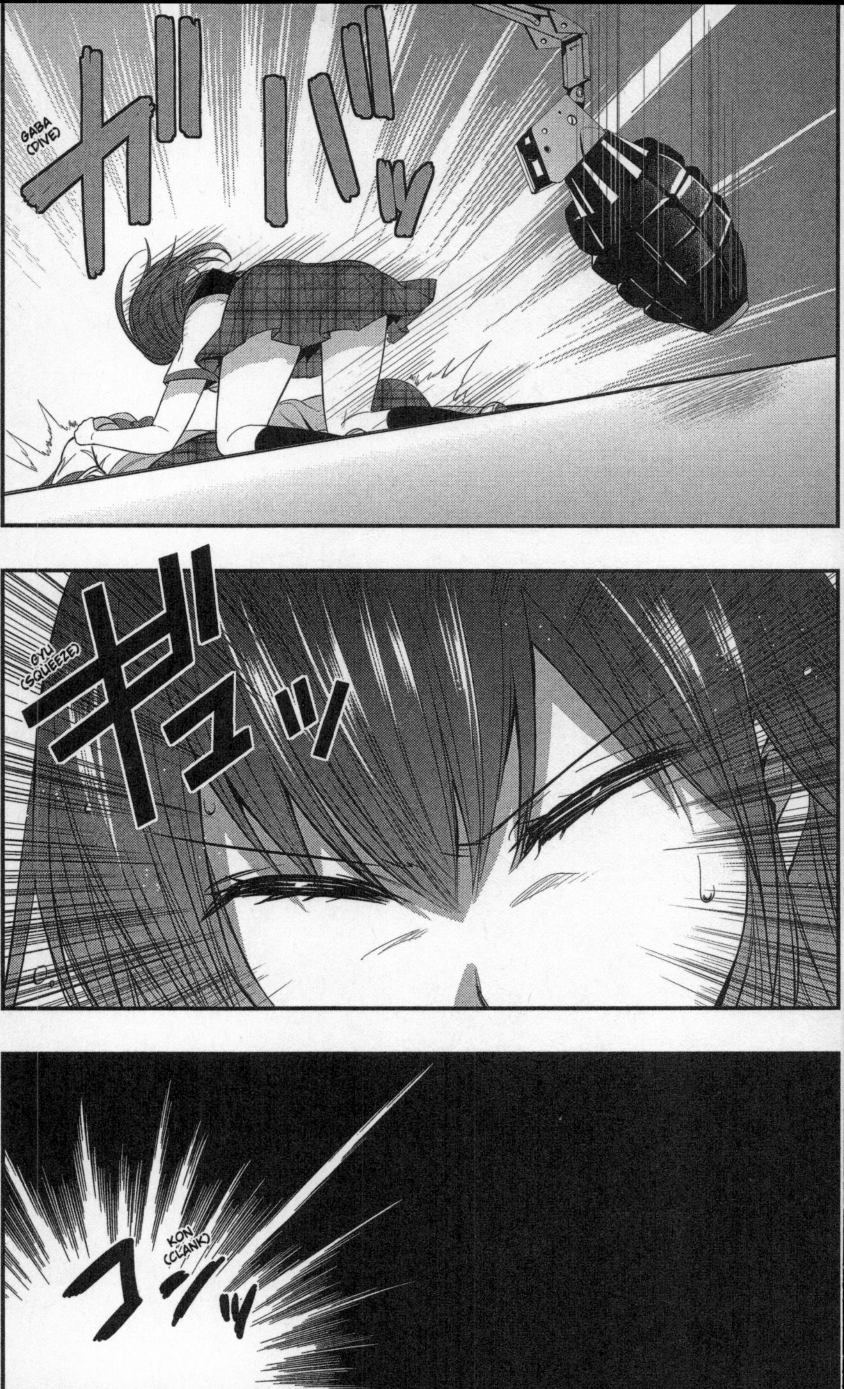
GABA (DIVE)
GYU (SQUEEZE)
KON (CLANK)

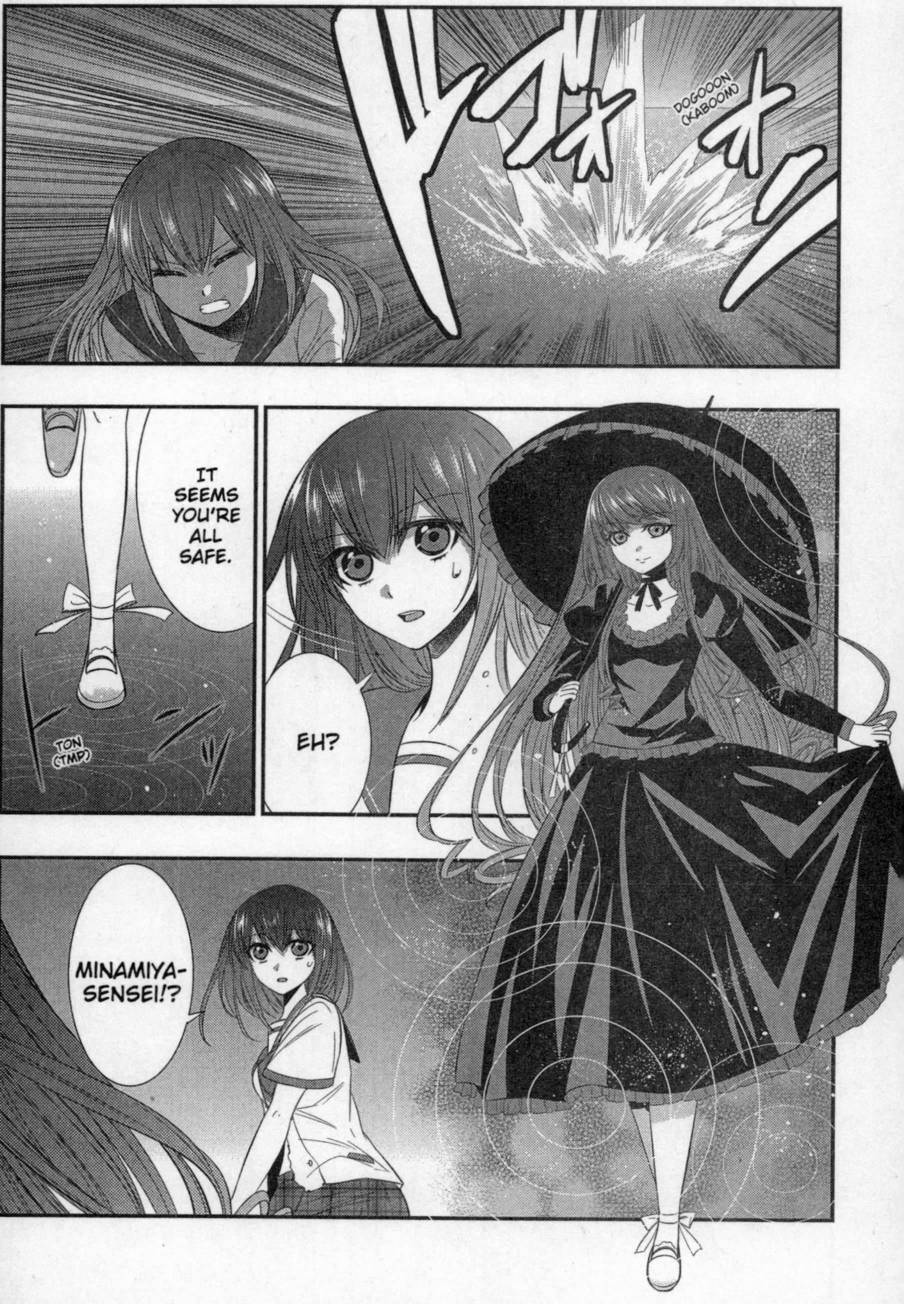
DOGOOON (KABOOM)
EH?
IT SEEMS YOU'RE ALL SAFE.
TON (TMP)
MINAMIYA-SENSEI!?

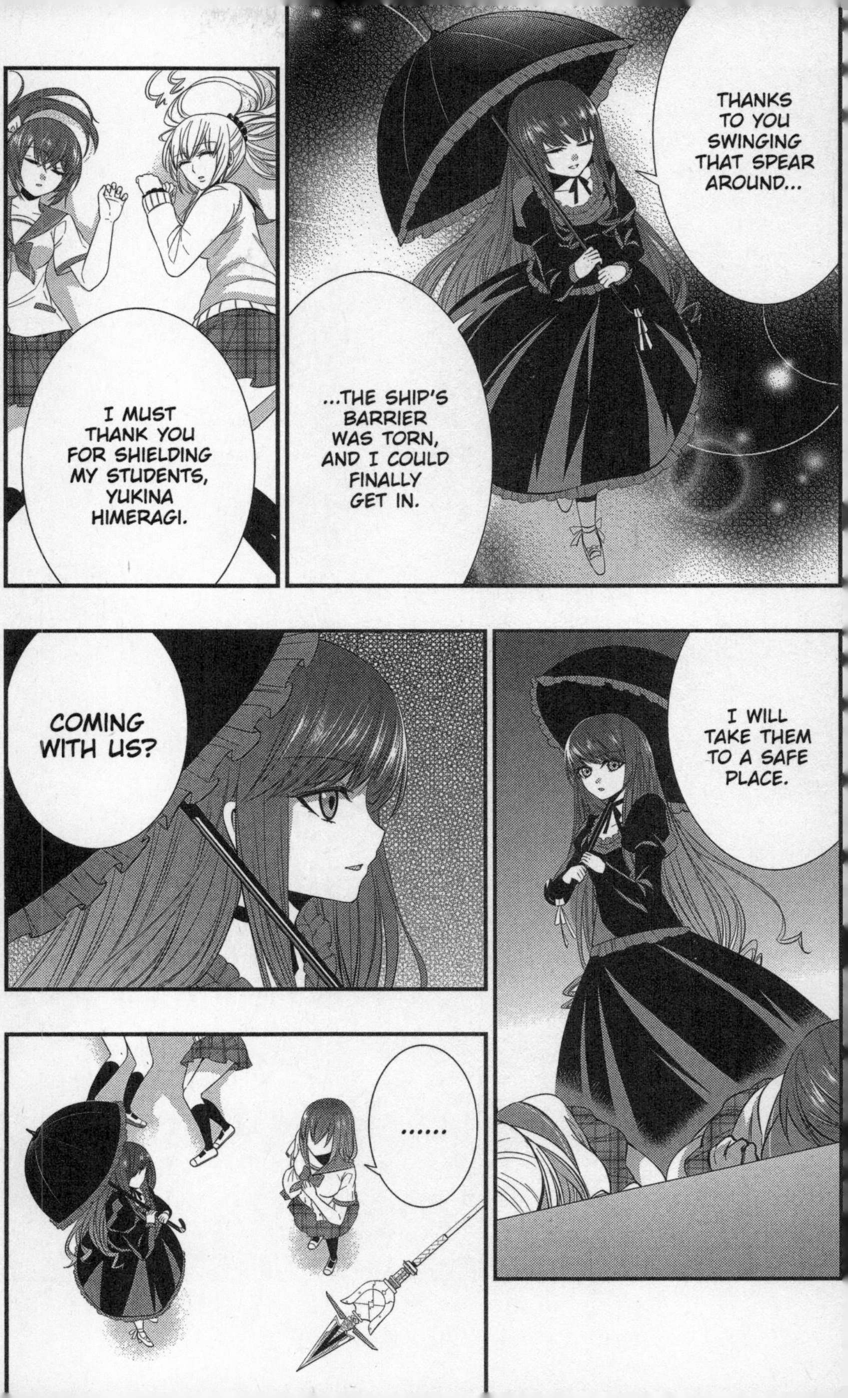
THANKS TO YOU SWINGING THAT SPEAR AROUND...
...THE SHIP'S BARRIER WAS TORN, AND I COULD FINALLY GET IN.
I MUST THANK YOU FOR SHIELDING MY STUDENTS, YUKINA HIMERAGI.
I WILL TAKE THEM TO A SAFE PLACE.
COMING WITH US?
......

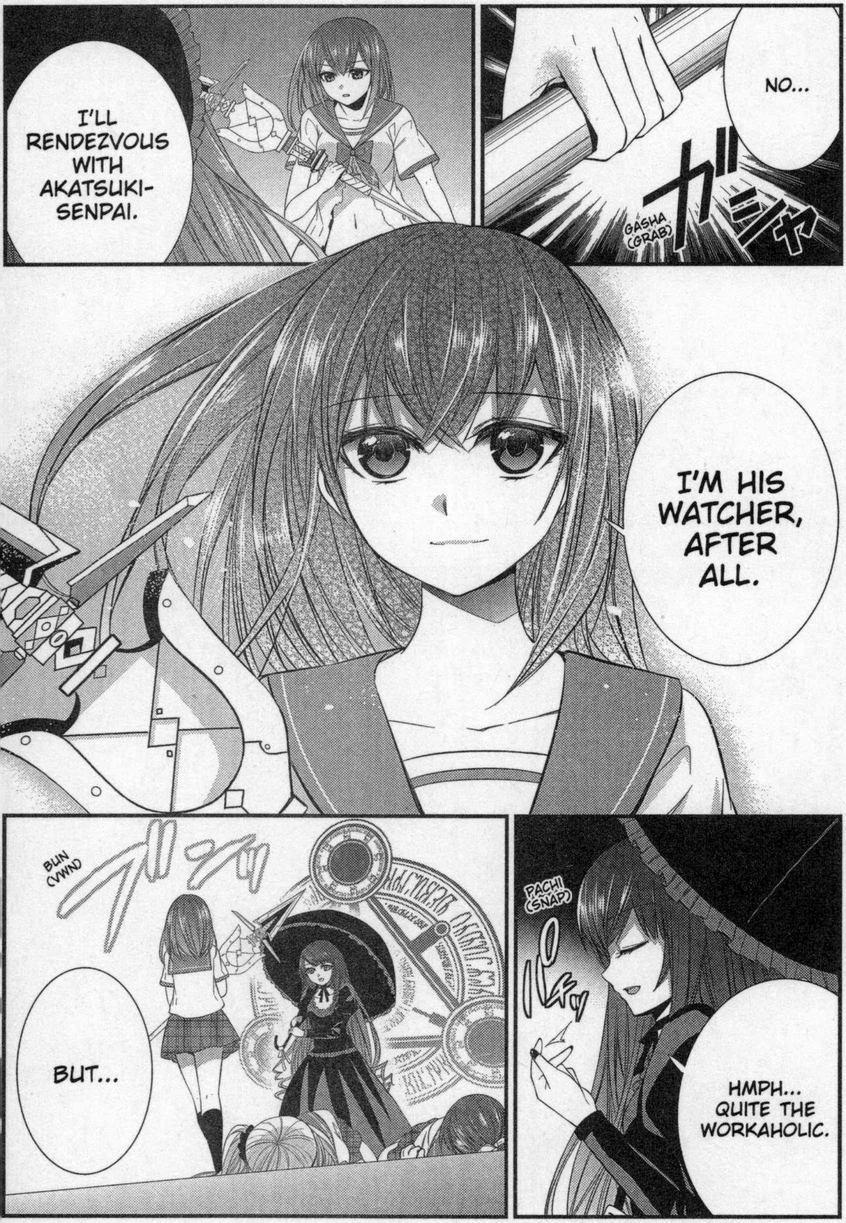
NO...
GASHA (GRAB)
I'LL RENDEZVOUS WITH AKATSUKI-SENPAI.
I'M HIS WATCHER, AFTER ALL.
PACHI (SNAP)
HMPH... QUITE THE WORKAHOLIC.
BUN (VWN)
BUT...

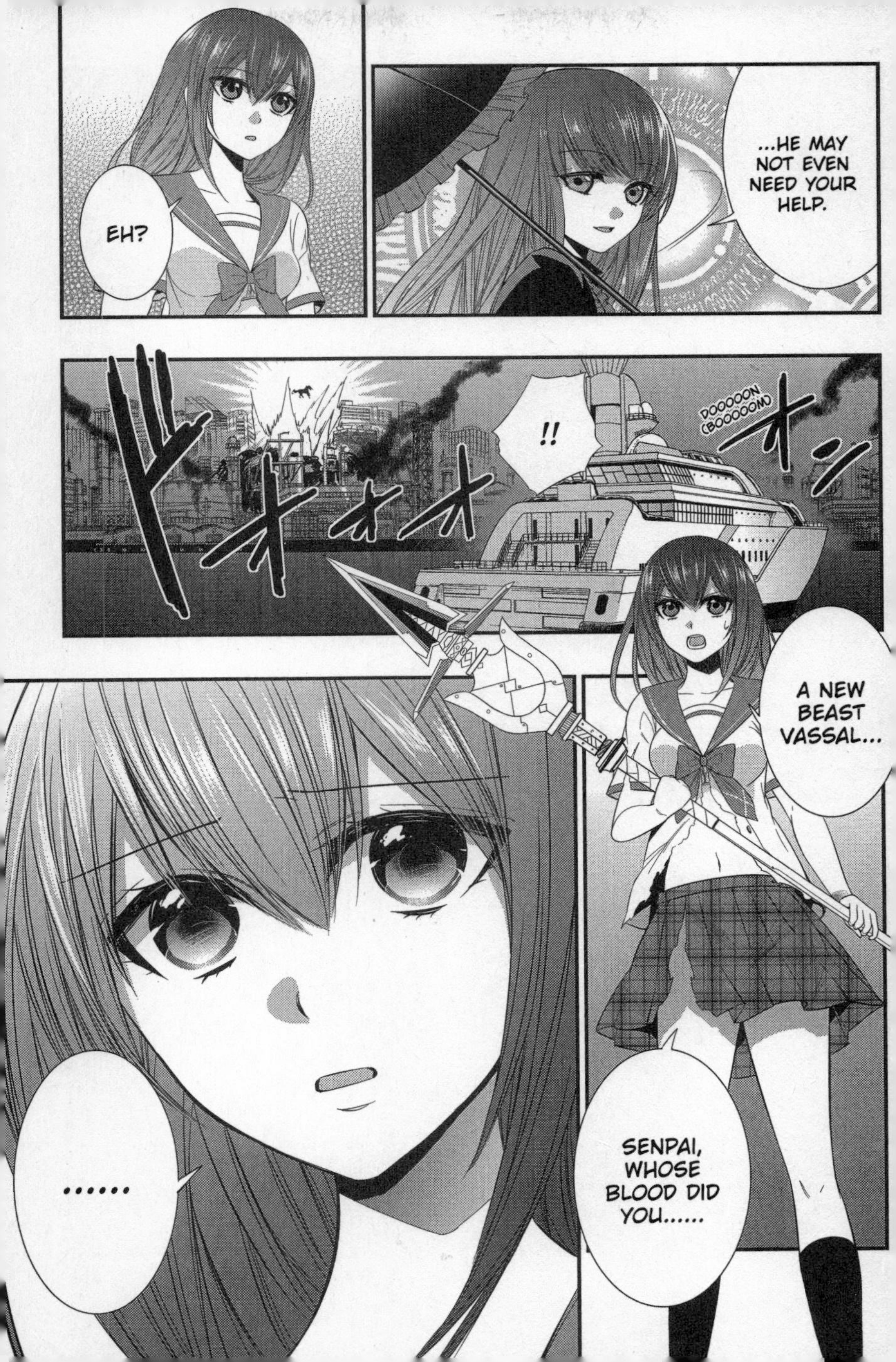
...HE MAY NOT EVEN NEED YOUR HELP.
EH?
DOOOOON (BOOOOOM)
!!
A NEW BEAST VASSAL...
SENPAI, WHOSE BLOOD DID YOU......
......

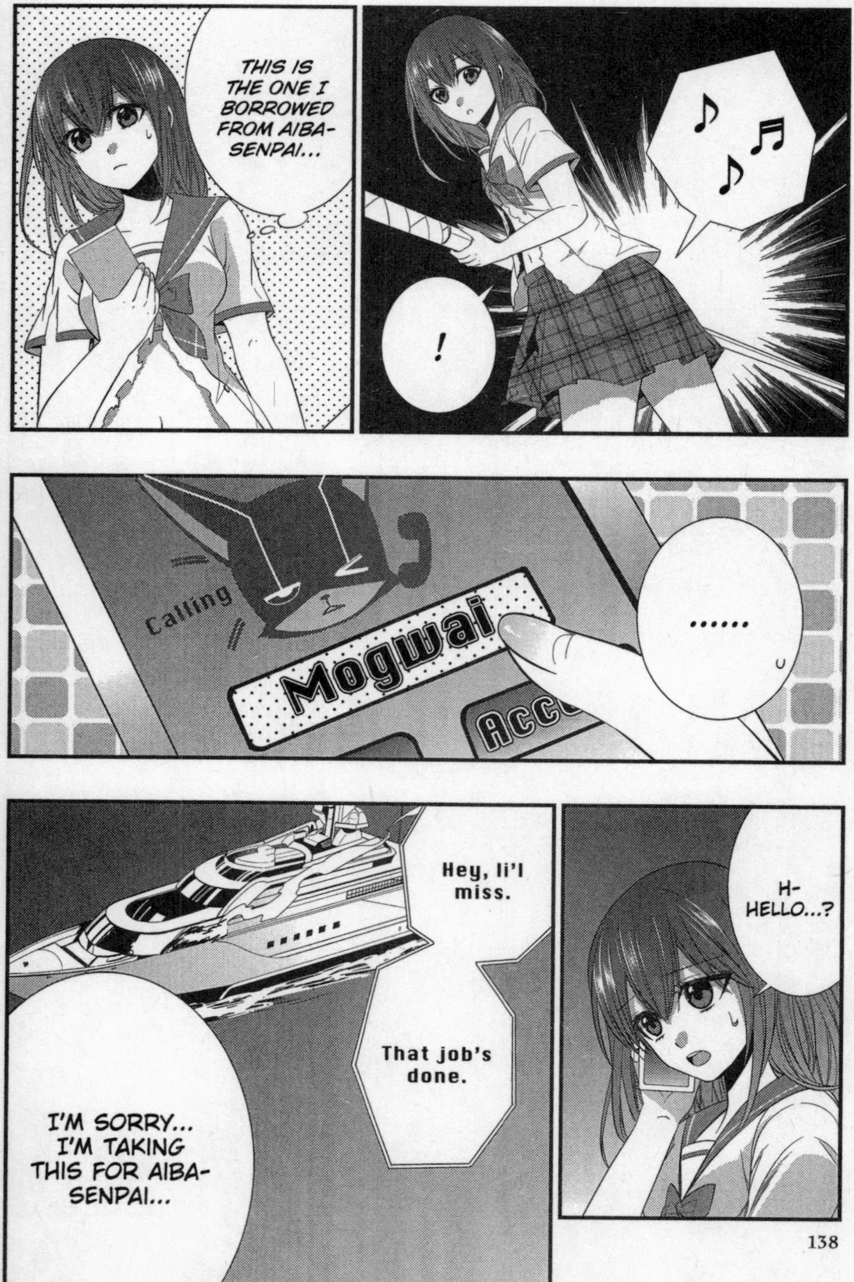
♪ ♫ ♪
!
THIS IS THE ONE I BORROWED FROM AIBA-SENPAI...
Calling
Mogwai
......
H-HELLO...?
Hey, li'l miss.
That job's done.
I'M SORRY... I'M TAKING THIS FOR AIBA-SENPAI...

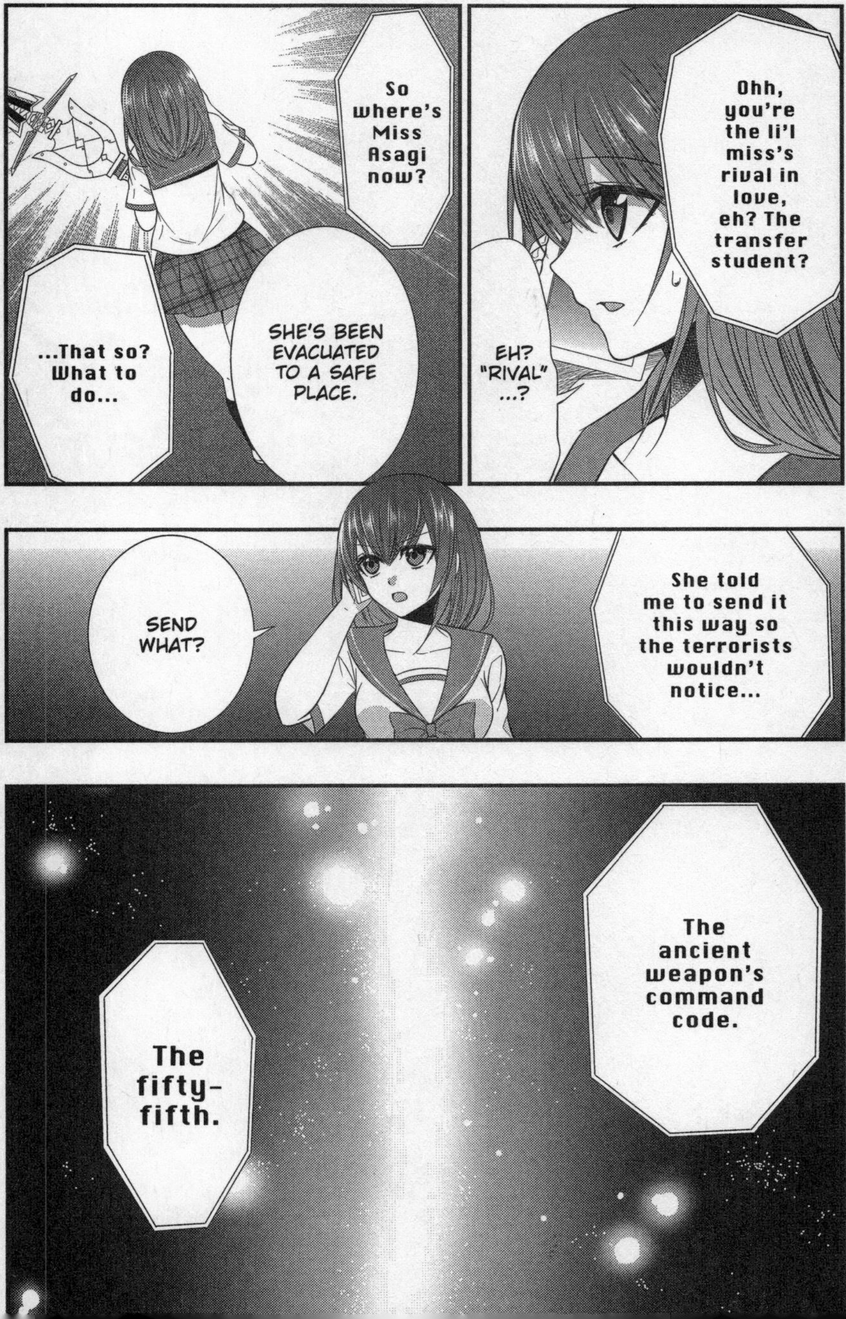
Ohh, you're the li'l miss's rival in love, eh? The transfer student?
EH? "RIVAL" ...?
So where's Miss Asagi now?
SHE'S BEEN EVACUATED TO A SAFE PLACE.
...That so? What to do...
She told me to send it this way so the terrorists wouldn't notice...
SEND WHAT?
The ancient weapon's command code.
The fifty-fifth.

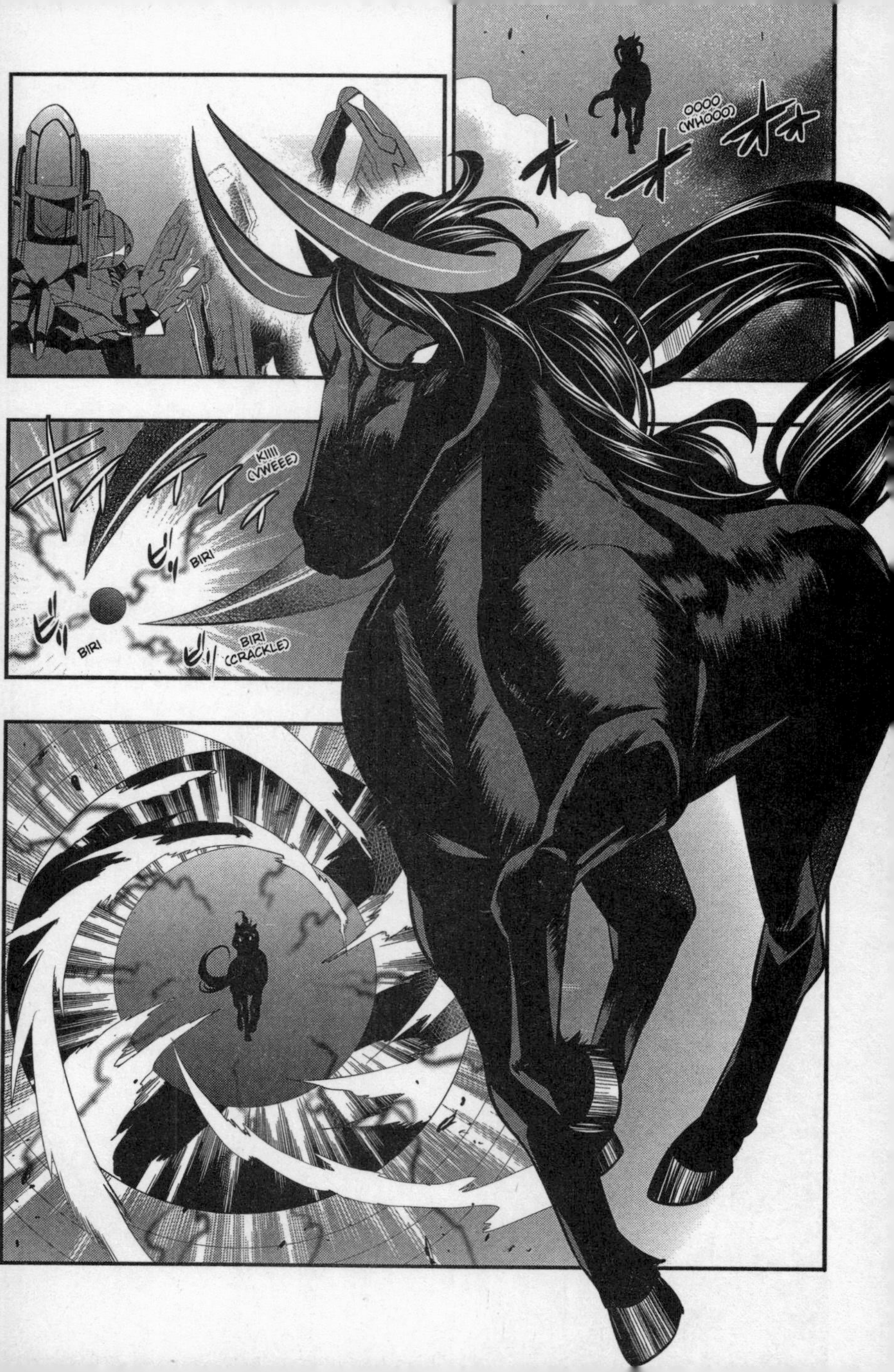
OOOO (WHOOO)
KIIII (VWEEE)
BIRI
BIRI
BIRI (CRACKLE)

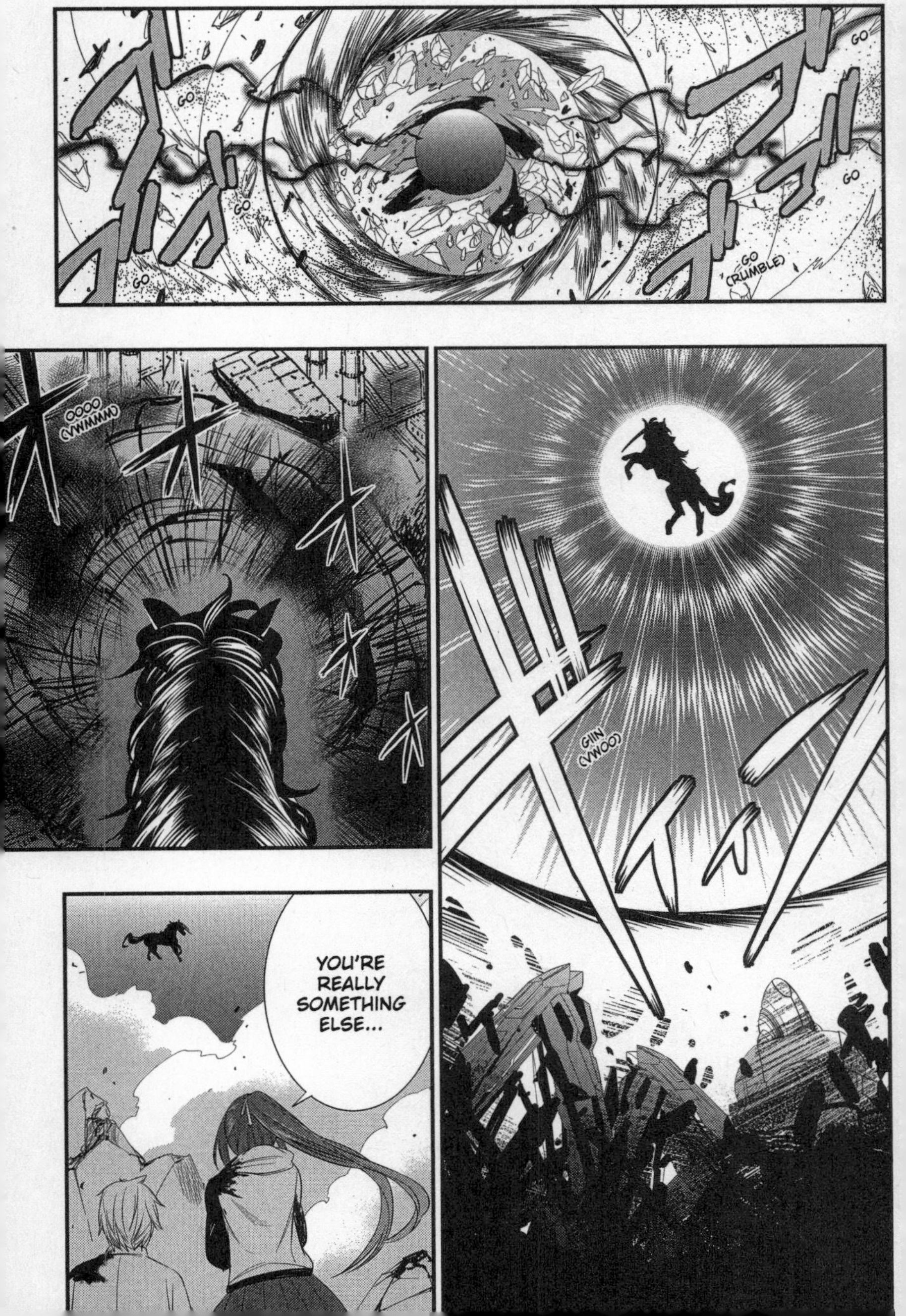
GO
GO
GO
(RUMBLE)
GO
GO
GO
GIIN
(VWOO)
OOOO
(VWMMM)
YOU'RE REALLY SOMETHING ELSE...

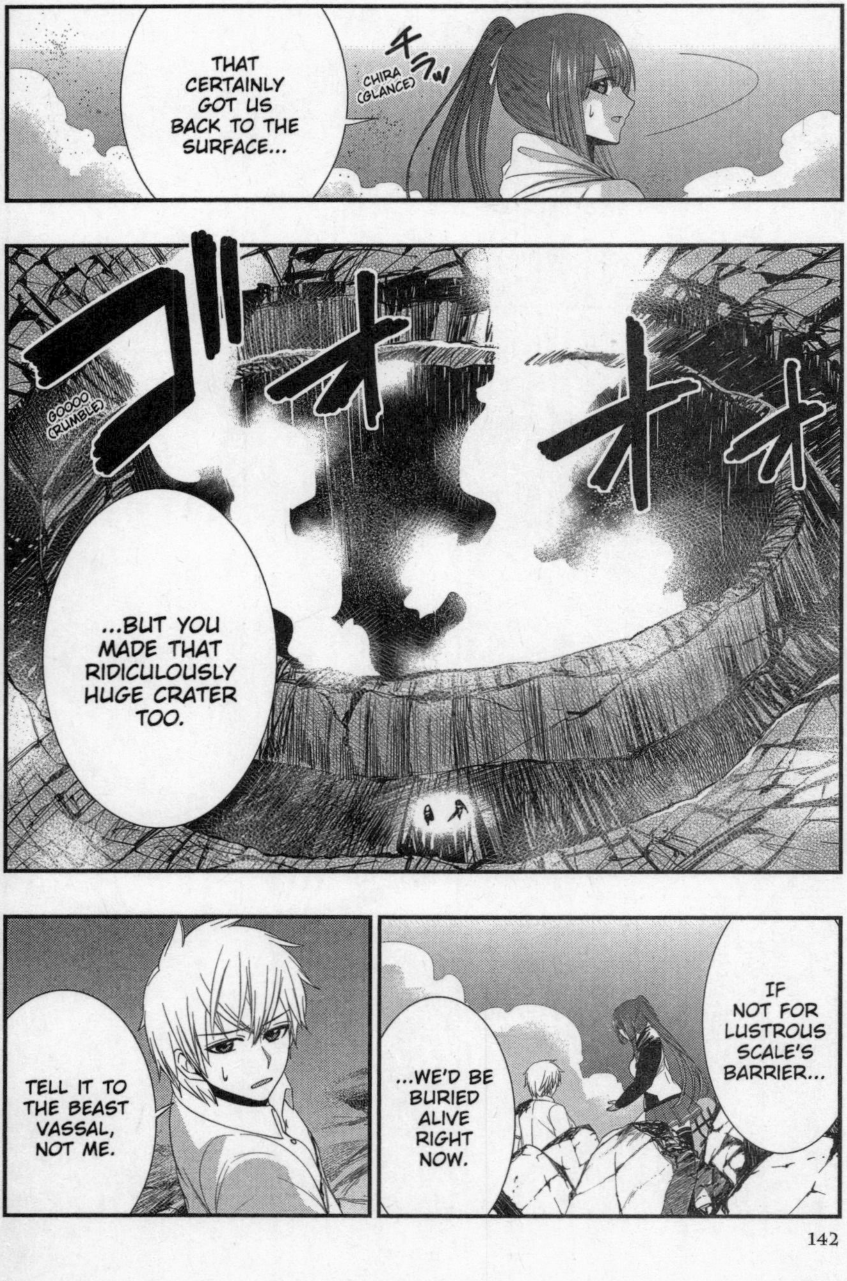
CHIRA (GLANCE)
THAT CERTAINLY GOT US BACK TO THE SURFACE...
GOOOO (RUMBLE)
...BUT YOU MADE THAT RIDICULOUSLY HUGE CRATER TOO.
IF NOT FOR LUSTROUS SCALE'S BARRIER...
...WE'D BE BURIED ALIVE RIGHT NOW.
TELL IT TO THE BEAST VASSAL, NOT ME.

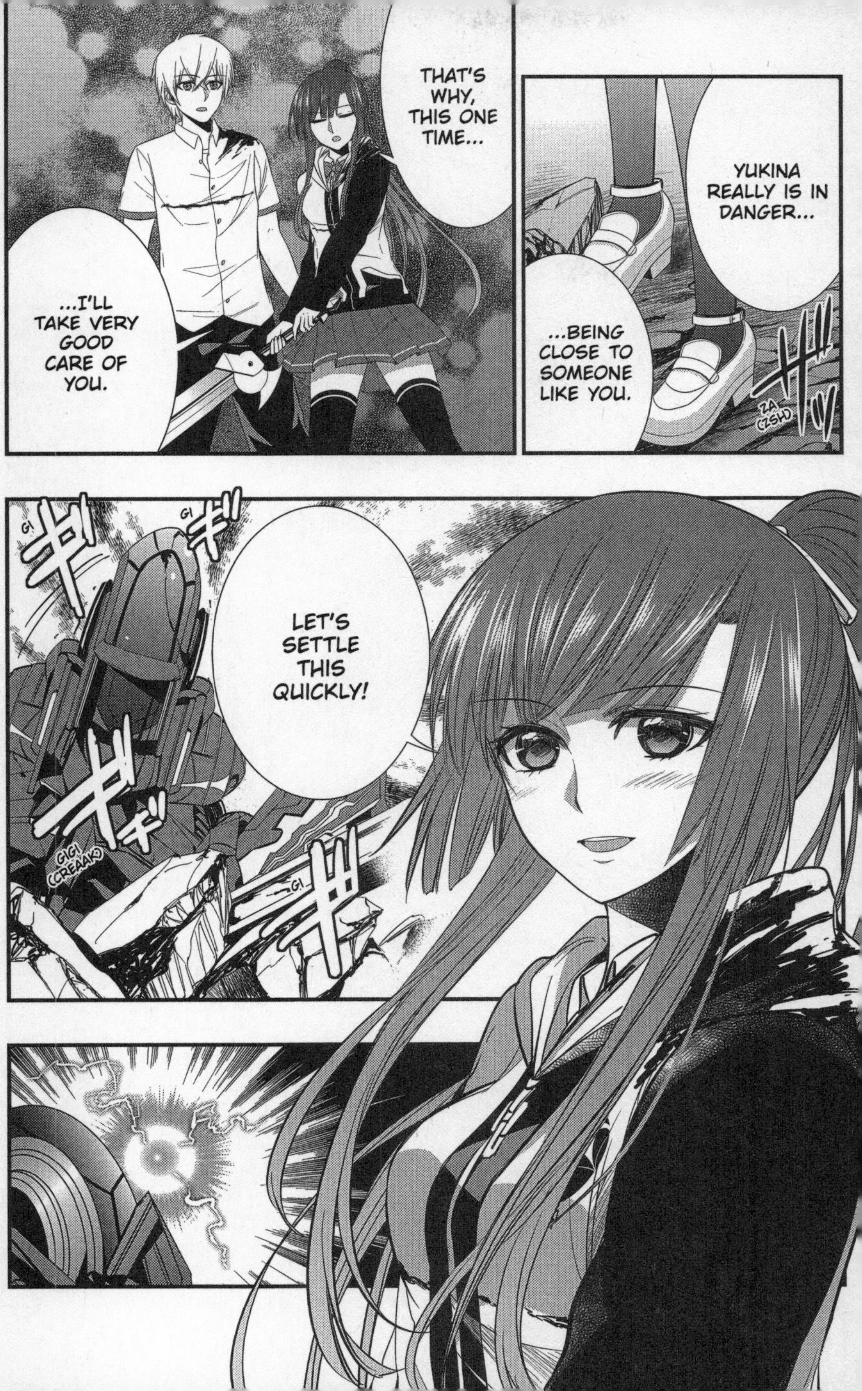
YUKINA REALLY IS IN DANGER...
...BEING CLOSE TO SOMEONE LIKE YOU.
ZA (ZSH)
THAT'S WHY, THIS ONE TIME...
...I'LL TAKE VERY GOOD CARE OF YOU.
GI
GI
LET'S SETTLE THIS QUICKLY!
GIGI (CREAAK)
GI

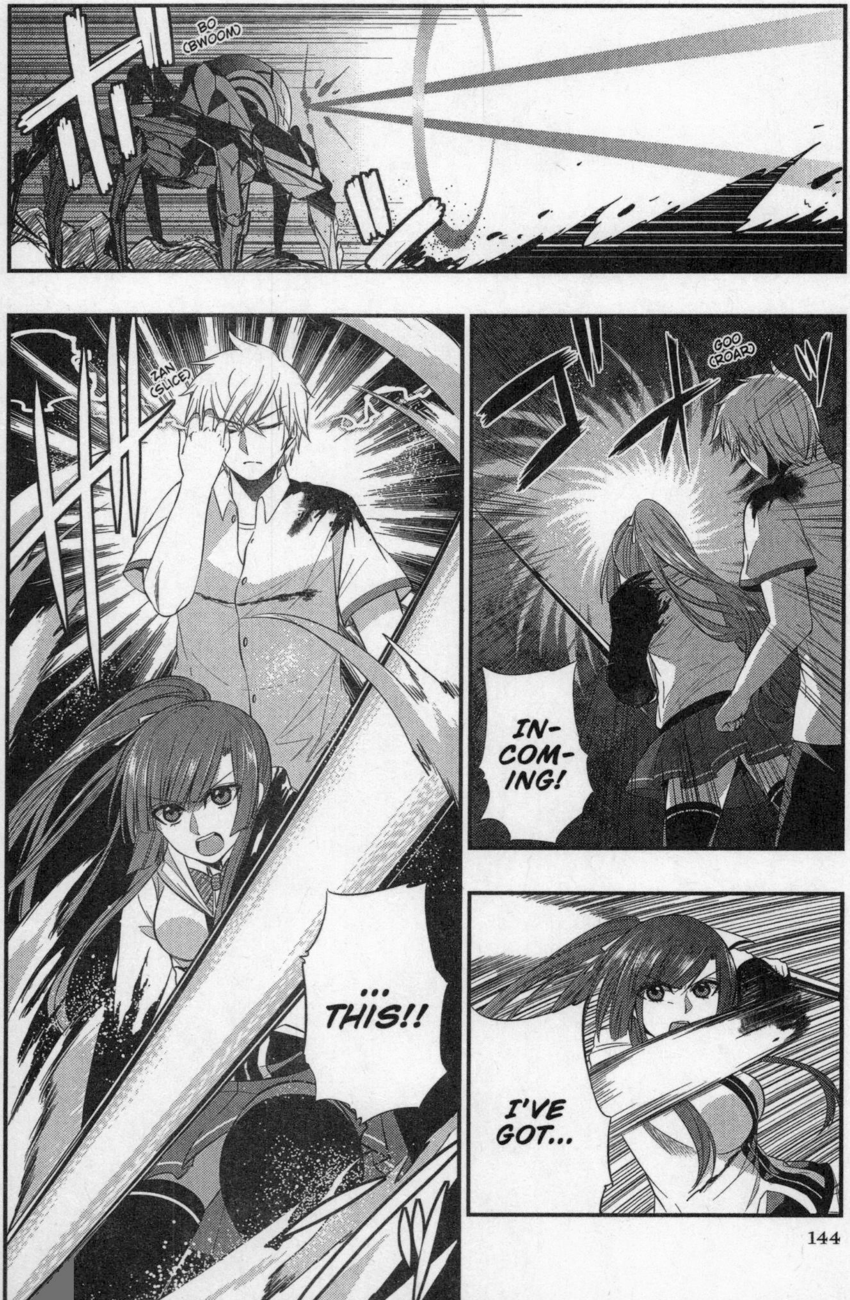
BO
(BWOOM)
GOO
(ROAR)
IN-
COM-
ING!
I'VE
GOT...
ZAN
(SLICE)
...
THIS!!

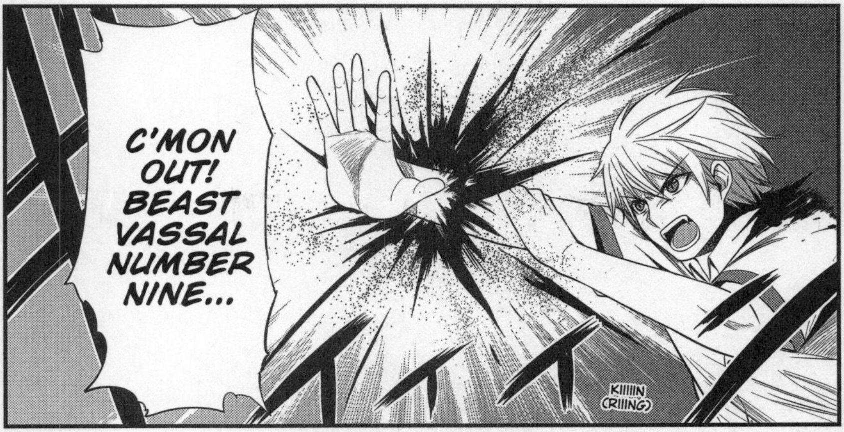
C'MON OUT! BEAST VASSAL NUMBER NINE...
KIIIIN (RIIING)
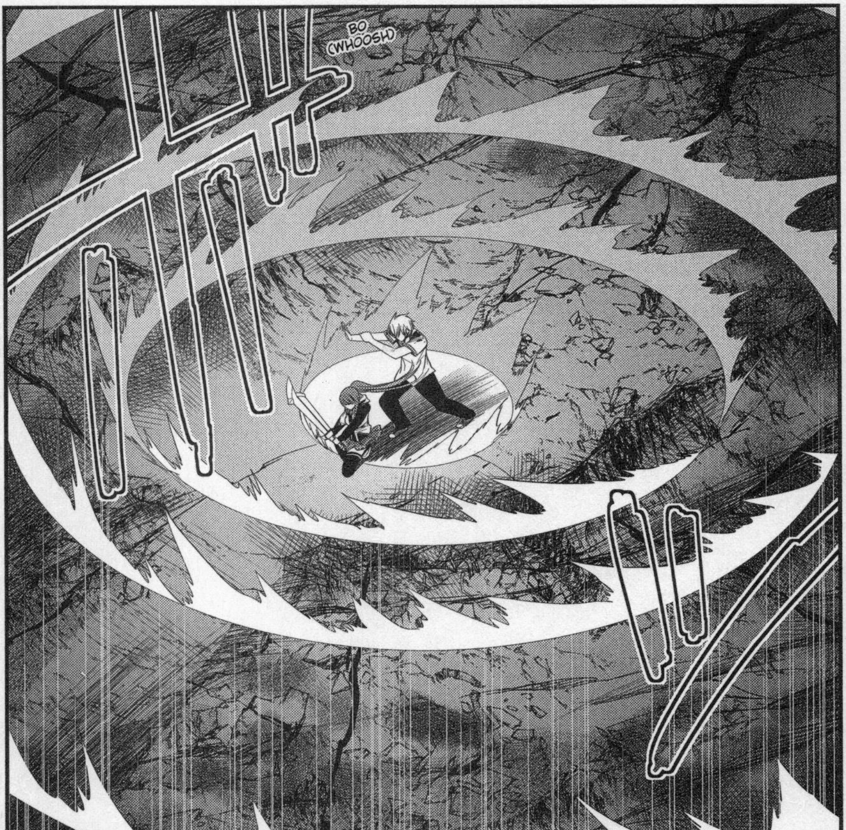
BO (WHOOSH)

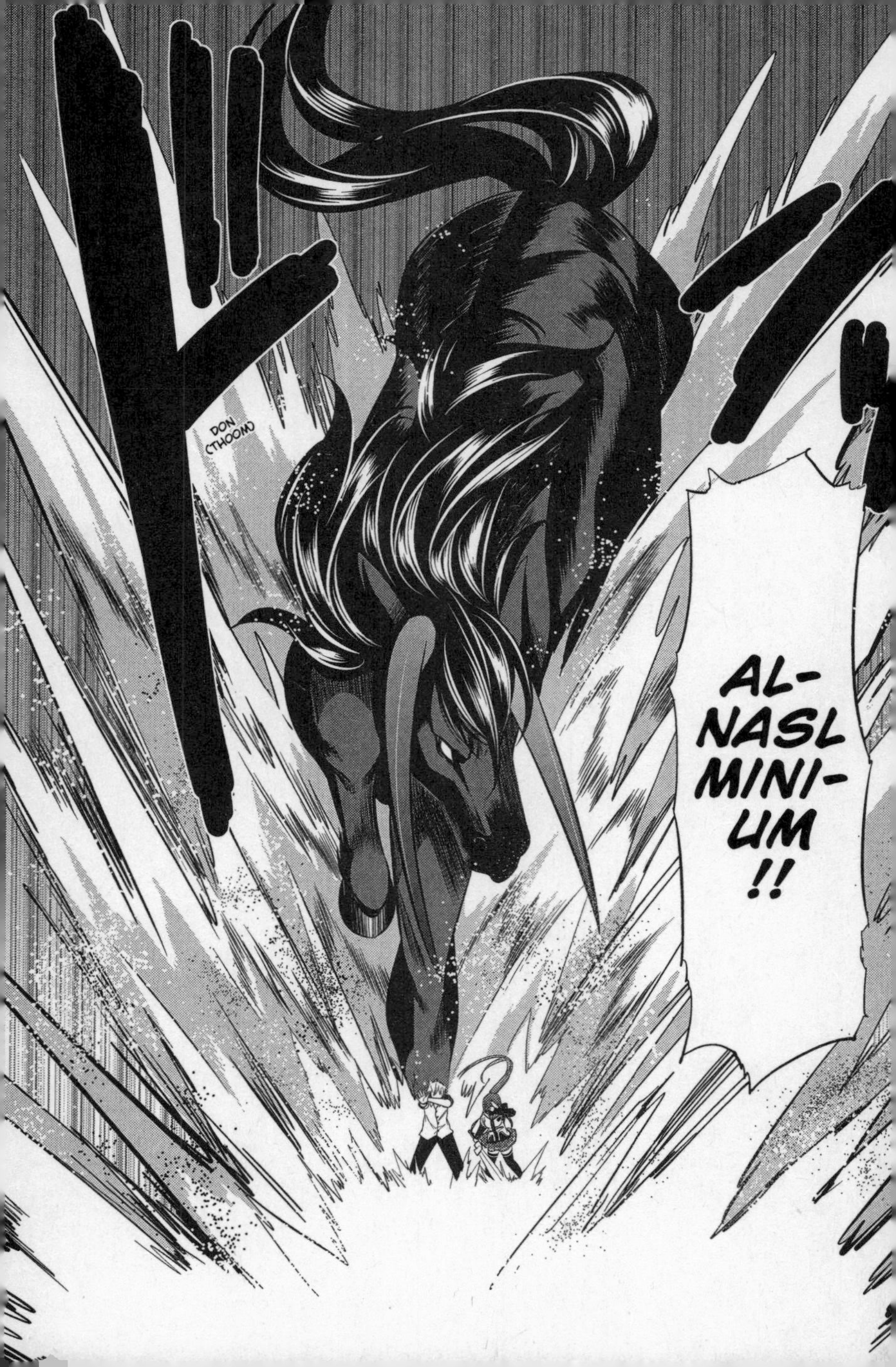
AL-NASL MINI-UM!!
DON (THOOM)

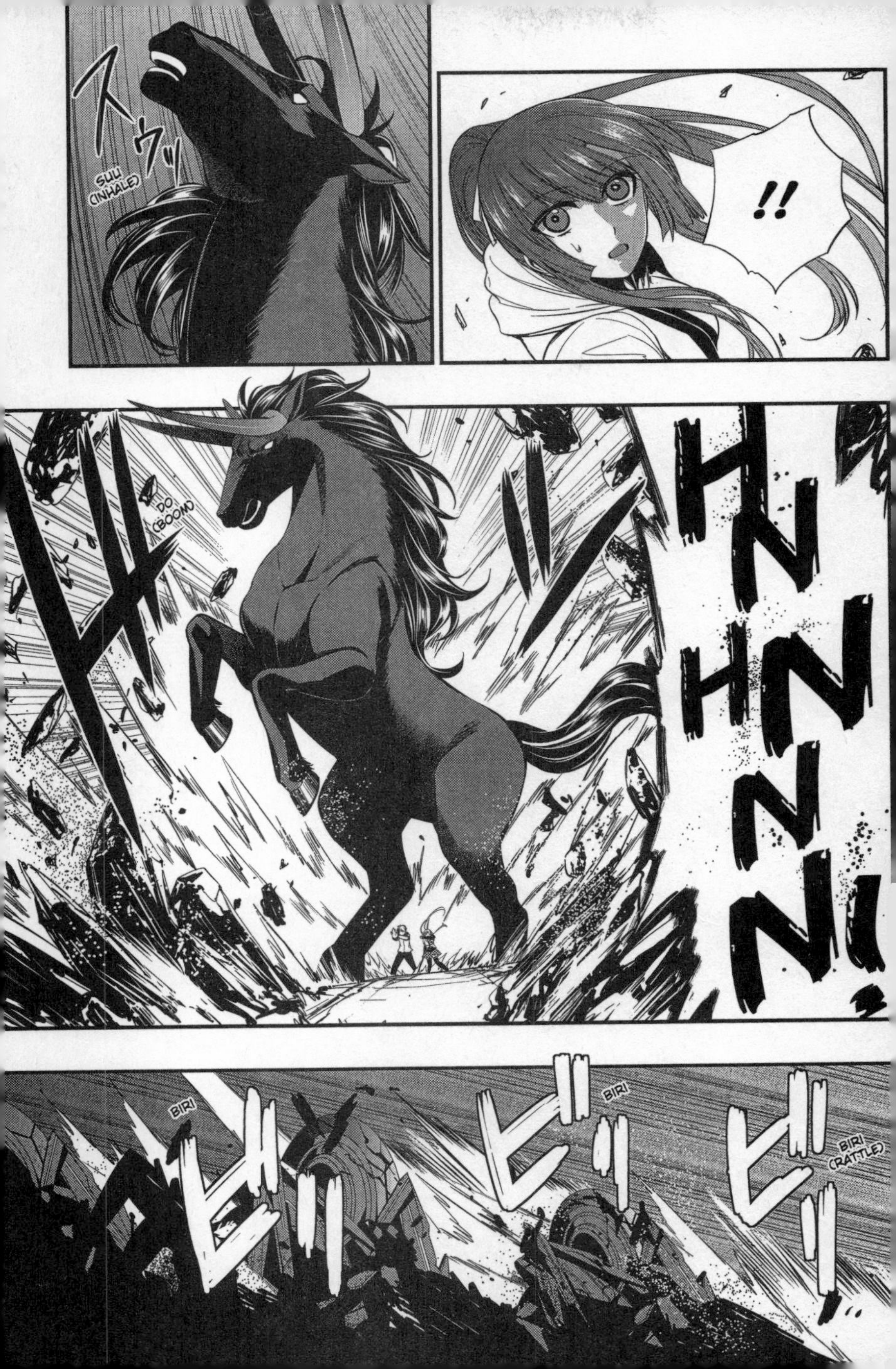
!!
スゥッ
SUU (INHALE)
HNHNNNN!
ドッ
DO (BOOM)
BIRI (RATTLE)
BIRI
BIRI

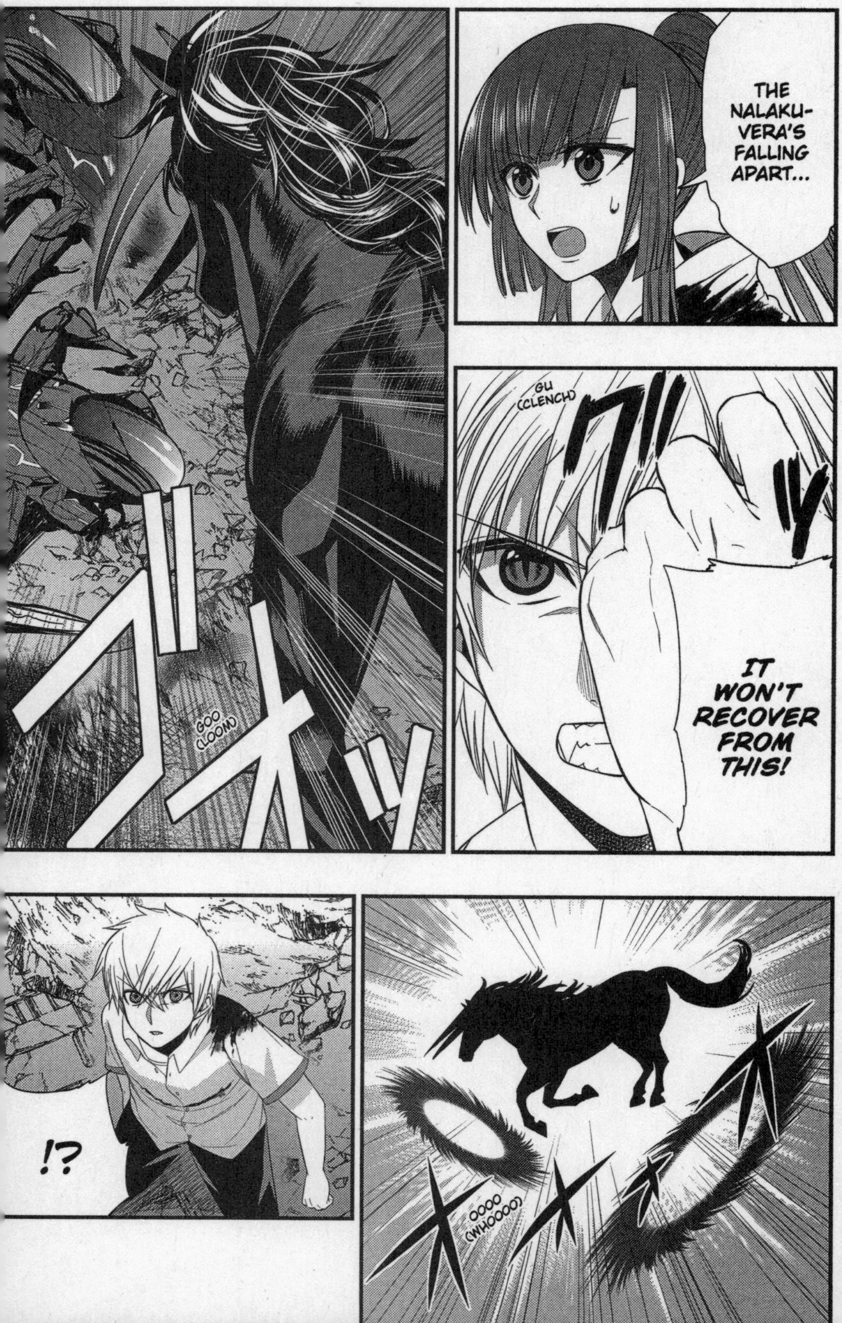
THE NALAKUVERA'S FALLING APART...
GU (CLENCH)
IT WON'T RECOVER FROM THIS!
GOO (LOOM)
OOOO (WHOOOOH)
!?

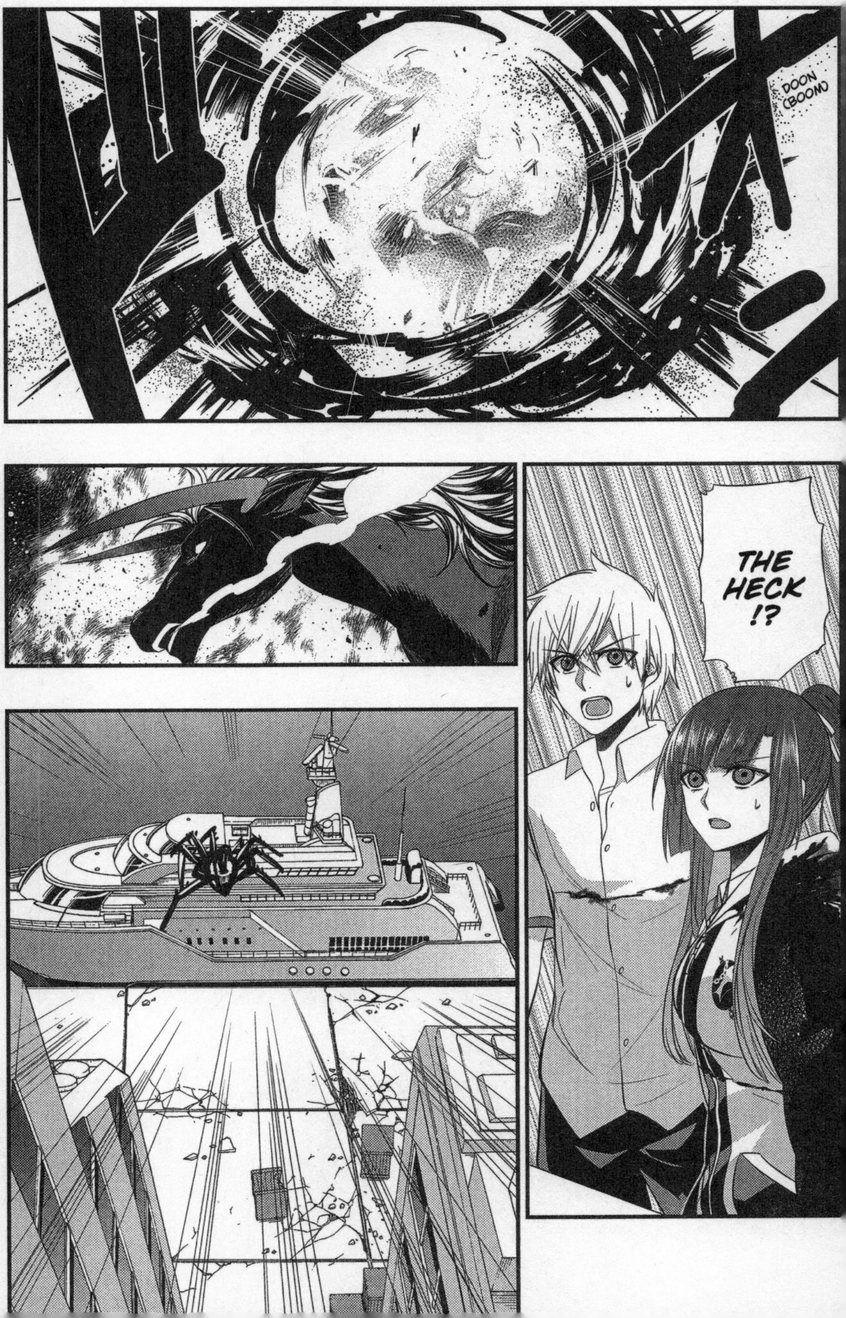
DOON (BOOM)
THE HECK !?

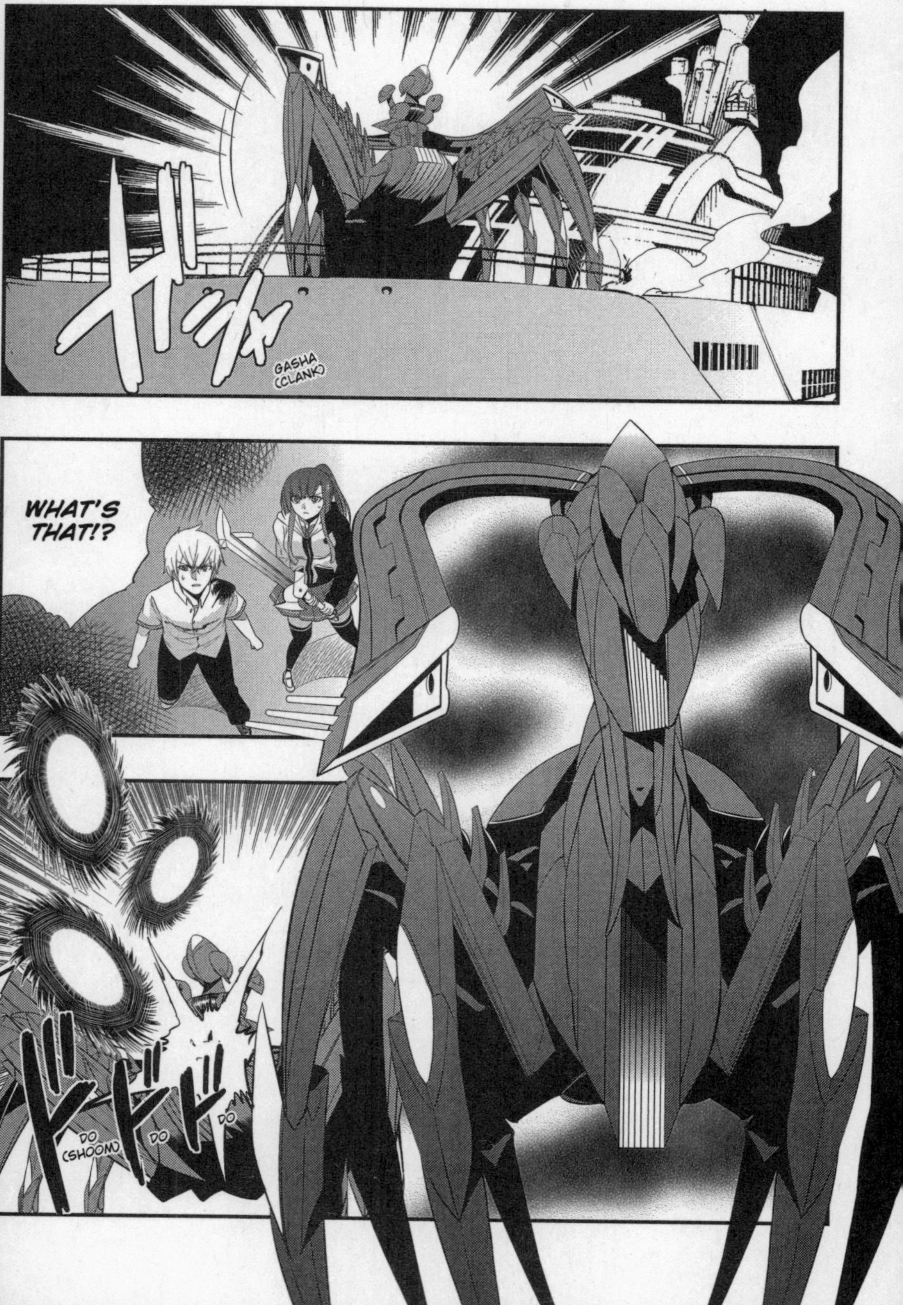
GASHA (CLANK)
WHAT'S THAT!?
DO (SHOOM) DO DO

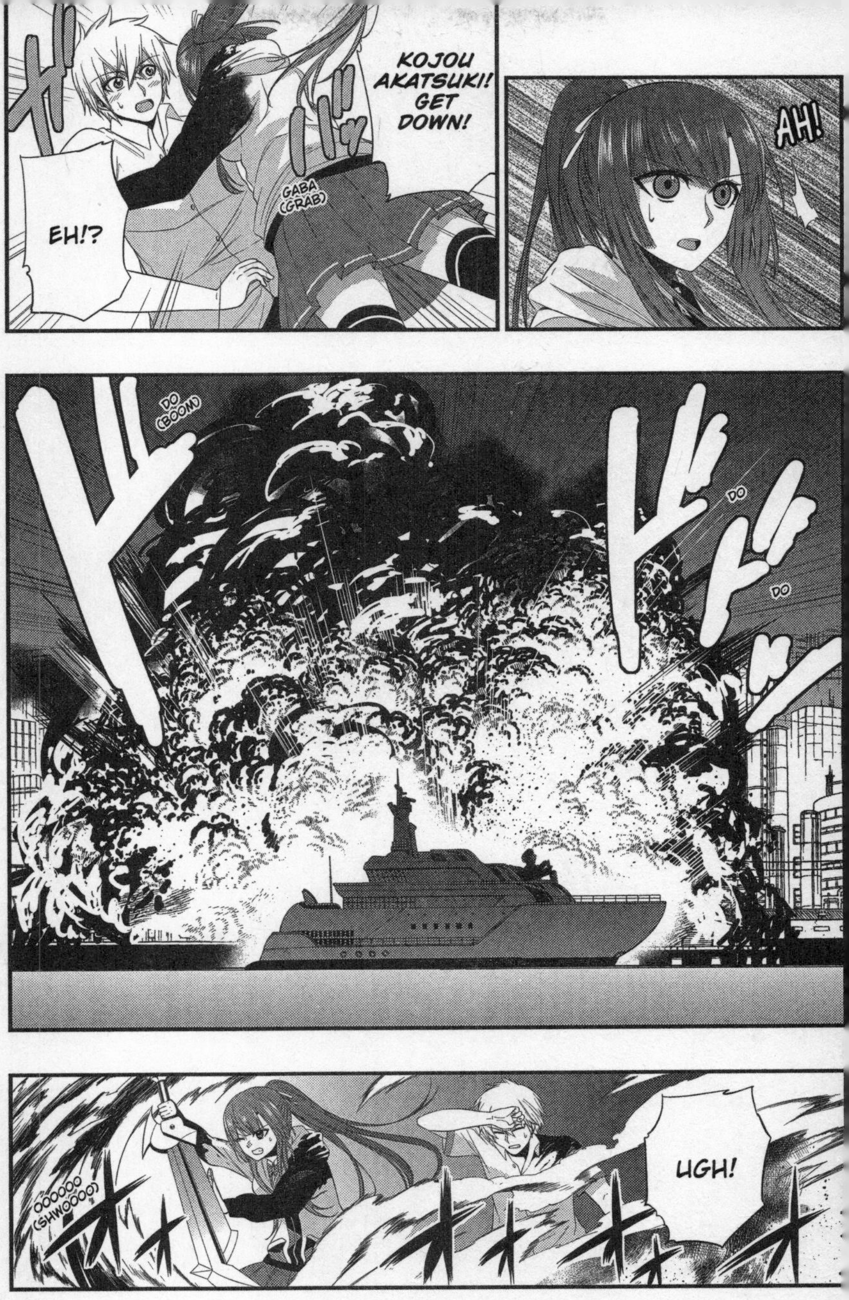
AH!
KOJOU AKATSUKI! GET DOWN!
GABA (GRAB)
EH!?
DO (BOOM)
DO
DO
UGH!
OOOOOO (SHWOOOO)

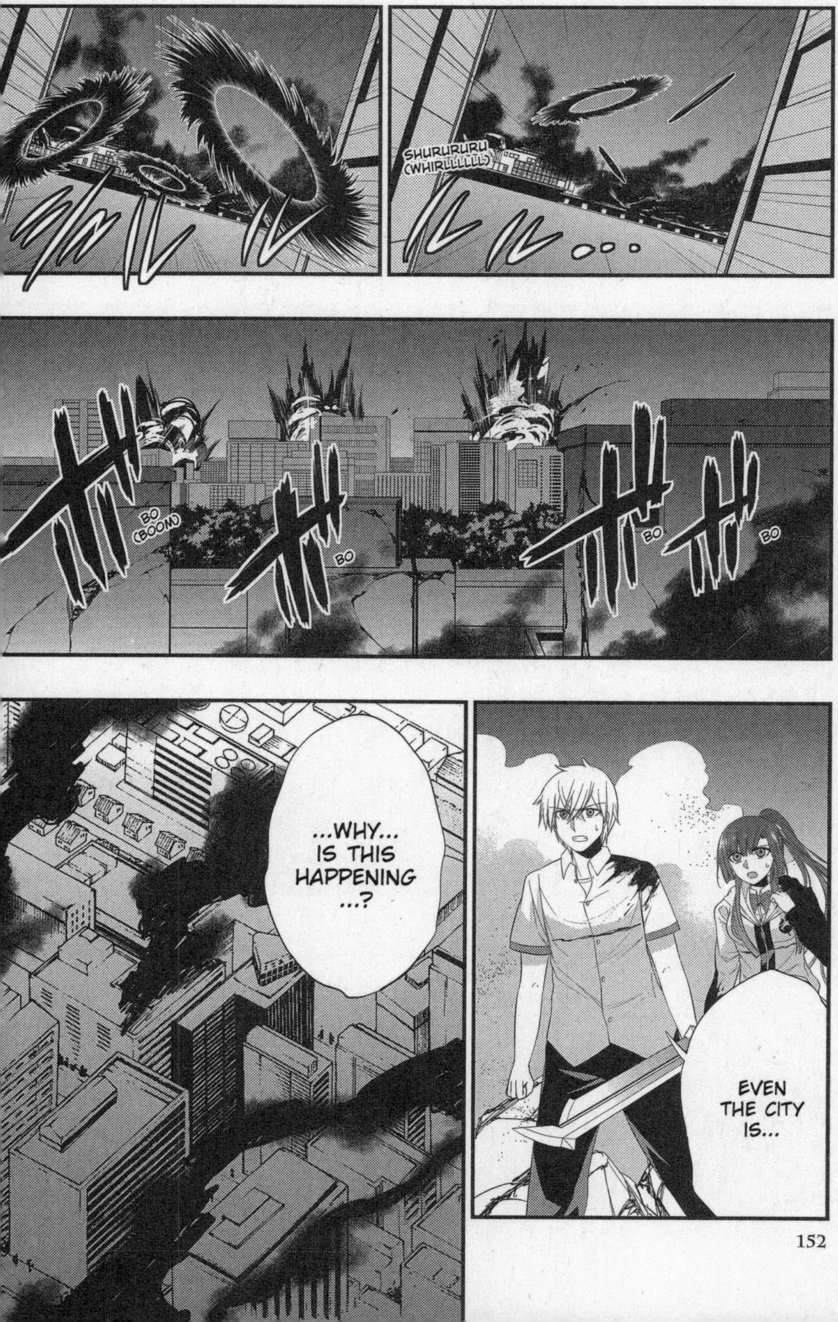
SHURURURU (WHIRLLLLLLL)
BO
BO
BO
BO (BOOM)
EVEN THE CITY IS...
...WHY... IS THIS HAPPENING ...?

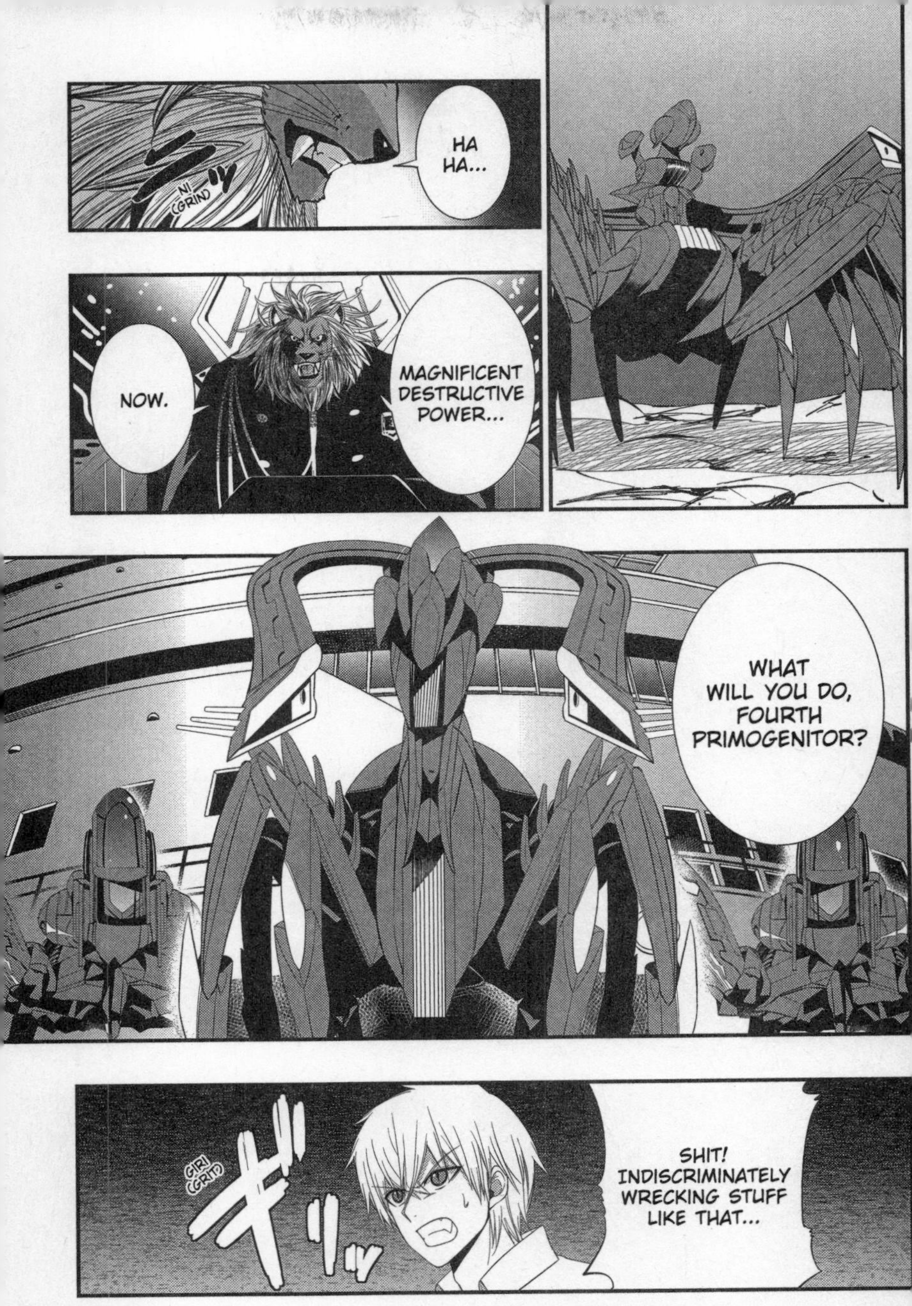
HA HA...
NI (GRIN)
MAGNIFICENT DESTRUCTIVE POWER...
NOW.
WHAT WILL YOU DO, FOURTH PRIMOGENITOR?
SHIT! INDISCRIMINATELY WRECKING STUFF LIKE THAT...
GIRI (GRIT)

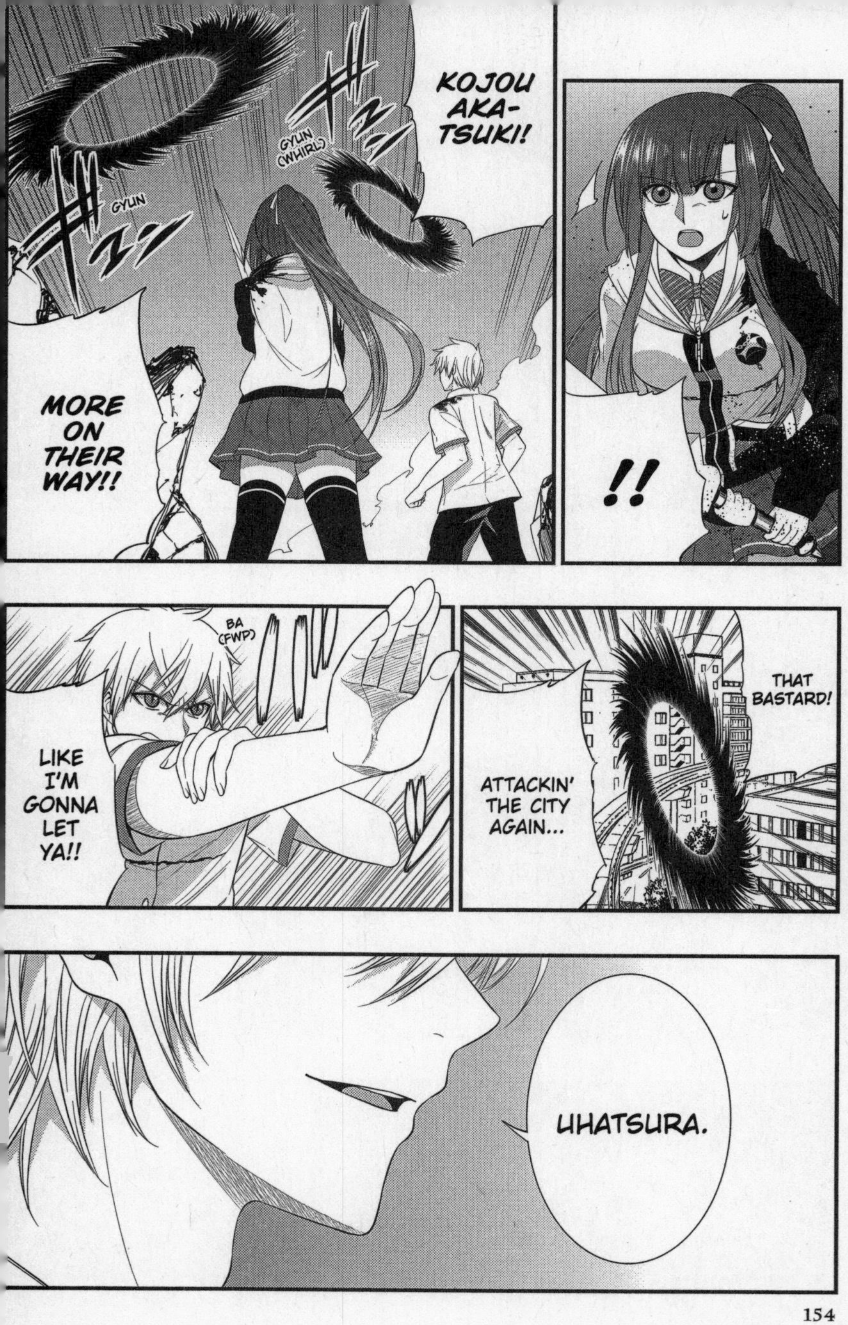
!!
KOJOU AKA-TSUKI!
GYUN (WHIRL)
GYUN
MORE ON THEIR WAY!!
THAT BASTARD!
ATTACKIN' THE CITY AGAIN...
BA (FWP)
LIKE I'M GONNA LET YA!!
UHATSURA.

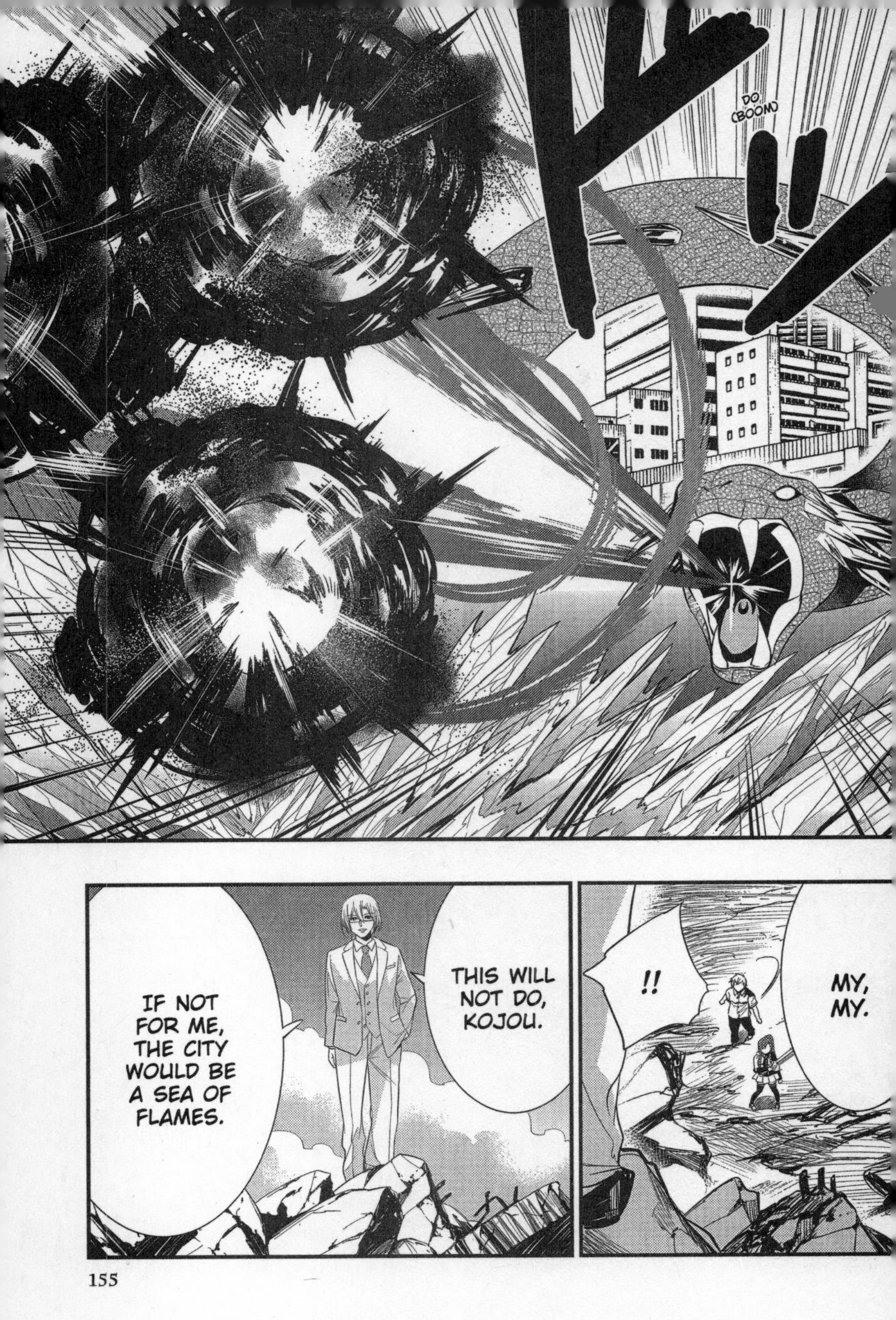
DO
(BOOM)
MY, MY.
!!
THIS WILL NOT DO, KOJOU.
IF NOT FOR ME, THE CITY WOULD BE A SEA OF FLAMES.

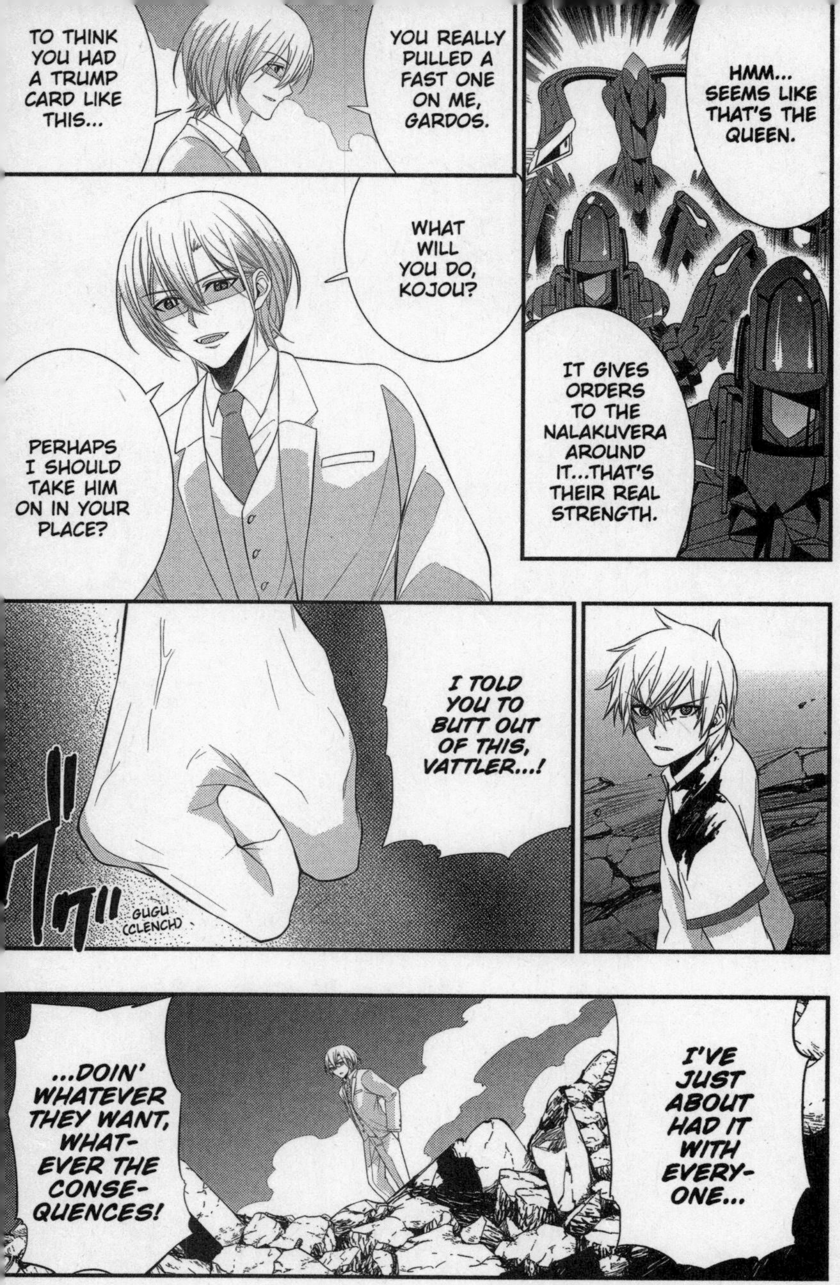
HMM... SEEMS LIKE THAT'S THE QUEEN.
IT GIVES ORDERS TO THE NALAKUVERA AROUND IT...THAT'S THEIR REAL STRENGTH.
YOU REALLY PULLED A FAST ONE ON ME, GARDOS.
TO THINK YOU HAD A TRUMP CARD LIKE THIS...
WHAT WILL YOU DO, KOJOU?
PERHAPS I SHOULD TAKE HIM ON IN YOUR PLACE?
I TOLD YOU TO BUTT OUT OF THIS, VATTLER...!
GUGU (CLENCH)
I'VE JUST ABOUT HAD IT WITH EVERY-ONE...
...DOIN' WHATEVER THEY WANT, WHAT-EVER THE CONSE-QUENCES!

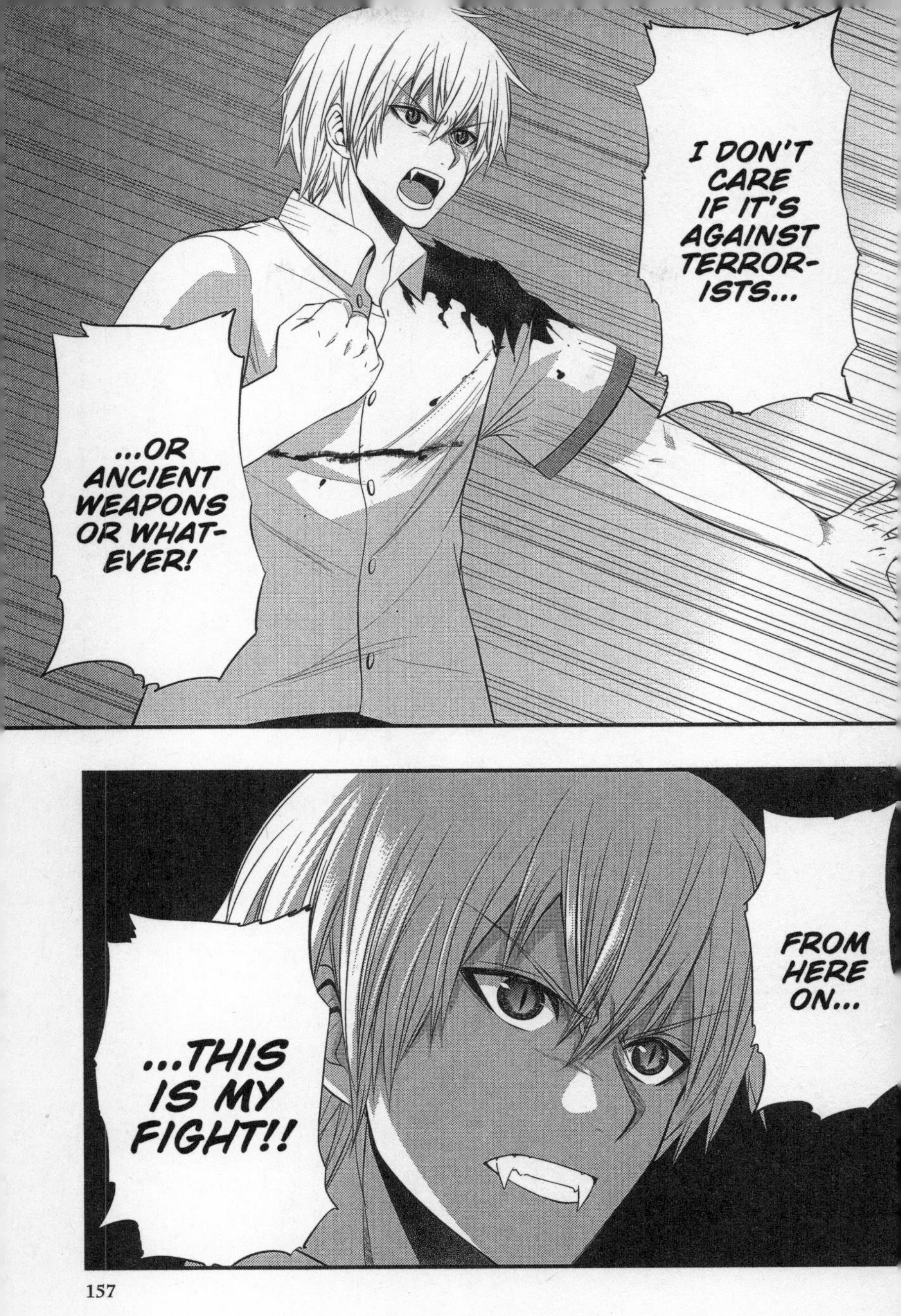
I DON'T CARE IF IT'S AGAINST TERROR-ISTS...
...OR ANCIENT WEAPONS OR WHAT-EVER!
FROM HERE ON...
...THIS IS MY FIGHT!!

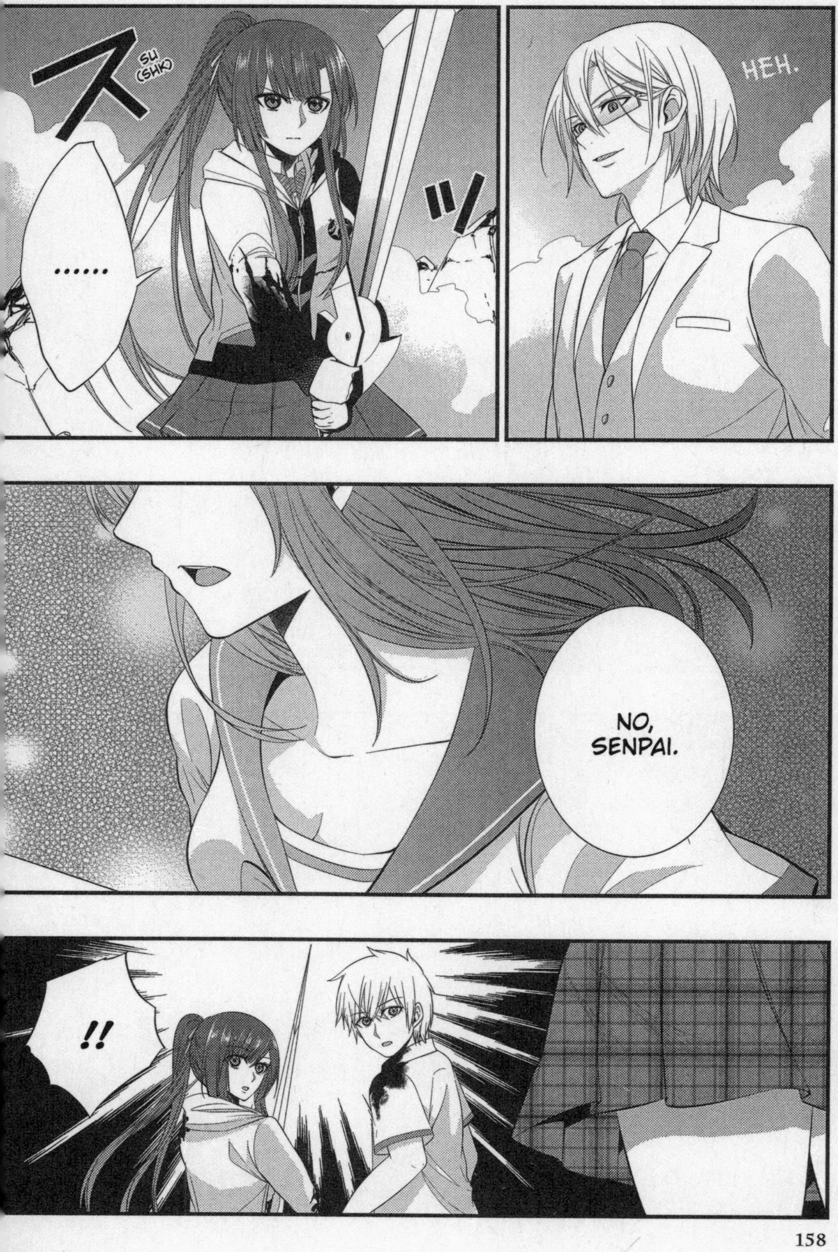
HEH.
SU (SHK)
......
NO, SENPAI.
!!

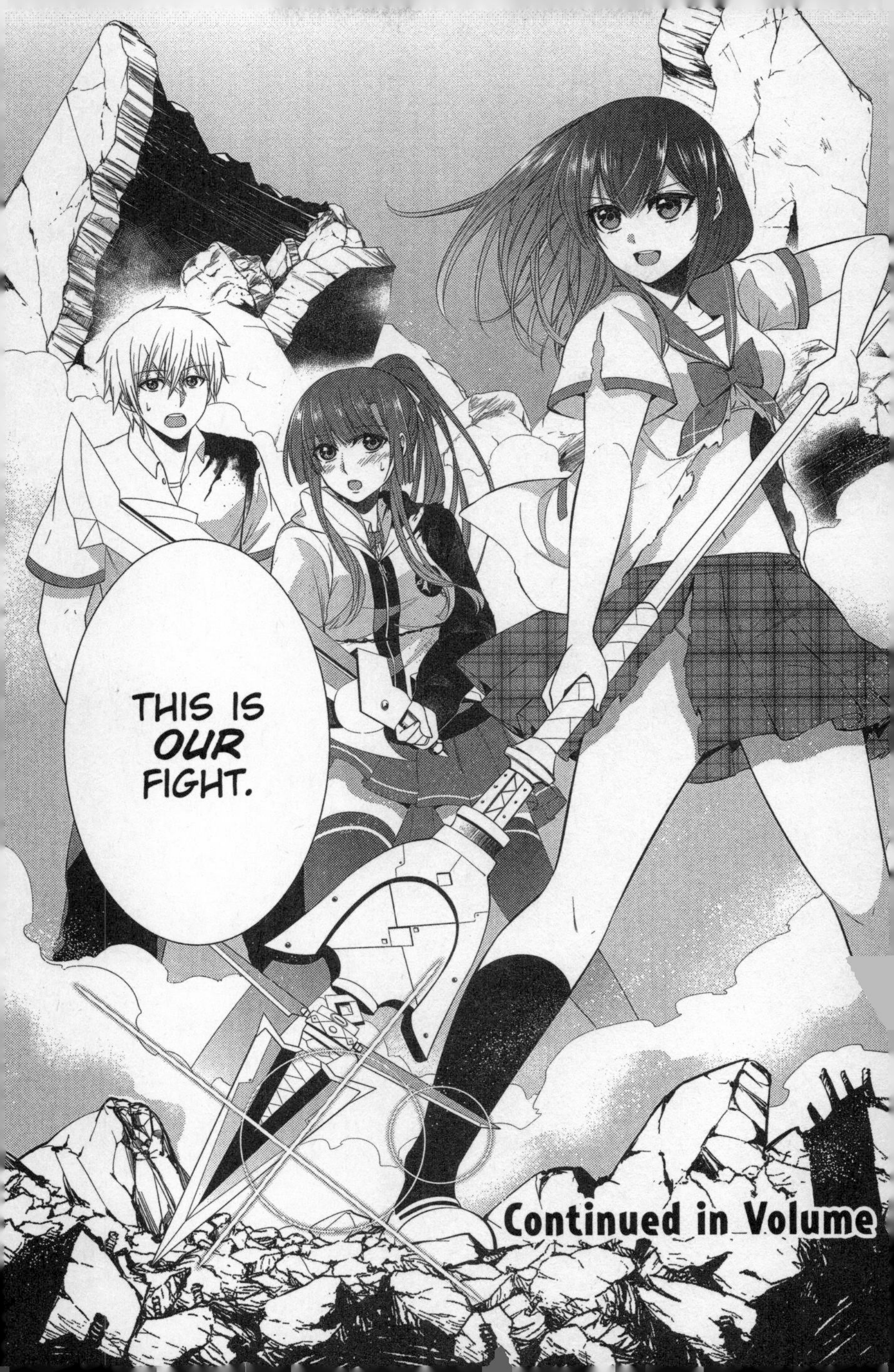
THIS IS OUR FIGHT.
Continued in Volume

Strike the Blood

DEFINITION

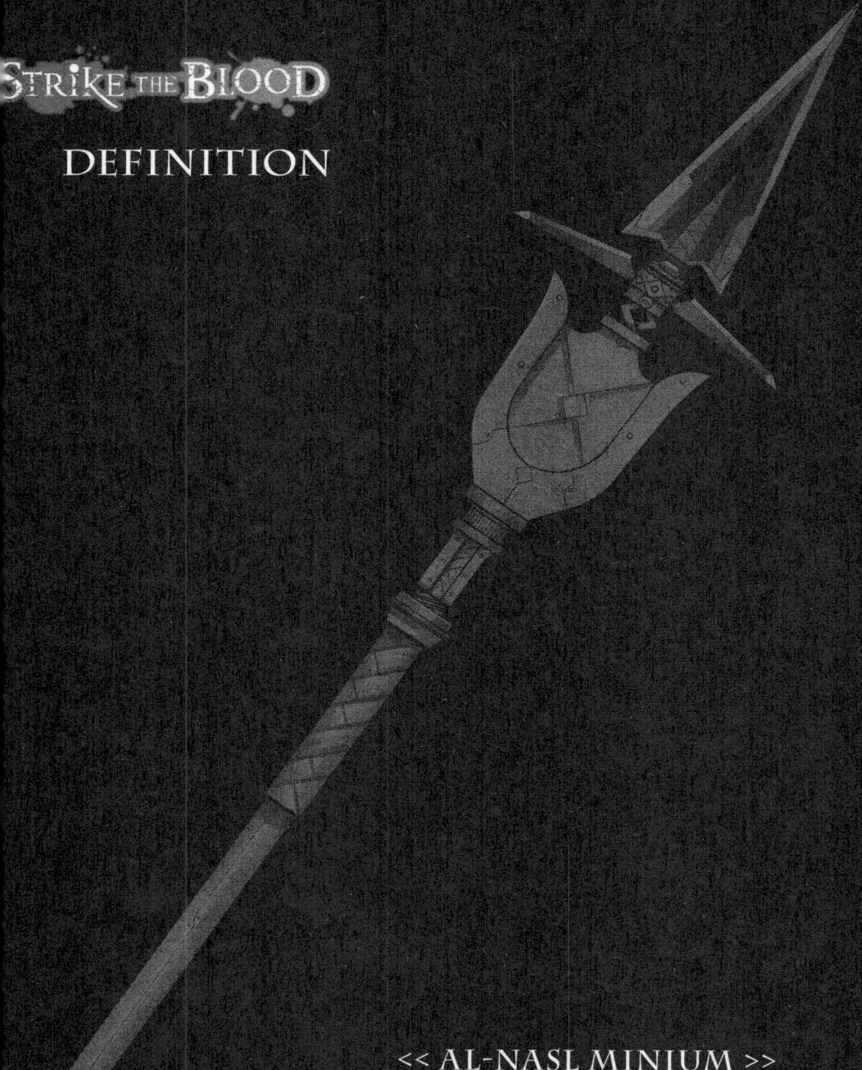

<< AL-NASL MINIUM >>

Ninth Beast Vassal of the Fourth Primogenitor. It takes the form of an scarlet, two-horned horse (bicorn). Its physical body is a solid mass of oscillations. The two horns act like tuning forks, between which the oscillations resonate before being released as a high-frequency wave. Its oscillations can pulverize solid rock and rip through metal.

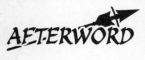

AFTERWORD

THANK YOU TO ALL OF YOU WHO HAVE PURCHASED THIS BOOK. I'M VERY GRATEFUL THAT, THANKS TO THE EFFORTS OF MANY, WE WERE ABLE TO SAFELY REACH VOLUME 5.

IT'S BEEN TWO YEARS SINCE SERIALIZATION, AND AN AWFUL LOT HAS HAPPENED IN THAT TIME. THE ANIME BROADCAST ALSO SAFELY REACHED THE FINAL EPISODE. THANK YOU TO ALL THE ANIME STAFF.
TO THE VOICE ACTRESSES WHO PARTICIPATED, THANK YOU: EVEN NOW, I CANNOT FORGET YOUR LIVELY, BEAUTIFUL VOICES.

I'M TRULY GRATEFUL TO MIKUMO-SENSEI, MANYAKO, THE EDITOR, ALL THE FRIENDS WHO HELPED, AND FAMILY.

I HOPE TO SEE YOU AGAIN NEXT VOLUME.

TATE 2014.9

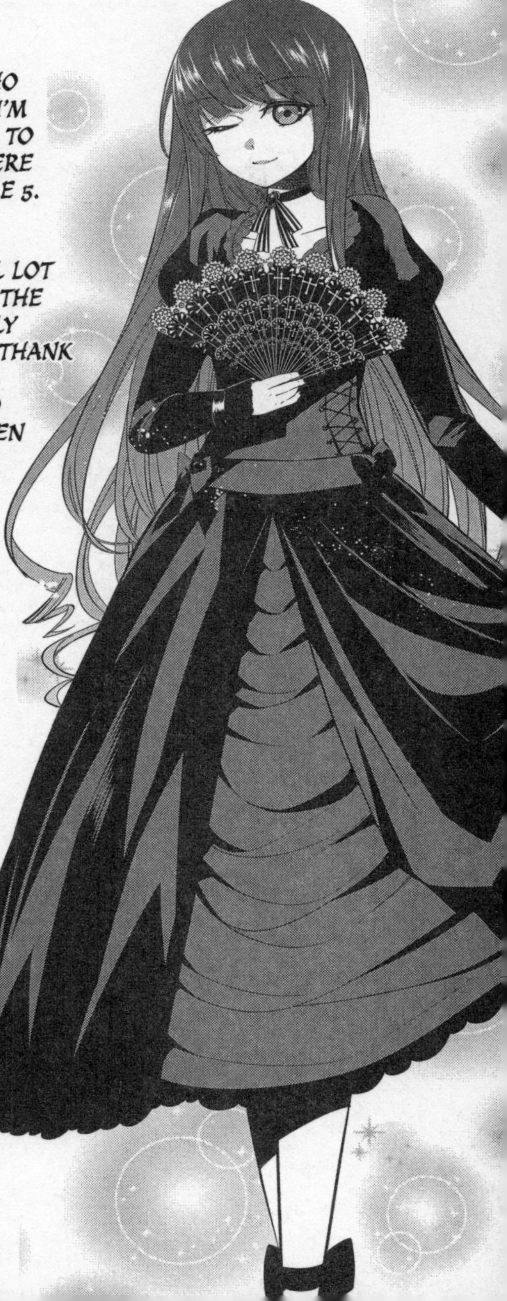

SPECIAL THANKS

GAKUTO MIKUMO-SENSEI
MANYAKO
WINFANWORKS
ISSEI / RYUU
KEI / KOJIMARU
KOMU / ALL THE FAMILY
...AND YOU!

STRIKE THE BLOOD ✦ 5

TATE
Original Story: GAKUTO MIKUMO
Character Design: MANYAKO

Translation: Jeremiah Bourque

Lettering: Xian Michele Lee

STRIKE THE BLOOD Volume 5
© GAKUTO MIKUMO/TATE 2014
All rights reserved.
Edited by ASCII MEDIA WORKS
First published in Japan in 2014 by KADOKAWA CORPORATION, Tokyo.
English translation rights arranged with KADOKAWA CORPORATION, Tokyo, through Tuttle-Mori Agency, Inc., Tokyo.

English translation © 2016 by Yen Press, LLC

Yen Press
1290 Avenue of the Americas
New York, NY 10104

Visit us at yenpress.com
facebook.com/yenpress
twitter.com/yenpress
yenpress.tumblr.com
instagram.com/yenpress

First Yen Press Edition: December 2016

Yen Press is an imprint of Yen Press, LLC.
The Yen Press name and logo are trademarks of Yen Press, LLC.

Library of Congress Control Number: 2016931008

ISBNs: 978-0-316-36185-9 (paperback)
       978-0-316-46612-7 (ebook)

10 9 8 7 6 5 4 3 2 1

BVG

Printed in the United States of America